THE TORN EARTH

Lesser Known Monsters: Book Three

RORY MICHAELSON

D1603818

rorymichaelson.com

LESSER KNOWN MONSTERS

BOOK THREE

THE TORN EARTH
LESSER KNOWN MONSTERS: BOOK THREE

A catalogue copy of this book is available from the British Library.

E-book edition ISBN: 978 1 8381660 9 0
Paperback ISBN: 978 1 7397775 0 0
Hardback ISBN: 978 1 7397775 1 7

Cover design by Dean Cole ©
Illustrations by Urban Knight Art ©

CONTENT NOTE

This book uses British English conventions, spelling, and grammar. Some colloquialisms may appear, but hopefully this just gives you some new and funny words to use in real life.

Please be aware this story contains sexual content and themes or events of anxiety, depression, grief, post-traumatic stress, toxic masculinity, violence, gore, and death (including main character death).

Endings can be a terrifying thing, especially because they are the beginning of so much more.
Thank you for being here with me for this one.

This one's for Oscar.

EXCITARE

In the darkness of grief, a moment can feel like a lifetime.

Years may pass before a fleeting sound, scent, or thought drives **sorrow** into your heart anew. So, if not by time passed nor tears shed, how can we measure **loss**?

Not by what changes or stays the same.

Not by vengeance taken.

In some ways, the world of those who loved **Oscar Tundale** ended at Stonehenge. What happened there changed them for all **eternity**.

But nothing ever *really* ends—least of all things, **trouble**.

So now, they must come together once more, for the sake of everything, forged by a bond of shared love and loss. Because no matter what has happened before, **the world will always need saving**. Perhaps if they can do *that*, they can also save themselves...

❧ I ❧
THICKER THAN BLOOD

RETURN TO ASH

Zara had always thought it strange that something as beautiful and bright as fire should be the destructive end of so many things.

Of so many people.

That so much could end in an incinerator like this, in a closed mouth full of burning teeth and death. She felt its oppressive heat, kissing her tear-streaked cheeks through the closed steel lips of its metallic door, even as it consumed her loved one's remains. Zara imagined the lacquered wood within crumbling, the body inside charring and igniting; fat, flesh, and bone bubbling and scorching until it was reduced to nothingness. It would take at least an hour, they said. She found it difficult to believe, given all that remained inside.

Nani Anjali had been so weak in the end.

Her withered frame had held little more than sagging skin on bones, her rheumy eyes misted with cataracts, dull but for the rare moments they were kindled by memories. Even at her sickest, they hadn't been able to put her in a home. Having over three hundred years of memories bubbling to the surface and spoken in several languages would have been unnerving for anyone but those that knew the truth.

Her lucid periods had grown thinner and further spread, like scattered jewels glimpsed beneath a flood of water washing them away. It had been a couple of weeks since Zara's last real conversation with Nani before she had died—brief as that was. She had taken her hand and stared her right in the eyes, as though she could still clearly see through the clouds fogging her sight. At first, Zara had thought she had been remembering something else, but...

"Don't lose yourself to sorrow, my brave girl."

When Zara had realised the words were truly for her, her breath had caught in her chest.

Nani's gnarled fingers had wound their way into hers, and she'd smiled sadly, as though she understood everything. It was as though she recalled every word Zara had said to her as she slept or drifted in and out of her current self. Everything Zara had confessed about what she had done...

"The world is constantly in peril, but no matter how dark the day may grow...nothing is as dangerous as a broken heart."

After that, she had sighed and fallen into a deep sleep.

She had not truly returned to herself again before she ended.

The last two years had taken their toll on Zara's mother. Her hair was more silver than dark now, the lines on her face deeper. She stood beside Zara, dabbing tears away from her eyes. Eyes Zara had barely been able to look into these last few days for fear that the relief she saw there might echo her own. Not relief that the burden of caring for Nani was lifted, but that the woman who'd done unknown good around the world had finally found peace. Unfortunately, no matter how Zara tried to rationalise it, that feeling still felt like treachery.

Zara's little brother, Hashim—still *little,* though he had shot up a foot to match her in height and was sprouting sparse hair on his top lip—was sobbing loudly beside her. His fractured, keening wails were almost alien within the sterile white walls and the cold, steel table and furnace before them. Zara squeezed his hand, and

4

her mother reached out and took her other as a gasping sob escaped her.

Zara absently wondered if she should be crying more.

It surprised her she had cried at all.

Not that she didn't mourn. It was the opposite, in fact. Zara felt *full*. Beyond full. She was so overloaded with emotions and memories that no one thing seemed to find a way out. She wasn't sure if she had all the tears wrung out of her, or she was just so deeply saturated with them it was impossible to pick herself up to squeeze them out.

It wasn't a new feeling.

It had been like that ever since Oscar.

Guilt seared through her again at her mind lingering on him now, at a time she should be remembering Nani. But she just couldn't help but imagine what it might have been like if they had gotten to bury him. Maybe if she had stood there, watching a box with her best friend inside burn, it might somehow feel better than what had happened. A finality instead of countless nights dreaming of his body being torn between worlds, lost forever, never to be laid to rest. On the worst nights, he was still alive—or something close—preserved eternally, drifting in an endless maelstrom of pain and misery.

The memory of Oscar flashed in her mind.

Not the memory she would choose.

Not of the thousands of times she'd seen Oscar laughing or happy, but the look of pained understanding in his eyes. That smile as he thanked her, forgave her for killing him. The hum of the willblade's hilt as she drove its blade into his chest.

Zara's chest felt tight, her breath rasping. She dragged her eyes away from the incinerator, where the only family member that had ever fully supported her with everything she did was being reduced to ash, desperately seeking anything to anchor her to this place, to take her away from those memories and centre her once more. She couldn't quite bring herself to look at her parents or weeping brother, so her gaze instead travelled across the white shirts and dresses filling the room and fell upon Cousin Rami, who stood between two uncles.

If Zara felt like she was bursting at the seams with everything that had happened, Rami looked overstuffed himself—in an entirely bodily way. He'd always had a thick neck and bulging biceps, but something had shifted in the last few months, ever since he lost his job with the police for gross misconduct. His square jaw jutted out stubbornly, coarse with scruff, and his dark eyes shone as he stared at the incinerator, a thick vein throbbing in his neck. His charcoal suit was so snug on his wide chest and shoulders, Zara thought he might have needed to be stitched into the thing.

More than once, she had wondered about steroids—that would explain the anger issues too. Rami always had a short fuse, but now he was more explosive than ever. That had been the reason for his dismissal. The civilian he'd *accidentally* put in the ICU whilst bullying a suspect happened to be the son of one of the police force's commissioners. He'd quickly found work in private security, of course, but as he frequently reminded her, his *real* work was yet to come.

As if he could sense her stare on him, his eyes met hers. Zara forced herself to meet them, keeping her gaze level. She could have sworn a faint smirk formed on his lips.

"Are you sure you don't want to come with us?" Zara's mother asked, pulling her into a hug in the sad little concrete carpark outside the crematorium. The forecast that morning had promised a clear spring day, but grey clouds lurked threateningly overhead. "We could put some uncles in a cab…"

"No, Mum, you go." Zara conjured a smile that was weak at best. "I'll take a cab. You'll never hear the end of it if you don't drive any of them yourself."

Her mother tutted and winked a bloodshot eye. "You really

think they would dare to cause a stir? I'm the matriarch now. You think one of them would have questioned your Nani's word if she told them to wear their clothes back-to-front one day?"

Zara's face cracked in a grin, and her mother's reflected it as she reached up to touch her cheek. "My beautiful girl. She was so proud of you."

Zara's breath trembled.

"Not to worry, Aunty," a familiar voice boomed from nearby. "I can drive her."

Her mother cast a doubtful look at the swollen bull of a man. Rami had once been the poster boy for the family, but now they finally saw him for what he was. Trouble.

"I'll give you money for the cab later," her mother said lowly from the corner of her mouth. The smile faltered on Rami's face, though he was surely too far away to hear what she had said.

There was a soft honk of a horn as her father pulled up. Her mother cast a harassed wave at Zara's father in the driver's seat before giving Zara a quick peck on the cheek and bustling to the passenger door. Zara waved and watched as the car pulled out onto the road and away.

"I'm sorry for your loss," Rami said stiffly. Zara took it as being as near a gentle tone as he could handle.

Zara sighed and turned to deal with him.

He didn't *look* sorry...

"Thanks," she said blandly.

"I know you were close. Today must be hard for you." Rami's thick brows knit in a fair imitation of concern.

Zara folded her arms. "What is it, Rami? What do you want?"

Rami raised his hands, wide eyes so exaggerated, it almost mocked innocence. "Nothing, nothing. Just showing concern. You've had a rough couple of years. It's natural for your family to be concerned about you."

Zara chewed the inside of her cheek.

"I know you and Nani were close, so I just wanted to see if there was anything I could do to help...like what we talked about before. It must feel like a good time now, so I just wanted to let you know I'm ready whenever." His eyes travelled down to his own body, lifting a thick arm as though surprised himself at its impressive size. "I've been training constantly. Just imagine what that thing inside you could do to help people in a body like mine."

Zara rolled her eyes, then glanced around to ensure none of the remaining relatives getting into their cars were close enough to hear her reply. "We've talked about this, Rami. You didn't do a great job of protecting people *without* powers. I need to be convinced you're ready. I need to know your temper is under control before I go making you strong enough to knock some-one's head clean off with a casual swipe."

Rami's face darkened. "Things change. That was a difficult time."

Zara's stomach twisted. *Right.*

Rami had claimed emotional duress because of Oscar's disap-pearance despite them not having even spoken, let alone dated, for years. Zara didn't know what she hated more: that he'd made that claim or that she automatically distrusted and rejected it. For all she knew, maybe he *had* been upset, but...

Zara scowled and pulled her phone out of her pocket, already flicking up an app for a cab. "Things change, Rami, but people don't. Not that easily. You have to put in the work for a responsi-bility like this. I already told you, I will hand it over, but you need to be ready—"

"But you're wasting it," Rami blurted out, his eyes widening in surprise as he did.

Zara closed her mouth and clenched her jaw, her gaze moving up to meet his. He was shifting those tree-trunk legs on the spot like a scolded child, but he continued.

"You have so much strength, and you're doing nothing but mope around and go to work. Think of all the people I could help, Zara. I would dedicate my life to it."

The truth of the words nettled Zara. She still patrolled occa-sionally, but in the last year or so, she hadn't had the time to follow up leads, even though the supernatural goings-on seemed to be remarkably quiet of late. She had finished her study, but taking on the advanced nurse practitioner role was a lot. And even with the Ghatotkacha's energy in her, she could only do so much.

Time and energy were only some factors, though. There was also the fact that she just didn't really want to host the Ghatotkacha anymore. She resented it. She hated its pounding torrent of energy and the way it made her temper flare and the dreams it gave her, even the ones that weren't memories seen through Nani's eyes. Even worse, it felt...*closer* now. Ever since that night at Stonehenge, sometimes...sometimes she could almost swear she heard its voice even when she was awake.

What she hated most of all was that, for all the power the spirit afforded her, it had failed when it mattered most. For all the things she could do, she couldn't save Oscar.

What Rami said might be true, and most days, she *did* think about giving up the ghost to him, but the time had to be right.

"I'm just saying, with me holding the power, things might be much better," Rami pushed. "Who knows, Oscar might even still be here if I'd have been the one to have it..."

A flash of fury and ice cold ran across Zara's skin. She stared at Rami, now hearing only the pounding of her heart in her ears. Rami's eyes fixed on hers, blinking in the realisation that he had pushed too far.

"I don't want to hear his name out of your mouth," Zara spat.

Rami shrugged his massive shoulders awkwardly. "I get it. It was a loss for me, too. I liked the guy. Me and Oscar—"

"Don't," Zara snapped. "You dated him for a couple of weeks and treated him like shit." Rami opened his mouth to retort, but she cut him off. "You need to leave."

She felt her power flooding into her, using her open fury as a channel to fill her with energy. It was crackling around her like static, and she knew her eyes glowed visibly, even in the sunlight.

"Zara, I'm sorry. I'm just saying—"

"Go! And I don't want to hear anything else from you for the rest of the day. You'd better be as quiet as the world's muscliest fucking dormouse at the funeral party."

Frustration flashed in Rami's eyes, and she thought she saw his fists flex for a moment before he huffed and turned away. He stalked over to his car, something black and shiny he probably shouldn't be able to afford on his current wages—yet another demonstration of where his priorities lay.

As Zara watched him, she felt movement against her chest. Not her pounding heart, but a tentative scrabbling from her handbag where it hung against her.

She was sure he'd been sleeping before, but now he was *definitely* awake.

He must be able to sense trouble brewing.

For a moment, Zara considered opening her bag and upending its contents to release the monster inside. She imagined him swelling and growing and chasing Rami as far as she could see.

She smiled in a way that was closer to just baring her teeth.

Nah, not worth it.

She heard a low whistle over her shoulder. "Jeez, bitch. You got mean whilst I was gone."

Zara froze.

No way...it couldn't be.

Slowly, hoping against hope, Zara turned around.

He was as handsome as ever, white shirt hugging his lean form, collar and cuffs oversized, black gems studding one ear. His umber skin was dewy and flawless but for a new, thin scar—paler than the rest of him—cutting a line down one side of his face, just beside his eyebrow. A short beard faded into his temples below tight dark curls.

He gave her that familiar grin, his russet eyes sparkling and white teeth flashing beatifically, and for a second, she felt like all the weight had been lifted from her heart.

"Marcus," she breathed.

Marcus winked, flourishing dramatically. "'Tis I."

TWO STEPS FORWARD

"What...what are you doing here?" Zara stammered.

"Wherever you need me, I shall be," Marcus sombrely replied before his face cracked in a mischievous grin. "Come on. The receptionist said we can use the consultation room, but I want to be out of here before she gets any ideas about me following through on the date I might have promised her..."

Some things never change.

Zara rushed after Marcus, who was already stalking on his long legs back to the oak double doors at the front of the crematorium.

"Marcus..." She held onto the relief of seeing him, though the anger at him for disappearing so long buffeted her like a tempest. "I haven't heard from you in eighteen months. You can't just show up at Nani's funeral like some kind of magickal glamour pirate and expect me to do whatever you say."

Marcus spun around with heavily lidded eyes and a deeply satisfied smirk. "I know. I look good, right?"

Zara sighed. "You look like a slutty magician."

"I *am* a slutty magician." Marcus waggled his eyebrows, and Zara couldn't contain a snort of laughter.

Jesus, she'd missed him.

Marcus strode through the entryway, opened the small door marked 'Reflection Room,' and gestured inside. "C'mon."

Zara wasn't all the way into the room when she spotted Song.

The ethernal was dressed in a full white suit, the perfect complement of Marcus. Their lapels glittered with black rhinestones, almost the same shade as their onyx skin. Zara opened her mouth to speak but was hit by a wave of emotion.

Regret. Sorrow. The anticipation of the end not really being the end at all. The faint satisfaction of a long life well lived. Hopefulness.

Zara smiled. Had she really hated that once? "Hi, Song. It's great to see you."

Song rushed forward, reaching out with their lithe arms, and pulled Zara against their tiny body with surprising strength into a fierce hug.

"Oh...wow," Zara murmured.

"Yeah, we're huggers now," Marcus said, casually pushing the door closed with a wave of his fingers. "Song really likes feeling people's slowly perishing mortal bodies against their shell. It gives them a sense of what futility might be like."

"Thanks, I hate it," Zara said dully.

Another feeling rushed over Zara, softer this time. Amusement. The sharp jab of a riposte at Marcus. Affection at a playful lie.

Marcus grinned. "Yeah, Song. You got me. They just like hugging. They think it's funny."

Song grinned broadly, a proud flash of white teeth.

"Oh." Zara found herself grinning back at them. "You smile now? You look incredible. And the puffer jacket is gone?"

Gratitude and shyness lapped at the edges of Zara's senses.

"Yeah, they were kind of attached to that look. Turns out they just hadn't found anything else they liked. We hit a couple of fashion shows since, though. They just have fancy-ass taste. Anyway, Zara, I gotta stop you flirting with Song before they decide they like you more than me."

Marcus dropped heavily into the worn leather chair by the window. Song moved to perch their tiny body on the arm, punching him in the shoulder playfully.

Zara put her hands on her hips. "Business? Does business include telling me where you've been the last year and a half whilst I've been stuck here alone?"

Marcus bared his teeth. "I'd like to say I had a choice, but we kind of got stuck between things. And by stuck, I mean literally, and by things, I mean a temporal flux in the Amazon."

"What?"

"It's a long story. Or a really short one, depending on how you look at it." Marcus shrugged. "Spacetime, huh?"

"Is that where you got the scar?"

"I will neither confirm nor deny the origin story of my cool ass scar."

Zara folded her arms. "Why do you even still have it? Can't you trade it with Song? Use the imperfection to juice yourself up some?"

Marcus shrugged. "I might've tried a few times. Turns out the scar isn't an imperfection. It's part of who I'm supposed to be, and for some reason...I know it."

Zara opened her mouth, frustrated with his nebulous answers. "I've been worried, Marcus. Do you really think with everything that happened, I didn't...need you?"

Marcus' russet eyes held sadness when he met hers, and he said simply, "I know. I needed you too."

Zara sighed. It would be two years next month.

Two years since she had killed Oscar.

Zara turned, stepping carefully around the low glass table to the tweed sofa opposite Marcus. As she sat, she wondered how many people had grieved in these chairs. How many people had held each other's hands as their lives fell apart?

That must be nice. The luxury of being able to fall apart.

"I won't ask how you are. Or how you've been." Marcus' eyes drifted awkwardly around the room the way they tended to when he was nervous. "We both know it's been shit. I can't tell you how many nights I've not been able to sleep thinking about it. But it is what it is, and this is what we got." He deflated slightly. "I...I wanted to be here. Not just to talk about things, but to be here for you. I'm sorry things got fucked up, Zara."

Zara shook her head sadly.

Sorry things got fucked up, or sorry I fucked them up? Maybe both.

"It's okay, Marcus. Like you said, it is what it is. And thank you. I appreciate you being here. I...I don't feel like I've really got many people on my side these days."

That's an understatement.

"How's Ed?" Marcus asked suddenly, breaking the stiff tension.

Zara smiled wanly. "He's fine. He stopped running back to Kinmount Street a few months ago. I think he finally figured out that Dmitri isn't there."

Isn't there and probably isn't coming back.

Marcus grinned. "I'll never forget that first night when I heard the banging. And he was trying to bash the front door down as the biggest poodle I've ever seen."

Zara laughed. "Yeah, that was pretty weird."

"You should probably let him out before he eats all your money or something."

Zara eyed him incredulously and was about to ask him how he knew when she realised her handbag was practically wriggling off the sofa beside her. She leaned over, opened it up, and a bubbling, shape-shifting ball of chaos poured out.

Marcus whooped in delight as a shivering teacup Chihuahua swelled into an energetic Yorkshire terrier and back—then something in-between—before inflating into a golden Shiba Inu and landing in Marcus' lap. His yips of delight were smothered by Ed's licks all over his face.

It was still strange seeing Marcus and Ed that way, considering the first time they met, the creature had used his head like a chew-toy when the three unwittingly broke into Dmitri's derelict house. That was before Zara gained the power of an ancient spirit inside her and Marcus soul-bonded to a transcendent being, of course...and before all the good and bad shit that happened thereafter.

"You'd better be quiet. I don't think all the flirting in the world would make the receptionist let you have a dog in here."

Marcus flipped Ed into his arms, cradling him like a huffing, excited, furry baby. "Oh, come on! Who could resist this guy?" He kissed him on the snout, and Ed shivered, his eyes closed in content ecstasy. "He's living at the flat with you? How's that going? Do I, uh...owe you rent?"

Zara grimaced. "It was a little tight at first, but I got a promotion, so I'm doing okay despite your disappearance." She still had the keys to Kinmount Street hanging up on a hook in her kitchen but couldn't face the idea of going in, let alone living there rent-free, even with London's property prices.

Marcus cringed, rubbing the back of his head awkwardly. "I'm sorry. Can I make it up to you? I'll give you my share of arrears. I have cash and some treasures from my travels that I'm pretty sure are technically priceless. I'm nothing if not a sharer."

"It's fine."

"Where do you even sell priceless things, though?" Marcus grumbled. "And if they're priceless, how can anyone afford them?"

Zara quirked an eyebrow. "So, you *are* a pirate now?"

"A little bit. I mean, a little manipulation of the ethernal has kind of given me access to resources and a bunch of bank accounts..."

"Marcus!"

"It's fine! All offshore tax scammers. I've even redirected a bunch to charities. Turns out I have a secret daddy fetish cos I love finding new ways to make the patriarchy suck my dick."

Zara smiled. "I'll allow it. But you said you were here to talk business, then told me everything but all the meals you've eaten in the last year."

"Right," Marcus snapped back to himself, chuckling. "Sorry— getting stuck in a time rift really messes with the old executive function. Not that I didn't have problems with that before, it's just now I seem to lose my train of thought more easily. And besides, I don't eat anymore. Well, except sometimes for fun. Had to trade in hunger and nourishment to get out of a nasty pinch in Malaysia." He tilted his head toward Song, who nodded gravely.

"Jesus, Marcus," Zara breathed.

"It's great, honestly! Kinda plays havoc with the bowels when I do eat, to be honest, but I reckon I'll trade that in next..."

Zara shook her head, staring not at Marcus but instead at Song. Though the ethernal looked timid, they were beyond powerful. An immortal godlike being that corporealised on Earth and formed a soul-pact with Marcus, trading their magickal energy for his perceived or actual human flaws. When they had taken enough of them, Marcus would...cease to be human anymore. He would become like an ethernal, and transcend. By anyone's reckoning, that was a lifelong process. But due to the hazards Marcus had endured, who knew how much wick was left on his candle to burn.

Zara braved the question. "How long do you have?"

"Oh, like an hour, but it's not too important," Marcus said casually.

Zara's jaw dropped, and she stared at him, horror-stricken.

Marcus stared back for a moment before his eyes widened. "Oh! You mean until I become all immortal and godly! Jeez, ages yet. I haven't even really gotten to the good stuff. I just meant I have an hour before I have to be somewhere else."

Zara let out a deep breath that had caught in her chest, and her body relaxed. She slumped back onto the couch. "Jesus, Marcus. Don't do that to me."

Marcus cringed, squeezing Ed, who was squirming out of his arms, and wrestled him back under control. "Sorry. But yeah, let's get down to business...to defeeeeat—"

"Marcus."

He sighed. "Did you see the news? About the landslides in Italy? And the tsunami in Indonesia?"

"Of course. It was all over the news."

"How about the five volcanoes that popped off in New Zealand a few weeks back?"

Zara nodded grimly. That had been big news. Building a city on fifty dormant volcanoes might have only been a small gamble, but that many injured and dead had really shaken the world.

"And the floods in China?"

"Yeah, it's been a real shitty year. What's your point?"

"In just a few weeks, there will be a series of quakes that will decimate California. Only a few days after that, another will obliterate half of Tokyo."

"Christ, Marcus. How do you...how can you know that? That would mean thousands dead."

"Millions," Marcus corrected. "And that's only the beginning. It gets worse. But what I saw gets a little hazy after that. I'm pretty sure that's a bad thing rather than a good—as in the world falling apart hits such a catastrophic level of cluster-fuck that it's impossible to pick one disaster apart from the other."

"What you...saw?"

"In the temporal rift."

"Right," Zara said, taking a deep breath and eyeing him carefully.

If it hadn't been for the events of the last few years, she might have thought Marcus had gone off the deep-end, but his wide and fervent eyes told her he was telling the truth. Song's sombre ethernal gaze beside him confirmed it was not just a truth that *he* believed, but *the* truth.

"Why are you telling me all this? It's natural disasters, right? Not anything to do with monsters that I can help with."

"Au contraire, ma soeur," Marcus said. "I speak French now, by the way. I can do all the languages. Get into it."

"How about sense? Do you speak that?"

"It does have something to do with monsters, though. In point of fact, it is *only* to do with monsters."

Zara's face scrunched up in confusion. "Are there like... monsters that can make disasters happen?"

"Oh Gods, no. That would be terrible, wouldn't it?" Marcus' face split in a wide smile. "But also, like, really *cool*." He sobered again. "No, that's not what's happening. It's specifically to do with Theia. Zara, the world of monsters is dying, and I think we have to save it."

THREE STEPS BACK

"Theia?" Zara repeated. Her skin tingled. "I thought Theia was already destroyed."

She remembered how Lyn had described it: if the earth were one side of a coin, Theia was the other—a place filled with things more incredible and terrifying than she could reckon.

It had been a while since she had thought about Lyn: the beautiful, fierce, intelligent doctor she had a short tryst with after...*after* saving Oscar from her clutches when she was trying to use him to end the world. It had been complicated, but there was definitely a tender spot left on Zara despite telling Lyn she didn't want to see her again two years ago. Lyn, of course, had kept good on the request.

"True, in some ways. Ever since the druids sealed the waypoints between Earth and Theia, pressure from energy trans-ferred from Earth—particularly hate—*has* been building up. Theia is totes broken, but from the Umbran crossing over, we know there is some sense of...existence there. Problem is, as things get worse, the whole place is finally crumbling under the pressure. And because of the interconnection between our worlds, the damage is finally showing on Earth. The veil is bulging, tearing at points that are shifting the Earth at its very core."

Zara stared at him numbly. "And what do you want me to do about it?"

"Zara, we need to stop it! If the pressure keeps building, eventually, not even too long from now...let's just say it will be a lot more than both the worlds at risk. The force will collapse Earth and Theia in on themselves with such pressure as to create something bigger than a supermassive black hole. It could destroy *everything*."

The Ghatotkacha hummed inside her. Before, with Rami, the spirit had gleefully rushed into her, attaching to her fury with its fierce energy to intimidate its opponent. But now, a deeper excitement thrummed. Now, it smelled what she had long suspected was its favourite thing.

It smelled battle.

She felt the pressure of it flexing against her. Driving her. It made her skin flush. Her insides boil. Bile burned the back of her throat.

"How?" Her voice shook from the control she exerted to speak normally when every cell of her wanted to scream.

Marcus wasn't smiling anymore. His eyes were fixed on Ed in his lap, who was making only the most perfunctory attempts to escape. Marcus absently booped him and cleared his throat. "Uh... well...that's why I'm here. I..."

Song cast Zara a sympathetic look, and she felt disappointment, confusion, and...

"You have no idea, do you?" Zara asked hoarsely.

Marcus cringed. "Nope."

The thrumming inside Zara eased, but not by much. More than anything, she wanted to let it out, to stand up and fling the sofa through the tall window, tearing through wood, glass, and brick. Not that it would fit, but she could always make it...

"Marcus, what you're telling me is that the universe is in peril, and you don't know what we can do to stop it. Have you tried—"

"The Bean-Nighe? Of course. I saw her straight away, and she's seen the same. But that's all. After that, she just kept saying the same thing: 'Too much death. Too much death.'"

"She can't see beyond death."

Zara remembered. The Bean-Nighe could see futures but hadn't seen Zara's destiny...because she had died before it came to pass.

Marcus nodded.

"So that's it? No one else with that kind of vision? At least... not with Betty Blumpkin dead?"

Marcus shrugged miserably. He'd never gotten to meet the squat, gruff drag queen—or otherworldly beauty depending which side of the glamour she was on—who had a skill for reading the past to guide the present. That would have been perfect right about now...but the Umbran had murdered her.

"There are a few people—monsters, I should say—that had foretelling in their skill set. There were even a couple lesser kinds in London, but by the time I got to them, they had gone missing."

Zara frowned. That wasn't a good sign. "Maybe they knew the danger and bailed?"

"To where?" Marcus shook his head. "The level of obliteration will destroy everything, including the in-between."

Zara grunted.

"I was in Guangzhou yesterday. There is a seer there that knows something is coming but can't see the details. She told me about a trio of prophets in Thessaloniki called the Nufates, but when I got there...it turned out they were a sham. Using monster blood to conduct low-level scrying. Had a Charybdis locked in a cage that they had nearly drained dry."

Zara frowned. "Wait, what are you talking about? How did you get there and here so fast, and—"

"And still look this good?" Marcus flashed white teeth and dusted off his shoulders. "I don't fly economy, sweetheart."

"Marcus, if you don't just tell me, I'm gonna spirit slap that grin off your face."

"Whoa, whoa, whoa." Marcus raised his hands in surrender.

"Spare my beautiful face. I've got some new tricks up my sleeve is all I'm saying."

Zara was about to ask what he was talking about when Marcus let out a low whistle through his teeth. There was a flash of movement from behind the leather chair he sat upon, and then from behind it waddled a duck. Its head was a beautiful, lustrous emerald green. The emerald spread down its proud, plump breast where either side split into mottled tawny wings.

There were three strange things about the duck. One was its beak; rather than yellow or orange, it was a shimmering gold. Next were its eyes. Zara had never seen a duck with blood-red eyes before. The third and final peculiarity was its legs—specifically that it had three of them.

"Marcus!" Zara gasped as the duck waddled forth and looked between her and Marcus with curiosity. Song reached down and touched their fingers to its emerald crown, causing the duck to close its eyes in bliss.

"Pretty fancy, eh?" Marcus grinned. "Found her on my travels. Only took a little juice for me to converse with magickal creatures. Less than getting pimples." He winked, but judging by his flawless, umber skin, Zara wasn't sure if he was joking.

Ed had perked up in Marcus' lap and was now desperately trying to get free, eyes fixed on the duck.

The three-footed duck.

Wasn't that part of what had gotten them into this mess? The childlike drawing that the Bean-Nighe had handed to them? The roughly hewn wooden token that Oscar had touched, handed to him by the ghoulish girl that had claimed Zara's own life-force before Oscar ended hers?

As if it could hear her thoughts, the duck gave a low inquisitive quack.

"Easy, buddy. I'll let you go if you're a good boy, okay?" Marcus said to Ed.

Ed went very still, wide eyes fixed on Marcus, and gave a heavy huff followed by a cough.

Marcus released him. Ed flipped off his lap and onto the floor in a heartbeat, already shifting into one of his more un-intimidating forms: a ridiculously fluffy Pomeranian. He pawed the rug tentatively, attention fixed on the three-footed duck, which seemed to *shimmer* slightly and gave off a nervous *quack*.

"And...it, uh...works?" Zara's voice was low. From what Lyn had told her, the three-footed duck was thought extinct—hunted too often for the properties of its blood. The ability to teleport anywhere *from* anywhere.

"Damn right!" Marcus grinned. "I couldn't tell you all the shit we've been up to thanks to Du—uh...her. Breakfast in Paris, followed by a morning walk on the Golden Gate Bridge. You might think that's irresponsible, but the way I see it, it would be irresponsible *not to* take advantage of such a beautiful gift."

"And it doesn't mind just...taking you places?"

Marcus shrugged. "Not so much. She likes a nice fluffy nest to sleep in, so as long as we get her lots of snacks and good pillows, she's alright. And, uh..." He cast a glance at the duck, raising one hand to cover his mouth and speak in a whisper. "She likes fresh meat. Other ducks especially. Our little travelling cannibal."

The duck took a tentative step toward Ed and let out a low quack again. Zara thought she saw dark, jagged teeth in its golden bill. It sent a shiver up her spine. "Well, *that's* horrifying."

"Yup," Marcus agreed, watching the duck with a mixture of affection, disgust, and concern.

The duck plopped down on its plump body, her beady red eyes fixed on Ed. He padded toward her, paused for a moment, then gave her a tentative lick right on her golden bill. The duck closed its eyes patiently.

Zara dragged her gaze away from the display uneasily. "So...not that it's not great to see you—I could have done with you around pretty much every day for the last two years. Or, you know, even a text would have been nice. But, if the world is fucked and we can't fix it, I assume you're not just here to show me some signposts and tell me we're on our way to hell in a handcart?"

"Universe, not world. And 'hell' would be the place *causing* it to implode, to be specific, rather than the destination. But yeah, I have some ideas for what we can do. There is a sect of druids in Japan. Apparently, they are an offshoot of the ones that put the seal in place that started all this shit. I'm going to head up there with my old golden-beaked pal here and see what I can learn. Only problem is...the Bean-Nighe said that things might go better with *you* there. Only, she didn't say that exactly. You know how she is with making sense and all—totally hates it. I just figured that since she mentioned it, I gotta catch ya. Get it? Got-a-catch-ya..." Marcus waggled his eyebrows, smirking.

Zara folded her arms, feeling an uneasy prickling between her shoulder blades. The last time she had seen the moon-eyed fate witch was the night Oscar died. She didn't exactly blame her, at least no more than she blamed herself, but thanks to the Bean-Nighe's vagueness, she was constantly haunted by the idea that she could have done more to save him.

"I don't know, Marcus. These things have a way of going south fast. After everything that's been going on...now isn't really a good time."

"It's all good," Marcus replied quickly. "Beanie said you'd probably say that. She also told me to pass on a message to you."

Zara's skin prickled. "Do I want to hear the message?"

"Want to? Probably not. But I do think you need to."

Zara sighed, steeling herself.

Marcus tilted his head, lifting his voice in a high sing-song way, a fair imitation of the pale doomsayer. "What was given to you is not always yours to give in turn. What you have might be kept, and who would take you can spurn."

Zara's heart lurched. Her jaw clenched, and she looked up at Marcus.

"I guess she's talking about your little ghost pal that makes you all sparkly smashy goodness, huh? And from what I caught, Rami wants to take on the spooky mantle..."

Zara did not reply.

"For what it's worth, Zara, I want you to be happy. Whether that means giving up your power or keeping it to fight another day. What I will say, however, is that when it comes to the end of the universe, I'd definitely rather have you at my back than that thumb-headed man-child."

Zara met his eyes and spoke carefully, "I...I don't know Marcus. Honestly. Ever since I got this, things have been hard. I don't know that they would be any easier without it, but...I just don't know if this is me. Sometimes, I don't know who I am anymore." Silence rung like a bell in her ears as she dropped her head. It hung for an uncomfortable amount of time.

"I know who you are, Zara," Marcus said finally, his voice soft. "And I think you do, too. Maybe you just have to remember..."

Zara felt tears prickle the corner of her eyes. She welcomed them for once, letting them run down her cheeks. "I'm not so sure."

Marcus leaned forward and grasped her hand. "You did the right thing, Zara." His voice was flat. "You had to...you had to do what you did to Oscar. If you didn't, none of us would be here today. Including him."

"I know," Zara said. The words were so solid and firm, she wondered if this might be the first time she had said it and really believed it.

"I don't think I could have done it. You're strong. Stronger than me. And that's why I need you to fight. So, I'm going to go to the sweet arse end of nowhere and talk to some secret witches, and you can take a little time to decide what you're gonna do. I'm hoping you're gonna suit up and come and fix this mess with me once and for all."

Zara laughed, releasing his hand and wiping the tears from her eyes with her palms. "Once and for all? That's wishful thinking. Usually, this shit just gets worse every time."

Marcus shrugged, grinning. "Yeah, you know me, ever the optimist."

There was a low knock on the door.

"Mr Williams? We have a family waiting for the room," the soft voice of a woman said from outside the door.

"Thanks, Lisa. We'll just be a minute," Marcus said loudly in return.

"Be sure to stop by the desk on your way out," the woman replied.

Marcus grimaced nervously, and a wash of amusement came from Song.

Ed was still licking the three-footed duck curiously. For her part, the duck sat and quietly allowed it.

"So uh, I get you don't want to come, but what about him?" Marcus asked.

It took Zara a moment to realise who he was talking about. "Ed? What, do you need something licked to death?"

Marcus arched an eyebrow. "We both know he can do a lot more than that. One of us first-hand. Besides, the Bean-Nighe said you were a low maybe, but Ed was a definite yes."

Zara felt a pang in her chest and looked down at the Pomeranian wiggling his tail in the air as he continued to try and lick the duck's face off.

Him too? Does everyone have to up and leave me?

"Sure. If you think he will be useful." She tried to sound nonchalant. "Just don't keep him too long. I need someone to eat my leftovers and climb on my head in the mornings to wake me up."

Marcus raised his hands. "No promises. I hope it's quick, but I don't know how things are going to work out."

"Just...no more temporal rifts. Don't want you coming back and me being a doddery old lady, do we?"

"I'll do my best." Marcus sounded, for once, solemn. It only lasted a moment before mischief found its way back into his voice. "Can I offer you a ride? I can take you wherever you wanna go." Marcus glanced toward the three-footed duck. "Singapore, Timbuktu, Alaska. Or ya know...home."

26

Zara smiled. "No, thanks. I'll stick with the cab. I'll leave the duck surfing to you."

"As you wish. Come on, Du—uh...buddy." Marcus stood, reached down, and hefted the plump creature up with both hands. It ruffled its feathers, adjusting in his grip as he righted himself.

Song got to their feet, golden eyes fixed on Zara's as they reached down and picked up Ed, who went still and quiet. They clutched him in one of their dark hands, the other linked through Marcus' arm.

Zara frowned, something itching in her thoughts. "Wait, Marcus."

"Yes'm?"

"You gave the duck a name, right? You've almost said it twice but stopped yourself."

Marcus stared back blankly.

"What is the duck's name?"

"I don't want to tell you."

Zara smothered a grin. "Tell me the duck's name."

Marcus looked away woefully. "The duck's name is...Ducky."

Zara had only just started laughing when they vanished with a pop.

TAXONOMY OF MONSTERS: THE SNALLYGASTER
(AVEM MORTIS)

A thing of scale, feather, and claw,
A thirst for blood within its maw,
A single eye to find its prey,
Seeking death in night or day,
It doesn't matter where you run,
That's how the 'gaster has its fun.

— ARTEMIS BEAN, 1917

4

THE MIRROR'S KISS

*Z*ara let the shower reach the edge of being too hot, relishing the heat as it flowed down her body. She'd thought that once she completed her exams to finish her master's and gotten her promotion, everything else would just fall into place. That had been three months ago. But things just *hadn't*...even before Nani died. She had no idea what exactly it was she needed to get herself back on track—or what track that was—but whatever trouble Marcus was trying to pull her into likely would only take her further away from it.

The brief lift of seeing Marcus again had been punctuated by the jarring news he brought. It wasn't exactly a surprise per se, just another thing to add to the list. Another reason to wake up tangled in sweat-soaked sheets...because the world was ending. *Again.*

It wasn't always the world-ending dreams that troubled her sleep. Some nights, she dreamt of the Ghatotkacha within its previous hosts, and those didn't feel like dreams at all. She relived memories. Sometimes she stood before a vast gold and red gate marked with symbols and heard the rumbling voice of the Ghatotkacha from within. It was becoming difficult to remember when she'd last had a restful night's sleep.

Marcus' visit and dark words had, however, left her gratefully numb to the afternoon gathering that followed Nani's funeral. Everyone there knew how close she had been with Nani, so there was a parade of distant relatives gripping her to them and spouting sorrowful words. They all seemed to say the same thing, hollow sentiments that skimmed over the void left below. When she fixed her gaze with theirs to decide who was being genuine, it was like trying to nail down a wounded animal and deliver the mercy blow, each of them squirming away with polite excuses.

On the other hand, the more she heard people talking about Nani, the more it brought back the real her. Not the soiled bed sheets and disoriented wailing, but the wry, wise, and whip-crack smart warrior of a woman Zara had known her whole life. It made the loss feel keener but also more distant. She hadn't seen *that* Nani for a long time, so really, the grieving had begun years ago.

Zara's mother had busied herself seeing after everyone, sorting out plates of food, and nipping interfamily conflict in the bud before it could really kick off. Zara recognised the busy work. She wondered again if her mother felt the guilt too—the guilt at the relief of not having to see Nani suffer any longer. A release from seeing the fleeting frustration in her eyes when she almost remembered who she had been before sinking into a fog of despondent confusion.

Despite all the years she had protected the family—and who knows how many others—from unimaginable threats when she had held the Ghatotkacha, she still died a long, quiet death alone in her bed. Zara sometimes wondered if Nani would have preferred to die in battle.

It made her wonder if she would rather go that way, too.

She closed her eyes and lifted her face so the hot spray of the shower plastered her thick, dark hair back, trying to imagine the misery washing off her like a film of oil.

At least Rami had kept his distance at the party, lurking at the edge of the room, though she had caught him watching her with that strange look.

That scowling, *hungry* look.

Spitting out a mouthful of water, Zara twisted the tap, irritated she couldn't cleanse her feelings as easily as her body. She used a little more force than was strictly necessary, and the metal groaned in protest. For a moment, she expected it to bust off, water spraying out in a torrent in its place.

It wouldn't be the first time.

Mercifully, not today.

Zara reached out and grabbed a couple of towels, wrapping one around her head and giving her body a cursory rub with the other before putting it on the hanger, then moisturising and donning a fluffy white dressing gown.

She made her way into the kitchen diner. Despite all the delicious food that family members had brought to the funeral party, Zara hadn't had much time to eat—what with all the facilitating other people's grief on top of her own.

Padding over to the window, Zara pulled the navy curtains closed, conscious that the dim light revealed her to the inky night outside without her being able to see back. She then made her way over to the tall fridge. One good thing about Marcus being gone was that the flat was tidy. Spartan, almost. She kept it that way because she didn't have much time to be sorting things out. She ate more meals out than in nowadays, and twenty quid a week got her a great cleaner that came every Sunday and kept everything nice. Zara approached the fridge and was debating if she had anything good to eat when she heard a low tapping.

At first, she wondered if the dull thud was coming from the refrigerator. She was well overdue for a replacement, and it was prone to making some interesting sounds. However, when she heard it again, she realised the sound was instead coming from the hallway.

Frowning and pulling the cord of her dressing gown tight, she turned and padded on still damp feet to the hallway. The lamp cast a glow that was eerie or cosy depending on context, but a mysterious tapping near midnight coming from nowhere near the front door fell firmly into the former.

Cautiously, Zara made her way down the hallway, her eyes immediately pulling to the full-body mirror there. A bunch of dill hung over the mirror's crown, its tips browning but still fresh enough to ward off unwanted visitors that might come that way. The mirror itself was clear, holding only the reflection of the opposite wall until Zara stepped before it and saw herself there, too.

She turned, deciding to check the door just for good measure, when it happened again, so close this time she jumped. The spirit within her awoke in a pulse of energy. She spun back to the mirror, finding only herself once more.

Then, slowly, her reflection changed.

Her golden-brown eyes lightened, becoming crimson like fresh, pooling blood.

Her tawny skin shimmered, turning alabaster, a shock of white, slicked-back hair now atop her head.

Her round curves faded, shifting to tall, lean sinew and muscle.

The figure smiled wickedly, raising her hand and tapping gently on the inside of the mirror's surface once more with black, pointed nails.

Zara's heart lurched in her chest, already galloping. The Ghatotkacha sang with excitement. She snatched the dill from above the mirror and spoke, her voice soft on the same word three times. A name. "Vandle, Vandle, Vandle."

The mirror shone, and the figure within reached out. The surface gave way to her long, pale fingers, like a bubble being flaw-lessly breached without bursting. Zara's heart pounded, but she didn't move as the woman people had once called Bloody Mary stepped forth.

"Zara, Zara, Zara," Vandle said, echoing Zara's summoning. Her tone was dulcet as always, deeper than you might expect, but softly spoken.

The dill had sealed this route for most that might mean to use it, but removing it and speaking Vandle's name thrice had opened it to her. The narrow hallway barely held them both, but Zara refused to move. She took up her space, forcing the other woman to stand close.

Zara opened her mouth to reply but found the pale woman's long fingers already wrapping around her throat, her breath already on her lips. Zara welcomed her, the soft touch of her mouth and the cool feel of her fingers. It had been weeks since she had last been able to visit.

Zara's hand knotted in the other woman's short, bone-white hair as those cool fingers found their way into Zara's dressing gown, hungrily rediscovering her warmth.

❧ 5 ❧

I SEE ME IN YOUR EYES

"It had been too long," Vandle drawled, her dark, pointed fingernail gently trailing its way up Zara's bare back.

"I blame you," Zara mumbled, face down into the pillow. She turned her head to look tiredly at the pale woman beside her. "You're the one with all the move and shake. You should have shaked it over here faster."

Vandle chuckled, running fingers through her now tousled hair. "Maybe if you let me smoke in bed, I'd be here more often."

Zara pulled a disgusted face.

"I'm immortal. It's not like they will make me sick...nor you."

"I know. They still smell and taste gross, though." Zara propped herself up on her elbows. The height difference meant she couldn't easily steal a kiss from those pale lips, so she settled instead for brushing hers against the curve of Vandle's breast. "Besides, you taste perfect as is. No seasoning required."

Vandle smirked, those red eyes fixing on Zara's. "How have you been?"

Zara sighed. "Hungry. You came just as I was trying to decide between leftover takeout or fresh takeout."

"Fancy."

"And if you're going to make a joke about me just having eaten—"

"No, Zara. I'm going to ask you how you are again. It was your grandmother's funeral today."

The smile slid from Zara's face. It wasn't as though she'd forgotten, not even for a second. It was just easier to pretend everything was okay, even if only for a little while. A few breaths without remembering the smiling picture of Nani amongst the flowers.

"I'm managing."

"Would you like to talk?"

Zara sighed and flopped back into the pillow, so her reply was muffled. "Not really, no."

"Understood," Vandle said simply. "But when you do want to, I am here. How is everything else?"

"Business as usual," Zara said tiredly, rolling onto her back. "Not much trouble to speak of around here. Though I'll admit I could look harder for it. How about you?"

Vandle grimaced at Zara's general evasion of the question. "New York is interesting. Much livelier than I remembered it being. Many of my kind make their homes there, and they are a diverse group. I haven't spent a significant amount of time there since the sixties, and it's changed. I suppose any city in a country with so many Theians in government would."

Zara's eyebrows shot up. "Huh. I mean...that tracks."

"Other than that, Paige is...formidable, as usual. I thought after Betty died, I would be short of things to do, but it seems she constantly has several pots on the boil. At times, I'm not sure if she is an agent of chaos or incredibly intelligent. Things go wrong about as often as they go right, but it's...fun."

Zara chuckled. That sounded about right, too. Oscar's sister had always been trouble, and after what happened at Stonehenge, she had taken an interest in Vandle from a purely business perspective. Vandle had been somewhat adrift since the Umbran slaughtered her psychometric drag queen partner. Now, she and Paige ran some kind of operation out of New York, sending Vandle on constant trips around the world to transport wares. Vandle wasn't telling her everything, but Zara got the impression that perhaps it was because Paige didn't tell *her* everything, either. Regardless, they could handle themselves, and it sounded like Paige was thriving. Zara had no desire to put a stop to that. Finding something to keep her busy after Oscar...it was important.

"There is something," Vandle said. "A *concern*."

Zara frowned. "What? Did something happen?"

"Almost certainly. Our kind are...going missing. Mostly cities, but there have been reports elsewhere, too. I have heard only whispers, but it seems like only parts of their remains have been recovered. The community is disjointed but agrees that something is...hunting them."

Zara froze. Her next breath came with great difficulty.

Monsters going missing and only part of their remains being found? That sounds like...

"An Umbran?" Zara's voice came out choked.

Vandle didn't meet her eyes; her fine silver brows were knotted with consternation. "Perhaps. Who can say? We don't know enough of them in their current state to be certain, but the remains found were...the wrong way around compared to last time." Her lips curled in disgust.

Last time, the Umbran seemed to be primarily interested in bones—to build a gate to destroy both worlds. That and the most delicious, fleshy morsels holding power to amplify its own.

"Like...whatever it is, is leaving the bones and taking the, uh... the meat?"

Vandle frowned grimly. "For the most part. Some bones have been found. Some innards and connective tissue as well. But I fear something sinister is happening. There are even more disappearances than last time."

Zara's stomach rolled. "That could mean that there is more than one Umbran through the veil."

Vandle nodded slowly but did not seem convinced. "Perhaps. Though it would take a significant rupture, which should not slip beneath our notice."

Zara puffed out her cheeks. "It may not have escaped notice as much as you think."

The last Umbran had ridden in a civilian called Harry Barlow, an emergency services operator for the police. Zara had wondered who the corpse the Umbran rode belonged to when the thing hunted them. She hadn't needed to wait long to find out. A few weeks after his disappearance, the police approached Zara regarding some pictures saved on his data cloud. They had found them whilst investigating his disappearance. After all, the Umbran left nothing of him when it was done.

The officers had shown her some quite disturbing and very stalkery pictures of them and Dmitri leaving his house. She had to tell them three times she had never met him before he disappeared before they stopped asking. It wasn't technically a lie. His name, his strange interest in them, and that his hate had somehow fuelled the Umbran was still all she knew.

Strangely, the latter concerned her the most. There was no shortage of hate on Earth to feed the once-cleaners of Theia, to fuel them into catastrophic, destructive forces of immense power.

"Do you have any leads?" Zara asked finally.

"I'm...not sure. Suspicions perhaps."

Zara leaned forward. "And?"

"Now is a bad time." Vandle looked troubled. "I should investigate more and tell you when we have more information. You have other responsibilities at present."

Zara shrugged. "Looking out for this shit tip called Earth is one of my responsibilities. At least for now." Her own words were barely out of her mouth before they nettled her.

Hadn't it been only earlier today that she had let Marcus investigate ways to save the worlds—no, the universe—because she couldn't take any more on? Today, when she had pushed Rami away as he promised to do more with the power to help others?

The uneasy feeling that maybe Marcus' warning and this were somehow connected settled heavily in Zara's stomach. "Vandle, I saw Marcus today. He had a premonition or something. He said that all the natural disasters lately are a sign that the veil is crumbling, that Theia is falling apart, and we have to save it or everything will end. And when I say everything, I mean...*everything*."

Vandle surprised her by just grunting thoughtfully.

"Uhhh...I was kind of expecting a bigger reaction?"

"Betty told me things might end this way. Not a foretelling, more an old prophecy and reading the pattern of the past. That is why she was so interested in the willblade."

A chill ran over Zara's skin as she immediately thought of Oscar. "What was the prophecy?" she asked numbly.

"The translation differed. There were similar texts in Tamil and Theian, and it was not clear which came first. Both speak of a wielder of a weapon forged from resolve. The rough translation was that the carrier will be broken, but in being so, they will save the worlds."

Zara sat bolt upright, staring at Vandle. "A prophecy about Oscar's death, and you didn't think to mention you knew this before?"

Vandle's look was severe. "I am to understand that you have been in a similar position yourself. Interrupting a destiny can change its path but usually not for the better. If one life can save many, changing fate...it is a risk that could never have been taken."

Zara sunk back on her pillow, huffing out a breath. "Well, fuck." She had nothing to say to that, so she stared up at the ceiling instead.

Oscar *did* wield the hilt, and he certainly had been broken. She had seen to that. She remembered the look in his eyes when she did it, when she drove the willblade into his chest.

"In any case, the prophecy may be speaking of you. You were a wielder, and you saved the world, Zara. And in doing so..." Vandle cleared her throat. "Broke yourself."

A nauseated feeling buzzed in Zara's stomach. "You think I'm broken?" she asked, voice stiff and eyes still on the ceiling.

"I think you have fractured who you are. Your love for your friend and your responsibility to the world. Divided as a consequence for doing the right thing. It is impossible not to be. Zara, the fact that it tore you apart is what makes you good; it is what makes you human."

Zara rubbed her eyes. The Ghatotkacha was dormant right now, as it often was after fighting or fucking. Sated and docile. But when the spirit was awake, she was not so sure about being *human* anymore.

"Are you angry? Should I leave?" Vandle asked. The uncertainty was strange in her voice, usually so cool and smooth.

Sighing, Zara tilted her head and rested it on the tall, pale woman's narrow shoulder. "I'm always angry, Van. Some things can't be changed. I understand that better than anyone. All you really have control over is what choices you put yourself in the position to make. Please, just...stay for as long as you can. You're just as blunt and wonderful as you always are."

"I'm...sorry," Vandle said.

"Don't be. You're also right, as per."

"I never tell you anything you don't already know."

Zara swallowed, forcing the next words from her mouth, her voice tight. "How about this? I've been thinking about giving up the Ghatotkacha to Rami."

The words burned on her tongue like acid.

Vandle's response burned her ears the same way. "I know."

Zara closed her eyes.

"I cannot imagine how it must feel. What you have had to endure," Vandle said. "But...I know you will choose what is right."

"Are you sure?"

"Of course."

"I'm not..."

"You will be." Vandle's slim fingers found their way under her chin, tipping her face to hers. She captured Zara's lips in a soft and luxurious kiss, broken by the sound of Zara's belly rumbling.

Vandle's lips curled in a smile against hers. "The stomach hath spoken. Let us eat."

A DOOR TO THE FUTURE

T he gate looked the same way it always did.

Zara closed her eyes and wished it didn't.

She wished she could be anywhere else, see any other gate—maybe even the one made of bones that haunted her other dreams.

When she opened them, it was still there: two vast, solid golden pillars and an arch, figures and shapes carved so ornately into it with such perfection, it must have taken hundreds of years. It dominated the summit of what was unlike any mountaintop Zara had seen in pictures before. Flat, worn stone lay beneath her feet, and in whichever direction she looked out, the edges dropped away from who-knows-how-high because all she could see was clouds. There was no pleasing vista or rolling landscapes or even other mountains. Instead, thick plumes of swollen cloud that promised to catch her softly should she leap before letting her sink through and fall for eternity.

Amidst the pillars stood the gate itself.

Two massive doors of solid, dark red wood.

Six golden symbols stood stacked upon one another, three on each door, each one unique but like the next in its own way. Among them, a thick serpent coiled around a broken crown, a perfect circle split in two with a crooked triangle at its peak, and twisted vines poured from an upended chalice. Each of the six was contained within what—upon first glance—appeared like a complete square, but on closer examination, was writing. The writing was so cramped and dense that almost all its edges touched. The glyphs hummed with power. She had gotten close but never touched them due to that warning buzz which practically made her hair stand on end.

"HELLO, LITTLE HUMAN," the Ghatotkacha said.

Its voice, if it could be called that, rattled her bones. A roaring, deep timbre, like splitting earth.

It didn't speak in English, or Hindi, or any other language she could tell. It forced its meaning. Not a sending, like Song, but a jarring thrust of intention, brimming with power.

Zara clenched her fists so tightly that her knuckles might have hurt if she were truly *there*. "Why did you bring me here again?"

There was a pause. Then it laughed, a great booming sound full of mirth.

"YOU TRULY UNDERSTAND SO LITTLE?" it said finally when its amusement had passed.

Zara bristled. She could feel the Ghatotkacha at the other side of the gate, feel its crushing power crashing against the wood like waves against rocks. "I understand enough," she snapped.

The Ghatotkacha laughed again, this time less mirthful and more wry amusement. "YOU REMIND ME OF HER."

A thousand needles prickled across Zara's skin, feeling it whether her body in this place was real or not. She did not need to ask who it meant.

Nani. Nani wouldn't have taken any bullshit from this thing, no matter how powerful or ancient it might be.

"TELL ME. DO YOU KNOW WHAT IS IT THAT YOU SEEK?"

Zara paused.

Every time, it asked this.

"No."

The same answer as always.

She didn't know what it wished to teach her, but somehow, she knew it wouldn't be good.

There was a rumbling sound of discontent.

"Maybe if you didn't act so fucking cryptic, I might give you the answer you wanted."

Silence.

"Whenever you're ready," Zara snarked, folding her arms.

Silence.

Then...the voice tore into Zara, louder and deeper than ever before, more than she could handle.

"IF YOU DO NOT KNOW WHAT IT IS YOU SEEK, PERHAPS YOU SHOULD STOP BRINGING YOURSELF HERE."

∾

WHEN ZARA AWOKE, gasping for air, she was alone.

She lay there for a moment, her heart slamming against her ribcage.

Deeper still, she felt the Ghatotkacha. Quiet, but...satisfied. Smug, almost.

Breathing heavily, she untangled her naked body from the sheet, kicked the empty pizza box out of the way on the floor, and padded to the bathroom.

After, she was disappointed not to find Vandle sitting in the living room but was at least slightly consoled by the fresh pot of coffee that she had left brewed for her. Filling up her largest mug with black, hot coffee, Zara sipped gratefully and dropped onto the sofa.

She had left a message, of course, as she usually did, scrawled in her untidy angular hand on the back of a receipt on the coffee table. The narrow slip meant there wasn't much room to write, so Vandle kept it short.

Sorry, P called. Stay strong. See you soon.

Zara sipped her coffee. The clock claimed it was almost half-past nine, but Zara felt like it should be later. Her body was full of energy, refreshed. Despite the dream and mental fatigue, she felt physically stronger than before. She always did when she visited the gate. That was one of the things that convinced her that place was more than a dream. It was as if some of the Ghatotkacha's immense power leaked into her through the gate. Like a battery recharged. She almost felt...*good*.

Then she remembered Nani.

The loss ached terribly, an all too familiar feeling in these last few years.

Zara forced it away and picked up her phone.

Time to get your shit together. Speak to Marcus, figure out how to help him with this Theia shit, then maybe consider whether to give Rami this beefy, creepy fucking ghost to haunt his dreams instead of mine.

Zara picked up her phone, thumbed her way to Marcus on the screen, and pressed call. The picture of him trying to fit a whole scoop of mint chocolate chip ice cream into his mouth and scrunching his eyes up in effort enlarged. The sight of Oscar's elbow in the image's corner sent another pang of pain through her heart.

She was immediately thwarted by it going straight to voicemail.

Two more tries, and then she left one.

"Hey, Marcus, it's me. I'm in. Come grab me for whatever you need to get done, and let's fix this Theia thing. Swing by with... Ducky." She couldn't help but grin as she hung up and put her phone down.

Right. That's 'universe in peril' checked off the list for now.

Zara's phone buzzed on her thigh, and she snatched it up, hoping it was Marcus.

It wasn't.

It was just about as Un-Marcus a person as it could be.

Sighing, Zara thumbed the answer call button.

"What's up?" she said, trying and failing not to sound too

44

irritated.

"Hey, Zara. It's Rami."

"Yeah, my phone warned me already about that, but I thought, fuck it, why not torture myself? What do you want?"

Zara thought she heard a low grumble. "I know you don't wanna talk to me, and I'm sorry if I hurt your feelings. Yesterday was hard for us all, but I just wanna help."

Zara pursed her lips. "Mhmm."

"I...I know I fuck up a lot, Zara. But I just want to do the right thing. I hope you can forgive me."

Zara sighed. "Listen, Rami. You're a dick. I've always thought that, and you know I have. I know you want to help, but you've got a way to go before you convince me you're somebody I want to give this much power to someday."

There was silence from the other side of the line for a few moments whilst he chewed on that.

"You...so, you do want to give it up?" he asked finally.

Zara suppressed a groan. Everything she said, and of course, that's the one fucking thing he heard. "Maybe."

She could hear Rami's breath, heavy on the other end of the line.

"Did you just call me to breathe at me down the phone?"

Rami grunted. "Okay. I get it. I...I understand, and you're right. I'll try to show you I'm the right man for the job."

Zara's eyebrows climbed in surprise, but she replied, "Good."

There were a couple of moments of stiff silence. Zara was about to turn her screen to check he was still on the line when he spoke again.

"Listen...the reason I called you. I know a couple of guys that are still on the force. They said there's been a flux of missing person cases in London the last few weeks. I was thinking it might be up your alley."

Zara smiled. Rami acting half-decent to take on the Ghatotkacha and a lead on disappearing monsters...two for one?

Maybe things were looking up after all.

TAXONOMY OF MONSTERS: THE HEADVYS
(CAPUT CANCRI)

"A many-legged creature known to attach itself to its victim's skull and feed on their fear. Its fangs, though terrible, are only employed if its hold is challenged, offering a painful paralytic to discourage attempts to remove it. It is said that once, a headvys attached itself to a human child in Denmark and remained in place for twenty-seven years until the host died of miserable exhaustion."

— ON CREATURES FOUL: ARTHUR'S NOTES ON
THE BEYOND

THE RAT-KING

Z ara felt strange being out in the cool night air, waiting to meet up with her cousin. It wasn't really something she imagined herself ever doing. They hadn't been on particularly friendly terms, even as children. The strangeness was increased by the fact she was standing in a carpark outside a ratty old collection of warehouses at a worn-down industrial estate for a lead on missing monsters. None of the huge, square buildings had any lights on. The cab driver asked her three times if she was sure before leaving her there and driving off almost an hour ago. She was finding it very difficult not to be annoyed, mostly because Rami had been awfully elusive about exactly *why* he needed to meet her here. Worse, now he was late too. And with every passing second, Zara was getting more and more pissed off.

Finally, a black four-by-four pulled in and meandered down to the carpark all the way to where she stood before pulling to a halt, its bright lights forcing her to raise a hand to cover her eyes. She tutted irritably.

"What the fuck?" she snapped at the driver as they stepped out, only feeling a small pang of regret when she realised it wasn't Rami.

Whoever it was, was even bigger.

His pale, hairless head looked like a peanut on his massive shoulders—more specifically, that one unusual peanut near the bottom of the pack that you showed your friend because it looked a bit like a head before you popped it open and ate the contents. His lower jaw thrust out, his pink ears looked like two misplaced battered wingnuts, and his beady eyes flashed at her dismissively, then to the person getting out of his passenger side.

Rami.

"Hey, Zara. Sorry we're late. Beeno wouldn't let us make it without stopping to get him a burger."

Zara wondered if the huge guy was 'Beeno', but a third person hopped out of the back seat. This one was white too and relatively prettier than the driver. He was smaller, though his body still looked to carry a significant amount of compact muscle. He clutched a burger in one hand and shot Zara a satisfied smile as he waved.

Zara did not wave back. Instead, she folded her arms. "So, I've been standing here whilst you and your gym bros bought burgers?"

"Nah, just Beeno. Me and Greg don't eat that crap." Rami chortled before catching Zara's arching brow. His face grew serious, and he cleared his throat. "As I said, really sorry. We're here now..."

Zara scowled. Maybe she'd have been less pissed off if they'd brought her a milkshake. "And why are we here?"

Rami waggled his eyebrows. "Clues."

Beeno took a happy mouth full of burger, and Greg smirked.

Zara stared, waiting for him to continue.

"A guy visiting one of the surrounding warehouses saw someone fitting the description of one of the missing persons being brought here." Rami gestured to one of the buildings located a little deeper on the estate. "These boys picked up on it, caught a stink of the supernatural about it, and volunteered to be the ones to investigate. They know all about the monstery things that go on around here and are great coppers, despite how they look."

Beeno guffawed at that, spraying burger from his mouth.

Rami winked, his head bobbing with self-satisfaction. "Greg here's last bird was part Siren. At least that's what he said. I reckon she was just far too good for him and shrieked a lot."

Beeno laughed again, with less of a spray this time, reaching forward to push at the giant man's shoulder. For his part, Greg just kept staring at Zara, but a slow smile edged onto his face. It didn't make him any prettier.

"We got the keys, courtesy of some smooth talking from these two but didn't want to check it out alone. Thought we'd call in some backup."

"Heavy backup," Beeno added, still chewing, and shot her a snide smirk.

Rami shoved the smaller man's shoulder, shaking his head.

Zara narrowed her eyes, scowling. "Fine, but let's get this over with. I have better things to do than wander around warehouses with you clowns."

"That's not very nice," Beeno said, swallowing and scowling at her. "We're esteemed officers of the law, you know? You should show us respect, sweetheart."

Zara forced a fierce grin at him, letting the Ghatotkacha pull on her anger. She felt its energy swelling within her. Beeno recoiled, and Greg's jaw stiffened as she felt the ethereal glow push from her pores like steam. "What I *should* do is get this over with. Now lead the way, *officers*."

Beeno stepped behind Rami, looking cowed, but the big guy just looked...strangely excited. The Ghatotkacha thrashed inside her, eager to fight. She pushed it down.

"Copy that, boss-lady," Rami said with a sloppy salute. He reached into his pocket, pulling out keys with a jangle. "Follow me."

～

Zara recognised the stink of death immediately.

Judging from the dark anticipation on her meathead companions' faces, they did too.

"We should spread out. Cover more ground that way," Rami suggested.

"No," Zara countered quickly. "If whoever...*whatever* is hunting people is coming here, it could still be here. You should stay close to me."

The big guy, Greg, grunted. Zara wasn't sure if it was in agreement, but he stuck close.

"Stay behind me," Zara whispered.

The warehouse was empty for the most part. The windows sat high, letting only a little moonlight spill in. She allowed the Ghatotkacha closer to the surface, feeling her body pulse with energy. The ambient light of the spirit rising brightened the empty room and also heightened her senses. She heard the men's heartbeats behind her; all three were racing. She smelled cheap body spray attempting to hide that at least one of them needed a good wash. The stale smell of rust and concrete hid below the metallic stink of blood and rancid excrement. Zara found it difficult not to gag.

An assortment of empty drink cans and greasy pizza boxes were scattered around. Who knows how long they'd been there. More concerning were the dark stains of what looked like old blood smeared on the concrete leading deeper into the warehouse.

"It looks like whatever is happening might be happening here," Zara said. "Nice work."

"Told you they were good," Rami boasted.

Zara's eyes, more sensitive than usual, spotted something in a gouge in the ground. She crouched down to pick it up.

"What the fuck is that?" Beeno breathed.

Zara turned it in her fingers. "A claw."

Probably torn from someone...something's hand as it was dragged through here.

"Maybe you guys should wait out front," she added.

"No way." Rami patted her shoulder with one large hand. "We got you. Just lead the way."

Zara nodded, unsure how much was visible to them in the darkness but hoping her glow gave them enough to see the gesture.

She followed the dark streaks to a door attached to a small portion of the warehouse with windows so dirty you couldn't see through them. The stink was heavier from inside; she smelled it wafting from under the frame.

"Be ready to move, and make sure you give me plenty of space," Zara said lowly.

"Yes, boss," Rami agreed quickly, close to her right.

Clenching her jaw, Zara reached out and gripped the cool, metallic handle. Gently twisting, she found it was locked. Spending just a fraction of the spirit's force within her, she twisted harder, hearing the mechanism crumple within.

"Three..." she whispered, "two...one."

She forced the door open.

The stench of decay hit her like a wall, but she forced through it, eyes scanning around the room.

It looked like it had been an old office of sorts, though the cheap desk in front of one wall had collapsed to damp and mould. Lined around the room, giving off a dull hum, were...chest-freezers. Nothing else. No one.

"What the fuck?" she breathed, stepping forward.

Zara reached out with her senses, forcing scent aside to scan the darkness with her eyes, to listen for breaths or a beating heart.

Nothing.

They were the only ones there.

The only ones alive, at least.

Zara strode forward to the nearest freezer. Quickly, before she could regret her decision, she popped her fingers under the lid and lifted it.

Inside was a body.

Large, yellow eyes, pale and unseeing, skin smooth. Their head bulged unnaturally, swollen above their brow like a mushroom. This was a type of monster that Zara had never encountered before. Frost gathered at the bloody stumps of their torso, each of their limbs removed with enough care that it was cut into the joint rather than torn.

Zara stepped back in surprise and disgust. "What the fuck?"

She knew the others were close. She could hear Rami's breath behind her, smell his cheap, acidic aftershave.

He moved nearer as if to get a better view of the thing, but as he moved, Zara felt a sharp, stabbing pain bite into her flank and let out a yelp of surprise. Heat spread from the spot, and she twisted to look at what had happened.

Rami's hand clutched something dark and pointed, pressing it into her flesh. Dark blood spread slowly around it as he pulled it loose.

"What the fuck, Rami?!" Zara shrieked.

She tried to raise her fists to strike him but found that her arm was suddenly heavy.

No, all her limbs were like lead. Uncoordinated.

"What did you fucking do?" she slurred, blood roaring in her ears.

Rami simply watched as she swayed on the spot, a smug grin growing on his blurry face.

Zara felt the concrete strike her knees first. Then, her head bounced off it, sending bright light flooding through her vision.

❈ 8 ❈

RIGHT IN THE STINGER

Zara blinked, her head thick and swimming, eyes blurry. Her body felt somehow...separate.

The Ghatotkacha was there still, pushing into her cells, thrumming with violence; it coursed through her veins like a fiery tempest. The only problem was she couldn't move her body at all. It was like she was a passenger in a floppy doll.

Rami's face appeared above her, leaning down, splitting and shifting in her doubled vision. She tried to focus but was only rewarded with that insufferable self-assured smirk, the thick vein in his neck throbbing as he grinned. "Alright there, Cuz? That looked like a nasty fall."

Zara snarled furiously. The effect was ruined somewhat by the drool she could feel leaking from the corner of her slack mouth.

Rami laughed heartily, and his huge, peanut-headed friend loomed beside him, clapping him on the shoulder.

"Fuckin' hell, Rami," Beeno said from somewhere out of sight. "From the strength radiating off her, I thought the stinger wouldn't put her down like that."

The stinger? That was the thing he stabbed me with?

"Oh, never fear," Rami whooped. "The stinger always wins."

Zara tried to glower at him, but the muscles in her face were just as weak and fuzzy as the rest of her. Apparently, Rami mistook her death-glare for an inquisitive look.

"Got it from some guy who had a weird scorpion body. Girta-billu or something like that. I don't know. What I *do* know is that this stinger did a number on old Greg here, and I figured that if it was strong enough to put *him* down...let's just say you're not the biggest catch we've had using it."

Zara moved her mouth, trying to get it to form words. They came out a mashed-up mumble with another trickle of drool. Rami and his friends howled with laughter.

The Ghatotkacha roared inside her, desperate to fight. Her heart hammered harder than she had ever felt it before. Her skin broke out in a cold sweat. Whether it was from the spirit inside her or the stinger's venom, she had no idea.

She tried speaking again. This time, she managed it. "Wha... what are you doing?"

"Oh, impressive! She can still talk!" Beeno howled. "Remember when it got you, Greg? You just laid there for a whole day. Pissed yourself and everything. We kept trying to feed you soup, but it just slid right back out your mouth!"

The big man shot him a dangerous look.

"We're just doing what we have to, Cuz," Rami said, still smirking. "You aren't strong enough to carry the burden. Don't worry, though. I got you. Sometimes we have so much pressure put on us, our bodies don't even know how to stop. Our minds won't even let us consider putting it down and giving up. Fight or flight. And credit to you, at least you chose fight." He hunkered down, getting close and bringing a waft of that vinegary after-shave. He was close enough that Zara could see the bloodshot colour of his eyes and the artery in his neck pulse. "But I'm going to help you, Zara. I'm going to take that baggage off you."

Zara spat on purpose this time. It spattered wetly across his face, and he closed his eyes, a look of dark fury replacing his smirk.

"Don't fuck with me, Zara. I'm doing this for your own good.

For *everyone's* own good. I see you all the time. Wasting your power. You sit all high and mighty, acting like you're better than me. You wanna play nurse when the second you took on the Ghatotkacha, this became something more important than your job. This should be your *life*."

He hocked and spat right back in Zara's face.

She screwed up her eyes and shut her mouth, but her blood boiled and screamed in her veins. She let out a feral roar.

When she opened her eyes, Rami was standing once more, looking down on her.

"I don't want to hurt you, Zara. But I will if I must because I'm willing to do what needs to be done. Without us, there would be monsters running roughshod all over London. All over the world. But we put together a resistance. We're strong. Mentally and physically. Not like you. You're just a little girl with a gift you don't deserve. A gift you never earned."

Zara felt tears of frustration leaking down her face.

That Rami would do this...would say this...was no surprise in a way. But that it might work?

No.

Every part of her, every helpless unresponsive fibre of her being, thrummed with the need to get up and make him eat those words and prove they weren't true.

They *couldn't* be true.

Because if they were...maybe someone else could have saved *him*.

Rami shook his head, and for a moment, he almost looked sympathetic. "I get it, Zara. It's been tough. It hurt me too...when Oscar died."

"DON'T YOU SAY HIS NAME!" Zara's words came out clearer than she expected.

Rami shook his head sadly. "It broke you, losing him. And that's okay. You aren't strong enough for this. So, I'm going to take it for you. Because we're family."

"And because you're a bitch," Beeno added.

Rami shot him a warning look as Zara blinked the tears out of her eyes. Her body was burning hot now instead of cold. She felt like her heart was throbbing in every cell.

"You just need to pass it on, Zara. Like Nani passed it on to you. I'll take everything on from there. You can go on, lead a happy life, and get on with your job, get a girlfriend or a cat or whatever the fuck it is that will make you happy."

"Kicking you in the balls is gonna make me happy..." Zara clenched her fist.

Beeno howled with laughter.

Wait...

Zara unclenched her fist and clenched it again.

The Ghatotkacha roared excitedly inside her.

That's what it was doing...making her heart race, making her body burn off the poison.

"And what are you going to do if you get it?" Zara said, letting the words come out sloppy.

Rami lifted his chin, speaking with false nobility. "I'm going to kill monsters, Zara, and protect the world for people too weak to do it themselves."

As he spoke, she tested her other hand. The digits felt hazier, still numb. She tried wiggling her toes; she could barely feel them at all, but her leg moved slightly when she tried.

"I..." Zara stumbled, realising that Rami was staring at her. The big guy was nowhere to be seen now, but her returning senses told her he was still in the room. She could hear his heavy breathing, the slight whistle as air passed through his previously broken nose. Beeno was the one that smelled bad, and he was still close for sure, but she resisted the urge to turn her head and find them. She didn't want them knowing how much she could move.

Not yet.

"I don't know how Nani did it," Zara mumbled. "If I can figure it out...I will give it to you."

Rami's eyes lit up.

"But...just one thing." Zara tilted her head the slightest bit to look at him. It moved more easily than she had hoped. Her heart still galloped desperately.

Not long now. Just keep him talking.

"What are you doing with this place? I'm assuming you killed that monster. That you've been doing this. Why are you keeping their bodies here?"

Rami sneered. "None of your business. Like I said, just doing what we've got to do."

"Are you...using them as bait?"

"I said none of your business!" Rami spat, striding toward her.

There was a distant click, and everyone froze. Zara took the opportunity to shift her head.

Beeno stood by the door, the big guy beside him. They looked at each other and then back out into the dark warehouse.

"What the fuck was that?" Rami snapped.

"Dunno. Probably a bird or something?" Beeno shrugged.

Rami grunted, seemingly appeased, but then there was another sound. The unmistakable sound of the warehouse door closing.

Zara didn't wait for another chance.

In one fluid motion, she twisted her body on the floor and snatched at Rami's ankle, yanking him with enough force to pitch him over before jumping to her feet.

At least that's what she had *planned* to do. He was the most dangerous. He still held the stinger that had numbed her body.

Her still sluggish body, however, had other ideas.

Instead, she flopped, narrowly missing his ankle as he strode toward the door with a curse. Zara pushed herself up, staggering to her feet and crashing into the chest freezer behind her, her fumbling grip on it the only thing stopping her from falling right back on her behind.

"Fuck," Rami snapped, eyeing her wearily. "Greg, see what that fucking noise was. Beeno, grab her so I can stick her again."

Greg grunted in dissent, skulking from the room even as Beeno advanced on her. "You're a bit bigger than my usual sort, but you still got a pretty face, so I don't mind grabbing you," he leered.

"Shut up, fuckhead." Zara pushed herself upright, swaying on her feet like a punch-drunk boxer.

She let the Ghatotkacha further out than she had in a long time. The room lightened with its glow. Her gait steadied. Her heart sang with the glory of battle.

Releasing this much of her strength was a risk, she knew. She was just as likely to tear off his arm as twist it, but she couldn't risk being put down again. She couldn't risk letting Rami get his way, not now that she knew the depths he was willing to drop to.

Beeno darted forward with a feral snarl.

Zara snapped her arm out with a quick backhand—fast enough not to miss, soft enough to knock him down or, hopefully, *out*. The spirit's ambient glow flushed out, a palm three times the size of her own swiping through the air at the man. Instead of the firm satisfying thwack of flesh, however, she only met air as Beeno rolled and darted to one side. Surprised, Zara whirled, staggering on the spot, and steadied herself against the freezer.

Impossible. How did he move so fast?

Zara wondered if she had more venom left in her system than she thought when he grabbed her from behind. She felt the heat of his body, the stink of the burger on his breath hot on her ear. "Not normally the position I'd go for, but if you insist."

Zara pushed back. The force she exerted should easily have gotten him off her or broken his grasp around her waist. Instead, he squeezed harder, winding her.

How was he so strong?!

"Oh, baby, I love when you wriggle," Beeno chortled, gyrating his hips suggestively.

Zara's rage boiled over.

Focusing her fury, she let a pulse of energy loose, pounding out from her body with as much power as she dared without shattering every bone in his body.

This time, he lost his grip, and she heard him clatter into the wall behind them with a cry. Zara turned, her heart beating like a war drum, and teeth bared.

Beeno had crumpled to the floor and was struggling to his feet, a look of shock on his face.

"Fucking useless," Rami snarled.

He was still somehow upright despite the blast of power, bracing himself against the doorframe.

"She's strong!" Beeno shouted, eyes wide.

Rami strode forward. "Not strong enough."

"Auntie Ama is gonna be real pissed if I break both your arms," Zara said, letting her eyes light up.

Rami smirked, readying himself in a combat stance and raising the stinger in his off-hand. "I wouldn't worry about that."

Zara moved first this time. She was prepared for it when Rami dodged her first blow. After a quick jab, she stepped forward into a front kick that should have put him through the stud wall behind him. But he was quicker than his size suggested. He stepped to one side, stabbing out at her with the stinger.

Zara let out a desperate burst of energy, not as strong as the last but strong enough to throw him off balance and keep the stinger from biting into her flesh again. He staggered back, steadying himself with a hand against the wall again.

"Why are you so strong?" Zara raised her fists.

Rami grinned. "Hard work."

"And a special diet." Beeno wiped his mouth, grinning.

"Been'!" Rami snapped, expression livid.

Zara tilted her head, confused. She cast a glance at the smaller man, who was shuffling to flank her, and he cast a nervous look at the freezer.

Her breath hitched.

Wait...

She remembered when the Umbran was hunting Oscar, and Dmitri learned how it had become so strong. He said that even higher Theians feeding on each other's flesh was taboo, but he had also said something about humans eating Theians, too.

The result of that is where many of the myths of demons come from.
Not all monsters of this realm have been Theian in origin.

"Rami...no," she breathed. "You're *eating* them?"

Rami's face grew smooth. He tilted his head, cracking his neck.

Slowly, he unzipped his jacket, switching hands with the stinger to help him slip it off. Zara watched with morbid curiosity as she heard Beeno's movements still, his breath quickening with anticipation.

Rami tossed his hoodie to the ground, standing tall and flexing his arms...his disturbingly muscular arms, the flesh mottled and raw. Growths, like small molluscs or tumours, sprouted out of them in several places.

"Rami...what have you done?"

"And just how long have they been eating *us?*" Rami raised his fists. "How long have they taken *our* strength, using it to control us from the shadows? It was past time to bite back. It's happening all over the world, Zara. Cells of our organisation, the Order of Helios, working together to take it all away from them."

Rami flexed his arm proudly, the veins and growths popping and oozing grotesquely. Amidst it all, just above the inner crook of his elbow, Zara saw a tattoo. A blazing sun, its rays etched like jagged barbs in a deep crimson.

Zara snorted. "Order of Helios? Rami, did you really go and join a cult?"

"You wouldn't understand," Rami snapped. "Your judgement is skewed. Poisoned by ignorance."

"Sounds like something someone in a cult would say. This isn't a fucking game, Rami. You're eating them? That's horrific. We might think of them as monsters, but lots of them are just like us."

Rami shook his head fiercely, pointing at her. "You've lost it, Zara. I'm taking that power, even if it kills you. You don't deserve to dirty it a second longer with your fucked up ideas of right and wrong."

Zara saw the attack coming before he even moved.

If she hadn't been amped up, she may not have been quick enough, but with the Ghatotkacha filling her, she tracked Rami smoothly as he feigned to the left and ducked in. She met him with a jab squarely across his jaw. This time, she didn't stop.

Zara lashed out with her arm, slamming it down and crashing it into his wrist, where he clutched the stinger. The force knocked his fingers loose, and the poison barb skittered somewhere between the freezers.

Rami moved back, spitting on the ground. The corner of his lip had burst open under the shining light of her knuckles.

The blow could have killed him, twisted his head to the side so sharply his neck snapped...if he had been a normal human still. Instead, bloody spittle streaked his chin when he moved forward again, lashing out with a left jab.

Zara swayed on the spot, sweeping out with a leg. But this time, it was Rami who was ready for her.

He leapt, twisting as he did, and swung his fist at her face, colliding solidly with her nose. Something popped in her face, and searing agony shot through her head.

Zara staggered back, tears stinging her eyes.

Through blurred vision, she saw him moving again, coming in with a big right hook. She raised her arms, blocking him from her face and body. Instead, he wrapped his massive arms around her. For a moment, she felt the heat of his body, the scrape of the growths on his flesh. Then he slung her like poorly handled checked luggage across the room.

She was weightless, sailing through the air. Even as it happened, the Ghatotkacha sung inside her, danced with the pleasure of battle—of pain and blood and the promise of hard-fought victory.

Zara tucked her knees up and curled her chin in. The hard, concrete floor thundered into her shoulder, but she was already rolling and twisting her body. She sprang to her feet, eyes searching for Rami. Fighting the disorientation, she readied herself for the next strike.

Rami was on his hands and knees, searching between the freezers. Beeno was keeping his distance, eyeing her warily from a few feet away.

Zara felt fresh blood running over her lips and chin. She grinned at him fiercely, knowing she must look positively demonic with her glowing eyes and blood-streaked face.

Beeno sneered at her. "Rami was right. You are a right little bitch, aren't you?"

Zara glanced at Rami rising to his feet, stinger in hand and a look of excitement on his face.

It's over if I let him hit me with that stinger again...

"Takes one to know one," Zara shot back, letting the power of the spirit inside her throb intimidatingly.

Beeno snarled and came at her.

The venom was nearly gone from her body. Even if she hadn't been prepared, her instincts would have done it.

She pivoted, catching his arm at the wrist and elbow. Twisting, she rolled him over her shoulder, releasing him higher than she should...but with good reason.

Beeno's muscular body spun through the air with a shriek very unbecoming of someone exuding such toxic masculinity. Right at Rami.

Rami dodged so narrowly that Beeno's flailing arm cuffed him in the face. Beeno crashed into the stud wall and, as Zara had guessed, tore through it. The result was much more satisfying than she expected. The entire wall gave way with a deafening crunch. The compact man tumbled into the wreckage, letting out a wail and wriggling in agony.

"Oh, baby, I love when you wriggle," Zara shouted his way before shifting her gaze back to Rami and raising her fists.

Rami was eyeing her, expression somewhere between caution and fury, clutching the stinger in his left hand. His arms bulged disgustingly, somehow even bigger than before. The mollusc-like growths on them were purpling, like they were filling with blood, and they looked...*moist*.

"I won't lie, Rami." Zara gestured at him with one hand. "This isn't your best look."

He ducked forward, moving so fast he was practically a blur. Zara lashed out, but he was too fast. He'd gotten stronger and quicker in just seconds. She barely had time to register the difference when she felt the stinger bite into her belly.

Zara cried out, doubling over as that terrible dragging weight piled onto her limbs again, her brain turning foggy once more.

Then she felt it again, jabbing into the side of her neck, and everything went white.

THE EYE OF THE FLAME

The gate stood before her.

Zara fell to her knees, solid stone jarring her bones.

She wondered what was happening to her *actual* body. Was the cold pain an echo of her falling in the warehouse? And if so, how long she would be out from now three doses of that stinger...what would Rami do to get her to take the Ghatotkacha.

He had been eating them.

Bile burned the back of her throat, real body or no.

"BACK AGAIN, LITTLE GIRL?" the Ghatotkacha rumbled through the gate.

Zara panted.

Could she taste blood in her mouth?

"I need it," she blurted.

Silence buzzed.

"WHAT?" the spirit asked finally.

"Whatever power it is that's being held back," Zara said firmly, looking up. "I need it now, or it's...over."

She could feel it.

Pressing against the other side of the gate. Like a silent storm swelling nearby.

"DO YOU UNDERSTAND WHAT YOU ASK?" the Ghatotkacha boomed.

"No," Zara said flatly. "But I want you to tell me. I know...I know it's probably something bad, but I'm not sure it's any worse than what's waiting for me back there."

The Ghatotkacha hummed thoughtfully.

"NO."

A chill ran over Zara's skin, and she wondered for a moment what she had done wrong.

"WE WILL BE ENOUGH FOR THEM."

Zara felt a flare of power.

"WHEN THE TIME COMES, YOU WILL NOT ASK. YOU WILL DO."

Zara shook her head, confused.

What does that even mean?

"FOR NOW...LET ME INHABIT YOUR BODY. I SHALL RETURN IT TO YOU WHEN THE FIGHT IS DONE."

"Fine," Zara replied immediately.

There was a moment of silence, followed by loud, booming laughter.

Zara gasped.

She was on her knees, Rami right beside her. Her body hadn't even toppled to the ground yet.

It seemed that less than a second had passed here.

Her arms weren't heavy anymore. In fact, she felt...weightless.

Everything seemed sharper now, even in the darkness. She could hear the strange, twisted beat of Rami's heart, echoed in the growths dotted all over his skin. She could hear the scrape of plasterboard on concrete as Beeno struggled. She couldn't sense the big man, but there was heat and movement nearby that may be him.

She heard the rub of flesh on flesh, the creak of ligament and joint, and the sharp exhale as Rami thrust at her again with the stinger.

But Zara felt a burning explosion from within her, the Ghatotkacha swelling like never before—closer even than it had been that night in Stonehenge when she had pulled on it too deeply. Closer than when she stood at the vast gate.

From the corner of her eye, she saw Rami.

He might as well have been walking through water for the speed he moved, a speed that just moments ago had seemed impossibly fast.

A hand caught his in the air.

It wasn't Zara's, nor was it the usual spiritual energy encapsulating her own that she manifested from the Ghatotkacha. This was a completely separate hand from a thick, translucent, glowing arm that had sprouted from beneath her own.

Rami's eyes widened as another joined it, plucking the stinger from his grip like a parent taking a toy from a child and crushing it to fine black dust in a single movement.

"What the fuck..." Rami gaped.

Zara's body rose to its feet. She did not command it; the Ghatotkacha had the wheel now.

There was movement from her other side. Beeno, she realised, a moment too late. He had struggled up and now rushed at her.

Two new hands sprung forth, the ghostly limbs bursting from her other side painlessly.

One batted Beeno's swinging arm aside, the other closed around his face, lifting him from the ground with muffled cries and kicking feet.

Zara felt a heady bloodlust rush over her, the thought of pulping his skull like a melon.

*No! Don't kill, just...*win.

The Ghatotkacha's energy roiled at her rebuke, ghostly fingers squeezing Beeno's skull, eliciting another cry.

FINE!

66

Smoothly, the Ghatotkacha tossed the little man back out into the rubble with a clattering squawk.

The other hand twisted Rami's arm, and there was a sickening pop as something dislocated. He roared in agony as Zara's body pivoted, her human fists flashing out under the control of the spirit, knuckles pumping several times into Rami's ribs and cutting off his cries in a huff of winded pain.

Then, the glowing hand released him, leaving him swaying on the spot, and she felt a surge of energy rack through her body.

A force of bursting light pounded into Rami and the three remaining walls with rattling impact. The ceiling groaned, and the walls buckled and gave out. As the ceiling of the small office crumpled and fell in, one of the ghostly fists punched up, releasing a burst of energy. The rush of power blasted the fallen debris up and out, leaving only a sprinkling of dust and shattered ceiling upon her.

Enough. Let's go.

The Ghatotkacha hummed with the will to continue fighting.

The fight is over. Give me my body back!

Instead, her spirit-piloted body strode out of the wreckage.

Behind her, Zara heard debris shifting. She turned and raised her fists, expecting to see Rami rising from the wreck.

Instead, Beeno staggered up, eyes wide with fury. "You have no idea who you're messing with," he spat, tearing his shirt open.

His pale body was marked with lesions and ridges like Rami's arms and shoulders but, additionally, thick, dark veins covered every inch.

Something moved under his skin, and Beeno screamed.

His body bulged, the left side swelling, inflating like a toad's throat. His skin stretched impossibly tight and began splitting, revealing raw muscle and tissue pushing out from beneath. The weight almost toppled him, and his swollen, split fingers had to push on the floor where his knuckles already grazed to keep him upright.

"I've only done this a couple of times before," he panted, skin coated in a sheen of sweat. "But it should make it easy enough to rip even you to pieces." He cackled wildly, his chest puffing up too, head twisting and bloody drool running down his chin. His left eye bulged in its socket, leaking serous fluid down his swollen cheek.

So, this was the power that eating Theians gave humans. It was...hideous.

The Ghatotkacha flexed her arms and the four other muscular, glowing limbs that had joined them. She felt the spirit rejoicing that the battle continued.

Someone stepped out of the shadows behind Beeno's half-mutated form.

At first, Zara thought it must be the big guy, Greg. She didn't look forward to seeing the size of whatever pumped-up party trick he was going to turn into. But based on the power that the Ghatotkacha was holding whilst using her body this way, they should be able to handle almost anything.

She watched as the figure reached out and took Beeno's lopsided head in their hands.

Beeno's eyes barely had time to widen in surprise before the man twisted viciously with a wet pop she would have heard even without her heightened senses. Beeno's head snapped way too far to the side. When his body dropped limply to its knees, Zara couldn't see the life leaving his eyes because she was now looking at the back of his head aligned with the front of his body.

Numb with shock, Zara looked at the figure that had killed him. Tall and broad, with a dark shirt and trousers fitted snugly to his body.

What?

"Who the fuck are you?" Rami roared as he struggled to his feet. "You just murdered an officer of the law. You're dead fucking meat."

"Two," the man corrected, his voice low and dangerous. He pushed out with a foot, nudging Beeno's corpse. Zara didn't know if she had expected it to shrink back to normal when he died, but there he lay, looking half dead man, half bizarre, badly made giant red sausage.

Zara swallowed. That meant the big guy, Greg, was already dead too.

Rami's eyes bulged, and his face contorted in fury.

Zara knew her cousin shouldn't be angry.

He should be afraid. He should run.

"Stop!" Zara barked.

Rami didn't hear her.

Whatever Beeno had been doing, Rami was much better at it.

He pounced forward like a stalking jaguar, his bulging arms already pumping up far too big for his body. Instead of his skin splitting and tearing, the purple, mollusc-like tumours dotting up his arms and shoulders...*opened*. Their small mouths were red and meaty and hissed out a foul-smelling steam as his body continued to bulge. Rami's chest puffed up as he dashed forward, using both his knuckles and his rapidly growing legs to keep himself balanced. He roared in fury and pain.

Zara wrestled to gain control back from the Ghatotkacha.

It was like hitting a wall.

For a moment, she thrashed against it and felt the spirit's amusement as it refused her physical control of her body.

"Rami, stop!" Zara screamed instead, but she knew it was already too late. Whatever he had become, he was too far gone to hear her now.

The newcomer stepped aside smoothly as the foul thing Rami had become barrelled through the space he had occupied not a moment ago, spinning something in his hand in a blur of metal.

Rami skidded, twisting, mouth wide and eyes bulging, veins protruding all over his skin. He was at least twice the size he had been before and still growing. He charged toward the man again, roaring.

This time, the man didn't step aside.

Instead, his hand moved in a flash, fingertips sharp with claws and forearm bristling with dark hair.

Those claws sunk into Rami's mouth, the thick talon of this thumb ramming his chin, stopping his massive form in its tracks.

Blood poured onto the ground, and Rami let out a strange squeaking noise. The man pulled with ferocious, sudden force.

There was a wet, tearing sound.

Zara closed her eyes for a moment, unable to watch. She heard the spray of gushing blood on the ground. When she opened her eyes a moment later, her swollen and monstrous cousin stood, eyes glazed and swaying on the spot. Lifeblood still pumped weakly from his torn throat. His mandible was missing, torn raggedly from his skull, tongue hanging loose and flopping against his ruined throat.

Then the man spoke.

"Nenorocitul Dracului."

Flames danced up the shape he had spun in his hand until they bathed the wicked curve of the axe. He moved fluidly, spinning and swinging with terrifying power and grace.

Zara closed her eyes again.

Only for a second.

When she opened them again, the top half of Rami was sliding off the bottom.

She expected blood, so much blood. But the flames that curled on the axe were eating his corpse, slowly and cleanly burning away each half from its severed edge.

Bile, horror, and disbelief burned Zara's throat, but she swallowed them down. She raised her fists and readied herself to fight the man. The axe went out, but the burning flames of fury remained in his eyes, sharp teeth bared. His hair was hacked short on top, one temple buzzed and the other covered in scorched ridges of scarred skin, ending at an ear curled from searing flames. His unruined ear was raised to an unnatural point.

The last time she had seen him, she had looked into his eyes, consumed by loss and misery.

She had feared it would come to this.

Feared that he would return to his monstrous ways.

Feared she would have to fight and kill him, too.

Every single time she remembered Nani's last words to her, she thought of this man.

This...monster.

Nothing is as dangerous as a broken heart.

"Zara," he said, tossing her cousin's ruined jaw into the burning mess of his corpse.

Zara heaved a breath and prepared to let the Ghatotkacha take over again.

"Dmitri."

TAXONOMY OF MONSTERS: THE GHATOTKACHA
(CALVITUM OLLAM)

Thought to be the son of a man and a Rakshasa demoness, the Ghatotkacha is gifted with incredible physical power and abilities to increase and decrease in size, and disappear from sight. The Ghatotkacha lived and died a hero in a war against demon-kind, after which his restless soul wished to continue the battle and began to bond with human hosts to continue his war. The bonding process seems to come along with the benefits of increased longevity, strength, and durability. Side effects appear to be temper flares, rash judgements, and a tendency to smash things (though this may depend upon the host subject). Aura appears to be rich orange, gold, and yellow lustre, but again, this may vary with possession.

— ORIGINAL TAXONOMY ENTRY, MARCUS
WILIAMS

II
THE LAST SUPPER

THE CREME DE LA THEM

When Paige pushed the door open, she was greeted with the stench of burnt toast, dirty grease, and cheap coffee.

It wasn't exactly the kind of place she *wanted* to be, nor was she dressed for it. Her dress—cut just above her knees—was scarlet satin by Valentino, and the gem-encrusted purse she clutched protectively to her chest was more expensive than everything else she owned added together. It was *not* the attire one would ever expect to see in a run-down little diner—a greasy spoon so greasy, no one would want to eat from it.

She'd heard the health inspectors were paid off so that the many obvious health code violations didn't get it shut down. The fact the prices were hiked so high no one would want to eat there anyway kept the place empty. It was all a front, of course, and a good one.

The cashier, a young woman with red hair and freckles that clashed hideously with her orange and yellow striped uniform, spared her a bored glance from where she leaned at the register. The cook, a white-haired man with a short, square beard the same colour, leaned against the counter, drumming his fingers on his generous belly through his grubby apron.

"Alright?" Paige said awkwardly, her eyes darting between the two.

The cook looked her up and down and gave her a smile she didn't like at all.

"Bathroom's in the back." The waitress gave her a disinterested nod of the head. "Be careful, though. Customer shit all over the place earlier, and Billy here didn't clean up yet."

Paige cringed. "Sounds lovely."

With a sell like that, there was no word for a password. Anyone that turned up looking like this and took up that offer had to be here for the wrong reasons.

Or the right ones.

Paige kept her awkward grin as she walked by, nearly losing her footing when one heel slipped in a puddle of mystery filth. The red-haired waitress smirked at that, and Paige hurried out of her sight.

She made her way through the opening beside the kitchen, swallowing and keeping her back as straight as possible, trying to regain her composure. The door for the ladies had an 'out of order' sign hanging on it—and it did indeed stink to high heaven.

Paige gave the door a tentative push with her foot, not wanting to touch the handle, but it was far too heavy. Sighing, she gave in and opened it up, fantasising about washing her hands at the soonest opportunity. But as she entered, she saw there were no sinks inside the bathroom. In fact, it wasn't a bathroom at all.

It was as though she'd stepped into the cloakroom of the nicest hotel she could ever imagine. The overwhelming stench of faeces disappeared, replaced with faint notes of lavender and vanilla and...something else far too expensive for her olfactory centre to place.

The walls were a midnight blue, their clean lines only broken by a scattering of pictures of tonight's host and proprietor with a handful of various world leaders and mega-rich celebrities. Paige was still gawping when her appreciation was interrupted by a long sigh. It drew her eyes to the woman sitting in a small booth beside a black door with a gold handle.

"Sourpuss!" Paige grinned and let the door close behind her, heels clacking on the pristine, white tile floor as she approached.

The brassy little delight of a surly-faced woman stared back at her with folded arms. Paige had met her numerous times at various gatherings but never learned her name. She was a pocket rocket at barely five feet tall in her black suit, golden-white hair in a no-nonsense bob, and a face like a fucking brick.

"He put you on...door duty?" Paige didn't try to contain her smirk.

The woman rewarded her with a slow blink.

This was their usual kind of interaction.

It didn't surprise her that one of the more trusted among Big Rudy's people would sit out here inside the supposedly dirty bathroom of the dive diner. The market had to have a front, and someone needed to protect the *real* entrance.

"Always a pleasure, Sourpuss. So, what's the damage?" Paige tilted her head at the woman.

The woman scowled, which was about the most emotion Paige ever managed to get. "You know the price."

Paige rolled her eyes. *Boring.* She could have at least had one of those amazing 'Die Hard' villain accents or something, but instead, the woman had a clipped transatlantic staccato that was difficult to place. "Twenty quid and a peck on the cheek?" Paige offered with a sly wink.

This time, the stern woman rolled her eyes.

That was practically a scream from her.

Paige clicked open her clutch, popped out a pleasingly thick roll of one-hundred-dollar bills, and thrust it at the woman. The woman barely even looked at it before she stuffed it into her pocket, forming an obvious bulge in her fitted blazer. Paige wondered how often they were cashing her out and where they kept the money.

She could always use more money...

Sourpuss waved to the door beside her.

"I bid thee a magical evening, madame," Paige bowed.

"Get in or go home," the woman grumbled like she didn't care which option Paige chose.

Paige was just laying her fingers upon the gold doorknob when a strange curiosity filled her.

"Just a question, Sourpuss. If it's just you out here, taking all that money, what if somebody were to...you know, misbehave?"

Paige watched and managed not to let her eyes bulge when, for the first time ever, the woman smiled. It was hard as nails and didn't go anywhere near her eyes, just flashed perfect, white teeth. "Got a button under the desk. One push and the merry little workers out there would be here in a flash to fill you with bullets. That's if I didn't beat them to it."

"Well..." Paige huffed a breath. "It's good to know I don't have to keep worrying about you, babe. See you in a bit."

～

DOWN THE NARROW stone steps and through the heavy red door at the bottom lay a different world. A different world from the dingy diner above, at least. But it was a world that Paige was becoming gradually accustomed to.

The pristine, white walls held fancy paintings, though, Paige had no idea who'd done them. Half of them looked like some old bloke had dipped his bollocks in a tin of paint and gone to town—those were probably the most expensive. The floor was laid in decorative tiles, gradually darkening with an increasingly intricate pattern around the edges of the room. A vast chandelier hung in the middle—almost low enough that she would have been able to touch it with her fingertips if she reached up—with smaller copies of it dotted around the rest of the room. A gentle, melancholic hum of orchestral music played from nowhere in particular. When you were rich enough, you could make magic stuff like that happen easily.

This place didn't smell like burned toast *or* shit.

It smelled like money.

Not just the place either, but the *people*. Suits that cost more than Paige's education—fuck, more than her whole family's education—and cocktail dresses of every fashionable shade and style surrounded her. Some stood in small groups talking, while others meandered around the long tables lined with immaculate place settings. Lingering around the edges of the room were the goons, of course. No black market would be complete without the goons. But even then, Big Rudy seemed to have gone out of his way to procure the...least goony-looking goons available. Half of them could practically be models. Fuck, maybe they *were* models. They were undoubtedly all carrying guns, but Paige was more worried one of them might put her eye out with a cheekbone first.

A pale woman sauntered past Paige, her hair a sleek, black cascade, her gown shimmering midnight, and a pink cocktail in hand. Without stopping, she scanned Paige's dress, eyes travelling over the large white collar down to her black pumps, and gave the barest of approving nods.

Paige nodded stiffly in return.

The woman was already moving on.

That was Valeria Sands.

Valeria Fucking *Sands*.

Big Rudy might be the top guy in town, but *this* bitch was the money.

She hadn't even looked at Paige before—not at any of the gatherings where Paige had glimpsed her—but tonight, she had somehow...*approved* her? Paige hadn't set eyes on such a jumped-up bitch since the day she met Tildy Smack-Her-Bottom or whatever her ridiculous name was.

Paige had gathered information about almost everyone in this room, all the shady deals inside of shady deals and dirty trading between almost all these fuckers. But there hadn't been juice on Valeria. That didn't mean the bitch was juiceless, it just meant she was too rich and too clever to let it escape—and that was something that Paige had to respect. But when Paige had dug deeper, well...what she had found was enough to upset the balance of everything.

"Paigey! Good to see you!" a gravelly voice rumbled from just behind her.

Paige plastered on her biggest false grin and spun around. "Rudy, you old bastard, how are you doing?"

Rudy Miller, or 'Big Rudy' as he was known, wasn't exactly someone whose people you wanted to anger, but Paige found he seemed to have a surprisingly high tolerance for her antics. Not bad to make friends with one of the most prolific black-market smugglers in the world.

Big Rudy beamed, teeth clenched on an unlit cigar and the top of his knobbly little head about level with her chest...his big, brown, watery eyes unsurprisingly fixed there. "I'm doing, I'm doing." He grinned, eyes never leaving her breasts.

Paige couldn't fathom what the fascination was, but if it kept his attention from the rest of her, she was willing to let it slide.

Despite his name, Big Rudy was a slight man, past his middle years, and had the mannerisms of a slightly nervous bird. He rubbed one hand through his sparse greying hair and, with the other, popped a black fedora on his head.

A fucking fedora.

She'd never even seen the perpetual cigar in his mouth lit.

He fancied himself an old-time gangster but had the bank account of a king. Paige knew the vast majority of shit he'd gotten up to. If there were any justice in the world, that soggy cigar he replaced his silver spoon with might just give him lip cancer.

"I heard you put a contract out for some Egyptian tomes," Paige said smoothly.

Big Rudy flinched, his eyes leaving her chest and meeting hers for the first time, palms raised in surrender. "Whoa, whoa, lady. I'm just trying to get the work done. You weren't in town, so I had someone else look into it." He carried over his gangster fantasy in the cadence of his speech, leaning on a faux American-Italian swing likely picked up from movies, despite being born and raised in boarding schools across Europe.

Yeah, he was one of *those*.

"Someone cheaper," Paige translated.

"Someone more readily available."

"Someone not as good."

"True, true." Big Rudy's beady eyes sparkled. "The best are always the most expensive, but you don't always gotta use your best tool in the box for every job, Paige. If you just want to hit a normal nail, you use a hammer, not your diamond fuckin' sledgehammer."

Paige arched an eyebrow. "Did you just call me a tool?"

"My best tool. Second best, maybe." Big Rudy smiled in a thin-lipped way that made Paige's stomach turn. "Where you been anyway?"

"Jakarta," Paige replied, folding her arms. "There was a showing of the Wonoboyo hoard. I wanted to see it."

"Sightseeing?" Big Rudy's eyes glittered greedily.

"Trying to figure out the easiest way to steal it," Paige replied.

Big Rudy laughed.

"Not planning to any time soon. Just worth scoping out. It's a lot of fucking treasure."

"Smart girl." One of Big Rudy's clammy hands touched on her bare arm, and she did her best not to recoil in disgust.

"Boss?" one of the cheekbone mafia asked, appearing and leaning down to whisper something in his ear.

Big Rudy bowed slightly to Paige, one hand nipping up to stop his hat from falling off. "My apologies. It seems the appetisers are almost ready, and I like to check everything myself. Since this is your first time attending one of our special dinners, would you do me the pleasure of sitting beside me tonight?"

Paige nodded stiffly in reply, though that wasn't what she'd planned at all. "I would expect no less. And of course."

Grinning, Big Rudy spun around and followed the pretty goon

away to where Paige suspected the actual kitchen in this building was. She couldn't imagine him serving anything to these people made in the kitchen upstairs.

"You finally made it," a deep voice said smoothly from over her shoulder.

A different kind of goosebumps spread over her skin.

"Where else would I come to have people continuously greet me ominously from just behind me?" Paige replied, trying to sound sharp but hearing herself sound distinctly flustered.

The man laughed huskily and stepped beside her. She got a waft of his aftershave, something rich and spicy.

He smiled at her. His amber and brown eyes twinkled impossibly as he brushed a rogue strand of curling dark hair from the stubbled angle of his jaw to behind his ear.

His perfect fucking ear.

His perfect fucking everything, really...

"Is this better?" he asked, voice like honey, stepping so close she could feel the heat coming from his body.

Unlike most of the room, Hunter Williams didn't dress up to dress up. He had no jacket, just a white shirt unbuttoned at the top and straining at the perfect fit on his broad shoulders and chest. He could pull it off and still look better than almost anyone in the room. It didn't hurt that he was one of the most famous actors in the world and probably owned more fucking houses than Paige did shoes.

Paige batted his arm—his delightfully fucking muscular arm. "Shut up. I don't need you being all creepy. I've been trying to get invited to one of these suppers for months."

Hunter chuckled. "Maybe you shouldn't have tried so hard. Big Rudy doesn't let anyone in until they've been around a while, or he has enough dirt on them to ruin their lives if things don't work out right. You're still a new kid on the block."

Paige tried to not let her knees wobble from the way he winked at her.

"Oh," she said, trying to look put out. She had known that,

and from her reckoning, she'd still gotten in faster than almost anyone else before her. "Rudy wants me to sit by him at dinner."

"So I've heard." Hunter smiled a perfect, white-toothed grin. "We can...catch up later. I'm glad you're here."

He popped something out of his pocket and held it out to Paige.

Paige stared at it blankly. "Is that..."

"Just a pretty flower for a pretty lady," Hunter said, smiling smoothly. "It's kind of a tradition."

Paige felt her face flooding with heat. "A tradition for people attending their first high-end black market supper party?"

Hunter spun the black rose in his fingers deftly and moved to fix it to her chest with the attached pin.

Paige stopped breathing.

He leaned in to whisper into her ear.

"A tradition for guys to do for girls they like when they're taking them somewhere special."

Paige struggled not to choke on her tongue and managed to spit out some words. "Technically, I came here myself."

Hunter chuckled again, leaning back. "As you seem to everywhere. You really are going to have to tell me how you do that one of these days."

Paige looked numbly down at where the black rose now sat just by her collar to evade the question. It wasn't something she was willing to share...not yet.

Somehow, she wasn't mad that he'd just made a hole in her very expensive dress.

"Besides," Hunter added. "I guess I'll have to make it up to you by really taking you somewhere nice. Are you free this—"

There was a gentle tinkling of a bell, and the room fell quiet.

An older man wearing a chef's hat, a pinstriped apron, and a ridiculous fucking twirly moustache cleared his throat. "If you would all kindly take your seats, supper will soon be served."

11

THE APPETISER

Paige shifted in her seat, making more effort to look natural than perhaps anyone in history had before.

Everyone else was sitting, chattering pleasantly. The seat on her right—Big Rudy's seat—was empty. To her left, a dour-looking woman with hair like wire wool and a sensational bronzed pantsuit was lecturing a young man that eyed her adoringly.

Across the room at a big-name table, which included Valeria Sands, Paige caught Hunter watching her. He winked, and she looked away as quickly as possible, hoping he would think she missed it. She couldn't be getting all googly-eyed tonight. Tonight was business.

A white-gloved hand slid something onto her lap.

"What the fuck?" Paige jolted, slapping the back of it and looking up at its owner.

A distinguished-looking waiter with thick, white eyebrows and a patient smile looked back. "Your napkin, madam."

Paige forced an awkward grin that felt slightly manic. "Oh, yeah. Of course. You just go ahead and put that napkin there." She waved at her crotch before she realised what she was doing.

Her eyes shot back to Hunter who was, yes, still watching her...and now smiling.

Her cheeks burned.

For fuck's sake...

"All settled in, Paigey?" Big Rudy's voice boomed as he appeared and started shuffling into his seat beside her.

Paige brushed a lock of hair behind her ear, trying to regain her composure. "Yeah, sure. Just got the shit scared out of me by one of your sneaky servers."

Big Rudy grinned, his fake-tanned face crinkling up. "That's cos they're not just waiters. Trained killers the lot of 'em. Can't have enough security around, in my opinion. And having them double up means I gotta keep fewer mouths shut."

Paige raised her eyebrows.

The cheekbone mafia and murderers were serving hors d'oeuvres?

This smuggling meet-and-greet was at a whole different level from anything she'd been invited to before. It was always good to know you just slapped a murderer's hand away from your lap...that surely would carry no repercussions.

"You're in for a treat tonight, sugar. I just checked in the kitchen, and everything is..." Big Rudy mimed a chef's kiss.

Paige cleared her throat. "What are we having?"

His expression was strangely dark. "Only the best. I serve my *special* guests only the most exquisite and delectable of dishes."

"So, like...prawns or something?" Paige replied, nonplussed.

Big Rudy burst out in a braying laugh that sprayed her with a generous helping of saliva.

"Excuse me," the steely-haired woman in the bronze suit said beside her.

Oh. Her voice...

"You're British?" Paige asked, pleasantly surprised.

The woman smiled as if that were obvious enough.

Maybe it was, though she was decidedly more Downton in her dialect than Paige was personally accustomed to.

"Are you Paige Tundale?" she asked.

Paige's stomach dropped. People knowing who she was rarely ended up being a good thing nowadays.

"It depends on who's asking."

"Margaret Dettweiler." She extended a wrinkled hand.

When Paige took it, the shake was far firmer and more vigorous than she expected.

"Nice to meet you." Paige retracted her hand, rubbing it thoughtfully.

"I was wondering if I might have a word with you at some point tonight. I imagine I have a not insignificant amount of work I could offer someone like you. All for substantial fees, of course."

Paige smiled. Substantial fees were always good. "What line of work are you in, Ms Dettweiler?"

The older woman's lip curled. "Catering."

Paige's eyebrow arched before she could stop it. "I'm...not sure if my skills are best suited to food."

The old woman winked. "Oh, I deal in rather rare ingredients..."

"Maggie here is the real deal," Big Rudy boomed, leaning forward. "It's all thanks to her we have this feast tonight."

There was a light tinkling of a bell once more, and Big Rudy's eyes lit up greedily.

"Perhaps we will talk more after you have...sampled some of my goods." Margaret smiled. She had a hard smile. Carved. Like she had seen no else do it in a long time and was doing her best to remember what it looked like.

"Alright," Paige said thoughtfully.

Catering?

These last couple of years after...everything that had happened, Paige had been in a dark place; broke, jobless, miserable. She wasn't sure what to do next—at least until she had struck up a certain friendship, all thanks to the timely saving of a life.

Vandle had been out of sorts, too. Her companion for what sounded like the last few centuries was gone, and she had no idea what to do with herself. Paige, however, had *plenty* of ideas of what to do with someone who could travel through mirrors and pop out of them wherever they liked—absence of dill or any other magickal deterrent allowing.

There was that, and the quirk of Vandle needing to be granted access to private property for her powers to allow her to use a mirror as a portal.

The interesting thing about a lot of museums, however, is that they are public property.

Anywhere else they needed access, all it took was a perfectly legal trip during the day with one word whispered three times, and the pair of them had full access after.

Bloody Mary? More like Bloody rich.

The waiter from before, the one with the eyebrows, appeared once more, a plate in each hand. He set one before Big Rudy and the other in front of Paige.

"Cerveau Velouté with wild mushrooms," the waiter said, shuffling away.

Paige leaned forward, took a deep sniff...and almost gagged.

"What the..." She turned, looking disgusted at Big Rudy, but his face was already inches from his...soup? He slurped at it greedily from his spoon.

Paige's stomach churned.

It stank. It smelled of mould and rot, which perhaps the mushrooms might have explained, but there was also a rank sulphuric smell that was now filling the room.

Paige turned to her left and found Margaret's pale, blue eyes piercing into hers with anticipation.

"It...smells funny," Paige said weakly.

Margaret smiled in a way that might have been motherly if your dear mother might be thinking of setting you on fire just to watch you burn. "You get used to it, dear. You should eat up. The benefits are astounding."

Paige frowned and picked up her spoon, stirring the thick soup.

A small brown nugget of mushroom bobbed at its centre unappetisingly.

Paige scowled at it, then looked up.

Hunter was watching her.

He looked...conflicted?

Slowly, Paige scooped up a spoonful of the soup.

"Tell me, dear. Did they ever find out what happened to your brother?" Margaret asked casually after swallowing a mouthful of the fanciful goop.

A chill ran down Paige's spine, and she froze. "What?"

"Your brother. What was his name...Oliver? He disappeared, did he not? Under quite mysterious circumstances? What happened?"

Paige turned and looked at the woman, whose eyes bore into hers.

For what?

An answer, or just to see how she would react?

Always the fucking mind games with these toffs...

Paige clutched her spoon tightly in her hand. "I...don't know," she lied.

Margaret's brow quirked, bemused. "So strange that it was around the time of a vast disturbance in the veil. I have a team of mystics who still won't shut up about it."

Paige frowned, turning away. "That's...lovely."

Something caught her eye.

From across the room, Hunter was shaking his head. Slightly, but quite definitely.

Paige carefully set her spoon back in the bowl.

"Excuse me, but I just need to nip to the bathroom."

She scraped her chair back, eyes still fixed on Hunter. He was looking away now, having started a conversation with the middle-aged man beside him, who had a trickle of stinky soup down his chin.

"You should eat it while it's hot, Paigey. All the goodness is leaking out of it already." Big Rudy slurped wetly through a mouthful.

"I'll be right back." Paige slid out of her seat, not missing the penetrating gaze of Margaret Dettweiler from her left.

The thick-eyebrowed waiter was passing by, and Paige clutched at his arm at the same moment she remembered he was a murderer.

"Oh...sorry. Where's the bog?"

He stared back at her in confusion.

"Uhm...toilet? I need a wazz," she mumbled, letting go even quicker than she had grabbed on.

The man gave her a very bored look. "This way, madam."

12

THE WIZ PALACE AND BEYOND

The moustachioed murderer gestured at a black door that said 'Powder Room' in fancy gold writing, flashing her a bored smile before sauntering away. Paige was just about to open the door when fingers closed around her wrist from behind.

She resisted the urge to wrench her arm free and instead glanced back over her shoulder with a look of cool surprise.

"Escaping already?" Hunter asked, raising an eyebrow and gently pulling her closer to him.

She allowed it, steadying herself with her free hand on his broad chest.

They weren't usually so overt with their affections. If word got out that Hunter Williams had been shacking up with some no-name Brit, it would be all over the tabloids. There were a hundred more tabloid-worthy secrets in the room beside them, however, and the small corridor off the main area afforded some privacy.

"Not exactly escaping." Paige twisted her lips. "I just needed a wee."

Hunter's face cracked in an uneasy grin, his eyes flitting to the door behind her.

"That alright with you?" Paige offered her own arched eyebrow.

Hunter's smile faded slightly. "Just checking on my girl."

Paige felt her cheeks flood with colour.

"Paige, I..." Hunter released her wrist, shifting awkwardly on the spot in a way that entirely didn't suit him. "I'm not sure that the food here is exactly...to your tastes. If I were you, I'd skip it. I'll take you somewhere for a burger after, or that place by the bridge you like."

Paige narrowed her eyes. "I knew it!"

A passing waiter shuffled by them, his dark eyes taking them in with curiosity, but didn't slow his pace.

Paige watched as he got further away and lowered her voice for good measure. "I knew it," she whispered harshly. "You were telling me not to eat it. What the fuck are they putting in this posh shit? Caviar? That's the little fish poop, right?"

"It's worse," Hunter replied. "Just...give it a miss. If I know you, you have your escape route in place like you do for any social situation that might get awkward." Again, his eyes shifted to the bathroom door.

A curious tingle ran over Paige's skin.

Wait...does he know?

I've never told him how we do it...

"A lady has her ways," Paige said flatly.

Another server passed by. Hunter's eyes followed until they were out of earshot. "Be careful."

Paige smiled. "Just careful enough."

His hand shifted to her cheek, fingers tracing her jaw.

Paige's stomach thrilled, and her heart beat faster as he leaned in. Then she caught the rank smell of that soup on his breath. Her stomach rolled, and she pushed him gently away with her palm on his chest.

"Easy now, lover boy. Dessert isn't until later. Besides, I really do need that wee."

～

THE BATHROOMS WERE EXACTLY what she expected, though Paige wouldn't have been surprised if the taps were tiny, gaudy cherub statues, and you washed your hands in their fountained piss. This wasn't that far off.

The walls, floors, and units were all the same: black, sleek marble, veined with gold. The sinks themselves, taps and all, were burnished gold. It smelled like lavender and honey, and gentle operatic music crooned from some other hidden speaker space.

In summary: this place was fucking ridiculous.

What Paige was most interested in, however, were the mirrors.

Vast, spotless reflective panels marched across the top of the sinks, joined edge to edge, and continued along the far wall above the fancy-looking black hand driers mounted there.

Perfect.

Paige briskly walked over to the sinks, clutch under one arm, and gave a cursory glance back at the immaculate stalls, all empty with their doors open. She did another quick sweep up above for cameras. Visible ones, at least.

They had discussed this before tonight. Likely, there was nothing set to record in this room, and it was almost as unlikely anywhere else. On one hand, Big Rudy would want to know everything that went on under his roof, but there was no way that the rich and powerful, the famous and fabulous, would come somewhere where their every move was being monitored. Of course, there were deals within deals and shady secrets wrapped in twisted little bows and tucked in the shadows. There was no way Big Rudy's clientele would remain so if there was zero secrecy available in the market. He didn't really have much choice other than to keep the cameras out.

Still, Paige couldn't shake the feeling that she was being watched.

But then, perhaps she was...

She slipped her clutch from under her arm and popped it open, taking out a small, flat stone. It was a dull cerulean blue.

You might not even pick it up if you saw it on the ground. But when it was in your fingers, it felt strangely satisfying, far smoother than you would expect, and unusually cool. That was, unless...

Paige carefully leaned forward and rested it against the closest mirror with a *clack*.

For a moment, nothing happened.

And then the stone got hot.

Not just hot, but *ohfuckthatshot* hot.

Paige dropped it with a yelp and stuck her fingertips in her mouth.

Dunnstone. Vandle said they were incredibly rare, found only where thinning in the veil had worn at rocks continuously over long periods of time.

When she picked it up, it was pleasantly cool again.

Tricksy little bastard stone.

But the reaction meant there was an enchantment protecting the mirror, and the hotter the stone, the stronger the magick.

Paige dropped the pebble back into her bag and popped her still stinging fingers under the faucet. As soon as she did, the bathroom door opened.

Paige didn't turn to look who it was at first, but she caught sight of her reflection.

"Sourpuss?"

The surly doorwoman didn't even meet her eyes and instead skulked straight into a cubicle and shut the door.

"A pleasure as always," Paige mumbled and let out a breath. That had been close.

She peered back into her clutch.

There was only one other thing in there, aside from her lipstick and the space where the wad of cash had been. And now *definitely* wasn't the right time to use *that*.

What was it Vandle had said about protective enchantments? They would have to be outside the mirror and not behind, else they didn't seal the way. So that meant that whatever seal had been placed was somewhere nearby.

Her eyes darted around the room.

This could take hours...

The chain flushed in the cubicle behind her, and Paige slipped out her lipstick and started making a show of topping up the ruby on her lips.

It didn't matter. Sourpuss came straight out and strode to the door, never approaching the sinks.

"Aren't you going to wash your hands?" Paige said in disbelief, but the woman was already out the door, and it was swinging shut behind her. "Wow. What a dirty bitch."

Paige sighed, recapped her lipstick, and dropped it into her purse.

She stared at the mirror once more.

Back to business.

Then she spotted something. Through the open door of the cubicle behind her was something that hadn't been there before.

A piece of paper?

She walked over and picked it up. It was a receipt, half crumpled. When she opened it, there was something scrawled in red pen in an untidy, cramped hand.

UNDERNEATH. GET OUT.

Her stomach dropped, and she spun around as though someone might be behind her.

Had Sourpuss left this for her? Swallowing, Paige strode back to the mirror, her mind racing.

Was it a trap? Well...if it was, she was already fucked. There was only one way to go forward in any case.

Stuffing the receipt in her clutch, Paige quickly ran her fingers underneath the mirror in front of her, followed by the one beside it. Then all of them.

Her heart hammered in her chest.

I've been gone too long. They'll be suspicious by now...

No...one more try.

What do I have to lose?

She started at the far left this time and more carefully traced her way underneath the panel. She was nearly the whole way across the mirrors when she found it.

At first, she thought it was a small piece of dried gum or maybe some glue from how they had affixed the mirror to the wall, but this had to be it. If it wasn't...

She pushed her nail underneath the edge of it and pulled.

Paige yelped as something popped. Her nail had split, but something else had happened, too. A small, metal disc had come loose and landed on the vanity beside the sink.

She picked it up, eyeing it. It bore a symbol.

Is that...a sun?

"Yes. Got you, you little motherfucker."

She dropped the disc into her purse and took out the dunn-stone once more.

She touched it against the mirror, bracing herself for her fingers to be burned, ready to drop it at the first sign of heat.

But nothing.

Paige smirked, popped the stone back in her bag, closed it up, and made her way to the door.

SHE WAS STILL TRYING to decide the best story to tell Big Rudy when she got back to the table. Diarrhoea currently seemed like the best option, but she hadn't gleaned the information she was hoping for yet, so it didn't seem prudent to likely get herself uninvited from every future event.

Big Rudy was up to something bigger than counterfeit art and statues, and she knew she had to catch him at the right moment in the right mood to find out what.

On the other hand, an excuse like that normally ended any follow-up questions, and maybe he'd stop giving her those lecherous looks.

A young-looking waiter with blonde hair tied up in a tiny man-bun staggered down the hall toward her. His pale skin was tinged greenish and slick with sweat. Grimacing, Paige stepped aside, but he still almost fell into her.

An older man followed, looking harried, and grabbed onto him firmly. "I'm so sorry, madam. He's feeling unwell."

The younger man gawked at him with wide eyes, mouth slack. "I can't believe they're—"

"Enough!" the older man barked, yanking him firmly.

"I'd speak to your union, mate. Don't come to work to get manhandled." Paige eyed them, trying to look mildly offended.

The older waiter tried to smother a scowl. "Apologies, madam. He's...new."

Before she could reply, the older man was half-dragging the younger man down the hallway toward what she assumed were the kitchens.

Frowning, Paige turned away but heard the young man's voice again.

"I can't believe they're eating it."

She froze, swallowing, and cast a look over her shoulder.

They were already disappearing around the corner.

Paige took a steady breath. *Eating what?*

She thought about the fact that she'd been gone for over ten minutes and that a group of the most powerful and deadly black-market traders would become highly suspicious, but she knew she couldn't let it lie.

Sighing, she turned around and followed the waiters.

PAIGE RECOGNISED THE EARTHY, sulphuric stink of the soup drifting from the kitchen even before she heard the muted din of its workers diligently preparing their meals.

The young, pale waiter had been led, now fully sobbing, into a room to the side. The strip lights of the kitchen, however, beckoned her toward the portholes of the grey double doors ahead. The smell grew stronger as she neared, and she cautiously peered through the porthole on the left.

A severe-faced man with a chef's hat passed by so closely that Paige jerked away, her soul almost completely leaving her body for a moment. But there was no alarmed inquisitive voice, no opening of the door. He hadn't seen her.

Silently, she moved forward again and looked in.

On the right, a couple of young chefs were stirring large pots with care. They looked tired, dark circles under their eyes and skin greasy from the kitchen's fumes.

Her eyes darted left, following the older chef that had passed by moments before. The kitchen was pristine—all white and stainless steel. A group of chefs gathered around one worktop. Six, no seven, of them toiled over something she couldn't quite see. Narrowing her eyes, Paige leaned closer, her breath misting the glass.

One chef moved aside, and Paige saw...a hand.

No.

A whole arm, dusky blue and tipped with long, dark nails.

Her stomach dropped, and as it did, one of the other chefs moved aside, shouting something at the first. She only saw it for a moment—the barest glimpse—but in that heartbeat, she knew she would never forget.

The monster's head was cracked open like a nut.

Half its wet, grey brains were gone.

The chef waved his hand, which held...

Was that a fucking ice cream scoop?

Somehow, the smell was stronger now. Overwhelming. A cold sweat broke out on her skin, her head swam, and she gagged.

She rested a hand on the door to steady herself, and it shifted under her weight. Paige let out a low yelp of panic, jerking herself upright as the door clicked into place. She stepped back, her heart pounding in her chest.

They were eating monster.

They were *all* eating monster.

Hunter...

A hand landed on her shoulder, and her knees almost gave way.

Barely stopping herself from crying out, Paige twisted around, her eyes wide and mouth agape.

It was the waiter from before, the one that had led the frightened young man. He watched her with calculating eyes. His other hand drifted to his jacket's opening.

A gun.

He's got a gun.

I'm dead.

Paige staggered backward, panic overwhelming her.

The waiter's eyes narrowed. "Madam..."

Paige didn't know if that formal means of address had ever sounded so dangerous.

She gripped the fear inside her and stamped it out, viciously forcing it down. She made herself stand up straight and lifted her chin imperiously, injecting every ounce of steel she had into her voice to stop it from shaking.

"Jesus Christ, Jeeves, you scared the fucking shit out of me! I just wanted to see the goods. Big Rudy and Margaret Dettweiler want me to move this meat, and I need to know how tight their operation is before I say yes."

The waiter stared at her, clearly judging, given his unchanged expression and posture.

"Everything seems to be in order, but lay a hand on me again, and I'll have your knackers added to my Newton's fucking cradle."

His posture relaxed slightly, and he bowed his head just a little. "Apologies, madam. Guests are not typically permitted here."

Nailed it. When in doubt, just act like the person who has caught you doing something wrong is doing something even worse than you.

Paige sneered dramatically. "I'm not a *typical* guest. I'm a business partner. Now, why don't you scamper off? I need to get back to my meal before it gets cold."

From the flash of irritation in the man's eyes, Paige thought she had gone too far, but he stepped back and gestured to her deferentially, teeth bared in a forced smile. "My apologies again, madam. I do hope that you enjoy your meal."

Paige bared her teeth in a rictus grin and strode back in the direction she came, wondering if a waiter's spit would even be detectable in a bowl of monster mash.

TAXONOMY OF MONSTERS: THE TIZZIE-WHIZIE
(SEPE MEDIOCRIS)

A hog of hedge and fox-tailed thing,
This creature fae can swim and sing.
With bee-like wings with which to fly,
Antennae wise to scout the sky,
It's said the only way to be its friend,
Are ginger biscuits—special blend.

— MARJORIE SHIM, 1952

13

THE EYE OF THE BEHOLDER

"Jesus Christ, Paigey, I thought you'd fallen in the John. I was about to send out a search party!" Big Rudy chuckled at himself as Paige settled back into her seat.

Margaret Dettweiler was making a show of keeping her back turned and was having an animated conversation with the nervous-looking red-haired gentleman seated next to her.

Paige forced a grin. "Serves you right for having such a fancy setup. I wanted to have a proper look."

"So I heard."

Paige looked at Big Rudy in alarm, eyes widening, and he let out a wet, braying laugh.

"No offence taken. Part of the reason I enjoy working with you is that you're a cagey broad. To be honest, I'd be kind of suspicious if you didn't snoop around to get the lay of the land. You do good work, Paige. And with that comes being a scrupulous motherfucker—which also means being paranoid."

Paige attempted a pantomimed cringe. "Am I that obvious?"

Big Rudy guffawed loudly, spraying her again with saliva. "Not at all, Toots. Another reason I like ya!"

"They took your soup, darling. Frankly, it's inedible once it cools," Margaret interjected, leaning over. "But if it means you were deciding whether or not we're in business, that's worth wasting a bowl or two." Her crinkled smile was like that of a well-fed cat, despite her wiry build.

Paige mirrored it with her own smile. "I've...not decided yet."

Fuck. They both knew she'd been peeping into the kitchen? These waiters moved fast.

Margaret's eyes hardened.

"She's not a convert yet, Maggie." Big Rudy waggled his eyebrows. "We still gotta win her over."

"With..." Paige cleared her throat. "The food?"

Big Rudy grinned. "Trust me, Paigey. Once you've tried it, you'll never want to stop."

Paige fought off a shiver at the thought.

"I suspected you'd been in touch with the other world from what I had heard of you and your family," Margaret said smugly. "And your lack of shock at our...*ingredients*. It seems you are aware of Theians and their activities in our world."

Paige's jaw clenched, and she gave a stiff nod.

"Of course, I've learned much from them. Fascinating how quick they are to turn on their own with their self-preservation under threat. Alarmingly *human*," the older woman continued.

So, Dettweiler has been hunting Theians based on intel from others she caught so she could eat them? But...why?

"Cancer," the woman said tartly, as though she could hear her thoughts.

Paige stared at her blankly.

"Stage three liver, metastasised to my lungs." She took a sip of wine. "I had three months to live. I was on a trip to Tokyo—quite frankly just checking off my bucket list—when I met a woman who told me that for five-hundred-thousand pounds, I could live forever. That was seventeen years ago."

"Prostate," Big Rudy barked gruffly. "Inoperable because they found the fucker too late."

Paige blinked.

Margaret gestured to the surrounding people. "There are

many reasons the people gathered here eat Theian flesh. Strength, power, beauty. But more than anything, *time*. If you ever wondered why certain actors simply seem not to age, it's not always because they found an impeccable surgeon. *Some* have improved themselves on a cellular level."

"What's the cost?" Paige breathed. "I mean, other than it smelling like cat sick."

Margaret and Big Rudy met eyes for a moment. Their gazes struck off each other like flint.

"There may be certain...physical consequences for some. It depends wholly on which parts and how much you consume with what regularity, in addition to how you use the energies that it provides. We take great care not to overindulge and only eat the highest quality fresh...produce. We wish to remain civilised and not surrender to our more primal urges. Think of it as a medicine. Too much can make you just as ill as being sick in the first place," Margaret conceded.

Paige frowned. That didn't sound so bad. Except for...

She imagined a Theian she knew on that butcher's block: Vandle's long, pale limbs, limp, with congealing blood leaking from her hacked-up body, red eyes staring, unseeing.

She swallowed. "The Theians—"

"Have it coming." Big Rudy shrugged.

"They have been feeding on us for centuries. Though by all accounts, they do not feed on their own, they treat us like cattle," Margaret spat, her eyes flashing dangerously. "For someone with your uncanny skills in location and procurement, you could help us locate and acquire more exotic samples to sustain this. We have plans for a breeding facility of sorts to make the entire process more convenient."

Paige nodded slowly. Better to keep her own thoughts on ethics quiet for this crowd.

But who's really the monster here?

"So, what do you say, Paigey? You with us?" Big Rudy asked.

He sat casually, but his eyes bore into her. She had no doubt that her answer very much impacted whether she would be lying in a nice comfortable hotel bed tonight or weighed down with concrete and sleeping with the fishes.

"I...I don't see why not," Paige replied, her voice cracking under the strain.

Big Rudy let out a whoop.

"Splendid," Margaret agreed, nodding magnanimously. "And perfect timing. Looks like the next course is here. We shall toast to it with a fine treat indeed."

A plate was laid down before Paige.

"Ah, great!" Big Rudy chuckled. "I was getting close to needing the old glasses again!"

Paige struggled not to heave.

Sitting on the plate was a delicate blini, micro herbs dotted around its edges. Upon its centre, a single eyeball and its dangling vessels and nerves stared back with an accusing glare.

14

JUST DESSERT

S he stared at the eyeball on her plate…and it stared straight back at her.

Big Rudy said something beside her, but his voice sounded distant and muffled in her ringing ears, like she was underwater.

She tuned back in for Margaret's words.

"Don't worry, dear. You don't even really have to chew if you think you can swallow it all at once."

Paige tried to look away from the eye but found that she couldn't.

From the corner of her vision, she saw Big Rudy snatch up the orb on his plate and pop it into his mouth as though it were a fucking pickled onion before gobbling it down.

"Tomorrow, you'll wake up with better than twenty-twenty vision if you didn't have it before. Shame you missed out on the brains this month. Though from what Big Rudy tells me, you are already as sharp as a tack," Margaret continued.

Paige turned, staring at the older woman in stunned silence.

It was difficult to put her almost motherly prattle together with those hard eyes and the fact that she was talking so easily about eating chopped up monsters.

"Wonderful," Paige managed, injecting false bravado into her voice.

Margaret smiled. Well, she crinkled her eyes, at least. She picked up her blini, with the eyeball balanced precariously on top.

Paige looked away quickly before she ate it.

"I invited you here, Paigey, not just because I want to offer you work, but because I want you to be part of the inner circle." Big Rudy was dabbing at the corners of his mouth inelegantly with his napkin again. "Most of these schlubs are just here to look pretty or stay fit, but there's a few that *really* come in on their returns. We're not just building better people; we're building a better world. One where the light of the sun burns through the darkness."

"Inner circle?" Paige picked up her fork and prodded at the eyeball tentatively, as though its vessels may coil around it and launch an attack.

"Who's a part of *that* is for me to know and you to find out...if you're interested." Big Rudy chuckled.

"What about Hunter?" Paige said suddenly. She looked up from her plate to where he'd been sitting.

His seat was empty.

He'd tried to warn her. But why hadn't he done it before tonight? Could she even trust him?

"Oh, I heard you were interested in him," Big Rudy said slimily, rubbing his delicate hands together. "Been around a while. He stays in line, but I don't know much about what he gets up to other than work. He's either real boring or real fuckin' sneaky. I'd put my money on the former. He's not what I'd really call inner circle material."

Paige frowned.

"That could always change, though. Having you working for me on procurement is one thing, but if you want a seat at the table, you really gotta become one of us. Then, who knows? Hunter could sit anywhere he likes as far as I care."

Paige stared at him as a zombie-ish drone echoed in her head.

One of us. One of us.

"And how do I do that?" she asked, suspecting she already knew the answer. "Become 'one of you'."

Big Rudy gestured at her plate. "Just...eat up."

Paige let out a breath and turned back to the staring eyeball.

Better than twenty-twenty vision?

No real negative side effects?

Maybe I could do it just this once.

I've definitely had worse things in my mouth.

Paige pressed the prongs of her fork against the filmy coating of the eyeball, angling it straight down at ninety degrees so as not to send it flicking off her plate.

Her stomach turned as, with a soft pop, the prongs slid in.

Big Rudy leered beside her. "Thatta girl."

Grimacing, Paige lifted the speared organ to her lips and opened her mouth.

GET OUT.

The hastily scrawled note in the toilets flashed into her memory as if in warning. She hesitated.

Only one person could have left it...but why?

At that exact moment, there was a crashing sound of breaking crockery and raised voices.

"I'M SO SORRY," Hunter said loudly, brushing the waiter's jacket emphatically and clearing off the meaty mess that had gotten all over him. Paige wasn't sure exactly what had happened, but something told her Hunter had done it on purpose.

Big Rudy was on his feet in an instant, scurrying over to investigate the commotion. Margaret Dettweiler, too, was curious, and the second her head turned, Paige moved.

She grabbed her napkin, slipped it around the eyeball on the end of her fork, and bundled it quickly onto her lap. By the time the older woman turned back, Paige was dramatically miming swallowing the thing, laying it on a little thick with a wincing splutter after.

The look of confusion on Margaret's face was quickly replaced with grim satisfaction. In that moment, Paige knew she had done exactly the right thing.

Whatever I do, I can't eat anything here. There's something more to it...something they're not telling me.

"I'm thrilled to be in business with you, Miss Tundale," Margaret said.

Paige schooled her features, resisting the shiver that ran through her bones. "I think it would be best if you and Big Rudy tell me everything that's going on."

Margaret gave a melodic laugh. "Why the rush? There are six more courses. We can talk everything through after with a nice brandy."

Paige's stomach turned to lead.

Fuck. I don't think there's room in this lap napkin for six more things.

As Hunter made his way back to his seat, he caught Paige's eye and winked. It was then that Paige almost regretted being there; she almost regretted all the manoeuvring, the months of hard work.

Taking a steady breath, she straightened her shoulders.

Now I know what they're up to. I just have to get through the night. Then we can figure out what to do about it.

"Sounds wonderful." Paige forced a smile. "Not sure if I have much of an appetite for more tonight, but I'm sure I'll build up a taste for it."

Margaret's eyes glittered at that. "Oh, I'm sure you will, love. I think you'll find that it can be rather...*addictive*."

Big Rudy was huffing and puffing as he found his way back into his seat beside them. "I swear to God, you hire trained killers as servers, and they still can't do the job right. Makes me look a damn fool. The guy swears Hunter just barged into him, like that makes any kind of sense."

Paige's skin prickled.

More servers were coming out, holding plates with more food.

"Ah, my favourite!" Big Rudy panted excitedly as a plate with some discs of bread and an odious grey-pink pâté was placed before him.

Paige struggled not to heave. "Lovely."

~

THREE MORE COURSES CAME, and Paige navigated them beautifully. A glob of pâté and what was certainly half of a kidney sat wrapped in her lap. She had straight-up said no to the weird, little tentacle thing that had come out, and Big Rudy had just laughed.

"Are you sure? Can be awful useful, that one!" he said.

Paige simply shook her head and told him all her tentacles were in ship shape at present.

When the elaborate cocktail glass filled with pale, unrecognisable, flaccid tendrils—like a prawn cocktail from hell—came out, Paige knew she was in trouble.

Big Rudy sucked them in like spaghetti whilst Margaret delicately coiled them around her fork. Paige leaned forward and took a sniff. They smelled...alright?

"You gotta eat this one, Paigey," Big Rudy muffled through a full mouth. "Delicious."

Paige scrutinised the tendrils.

These would be very hard to hide.

"I'm actually getting kind of full," she said.

Big Rudy quirked an eyebrow, one monster noodle dangling out of his lips.

"I'm not sure that it's all agreeing with my stomach, to be honest. Maybe I should sit the rest out. I'm sure next time I'll manage the whole lot."

He slurped the rest of the monster part in wetly, swallowing and eyeing her doubtfully. "I've never heard of it bothering anyone's guts before. Usually, this stuff makes you feel better than ever, not worse."

"Oh, I have a *really* sensitive stomach." Paige winced. "Half the time I go anywhere new on holiday, I spend most of my time on the toilet."

Wow. Really bringing out the big guns now. Trying to cringe talk my way out of a corner right at the dinner table.

"That's even better." Big Rudy smiled. "These are for your intestines. Eat up, and you'll feel right as rain almost immediately."

Paige's shoulders sagged. "Wonderful. But maybe I...I think I just need to nip to the bathroom first."

Big Rudy's beady eyes bore into her.

Carefully, she stood, taking care not to let the contents of her napkin unbundle.

That'll make the trip to the toilet worthwhile...some stuff to flush.

Paige tried to inconspicuously bundle it against her hip and reached to pick up her purse. As she did, something slipped. She gripped onto her purse as though that was what had slipped from her grip, but it was not. It caught her eye as Big Rudy and Margaret Dettweiler turned their heads in interest.

The eyeball landed with a plop onto the beautiful floor, bounced once, then rolled to a stop at the tip of her shoe, leaving a gelatinous smear on the tiles behind it.

"That's—" Paige began, looking up at Big Rudy. His face had paled, and his eyes were wide.

The kidney and pâté slipped out together, landing with a splat beside her.

Paige sighed and let the napkin fall, too. It flapped delicately and landed over the top of her spilled mess, as though a burial sheet over a fresh body.

It may as well be the burial sheet over my *body.*

Big Rudy's face was shaking now, the paleness giving way to pink fury.

"Well, well, well," Margaret said, sounding amused. "Looks like someone is a liar as well as a sneak."

Paige raised her hands. "I can explain."

Big Rudy let out a single, sharp whistle, and several of the server cum murderers suddenly snapped to attention, making a beeline toward Paige.

Fuck.

Paige moved to open her bag.

Last resort time.

A firm hand closed around her forearm, pulling it to one side, as another found her opposite wrist. Her handbag dropped to the floor.

"I'm sorry, Paigey," Big Rudy said, looking genuinely sad. "I really wanted you to be in on this, but if you aren't all the way in, you're all the way out."

Paige opened her mouth to reply, to say something quick and clever, to disarm him and get back into her seat, but nothing came.

Well, if you can't calm the storm, may as well throw a fucking hand grenade in.

"VALERIA SANDS!" Paige cried.

The room was already near silent, with most of the diners turning to see what was happening to her. But when she shouted that name, it was quiet enough to hear a penny drop. Even the servers froze for a moment. There was a good fucking reason for that.

Valeria Sands herself stood.

She had been sitting behind a rather enormous man with a moustache like a walrus. She gave Paige a look somewhere between confusion and mild interest. "Yes?"

Paige took a breath and announced, "Valeria Sands has paid off more than half of your crew, Rudy, and killed more than a few who were too loyal to turn. Valeria is planning on taking over your trade and getting rid of you in the process. Half the people in this room are already backing her."

Silence.

Stunned faces looked around at each other, some as though in disbelief, others in hostility, but more with knowing...even more with understanding.

She saw a couple nod at each other.

Valeria's eyes had widened at first, but now a broad and satisfied smile was working its way onto her beautiful face. The waiters released Paige's arms abruptly.

Valeria purred, flicking a hand in irritation. "Fine. The jig is up. I suppose there really is no time like the present." She pointed a single, immaculately manicured finger at Big Rudy, who sat gaping at her in shock. "Take him."

And then...all hell broke loose.

15

YOU ARE WHAT YOU EAT

The cheekbone mafia members that had gripped Paige moved with certainty toward Big Rudy, drawing their guns. One woman, clearly not privy to the intentions of either side of the equation, started screaming a piercing scream that seemed to go on forever.

A handsome, dark-skinned waiter stepped in front of Big Rudy, barring the others' path, and launched straight into one of them with a kick. Before his companion could draw his gun, the waiter had him in an armlock, and they twisted onto the ground together.

Paige stepped back. Something popped under her heel, and she tumbled to the floor amidst a tangle of arms and legs of people trying to get up from the table—some to get away and some to get to Big Rudy. Rolling onto her hands and knees, she glimpsed the remnants of the pulped eyeball on her heel.

"Fucking delightful," she grumbled, snatching up her purse.

"Wait, wait!" Big Rudy was wailing. He had stood to his full size of five-foot-not-much-else and was shouting over the rising din in a way that did not speak of control.

Margaret Dettweiler leapt to her feet beside him and brandished her table knife at anyone who came too close.

All around the room, fights were breaking out. There was screaming and shouting, and more disturbingly, noises that sounded like growls and roars, punctuated by the occasional loud crack of a gunshot.

Paige quickly opened her purse and snatched out the small trinket that Vandle had given her for emergencies because this was certainly fucking one of those. She shuffled on her hands and knees, more than one panicking partygoer tripping over her as they tried to fight or flee.

"DETTWEILER!"

Paige heard Valeria Sands cry over the noise and scuffling. She froze and slowly peered over the table's edge.

She saw .the beautiful Sands standing in the middle of the room, surrounded by three waiters, two of them women and one a large man, each aiming guns at anyone who might be a threat.

There was a crack when an elderly guest came too close and the man pulled the trigger. The guest fell to the ground, clutching his leg and crying out.

Despite her better judgement, Paige looked back to Big Rudy and Dettweiler, who were becoming increasingly surrounded by hostile guests and waiters. Several suited bodies lay on the floor, most in pools of blood.

"We will honour whatever your contract is and better. Double it if you tell us everything that pig of a man has been up to." Valeria smiled sharply.

Dettweiler's eyes flashed from Valeria to Rudy.

"Maggie, no..." Big Rudy groaned, raising his hands.

The old woman moved in a flash, driving her table knife into his throat.

Big Rudy's eyes bulged, and blood pumped from his neck and between his lips. A second later, he fell face-first onto the table in a clatter of plates and silverware.

Fuck.

Paige twisted and was moving again as she heard the old woman scream, "I told you never to call me Maggie!"

Well...he was pretty annoying, and he did probably deserve that, but—
"WHERE'S THAT LITTLE RAT TUNDALE!" Valeria crowed this time.

Paige tried to make herself as small as possible and continued slowly winding through the guests, following others who seemed to rush toward the door.

There was another crack, and the bullet sent a spray of plaster showering from the wall above where she crawled, scattering into her hair.

Paige froze.

"Yes, I see you down there, you little vermin. Stand up, now!" Valeria demanded.

Very slowly, Paige stood, raising her hands, one still holding her purse and the other still clenched tight around the trinket.

"Did you really think you had escaped my notice? Did you really think I didn't know all this time what you were up to? How you were so good at getting places no one should be able to get to so fast?"

Valeria gestured with one hand, and the two women guards moved to put an end to a still ongoing struggle between two of the guests. One of them looked to have changed. He was swollen up like he'd eaten a hundred bad shellfish as bright pink skin tore through his suit.

Was that what eating too much monster flesh did?

Paige's heart hammered against her ribcage.

"I know precisely who you are." Valeria sneered. "And now I will tell you what it is you will do to live a few moments longer."

"Do you know *precisely* what I have in my hand, though?" Paige replied, voice shaking.

"What?" Valeria frowned, tossing her perfect hair. "That cheap purse?"

Paige cocked her head.

Cheap? This bitch...

She shot the woman a feral smile. "No. This!"

And she threw it.

To Paige, it looked almost like a marble, a perfectly spherical glass ball barely the width of her fingertip. It was beautiful to look at. Red and orange, white and blue, coiled through it like liquid captured in flickering motion. Or flames.

Vandle had told her that if she ever had to use it, to make sure she was already running far away. But she couldn't exactly do that for fear of catching a bullet in the back of her head.

So instead, she watched the marble, or as Vandle had called it, the hex-stone, sail through the air as Valeria Sands and her body-guards stared in abject confusion of the audacity of such a thing.

Right until it shattered at her feet.

A bright burst of flames erupted from it like someone had switched a burner from nothing to full right beneath the glorious woman. Her body immediately disappeared in a geyser of flame, and a piercing scream filled the room. The large bodyguard was screaming, too. The flames seared his arm and the side of his face, and his suit was alight. He flapped his arm, screaming, and set two other people close to him ablaze.

Paige ran.

One of her heels broke, causing her to jar her ankle painfully, so she kicked off the shoe and half galloped to the door wearing only one high heel.

"STOP HER!" wailed a reedy voice.

Paige turned and saw Dettweiler pointing at her with one finger. There was blood smeared over her face, and her eyes were wild with the thrill of death.

Paige spun back and ran faster. As she approached it, the front door burst open, and a swathe of new bodies flooded in—the red-headed cashier, the cooks from upstairs...all bearing heavy firearms.

Paige almost fell over trying to stop her momentum, and lost her other shoe.

Thankfully, because of the chaos, the new arrivals hesitated. Taking advantage, Paige bore left down the corridor to the toilets and kitchens.

Time for plan B.

She sure as shit wasn't getting out of the main door right now.

Dettweiler's voice screamed again. "I SAID STOP HER!"

Paige ran, feet covered in someone else's blood, slipping on the tiled floor as she did.

The door to her left opened. Somebody lunged out and grabbed her, holding her to their body with too much strength as they pulled her into the bathrooms. She let out a horrified squawk and tried to fight back, pushing her fingers into her assailant's face desperately.

"Stop, stop!" Hunter urged, releasing her body and taking a hold of her hands before she could do any actual damage to his perfect face.

"What the fuck are you doing?" Paige spat, pushing him away.

"Saving your sweet ass!" Hunter's eyes were wide with panic. "There's no way out down here."

"That's fine. I have a backup," Paige panted.

He grinned wildly. "I know."

Paige tilted her head, the shouting from outside getting louder.

Hunter threw himself up against the bathroom door, blocking it with his body.

"Why didn't you warn me? What the fuck is going on with you?" Paige gasped.

"When we get a minute, I'll tell you. But until then, let's concentrate on making it that far. You get out; I'll hold the door as long as I can."

"And you?" Paige asked.

"I'll lie." He grinned. "I'm a great actor."

Paige cringed. "Are you, though?"

Hunter's eyes widened in surprise, followed by a delighted smirk flashing onto his face...then his body lurched violently forward as someone barrelled into the door.

Hunter grimaced, bearing down against it, and he...*grew.*

His handsome face became a little less so. His skin blushed, and his eyes grew very bloodshot. Hunter's shirt burst open, and his muscles swelled disproportionately until they threatened to split his flesh, pulling it taut and shiny.

"Go! Some of them are stronger than me, so just go." His voice had changed too, deeper now, almost a guttural roar.

Paige stumbled back.

The massive force hammered into the door again, launching Hunter's body and sending him crashing into the nearest stall, tearing the cubicle completely apart. She lost sight of him somewhere under the collapsed door and fallen wall of the cubicle beside it.

"Paige fucking Tundale," a voice rasped.

A woman, more blistered flesh and char than skin, strode into the room, the tattered remnants of a gown barely clinging to her body. Much of her silky hair was gone, leaving a seared scalp with patches of darkened bone beneath.

"Valeria?" Paige breathed. "You look...hot."

Valeria hissed. "You think you're funny, don't you, bitch?"

"Oh, I'm not joking. At all." Paige stepped back. "Want me to rinse you under the tap for a bit?"

Valeria put one blistered hand on her hip.

Were the patches in her scalp growing smaller?

Not only that, but her split and bubbling lips were healing too, right before Paige's eyes.

"I've eaten far too many Theians to be killed by a trick like that," Valeria sneered.

More bodies were filtering in around her.

One vast, hulking form couldn't fit through the door, but five or six of the cheekbone mafia slid in, raising their guns.

"I want her alive." Valeria smiled. "At least for now. I want to make her feel every bit of pain she has caused me tonight. I've always wanted to know how much pain it takes to actually kill somebody rather than merely injure."

"There's just one thing, though..." Paige raised her hand again.

Valeria flinched, and the goons raised their guns.

Paige opened her hand, revealing nothing inside. "Made you look."

"ENOUGH!" Valeria howled.

As she did, Paige took the chance to say three words.

Not three different words, but the same word three times.

"Vandle, Vandle, Vandle."

The lights flickered.

The first of the goons was stepping forward as a lithe figure in dark leathers loomed from behind Paige, quick and graceful.

"What the f—" he began. But his words ended in a bubbled gurgle as Vandle's knife slid across his throat so quickly it was almost a blur.

"Catch her! Don't kill!" Valeria screamed at the same time as she was trying to get out of the room.

In the time it took her to say it, Vandle had already gutted another of the goons.

A third opened fire, but she leapt into the mirror on her left, reappearing in an instant a few paces away, springing out from the mirror and flicking her wrist. She threw her blade so fast, Paige didn't even see it; it seemed instead that the hilt sprouted from the man's eye.

Now the other goons were panicking, trying to get out of the room and follow Valeria, but Vandle wasn't so keen on that idea.

She ducked under a man's firing gun, twisted his arm with an audible pop, brought one booted foot up behind her like a scorpion's stinger, and kicked him so hard in the face, it left his features a bloody pulp. She twisted around his falling body and punched the last of them square in the throat.

Paige heard the delicate structures in his neck crumple.

Squeaking, the man fell to his knees, dropping his gun onto the floor with a clatter as he died.

Vandle kicked the weapon away.

"Come!" she barked at Paige, reaching out with a hand.

Paige took it, and Vandle swept her into her long arms with ease as they leapt into the mirror.

TAXONOMY OF MONSTERS: THE MANANANGGAL
(SUI SEGMANTI)

A being who wishes not to disclose her true age and is seemingly related to other legends (see Malaysian Kephn, Penanggalan, Langsuir, Indonesian Leyak, Japanese Nure-Onna, as well as overlap with British Black Annis). Possesses the unusual ability to function, then re-join or regrow following separation from body parts. Incredibly powerful and with an apparently carnivorous diet, it is unclear if there were ever more of this being or if she is a unique development from millennia of existence. Aura appears to be pitch-black and molten red. Predatorial behaviours may be apparent, though should they be able to be recruited as an ally with the correct motivation, they should provide a valuable (if difficult to trust) asset.

— ORIGINAL TAXONOMY ENTRY, MARCUS
WILLIAMS

III

THE POWERS THAT BE

16

NEW, OLD FRIENDS

The gentle chime of the bell over the door indicated the arrival of a new customer.

It was a middle-aged man with bushy eyebrows in a flat grey suit.

Marcus focused on him, staring into and past him at once, almost like solving a magic eye puzzle. That was the best way to read someone's energy, or auras, as some called it.

A placid orange swirled around him, smooth and simple, about as flat as his suit.

Not a Theian...not even a monster.

Song slurped happily beside him as the man sat down and ordered a bowl of ramen. There were only six seats in the restaurant, four lined up across the counter and two on the other edge of its L-shape, partially obscured by cooking equipment.

The air was heavy with the rich steam of pork bone broth and the hiss of sizzling rose dumplings. It was *almost* enough to make Marcus hungry. It was already enough they left Ed back at the hotel, sulking on the floor by the penthouse suite for fear he may not behave himself. At least there was a wary Ducky sitting on a plump pillow observing him regally.

Song had no such issues with digestion. They had found that

since sampling Marcus' hunger, they could almost taste things. Not quite the full experience, but more like breathing in the air above a plate of fresh food and having its notes play across your tastebuds—stealing its essence. That experience for Song, however, was vivid and new. So, of course, now they loved to eat everything they could get their hands on. The molecules they consumed were broken down and absorbed into their energy expenditure to help maintain their corporeal form, which Marcus realised wasn't really that different from what happened when anybody ate.

Song looked up from their bowl of ramen, golden eyes sparkling with pleasure.

"Good, huh?" Marcus grinned.

They nodded emphatically. A vague sense of guilt washed over Marcus.

"Don't worry," he said. "I'm good."

Song picked up their bowl in both hands and slurped at the broth, eyes never leaving his.

A little of it splashed on their blazer, today's choice an almost impossibly crisp white, matched with a pastel purple shirt and pale yellow bowtie. That, along with the almost onyx black of their skin, meant that no matter where they were, Song would have cut a memorable figure. But in Sapporo, Japan, basically everyone's attention followed them constantly. Marcus couldn't let them have *all* the attention, so he wore a pale pink shirt, powder blue trousers, and a white sequinned tie. They had been quite the popular figures in Tokyo earlier that day, where fashion hungry folk had all but swarmed them. But on the more traditional island of Hokkaido, many of the looks were curious rather than admiring.

The chef, a young man with a beakish nose, handed a bowl of steaming ramen to the new arrival, who was tentatively peering at Song from between the water dispenser and cash register perched on the counter.

Can't really blame him...

"Are you sure I can't get you anything?" The young chef had turned back to Marcus, smiling.

"No thanks. We're just waiting for a friend, and we'll be on our way," Marcus replied.

The chef bowed, his eyes drifting to Song, then turned and busied himself cleaning the counter.

The entire exchange had taken part in Japanese, of course, but with the number of languages Marcus had access to, the differences had sort of stopped meaning anything. Song had told him that being able to understand every language would have overloaded his cognitive function, so instead, they had essentially reprogrammed him with an internal translator. To speak a language, he just had to get the gist of which one and open his mouth, vaguely wanting to respond in the same fashion. Understanding was more fluent; after the first few words, he caught on. Dialects could sometimes be an issue, and it could take a few sentences to adjust to unfamiliar composition or colloquialisms, but the removal of language as a barrier was...liberating. It had only taken him a few hours to realise that Song themself didn't face the barrier of words altogether, instead using the direct sending of intent, emotions, and desires. The fact that was likely his next significant progression filled Marcus with both excitement and incredible anxiety.

Their escapades over the last two years had taken a significant toll. Marcus burned through the perceived flaws in his humanity that Song could feed upon far faster than he ever expected— around twenty years' worth in a matter of months, in fact. On one hand, this horrified him. On the other, it didn't surprise him at all. He had always been incredibly quick on the uptake. Once he had a handle on the exchange and the incredible abilities they could grant him, it brought an overwhelming urgency to need to take the next step.

Then the next five.

And now?

Not only did he not need to eat to sustain himself anymore,

but he didn't get tired either. He still *needed* to sleep. Song had insisted on not taking that away from him yet, but now he had to set a series of reminders to make sure he rested. There were countless other things he had given up, too—his fear of heights, his anxiety in crowds, and his irrational panic when any flappy thing flew at his face, to name a few. Now, he found himself weirdly wishing he'd seen more imperfections to keep trading as the final destination of transcending his flaws got ever closer. At that point, he would cease to be human anymore...and become like Song.

The little bell over the door chimed again.

The half-boiled egg that Song was just trying to put in their mouth all at once slipped, falling back into their bowl of steaming broth with a plop.

Marcus narrowed his eyes.

The man who had just entered was elderly. His hair was white as bone and face a deep and kindly map of wrinkles, but the space around him hummed with spiky, glittering, silver and midnight blue energy.

Marcus smiled.

Now, here's our monster.

～

Mr Sato was an informant of sorts.

Marcus wasn't sure exactly what *type* of monster he was, but the fact that he didn't smell of death was good enough to attest that he wasn't one who sought to bring ruination on man-kind— or gobble them up—at least for now.

The strength of his energy field was so jagged, Marcus wondered if he was Theian, though it seemed to be blocked by something. Disguised perhaps?

The old man didn't give Marcus long to wonder.

"Greetings, my friend," Mr Sato said, bowing carefully.

"Sato-san." Marcus stood quickly, bowing in return.

Song remained seated and watched the exchange with interest, slurping another noodle into their mouth.

"Please, call me Sato." His eyes shifted to Song and sparkled with amusement.

Marcus winced a little and opened his mouth to explain.

"Do not worry, my friend. I would not trouble a being who does not abide by this planet's conceived rules of space and time to observe the futile pleasantries we force upon our mortal selves," Sato said quickly.

It took Marcus a moment to realise the old man had said it in English.

"Perhaps it is best we converse like this? It might be more difficult for others to follow, I think." Sato winked mischievously before sitting down beside Song with a smoothness that did not match his age at all.

Marcus felt a gentle sending as he took his seat once more, just for him, imperceptible to Sato, the businessman, or the chef. Curiosity and a hint of warning. Song didn't even look up from their bowl.

Sato chuckled. "I mean no harm. I am far too old for that kind of thing." He winked again, his dark eyes twinkling. "And by any means, trouble is not the business we have today. Rather, information is on the menu."

Marcus stiffened, and Song stopped slurping their noodles for a moment.

He shouldn't have felt that...

"Do not fear. Not all reading happens between minds and souls." Sato smiled. "I was simply observing your body language."

Marcus eyed him.

The chef had approached, bringing the old man a glass of cold water. Sato gestured with three fingers to the menu, ordering with the hand signal alone as he bowed his gratitude.

"You know what we are looking for?" Marcus asked stiffly.

The old man chuckled. "That's the funny thing about tracking down a contact like me. Once you start searching, word gets back.

Like flies vibrating a spider's web. Mora is a dear old friend, and she told me everything you told her, and likely a little more."

Marcus grunted. Mora was an old spiritualist from the Isles of Scilly. She looked even older than Sato, and her small cottage had all manner of herbs and freshly dead things dangling from the rafters. She had refused to talk to Marcus unless he let her read his tarot, and once she did, she refused to tell him what it said and just laughed before repeating it twice more, her eyes growing wilder and more excited each time.

"You search for a foothold between worlds," Sato said, bowing gently as the chef set a bowl of steaming noodles down before him. He picked up the bowl and boldly gulped half its boiling contents in a few mouth-fulls.

Marcus gaped.

The man must have a mouth and throat like asbestos.

Sato set down his bowl, cheeks puffed out with scalding pork and noodles, chewing.

Song watched with interest as he swallowed.

"Delicious!" Sato said loudly, raising a hand to the chef.

"More than a foothold," Marcus said. "A way to form a breach, but filter what comes through."

Sato laughed merrily. "They are *worlds*, boy, not dirty tap water."

"I don't think those differences matter as much as you might first think," Marcus replied quickly.

Sato grinned. "I agree, but it's all about—"

"Scale," Marcus finished.

Sato smiled, moving his hand deftly to sweep misplaced strands of white hair behind his ear in an almost feline motion. "Precisely. What you are seeking isn't like turning a tap. It's like trying to drill a hole into a dam made of glass that's holding back an ocean as vast as a world itself. Tapping at the wrong point too hard or too fast can shatter the entire thing. And then everyone is *very* dead."

Marcus frowned.

Mr Sato had come highly recommended. Apparently, he was a renowned professor of astrophysics and, of course, probably ancient himself. So surely, he knew...

"I was recently trapped in a time rift in Peru," Marcus said.

Sato's face was hidden by his bowl, slurping deeply from it once more.

"Whilst I was there, I saw the space between worlds. The potential space, I mean, rather than actual. Outside of our linear understanding of time, and with myself removed from its context, I could understand some things. Not as much as I'd like, but—"

Sato put his bowl down with a thud, swallowing, and belched loudly. "You should be dead."

"I probably would be if I hadn't already been with Song for so long," Marcus admitted. "It was a close call as it was. My brain couldn't absorb it all. It was like holding a sponge under a waterfall. Only some of the liquid could get sucked in, and the rest was just overflow until it pushed me out. Thanks to Song, I'm a pretty big sponge, though."

Sato chuckled.

"But I saw that if we do *nothing*, that dam made of glass is going to shatter. The pressure of that ocean is getting too high."

Sato smiled thoughtfully.

"I also saw that there were some spaces that met in that potential space—old wounds healed cleanly, that could be re-opened once more, their edges toughened by the scarring, making things less likely to break."

"Interesting," Sato admitted, rubbing the back of his hand across his mouth.

"So, what I need from you isn't advice. It isn't for you to tell me what I can and can't do. I may destroy everything, but if I don't try, everything will be destroyed anyway. I don't need the what, where, or when. Just the how. I guess whether you want to help depends on whether you want to help me try to stop that dam from bursting at the risk of breaking it a bit earlier than it would otherwise."

Sato gave a long sigh. "One might say that perhaps it is past time for that. But I am...rather fond of this place."

"Me too," Marcus agreed. "And the people in it."

He felt a gentle nudge of affectionate agreement from Song. They had finished their bowl and were watching Sato intently.

"What I need is a tool. A blade to part the veil, or the means to make one."

Sato remained silent, his dark eyes hard and fixed on Marcus for a long time.

"If you won't help me, there are others—"

"No," Sato said simply.

Marcus' mouth shut so quickly his teeth clicked. He huffed. "No, you won't help us?"

Sato's smile was sharp. His eyes twinkled. "No, there aren't others. I am quite sure that I am the only one that can tell you what you must do. Any others who might *help* do not have the full cut of it. And those who do may already be dead."

Marcus' jaw clenched. He really didn't want to have to force information out of the old man.

"But I will help." Sato nodded finally. "It's been a long time since I have been involved in such excitement, and I am certainly invested in the success of your venture."

Marcus released his breath, not disguising his relief.

Sato chuckled again, picking up his bowl and draining its dregs, smacking his lips noisily. "But first, how about you take me for a nice whisky or five and tell me all about this rift?"

❧ 17 ❧

SEE ME WITH THEM HANDS

Sato could *not* hold his liquor.

After three rounds, his cheeks were flushed and his twinkling eyes slightly glassy.

He asked Marcus questions almost as fast as he could answer them, and in an order that left his head spinning—everything from the direction of the wind to the exact coordinates where he first discovered the rift.

Now, they wandered down the dimly lit back-streets of Sapporo.

Sato had insisted on walking Marcus back to his hotel to get as much information as possible out of him. In Sato's words, 'You are clearly a busy man. Who is to say where you will be tomorrow, should we all still be living?'

Sato never seemed pressed about the impending doom, instead fatalistic. It seemed at once consistent and conflicting with his peaceful attitude to the world around him.

Marcus could see the pale glow of the plush hotel—where he and Song had the penthouse—looming nearby.

"So, Sato-san. This has been wonderful, but you still haven't told me what I'm supposed to do next."

Sato's eyes crinkled, his nose very pink. "I never said I would tell you what to do next. I only intend to ensure I point you toward the general direction of success."

Marcus paused, rolling his neck. "Sato..."

The elderly man chuckled. "Do not fear. Something tells me that once you know the means, the way will make itself clear."

Song was wandering slightly ahead, peering with interest down the nearest alley. Knowing them, it could be because of anything from a stray cat to a dead body.

"Then tell me the means," Marcus grumbled.

Sato's smile was sharp, given his inebriated state. "I am aware of the events that occurred at your Stonehenge not so long ago."

A chill ran over Marcus' flesh.

"Oh, come on now. You can't imagine that word of something like that wouldn't get out. As it is, someone visited before you, asking me questions such as this. My experiences with him were... far less pleasant. Though I gather the relative recency of the situation made him somewhat under duress."

Marcus stared at him for a moment before grunting with realisation. "Dmitri was here?"

Sato's smile faded. "He was...a broken thing, willing to risk destroying anything and everything for a chance to find what it was he lost. *Who* it was, I gathered."

Marcus nodded stiffly.

"I counted my blessings that I survived that encounter. He knew I was not telling him everything, and I feared he would go to any means to get that information out of me. I tried to persuade him. I can be *very persuasive*." For a moment, Sato's eyes shone a strange yellow, shimmering in the moonlight. Marcus knew better than to wonder if it had been a trick of the light. "Alas, even my wiles were not enough to calm the man. I fortunately escaped, but it was some months before I could resume my activities and be certain he was not still seeking me."

Marcus' stomach clenched. He had traded in panic some time ago for power, but this wasn't that. This was *dread*.

Put that fucker on the list to get rid of next.

"Dmitri is...*was* a good guy," Marcus said.

"Grief can do terrible things to a soul." Sato looked much older for a moment as his shoulders sagged. "I fear he is no longer the man you knew. He was...desperate. Lost. What of *you?*"

"I..." Marcus looked up at the moon. "I believe that some things are not under our control. It may be impossible to move on from pain like that, but we can learn to carry it, even if we need help, move slower, or take time to sit and rest more often. I think sometimes carrying that pain forward with us is all we *can* do..."

He felt a wave of confusion followed by a spike of concern from Song nearby and turned to find them.

They stared into the darkness of the alley, head cocked.

A flash of a memory replayed in Marcus' mind. The memory of Song's corporeal body being destroyed with rows of spikes from the Umbran in the cemetery.

Come away, he sent back urgently.

Song heeded him, stepping in his direction briskly.

The hair on Marcus' arms rose. He smelled magick in the air, dark and heavy, like rotting berries and sour cream.

There was a hissing sound, and Marcus realised with alarm that it was coming from beside him. From Sato. The man's body was rigid, his face contorted in fury, narrowed eyes a vivid yellow, and teeth sharp as nails.

From all around them, the shadows burst loose.

Marcus was ready.

Some part of him was always ready now. His hands were up in a flash, fingers dancing in the air with uncanny dexterity.

The things that burst from the shadows were what Oscar had called flecks. The weakest forms of Theian life, barely able to take shape themselves without a surge in power or time to grow—the intentions of a new being gradually forming into reality.

A vast serpentine shape uncoiled, its head like a sabre-tooth tiger with a lion's mane. Marcus' hands twisted, stiffening the air around it like set jelly. From behind it, something the size of a car with enormous tusks unfurled its bat-like wings. Marcus adjusted his stance, capturing that one, too. But more were coming.

"Sato, you should—" Marcus began.

Beside him, Sato's body was shivering, rigid as though a thousand volts were coursing through him. The elderly man was...*melting*.

Grunting, Marcus pulled his hands apart, tearing the space where he clutched onto the two flecks. They dissipated like bursts of thick, dark smoke torn apart in a gale. The forms that followed were strangely humanoid but with long, dangling arms. Their slender fingers almost touched the ground as they moved with clumsy speed. Marcus lashed out, moving a flat palm like a blade. The air crackled around them, and he thought he heard them groan as their forms shuddered from the blow, yet held their shape.

Sato let out a low, gurgling growl. His slitted pupils rolled back, and his wrinkled flesh turned smooth. The white hair he sported turned thick, dark, and lustrous.

What the...

Marcus thrust out at the flecks again, harder this time. His attack ricocheted through them and off the wall behind them, blowing off dust and dirt with a sound like a cracking whip. Still, they held their shape.

This time, two staggered forward. Marcus snatched out at them, trying to use the air around them as a crushing force. One of them burst, but the other was disturbingly solid. He felt a trickle of blood leak from his nose.

From the darkness, even more shapes loomed forth.

A numb sense of shock spread in Marcus' chest.

There!

The thought was from Song. A wave of realisation and accusation all at once.

Marcus spun and scanned the surrounding space. He zeroed in

on movement across the street, a flash of pale skin and red hair, but nothing else around it. The flicker of a humming crimson aura.

"Gotchya!" He snatched out with his hand.

Whatever it was yelped loudly, and he felt power bucking and writhing in his grip. Powerful, but contained.

Marcus turned his attention back to the alley. The dark shapes were fading and easing back into the shadows. He faced the culprit again as it pressed on his binding, thrashing desperately but seeming to tire.

Beside him, Sato had fallen to one knee. His suit was baggy on his now lithe body, one that spoke of agility and speed rather than wizened fragility. He was panting, and a sheen of sweat glistened on his skin.

"Did whatever just happen make you...*younger?*" Marcus asked.

Sato looked up, sweeping a curtain of inky hair away from his handsome face, and blinked with those yellow eyes. "It undid my glamour," he said raggedly, standing straight on shaking legs. "Or should I say *she* did."

Sato was still quite small, almost the same size as Song, who was very close to him and seemed to be...sniffing him?

Sometimes Marcus didn't even bother to question what exactly they were interested in, but he was pretty certain it was just *everything*.

Sato eyed the space across the street warily. "Proceed with caution, my friend. It seems the way found us before I could tell you the means."

Marcus bared his teeth, squeezing his grip again and hearing her cry out. With his free hand, he wiped away the trickle of blood from his nose.

"Alright," Marcus replied, maintaining his grip and striding to the space where his captive was held. "Let's see what kind of little fishy we caught."

A coil of bright red hair flailed strangely out of nothing in the night.

Marcus reached forward, partially removing his casting, until his fingers made contact with some kind of leathery fabric. Gripping it, he pulled.

The girl underneath was a few years younger than him, but any semblance of innocence was vanquished by the fierce glint in her eyes. She spat and wriggled in his grip, eyes flashing murder.

"Oh, hello there, little one." Marcus smiled, quickly assessing her. "And what brings you out trying to high key murder us with some mysterious monster powers on this fine evening?"

She wore a baggy, green hoodie that clashed with her red hair and the smattering of freckles of almost the same colour across her button nose. Her aura flared around her, jagged, like flaming radio static. "You don't know who you're dealing with. Let me go now or you'll regret it!"

Marcus cast the leathery cape aside. Now that it was off, he could see it was a strange, mottled brown, with different patches poorly matched together to craft the oversized shroud. It was almost like it was made from...

No. Impossible.

Song was already examining it with interest on the ground beside him.

"Can do, firecracker." Marcus' eyes found something that brought that dread back again.

Yes, that cape is definitely *made of skin because...*

Marcus released his grip on her, his fingers dancing and snatching something long and thin out of her left hand.

She cried out as it was wrenched from her fingers, and Marcus drew it toward himself, suspending it in the air a few inches from his face.

The bones were black as coal but too perfect to have been charred. The perfect, smooth shaft of the radius was interrupted by the pale brass of the wire that bound it to the ulnar. Shiny metal was intricately wound around the unusually large wrist bones, fewer than you would find in a human. The entire arm was about half the size of Marcus' own forearm and tipped with three long claws. It made for an eerie wand.

The red-headed girl hissed in fury, and her aura shuddered... but she was very much human.

Marcus smiled grimly, looking back over his shoulder. "Sato-san, looks like our nice evening is over. Can I interest you in a chatty nightcap back at the hotel with our new friend here?"

❧ 18 ❧

BE OUR GUEST

Two hours later, the girl's pale face was still pink with anger, her bottom lip thrust out and her arms folded where she sat in the hard-backed chair. Her aura was a deep, violent red with sparks shooting through it.

Getting her up to his hotel room had been a cinch; Ducky had been just a whistle away for that. Now, the mallard perched back on her pillow on the bed, gobbling down some dried meat. Ed stood beside her, trying to inconspicuously sniff her meal, whilst Sato sat cross-legged on the bed beside Ducky, looking strangely much more *himself* in his current form.

More interestingly, Sato had taken off his now oversized jacket and shirt, wearing only a vest with his baggy trousers. His arms were covered in the most beautiful tattoos Marcus had ever seen, inked a deep, faded blue that looked as though it had been in his skin for decades.

Song was standing extremely close to their unwilling guest, who was sitting on a chair by the foot of the bed, smiling strangely at them.

Marcus paced back and forth. The cape made of flesh and the bone wand were both on the floor. He hadn't wanted to touch either again, at least not after unintentionally grabbing the former. His fingers still somehow felt dirty from the contact.

"I have to say, it's rare an assassin would be treated with this much hospitality. You're not tied up, and I even offered you some bloody tea, so I really think you should tell us exactly why you were trying to kill us," Marcus said tiredly. It might have been the hundredth time he'd asked.

The girl just scowled.

"You know, I could just have Song here help me make you a little chattier. Your tongue would be a little looser if we laid open your cognitive mapping to lower your inhibitions."

The girl scoffed. "You think I'm a fool? I have no pact. They cannot tamper with my truths."

Marcus quirked an eyebrow. "What makes you so sure? How many have you met? Because I've got a bloody spectacular understanding of what we can and can't do to someone like you. I'd feel a little guilty about destroying your mind, except you just tried to kill us."

There was a flash of doubt in the girl's eyes.

Marcus allowed his smile to darken.

He was bluffing, of course. She had the right of it, but it was good to see where the limits of her knowledge ended.

"I would gladly give my life in service," the girl said as if by rote, her fervour returning.

"You might yet." Marcus shrugged. "But how about you give your name first?"

The girl's eyes narrowed.

"It doesn't have to be your name, but whatever you would like us to call you."

The girl eyed him suspiciously. "Isla." When she spoke, it was so fast it was like she'd spat out a curse word.

Marcus rubbed the hair on his chin.

"Alright, Isla. I want you to know I'm not keen to hurt you, despite what you did. You certainly seem to know a lot for someone your age, and those tricks back there with the Theian remains were very...impressive. I gather you are not working alone."

"I might be." Her chin rose confidently.

"If you were, there wouldn't be much for you to die in service of, like you just said."

Isla did not answer that. Instead, her bottom lip thrust out again petulantly.

"The Filii Terra," Sato said placidly from the bed.

The colour in Isla's cheeks darkened.

"Children of Earth, huh?" Marcus frowned, eyes moving between Sato and Isla. "I've heard of 'em. Sealers of the veil and all that?"

"That's them," Sato said. He reached out tentative fingers to pet Ducky, who allowed the affection with regal poise.

"So, you're the ones that messed everything up..." Marcus sat on the edge of the bed, meeting Isla's eyes.

The girl shook her head. "Without the seal, Earth would have been overrun. Everything that has been is thanks to us."

"So, you're trying to kill me, what, because I'm trying to breach it?" Marcus asked.

"I'm trying to kill you because it was what I was ordered to do. It is not my place to question, only to follow."

"Lack of past tense, duly noted. Your nasty little wand privileges remain revoked. Don't make me go all 'I bind you, Nancy, from doing harm' on you."

"If you open the veil—"

"If I don't, it's all over," Marcus cut in. "If you're really so interested in protecting Earth, you should be helping me rather than using some creepy little hand-wand to get flecks to rip me apart."

Isla huffed. "I don't know what you called them that for, but they weren't truly shadowlings. More like echoes of them."

"How does that work, anyway? Some kind of...enchantment?"

Marcus' mind wandered back to Dmitri's flaming axe, only *this* wasn't really anything like that.

"Of sorts," Sato said. Isla's eyes shot daggers at him as he continued, "The Filii Terra have mastered the art of using Theian remains as vessels of power. It is distasteful but...effective."

"So that cloak *is* made of skin." Marcus' eyes drifted to where it was heaped by the door. His stomach rolled.

"Indeed," Sato said. "The cloak is likely made from the flesh of my kind who can use glamours or their natural abilities to remain unseen. There are several creatures that humans believe originated on Earth—mostly ocean-dwellers—that can do the same, though I imagine their power is too weak to hold the enchantment even if cast immediately after their death. The wand is more difficult for me to specify. It's from something much older, pure Theian, with the high power to command shadows and even stun those of a higher function such as myself."

"Say what you like, act as clever as you want, but you are nothing but a *monster*," Isla spat, her aura pushing out in even wilder spikes than before. "You do *not* have a higher function than that."

Sato arched an eyebrow, offering a handsome smirk. "I have lived for several of your kind's lifetimes. I have watched regimes rise and fall—helped a few tip the right way, too. Countless people I've loved have died, and I've spent ten times your current age studying the cosmos alone. I'd thank you kindly for not dismissing me when you are the barbaric newborn wielding bones of the fallen for your violent delights."

Marcus thought Isla was going to leap from her seat, and he considered thickening the air around her once more as her face went almost the same red as her freckles. Instead of acting, however, she folded her arms stiffly, her eyes welling with tears.

Marcus felt a flash of irritation.

"Listen, Isla. I know you think you're doing the right thing, but you're not. I won't hurt you, but I can't let you get in my way."

A tear rolled down her cheek.

"And frankly, you trying to kill us and then sitting here acting like the victim because things didn't go your way kind of makes me sick. But I'm trying to work with the only option we have here, so I'm going to make you a deal...and it's not really one you can say no to."

Isla sniffled, looking up at him and rubbing away her tears with the heels of her palms. She didn't look angry now, but *relieved*.

As much as she said she would die for her cause, she clearly didn't want to.

"Take me to the Filii Terra. We can get this all cleared up and help them understand what needs to be done. That means you won't all have to try and kill me again but also that we can hopefully save the worlds."

Isla blinked.

"For my part, when we get there, I will listen to what you all have to say. I can't say any fairer than that." Marcus raised his hands. "For your part, no more hiding in the shadows, making little suits of dead monster skin and doing creepy stuff."

Isla seemed to think about this for a moment. Her eyes drifted to the cape and wand by the door. Marcus' fingers twitched at his side. She'd never make it that far, and things would work out much better if she complied.

"Fine." Isla took a shaky breath, regaining her composure. "But no promises. If the Filii Terra command me to execute you, that's what I'll do."

"What you'll *try* to do," Marcus corrected. "You won't get the jump on me again like you did tonight. And to be honest, I'm an awful lot less kind the second time someone tries to kill me. I'm less likely to offer you tea and more likely to let Ed over there eat you."

Isla's eyes drifted to the snoozing poodle nervously. One of his eyes opened knowingly, and she flinched.

"That sounds just wonderful," Sato said, hopping up from the bed. "I wish all of you the best with your future endeavours."

Marcus turned, surprised. "You're leaving?"

"Of course," Sato replied. "The Filii Terra and I have an unpleasant history. As you can imagine, the ability to change shape is a rather desirable thing they would like to imbue themselves with, so I have no desire to visit them in their home territory. But I believe they will have the tools you need to complete your task."

"Wow." Marcus frowned. "You really were barely any help at all."

Sato winked dashingly, tucking a dark lock of hair behind his ear. "We had a nice time, at least. There is a number where you can contact me in my jacket pocket, should my services be required. I dare say I may be of some assistance yet. And, as I say, I really would rather the planet weren't obliterated. It's where I keep all my stuff."

Marcus grinned. "I'll bear that in mind. But aren't you taking your jacket with you?"

Sato shrugged, his eyes shifting from that dark brown to yellow again, and turned to Song. "It was a pleasure meeting you, Song. Always a delight to meet an ethernal." He turned and bowed toward the bed. "And a pleasure to meet you, Lady erm...Ducky."

Ducky let out a drowsy quack in reply.

"Dog," he added toward Ed.

Ed's nose twitched, and he gave a low bark.

Sato took a few strides, not toward the door but the half-open window. He gave a brief salute, then disappeared into a bundle of his own clothes.

Marcus opened his mouth, gaping in surprise. A sleek black cat slunk out of the pile of clothes and sprang out the window and into the night. Marcus lost sight of him almost immediately. "Well, shit."

Isla stared at where he disappeared, lips curled in disgust.

Marcus felt a strong sending of delight from Song and turned to find them watching him with a brilliant grin. He couldn't help but mirror it.

"Alright, gang." He planted his hands on his hips. "In the words of every dad after they've paid a bill at a restaurant: let's rock-and-roll."

TAXONOMY OF MONSTERS: THE WOLPERTINGER
(SILUESTRIBUS MEDIOCRIS)

Thought at first a marvellous wonder
Of taxidermal combined plunder.
A head of hare, though lacking paws,
A squirrel's thorax, pheasant's claws.
Deer's antlers sit upon its crown,
Earning praise and great renown.
But many rushed to hunt their kind,
Making them now quite hard to find.

— IMKE SCHWARTZ, DATE UNKNOWN

IN PLAIN SIGHT

Everywhere Marcus could see, vast, glorious mountain peaks rose like mandibular fangs from the earth. With no street-lights, the moon and stars glowed with a wonderful brightness. It was impossible not to take another full spin, taking in the natural architecture of it all.

In the darkness, Marcus' enhanced eyes could pick out almost every detail under the canopy of stars. The cool night air lapped against his skin, bringing the scent of unspoiled nature. Water flowed from the snowy mountains, the earth remaining untrodden, and the foliage still wild.

And something else.

Magick.

It was...*everywhere.*

Song lay on the ground amidst some wildflowers and over-grown grass, their eyes closed as though in rapture, limbs splayed like a starfish. The usual hum of the connection Marcus felt from them was oddly muted, absent of their typical intrigue and amusement. Ed had promptly plopped to the earth beside their legs as a sheepdog and was panting happily.

Marcus wondered whether it was the location or the magick that did it.

Something about it all just felt so *relaxing* despite their circumstances.

"We're close," Isla said sulkily. Her arms were folded as she stared up at the moon.

"You're really telling me that somehow, some kind of commune of Neo-druids has an entire community built here in the middle of nowhere?" Marcus gestured at their wild surroundings.

A smug smirk challenged the scowl on Isla's face. "You may have an ethernal filling you with power, but it would do you well to remember that *real* power is in knowledge."

"Oh, shut it," Marcus chuckled, taking another deep breath. "You are fully the moody little twit who tried to off me with an evil wand like ten minutes ago whilst *I'm* trying to gain information to save humanity. You don't get to act all brainier-than-thou just cos you have a bloody secret."

Isla's cheeks reddened, but she looked more embarrassed than angry.

She really didn't look much younger than they had been when all this monstery stuff had started.

She definitely acts younger than us, though...or is it that I feel that much older now? And why is it that, despite both of us, I want to like her?

He looked at Song, their face perfection while in peace.

Sensing his awareness upon them, their eyes opened, revealing large golden pools of eternity.

Marcus smiled.

"Is what you said really true? Is...are the worlds going to end?" Isla's voice was measured with the effort of trying to sound civil.

"Not if we can help it."

Isla's eyes narrowed. "We?"

"Sato said I needed your help to part the veil. I won't lie; your practices seem..." He twisted his mouth. "Unethical. But that's something we can discuss later. The fact that existence is going to end needs to come first. And if the Filii Terra send you out packing heat like you came at me with?"

The creepy wand and skin cloak were bundled into a rucksack and in Ducky's custody. It made Marcus a little nervous, leaving them with her, as the duck seemed *very* interested in the cloak, eyeing it hungrily.

"I deduce you lot might be pretty helpful in whatever battle we're going to have on our hands to, you know, save——"

"Humanity," Isla breathed.

Marcus shook his head. "Everyone."

"You really care about saving...those things?" Isla's pale blue eyes drifted to where Song and Ed lay.

Marcus felt a stab of anger. "Careful now. That's my family."

Isla grimaced in disgust, and Marcus felt any empathy he had for her evaporate.

"I thought stuff was simple, too, once," he said stiffly. "Turns out they're beautifully complicated. Now, I've probably met more bad people than I have bad monsters."

"They kill people," Isla snapped.

"Not all of them. Besides, *people* kill people and for far worse reasons than needing to eat to survive. I'm not saying it's right, it's just——"

"They killed my family." The words tore out of Isla's throat like she had no choice in the matter.

Marcus closed his mouth, his eyebrows drawing together. Isla stared up at the moon. Her pale body was stiff, jaw clenched, and eyes watery.

"I'm sorry that happened, Isla. I truly am," Marcus said, trying to soften his tone.

Isla sniffed. "I know what you're thinking. That if he was in the Filii Terra, maybe one of them killed him in self-defence or something, but it wasn't like that. It was when I was small. We weren't even part of the sect then. Mum had a normal job, a normal life. Until one of them ripped her to shreds in an alley for no reason. The Filii Terra...they took me in, taught me how to take care of myself. My dad wasn't around when I was younger, but I found him later. I didn't know how to talk to him, what to say, or even if he ever wanted me. But then he disappeared. I just...I know they killed him too."

So that's why she hates monsters so much.

"That sounds horrible."

"Horrible? It's worse than that. You've clearly never lost someone."

Marcus' stomach dropped.

"You're right," he said numbly. "It *is* worse than horrible. Like a part of you has been taken away, except it's not a part you didn't need. Part of what *makes* you. Every time anything happens after, it's worse because they're not there to see it or for you to tell them about it. It's like there's not enough air left in the world, and your feet don't touch the ground right anymore. It's the worst thing that ever happened, and it always will be. Even when you lose someone else, it doesn't cover it up; it's just a new hole in the fabric that makes you, and you just feel like...you're going to come apart all the time. It never goes away. You just get more used to it every day, and that...that feels so wrong."

Marcus trailed off, the words burning like bile in his throat. He felt tears prickling his eyes and blinked them away. "But losing them doesn't mean we can take from others. It doesn't mean we can give up either, even if we want to sometimes. Isla, I'm sorry for the way it went for you, I really am, but...I've been through hell. Fuck, even before I knew about monsters or before I lost anyone special to me, I've had to fight every day just to be myself. I had to fight *myself* for feeling like I *wasn't* myself...and all the people telling me I'm wrong. I've had to deal with people who decided who I was before I was even born or who didn't understand why I can't just be *normal*." That word left a foul taste on his tongue like it always did. "I don't try to be good or better for the people who want to judge me. That's their problem. But I *do* want to be better for *me* and the people I love, and now...the ones that I've lost."

There was a long moment of silence as the air sighed through the surrounding mountains.

"I'm sorry." Isla's voice was brittle.

When he turned to her, her attention was still on the moon.

"Who was it?" Her voice was little more than a whisper.

Marcus cleared his throat. "Someone very important to me, who I'd been through a lot with. I won't call him my friend because he was more like family. He died because of a Theian called an Umbran."

He thought he saw Isla's eyebrow twitch. "You said that before about...*them*. Calling people your family that aren't related by blood..."

"Of course." Marcus frowned. "I know you lost your family... but the Filii Terra, aren't they kind of like your family now?"

Isla looked at him, her brows drawn together. "I...don't understand what you mean."

"I mean that they're people who have my heart. People I love and trust, and I feel like as long as we have each other, everything will be okay. People I'd die for and die with, and when we laugh together, it's like the world stops turning, just for a second."

Isla blinked. Her eyes sparkled like diamonds in the moonlight.

Marcus shook his head, finding it difficult to believe. "You must have someone like that. I don't know how I would have coped without them or Song."

Song sat up smoothly, settling into a cross-legged position, tilting their head.

"But they're...one of *them*." Isla sounded more confused than angry.

"Song isn't Theian, but they're not from here either. Not that it matters. My...the one who died. He loved a monster. And I don't think I've ever seen anyone love anything as hard as that monster loved him back. I just think if anyone can love that much, how can they be bad? If Song and I can love each other like we do, when that's an inescapable truth that brings us together, how can any of them be completely bad?"

Isla turned to him, tilting her head curiously, but she said nothing. A gentle breeze teased her red curls in the night.

As the moments passed, Marcus thought she might say something several times. Words seemed to dance on the tip of her tongue until she finally spoke. "We should go into the homestead."

Marcus waved toward the mountains grandiosely. "After you, milady. Mostly because I don't bloody know where we're going."

A sly smile crept onto Isla's face. "We don't have far to go."

She raised her hand, her sleeve falling back.

Marcus watched her curiously.

Then he saw it.

On her index finger sat a ring...made of *bone*.

He raised his hands quickly, ready to fight, but he was too slow.

She rapped her fist three times in the air, and it rippled like the disturbed surface of a perfectly placid pool.

Marcus stared at her in confusion, then his jaw dropped.

As the ripples spread out, the patches of shivering air changed shape. Solid buildings of stone appeared from the bushes nearby. Glowing torches awoke from nothing and dotted around the clearing. Up ahead, a vast building took form, an enormous flag hanging over the doors. The flag bore a strange symbol, almost like a crosshatch with a triangle over it.

Figures formed from the darkness.

Marcus thought they were flecks again but only for a second. They moved with too much benign and regular purpose. Their aura's, like Isla's, were human but with the same strange sparks. They stood in small groups and seemed to converse with one another.

Soon, their features became clearer. They were people of all kinds. One formed nearby, a kind-eyed Black woman with pale and milky eyes. The sapphire tunic that covered her stooped, diminutive frame complimented her heavy mauve aura.

Behind her stood a massive man with ruddy skin, and a long,

blonde beard plaited down the middle. His aura was pale yellow and so faint it was barely visible. Marcus had never seen *that* before and didn't know what it meant.

Nearby, a tall, willowy woman stepped forth, her hair straight and golden down her back, features pale and pinched. Her aura was constantly shifting, tones of red earth like a muddy pool.

As the shimmering air smoothed, it was as though everything shuddered, settling into its rightful place and locking in. Marcus felt a warm rush of delight from Song and turned to find them leaping up from the ground, clutching a confused-looking Ed in their arms, who was now a Pomeranian.

"Good evening," the golden-haired woman said, smiling. Fine crinkles around her eyes said she was older than she looked, and her icy-blue eyes themselves were implacable.

Her voice was confident.

"My name is Linda, Matriarch of the Filii Terra. We've been expecting you, Marcus."

❧ 20 ❧

THE SEAT OF THORNS

Marcus couldn't stop looking around. "Where the sweet fuck were you hiding all this?"

The Matriarch wore a long, emerald cape that draped to the floor. Beneath it was a loosely fitted aqua garment from some natural-looking material. "From what I hear, I could tell you, but if I give you a few minutes, you will likely figure it out yourself."

Marcus met her cool, blue eyes. They reminded him of chips of ice.

Was that a challenge?

A thought from Song pressed against his mind.

An offer.

No, I want to do this myself.

A reply of warm confidence and pride.

"It isn't glamour," Marcus said confidently. "Otherwise, you would risk us walking straight into a wall as we passed through, no matter how rare it is for people to come around these parts."

The corner of the Matriarch's mouth quirked in an amused smile.

"And you haven't put it in the in-between. If you had that kind of reliable control over the veil, there would be no telling what other kind of power you had, and there's little chance that I'd be alive after an assassination attempt on your behalf."

She tilted her head.

"So, I'd say it's a low-level forbidding; a repulsion charm of sorts, to disincline passers-by from continuing this route but basically make them think it was their own idea. Maybe a high-level obfuscation charm, making people not want to see it at all, making them feel calm, almost disinterested. Probably works best on people with no knowledge of its presence or purpose."

The Matriarch's face cracked into a full smile, showing pearly white teeth. "Excellent, though you are incorrect on one thing."

This time, it was Marcus' eyebrow that quirked.

"It was not an assassination attempt."

Marcus opened his mouth, but it was Isla's voice that rang out. "What?" She stared in disbelief.

The Matriarch didn't meet her eyes. "I wanted to see precisely what you were capable of and how far your bond with your ethernal had progressed. I wanted to gauge your intentions and have you brought here, to me, to discuss how we might move forward together."

Isla gasped and opened her mouth angrily, but she never got the chance to speak her mind.

"Enough, Isla. You may be the most promising youngster in the order, but you are a Child of the Earth, and you shall act as one." The Matriarch's voice wasn't unkind, but it was firm.

Isla let out a breath, and her shoulders sagged.

"How did you know I wouldn't kill her?" Marcus said, his eyes narrowing.

The Matriarch waved a dismissive hand. "Oh, I have been keeping tabs on you for some time. I was quite sure you were not that kind of person."

Marcus' skin prickled. Taking the time to look at her, he saw things that made his skin crawl. Her ears were each studded several times, not with silver or gold but splinters of bone in various shades and sizes. A blackened bone dagger hung at her hip, slightly curved, and it looked to be razor-sharp. Around her neck, he saw thick joints of some dark material that disappeared under her loose clothes. There was no telling what kind of Theian remains she had around her or what she was capable of.

He squared his jaw. "Bold of you to assume I'm completely a person anymore. I may have had my sense of remorse removed before I met Isla—"

"If you believed remorse was a flaw, you wouldn't have made it nearly so far as this. Even if greater human moral attributes could be seen as a flaw, their trade would certainly indicate the end of the soul-bonded's humanity and herald their ascension."

Goosebumps raised on Marcus' skin.

This woman knows so much about...

"I can tell you more, my child. All that you wish to know. More than any other might—even the ethernals themselves."

A strong feeling of distrust pressed upon Marcus, and he felt small fingers link into his own. He didn't need to turn to know it was Song, but he wasn't sure if the distrust came from him or them.

"I'm good, thanks." Marcus forced a smile. "We have more important matters to attend to."

A fleeting look of surprise spread across the woman's face but was rapidly replaced with that amused smirk once more. "Very well. Isla, go with Anabelle to be debriefed." She dismissed the girl, then gestured toward a large building made of wood. "Marcus, we shall speak in the grand hall. Would you like for your...*creature* to be watered and fed?" the Matriarch asked, sparing a brief glance of distaste for Pomeranian Ed, still in Song's arms. He was shivering.

"No, thanks," Marcus said stiffly. He exchanged a glance with Song, and they shared the sending with Ed. The mimick-dog calmed as Song set him on the ground, and he bolted in the direction that Isla had gone.

The Matriarch's eyes followed disapprovingly.

Marcus cleared his throat. "Let's just get this over with."

THE INSIDE of the grand hall, as the Matriarch had called it, was not particularly grand.

Four structural pillars supported the roof and were spread out in the modest space, the horizontal wooden slats of the wall mostly hidden by ornate tapestries. The floor was covered in blankets and cushions, and the whole place smelled of herbs and spices...and something darker and damper than it ought to.

Beside him, Song wrinkled their nose.

The man with the plaited beard followed and stood behind them, blocking the doorway ominously. It was just as well; Marcus wasn't easily intimidated nowadays. Isla had disappeared with the elderly Black woman, Anabelle. Before she left, she shot Marcus a strange look, her eyes wide, brows drawn, mouth a straight line.

"So, Marcus. I gather that you have identified the potential for a cataclysmic event that would threaten the status of the very world?" The Matriarch moved to take the only seat in the room, a high-backed chair that looked to be made of simple wood. Its ornate back, however, was carved with vines and large, sharp thorns that stuck out in all directions so they would stab the one seated if they moved too far back.

"Don't mind this," the Matriarch chuckled, catching his gaze. "This chair is to remind the leader of the Filii Terra that this is not a role one can relax in. I am here to serve and must always focus on doing what needs to be done."

Marcus raised his eyebrows. "Because without a pointy chair, you might, what, turn evil or something?"

The Matriarch raised her chin. "Power corrupts, my child. And absolute power..." Her eyes drifted to Song. "Did you ever hear what the ethernals did to Theia?"

Beside him, Song stiffened. A deep sense of uncertainty throbbed around them.

"What?" Marcus said.

"Far before the veil was sealed, before humans even walked

this rock, Theians had an understanding with the ethernals," the Matriarch said. "They shared their pain, their sorrow, their hunger, and like the soul-bonded humans after them, they would ascend and become a part of the great ethereal consciousness within the universe."

Marcus clenched his jaw, looking at Song. Their eyes were wide, confusion buzzing through their bond.

They...don't know this? How?

"The ethernals betrayed Theia. Monsters are more powerful than humans, of course. They live longer and do not cling to fear. Gradually, convinced of their own superiority, the number of Theians willing to suffer the bond dwindled. So, some ethernals began took what was *not* offered to them. To indulge."

A deep ache shook the bond.

"You're lying," Marcus breathed.

The Matriarch smiled sadly, shaking her head. "Unfortunately, it is all in the ancient texts we protect in this place. When the ethernals who violated Theia reconverged with the higher order, their indiscretions were immediately discovered, and both they and the knowledge they bore were obliterated. Their direct link to Theia was sealed, and the veil has always repelled them."

The woman's attention turned to Song. "You must know I speak the truth. Why else would one with almost endless knowledge and power not be able to see into a world and have no knowledge of why?"

Song's mouth hung open. A deep sadness flooded through every fibre of Marcus' bond—his eyes welling up from the force of it—and he squeezed their hand.

"The Theians did not forget, of course," the Matriarch continued. "I fear that is why, when humans arose far later, the distrust of other species resulted in some...base animosity."

"Why are you telling us this?" Marcus' voice shook. "You know why we're here."

"I am telling you this for one simple reason." The Matriarch sat back, placing her arms on the thorny armrests. Marcus watched the spikes dig into her skin, yet her facial expression didn't shift from placidity. "You know that your bond with the ethernal is a beautiful thing. But it, just like them, is neither pure nor infallible. If you wish to save the world, the powers you must draw upon require sacrifices you do not wish to give...but give you must."

The flood of sadness stopped.

Marcus looked beside him, where Song watched the Matriarch, golden eyes blinking.

"What are you talking about?" Marcus' voice was stiff.

The Matriarch looked between them solemnly. Her aura seemed to throb in anticipation. "If you wish to stop the end of everything, you must give up your bond."

✤ 21 ✤

HEAVY IS THE HEAD

"**B**ullshit," Marcus snarled.

The Matriarch simply blinked.

Marcus squeezed Song's hand. To him, Song always felt physically small...but never fragile as they did right now. Even when they weren't actively sending, they emanated a presence, but now...now it felt like they were retreating into themself.

"Why? Why would severing our bond help? What does that even have to do with anything?"

"The bond brings a powerful magick, but it *is* finite. Even with you as a conduit, the exchange means you cannot sustain the power necessary to pry open the veil and hold it for long. Your humanity would be gone, and your elevated being would be forced apart by your absolute power. Once discorporate, it might take you hundreds of years to will yourself into a physical presence again. And even then, expending your power through a physical manifestation would just cause you to come apart once more."

"But why does breaking the bond change any of that?" Marcus shook his head, confused and angry.

The Matriarch gave a gentle nod to the huge, bearded man, and he moved to the left, rounding her thorny throne, and picked something up from behind it.

He held a circular, flat, white object. It looked to be made from the same bone as the small wand Marcus had stowed with Ducky.

When he realised what it was, his blood ran cold.

"Think of it as jewellery. Your companion donning this circlet will tether them to this realm and enable them to use a higher concentration of their power for a sustained period."

"Tether them to this realm? That's not something they should be forced to do."

"I concur," the Matriarch said. "But desperate times..."

Something pulsed through the bond, and Marcus' eyes snapped to Song. They stared at the circlet as though transfixed by its existence. Their sending was nervous hesitation, like standing on the edge of a cliff and longing to leap off no matter the consequences.

No, you can't do this. It's...not right.

Song turned those golden eyes on him, and the sadness within them required no sending.

Marcus' heart sank.

"I will be honest about the consequences. Tethering themself will cause the ethernal's bond with you to be broken. What exchanges have already been made will remain, of course, but should any more exchanges attempt to be made in their tethered state, the consequences would be dire."

Marcus stared at the Matriarch. Stunned, he swallowed—it was like swallowing blades. "What do you mean, dire?" he managed.

"So far, your exchanges have been measured transactions. Should the ethernal try to remove the relic or exchange with you in their tethered state, unbonded, it will be less like sand running through an hourglass and more like throwing that hourglass against the wall. The action would break them apart and scatter them to the furthest reaches of possibility. They may never recorporeate or even form in a semblance of their previous identity. It is exceedingly difficult for an ethernal to be destroyed, but that's about as close to it as it gets."

Marcus didn't think his heart could sink any further, but it did.

"Besides this, you will know power unlike you have ever known, but only for a fraction of a second before you are separated from the fabric of this realm. Most likely via a very messy bodily explosion."

"No," Marcus said firmly at the same moment Song stepped forward.

Song stared at the circlet resolutely.

"Song, no. We can't do this. You are..." Marcus choked. "You are everything to me."

He tried to press the entirety of what they made him feel.

Safe, joyous, seen, understood, fulfilled, complete.

Everything that didn't have words, the deep realisation of belonging in his bones.

He felt Song receive them, felt them embrace his sending, and envelope his soul in warm recognition.

They turned slowly, and he saw their cheeks wet with tears but eyes hard with resolve.

His breath was tight in his chest.

The Matriarch stared at Song, her mouth hanging open with shock. "I...I have never heard of an ethernal weeping. They must have learned much from you. They are far more in tune with humanity than any I have ever seen before."

Marcus bit back a sob.

Song's sending came, wrapping him in its warmth.

Reassurance. A completed embrace. The knowledge that no matter what happens, we will always have each other.

Marcus felt tears rolling down his cheeks.

"It seems their love for you has extended to the rest of this world, and they are willing to sacrifice much to ensure its survival. And yours." The Matriarch smiled beatifically. "Come, honoured ageless one. Receive the relic, and you shall have the power to save reality."

Song wiped tears out of their eyes with one hand. Still looking at Marcus, they turned to the man holding the relic and stepped forward.

Marcus watched, unable to speak, as the man held up the bone circlet. Song closed their golden eyes and stepped forward once more. Then, the man settled it upon their head.

FOR A MOMENT, nothing happened—nothing other than Marcus' heart breaking.

Without warning, Song's body convulsed, and they lurched forward.

Marcus took a step toward them to help but felt like every inch of his skin had been ripped off at the same moment. He let out a scream, falling to the floor. His bones turned cold inside him as he gasped and writhed. His eyes bulged, tears streaming down his cheeks and every muscle in him freezing while he tried to twist to see Song.

Song was on the floor, too, on their hands and knees, shivering.

The searing heat of his flesh and ice at his core slowly subsided, and all at once, he felt...nothing.

He felt alone.

The warm presence that was always there—that he was so sure had always been there—was *normal*.

It was as if every nerve ending in his body was dulled. Like he was half-awake from an anaesthetic and was sure nothing would ever be clear or complete or meaningful again.

Wretched despair tore through him, and he spasmed again, letting out a sob as the loneliness took hold. He pushed himself to his elbows and knees. He tried to move toward Song, but his body shook.

"Get up," the Matriarch said.

Marcus panted.

What?

"I said, get up." Her voice was cold as stone.

Marcus twisted on the ground, looking up. She was not talking to him.

Song struggled to their feet mechanically, their golden eyes wide with panic.

The Matriarch reached out with long, pale fingers and touched them first to Song's cheek, then their platinum hair.

Fury sparked in Marcus, almost searing away the pain and loneliness inside.

"What are you doing? Get off them!" he roared.

The Matriarch shot him a contemptuous smile. The expression changed her face completely. Before, she had seemed patient and poised. Now, she was cold and spiteful. She patted Song's cheek once more as they shivered, frozen in place.

Marcus forced himself to his feet. He thought he might throw up. His head was light, and he staggered on the spot.

The huge, bearded man moved toward him and took him firmly by the arm. The grip steadied Marcus, but something about it didn't feel like it was a considerate move.

"I am sorry that this is how it must be. I truly am. But if the world must be saved, we should be the ones to do it. Children like you cannot be trusted with such an important task."

"Children?" Marcus sputtered.

"Step forward," the Matriarch commanded.

Song didn't even hesitate this time before they followed her command, taking a single step forth.

Marcus' blood boiled. "What have you done?"

"If you cannot even navigate a situation like this, how could you be trusted to avert the end of the world? Do you really think us fools? *Us*, druids, with the ability to read the signs and divine events through history and commune with the very nature of this world? Us, with the ability to use monsters' bodies to instil power to protect those in need? *That* is why you cannot be trusted with a task such as this...so I have relieved you of your responsibility."

Marcus raised his hand and pushed at the man beside him with crushing pressure. The massive man didn't even sway. Marcus frowned and tried again.

"I would not trouble yourself with that." The Matriarch's smile was thin lipped and razor sharp. "Those tattoos on Birger's skin mean magick does not affect him. He cannot use relics or enchantments, but it's times like these when his talents are truly worth their pound of flesh. He was a fine vessel to hone a craft we have now been able to offer to some other worthy allies."

Marcus tried to pull free of the man's grip, but it was like steel.

Instead, he raised his free hand at the Matriarch.

"Negate any of his castings," she said quickly. "Block his power completely."

Song stiffened, their mouth opening in a perfect 'o.'

Marcus froze as a cold feeling settled over him. He teetered, suddenly weak in the tattooed man's arms.

"What have you done?" he moaned.

The Matriarch lifted her chin proudly. "The circlet gives me full control of the ethernal's tethered state."

Marcus hissed.

"Do not fret. I will ensure that the world is saved." She tapped at the black bone dagger hanging at her hip. "This is the key to ensure that. You need all the correct tools to do a job right, you see. I have the key, and now the power to use it. Next, I just need to find the correct way to access the lock—a break in the fabric between worlds, with the right link to allow clean access."

Marcus twisted angrily in Birger's grip. The large man scowled.

"But that's not for you to worry about." The Matriarch tapped her pursed lips thoughtfully. "You are just a liability now. Too emotionally tied to the solution to see sense. I think it is safest to simply dispose of you."

Marcus' heart sank. His mind raced with potential solutions, coming up blank.

She has Song.

No matter anything else, that single fact meant the woman held Marcus' heart in her fist.

"Release him, Birger. Let him meet his end on his own two feet. We owe him that, at least." The Matriarch gestured a careless hand, as though she was beneficence incarnate.

Birger's grip eased, and Marcus swayed on his feet as he stepped away.

Song's eyes met his, wide with desperation and sorrow.

"It's okay." Marcus forced himself to grin. "Everything is going to be okay."

He raised his hands into the air, making it clear he had no intention of fighting back.

"Farewell, young traveller," the Matriarch said with a nod. "May we meet in the next life on better terms."

Marcus took a deep breath.

The Matriarch rested one of her hands on Song's shoulder. "Destroy him."

Song opened their mouth as though they wanted to cry out in pain, but their hands were already rising, crackling with blue energy.

Marcus pursed his lips and whistled.

There was a pop, and he felt feathers in his fingers.

"Go!" he cried.

He saw the Matriarch's eyes widen in surprise and the large, bearded man lunge toward him, even as he saw the lightning burst forth from Song's hands.

But he was already gone.

TAXONOMY OF MONSTERS: THE SEELEY BUG
(CARO EXHIBUIT)

"This parasite's venom acts as a local anaesthetic to dampen its host's senses before it uses a bladed tail to create an opening for it to crawl under its victim's skin. From then, its metabolism is sustained by the warmth and some carefully consumed tissue, keeping its victim alive as long as possible. Removal requires burning the host's flesh to draw the seeley bug to the surface and allow forcible extraction."

— ON CREATURES FOUL: ARTHUR'S NOTES ON
THE BEYOND

CHANGING HEARTS

S patial magick was a funny thing.

Marcus' understanding of space and time before meeting Song had been that it was, first of all, unfathomable, and second, non-linear. And on both those accounts, he had been right.

Human scientists and philosophers had long since used understandable language and concepts to embed a rudimentary yet flawed perception of reality into common understanding.

The funny thing was, that was true, too.

When the group first visited Dmitri's house and Marcus fell into the basement, Dmitri used pheromones on Oscar to alter his perception of events, compelling him to believe something else. Dmitri had no control over *what* Oscar believed, but gave the powerful suggestion that it wasn't what had happened. When they talked about it later, Dmitri explained the new truth that Oscar's brain generated was purely synthetic, and his memory and senses had adapted to gain some concrete understanding of reality.

That was exactly what happened when a human mind transcended the fundamental understanding of space and time, as well.

The difference was now, Marcus knew that's what was happening.

He knew that though his body had momentarily ceased to exist on a tangible level in the physical world, he was still very much intact. It was exactly like the moment he shifted into the Bean-Nighe's realm. He was, in fact, nowhere. But the potential for where he would be at the next given moment was almost endless.

To make sense of this, his mind perceived this state as an infinite tangle of sparkling threads suspended in the nothingness, like shimmering angels' hairs flowing in a boundless void. Each came with a unique sense of place and purpose, sometimes familiar, but mostly beyond his scope of knowledge. As such, he usually depended on Ducky, or even Song, to help guide the way to where he wanted to be. They both had the inherent awareness of each thread's meaning and could guide the way to help him appear anywhere. The problem was, he hadn't told Ducky to take them to any one place in particular—simply to *go*.

This carried the risk that Ducky may take them into freezing space or embed him within a wall. Ducky, fortunately, was lazy. She simply brought them here, instead: to the in-between, hanging between possibilities.

Marcus felt the threads touching at him, distant and near.

He could go...*anywhere*.

He could go for help.

He considered Zara. She'd do anything to help him out of this. At least he thought she would. But would brash blasts of spirit energy help against the magick the Filii Terra were using?

He considered the Bean-Nighe. Would helping him with this err too far from her chaotic neutral? Would he get anything but strange riddles and sad smiles?

He could run.

But...

Song.

His senses lit the flowing strands that kept them near. The despair in his deepest self was extinguished by solid resolve.

I won't leave them.

I'll never leave them. No matter what.

He drew the threads closer, choosing where it would be best to appear.

Close, but not too close...

The other threads, each throbbing with its own unique presence, shifted around. Among them, he felt another familiar presence.

Decisively, he grasped on to that sparkling thread of power and dragged himself from the nothing and back into reality.

MARCUS GASPED like he had just surfaced from deep, cold waters, an icy sweat coating his skin.

He didn't have time to gather himself before something hard smacked him in the middle of his face. Thankfully, it was soft.

A pillow?

"What the fuck are you doing here?!" a snarling mass of red curls hissed.

Isla stalked toward him, face almost the same colour as her hair once more, clutching her nightgown around her.

Marcus quickly lowered Ducky and set her down. He reached out for Isla, but she danced away.

Ed barked happily nearby. Marcus had given Song a sending for the mimick-dog to keep an eye on the fiery redhead, and now he seemed to think these antics were some fantastic game.

"Shhh," he begged, putting his finger to his lips. "Both of you. Don't make a noise. They're after—"

There was a loud buzzing crash, followed by yelling.

That must have been the blast of energy Song had been sending his way.

Glad that didn't hit me.

Isla's eyes widened as she looked to the window, panicked. "What the—"

"Your Matriarch, she..." Marcus shook his head, chest tightening. "She did something to Song. Took control of them."

There was more yelling from outside. Among them, Marcus heard the Matriarch's voice calling out, imperious.

"CHECK EVERYWHERE! FIND HIM!"

Marcus' heart lurched in his chest. "Ducky, the bag..."

There was a soft pop, followed by another a moment later, and the mallard appeared once more, this time sitting atop a drawstring bag.

"I should call for them...I should have them take you. What have you done?" Isla snapped.

"What have *I* done?" Marcus hissed, pulling open the bag. He reached in, surpassing a shiver when his fingers closed around the leathery feel of dead flesh as he dragged out the cape. "The Matriarch is some kind of Mega-Karen, and she thinks she can open the veil herself using Song."

Isla's eyes opened wide. "She wouldn't."

"She knows I'm right and that we need to do it, only *she* wants to be the one to do it. *She* wants the power."

Marcus wanted to heave as he draped the flesh-cape around himself. It smelled like stale sulphur and dank rot.

"Go," he urged Ducky. "And take Ed with you". Getting irritated with all the commands, the three-footed duck took a lazy lunge, trying to bite his fingers with its toothy bill.

Marcus, used to that, dodged it deftly before she disappeared with another pop, taking the bag with her. A couple of pops and a surprised yelp later, and Ed was gone, too.

"She's the Matriarch..." Isla began.

"She lied to you, too. She sent you to kill me, risked your life to trick you into bringing me here so that she could get control of Song. I'm guessing from how annoyed you were, that's not the first time she's lied to you?"

Isla's mouth closed so quickly it was a wonder she didn't bite her tongue.

That's what I thought.

That's why I came here.

The footsteps and yelling were getting closer.

"Quick, how do I make this thing work?" He yanked at the stinking flesh cape.

Isla stared at him before her eyes drifted to the door indecisively.

"Isla, I won't ever lie to you, but I need you to help me..."

"Envision you pushing your energy into it, sharing some of your power," she said quickly, coming to her decision. "Imagine it's your own skin, and imagine no one being able to see you."

Marcus imagined the bright light of his aura, the golden, luminous sunshine yellow that he knew it was, spreading into the cape.

As he imagined himself becoming invisible, the door opened.

Marcus clenched his jaw so tight it hurt, pulling the cape completely over him and holding his breath.

The Matriarch strode in.

"Isla," she said firmly.

Isla spun to face her, face still pale and eyes wide. She hesitated for a moment, but when she spoke, her voice was harsh with irritation. "What do you want from me? Haven't you used me enough for one day?"

The Matriarch's brow twitched with anger as Birger and Anabelle entered behind her, followed by...

Song.

Marcus' heart twisted in his chest.

Their eyes found him unerringly, staring at him, their face unchanging.

Marcus tried to let out a very slow breath.

"Now is no time for your nonsense," the Matriarch sneered. "The boy has fled. He could be dangerous. You will come out at once and help us begin the search for him. Quickly. There are preparations to be made."

"Oh, you're actually going to share your plan, are you? Rather than lie to me and what? Befriend someone's soul-bonded ethernal or something? How are they even here if he's gone?"

The Matriarch's back straightened. "I do not answer to you, girl. This one knows where they will serve best. *You* will do your duty. It is not your place to question me."

"Fine," Isla snapped, folding her arms sulkily. Marcus wasn't sure if she was acting or if being this petulant just came naturally. "I'll get changed and come as fast as I can."

The Matriarch spun on her heel. "Be quick."

Isla stuck out her tongue as the woman stalked out, followed closely by Birger.

Song was still staring at Marcus, their eyes wide with fear.

"Come!" the Matriarch barked from outside.

Song winced as though in pain, then stiffly followed like a marching doll.

Anabelle stood firm, her heavily wrinkled face scrunched in thought and her small beady eyes searching the room.

Marcus tried to keep his breath low and steady as her eyes travelled to the corner where he huddled. She frowned, staring at the space he hid.

No...it's like she's staring right at me.

Her fingers tightened around her cane, and she looked back to Isla, who stood stock-still, breathing heavily.

He thought he saw her give the barest of nods before she slowly turned and hobbled out after the rest, closing the door behind her.

Isla stomped forward, locking the door behind her, and turned, still breathing heavily, to stare at Marcus' corner.

Shivering, he wriggled out of the stinking cape and threw it aside.

"What do you want from me?" Isla asked a little breathlessly.

"Nothing more than what you *want* to do," Marcus said. "I just need you to do the right thing, that's all."

Isla scowled.

"That's what you always think you're doing, right? When you do whatever it is she tells you to do? When you tried to kill me and Sato? You just thought you were doing what you were supposed to. To help the world. Isla...we can't let her use Song like that. The Filii Terra got us into this mess when they sealed the veil. Let me be the one to fix it."

"I...I..." Isla struggled.

"You've lost people important to you. You wanted to fight. To make it so it didn't happen to other people, right?"

Isla nodded, regaining a little of her fierceness.

"Then help *me*. Song...Song is the most important person in the world to me, and together, we're trying to save everyone." Marcus' voice cracked. He took a breath and tried again, tears stinging his eyes.

Isla stared at him, looking torn. "But they're..."

"Not human?" Marcus asked. "That may be true, but they still love me, and I them. They still feel, and laugh, and care. Does the fact that they're not the same as us make that any less real?"

Isla opened her mouth to speak but apparently had no words. She shook her head, confused.

"Song is the most beautiful soul I've ever met. And the Matriarch has..." He trailed off, sick to his stomach.

Isla sank to the floor, putting her back to the door. They sat in a dark, uncomfortable silence.

"Has she done things like this before?" Marcus asked finally.

Isla remained silent, then nodded.

"What makes her any different from the so-called monsters?"

Isla stared at the floorboards.

"You know she can't be right. *This* can't be right. You want to fix things, and so do I, but neither of us is going to succeed doing this alone, Isla. We need to do it together. The monsters...lots of them were born in this world. Some of them love humans and

Earth as much as anyone else on this rock, and they have just as much to lose.

"You want to do the right thing, but I'm not so sure your Matriarch feels the same. She just wants to do what *she* thinks is the right thing. You and I, if we work together, think of all the people we can save. Think of how many people won't have to feel that loss we've felt. You can't help the world by just putting out spite. If you really want to make a difference, then you need to find what it is you want to love and protect."

Isla's eyes teared up. "She...when I joined the Filii Terra, she was different. I think she wanted to help people. But now, she works for some bad people, making them charms and protection seals. I think she's more interested in power and control than doing what's right."

"Does anyone else feel the same?" Marcus asked.

"A few. I think...Anabelle does. She was the wife of the previous Matriarch. She's never quite seen eye to eye with Linda as Matriarch but keeps her peace to try and steer her as an advisor."

"The old lady that was here before?" Marcus shivered. "I felt like she could see me."

"She probably could." Isla shrugged tiredly. "She's worked with the veil for so long and is half-blind, but she says that she's only half-blind here because the other half of her vision is looking somewhere else."

Sounds promising.

"Why does it matter?" Isla said. "There's nothing you can do. The Matriarch is too strong. She has multiple relics, and now she has your ethernal."

"I reckon we've got a chance if you're willing to help me," Marcus said.

Isla narrowed her eyes.

"I know, you're thinking 'what's in it for me'—"

"Show me how to have what you have," Isla said quickly.

Marcus eyebrows raised in surprise. "What?"

"You said those people were your family. I want that." Isla's eyes burned as fierce as her words. "The Filii Terra...mostly they're just using each other or stuck together in the same space for too long. They don't really care about each other...except maybe Anabelle. I want to have people like *you* do."

Marcus' heart ached for the girl. "Isla, it's not that simple. I can't show you—"

"Then work it out," Isla snapped, tenacious tears brimming in her eyes. "If you want me to help you with your hopeless fight, then figure out how to help *me* in return."

Marcus smiled sadly. "There's always something you can do, no matter how bad the situation. Problem is, sometimes what you do makes things worse. But fuck it, it's still something."

"Is that your way of saying we have a deal?"

Marcus took a deep breath. "Sure. If we make it through this and what's coming, I'll help you with your problem."

A hopeful smile lit up Isla's face.

"It's going to be fine," Marcus said. "The Matriarch isn't as high and mighty as she thinks because there are people here who don't want her in power. She might not even know—"

Isla huffed. "She knows. She just doesn't care."

"That's even *worse*." Marcus' grin widened. "Or better, depending on how you think of it. The cherry on top is that she has wildly underestimated me."

Isla cocked her head. "How do you figure that?"

"Because she thinks I'd go anywhere without Song," Marcus said, still smiling. "And because she basically told me her entire plan like a cartoon villain and automatically assumes I won't do anything to stop her. And most importantly: because she has no idea how much trouble I can really cause."

23

BREAKING THE RULE

The stars above seemed brighter than ever as Marcus strode through the village.

It only took a couple of moments before the cries went up.

A middle-aged white man with a grey moustache ran at him, spinning a kind of carved bone staff that blasted a gust of wind out, kicking dust and debris in a torrent.

Marcus had nothing. Whatever the Matriarch made Song do to his powers still held.

What he did have, was backup.

Serpents of darkness curled from the shadows around the man. They snatched the staff from his hands and wrapped around one of his arms and legs, catapulting him through the night into a nearby tent, resulting in a series of screams from within as it collapsed.

"Sorry!" Marcus called out, before adding more quietly, "Go easy, will ya?"

"That's Edward. He's an asshole," Isla's disembodied voice said.

Marcus shrugged. "Fair enough…"

A stocky woman with wiry black hair came toward him, raising her hands. Each of her fingers bore a matching bone ring, dark and cut in a jagged shape. The air crackled between her palms.

"Wow! That's cool!" Marcus beamed.

There was a flash as a bolt of lightning sparked from between her hands.

The shadows around her feet swelled like a violent wave, closed around the flash of power, catching it in the air, and...*squeezed*.

The woman's hair stood on end, and she let out a shriek as the energy was forced in on itself. It burst apart with a crack and sent her tumbling into the nearby shrubbery.

Marcus' eyes widened.

"Miriam. She makes awful soup," Isla whispered.

"Do you even like anyone here?" Marcus shook his head with a rueful grin at the empty space beside him.

He thought he heard a snicker.

Marcus quickly made his way to the central point, where they had first broken through the glamour. It was close by, and the large, blazing fire there guided the way.

No one else attacked after they saw what he had done. Birger, however, emerged between some tents to the left. The man stalked him like a giant, bearded mountain cat.

"Anything I try will slide right off him," Isla hissed in warning.

"I got it." Marcus smirked as the man grew closer. He raised his hands in a grand, mysterious gesture.

The large man's eyes narrowed, but he did not slow his pace.

"ABRA CADAVER," Marcus shrieked, thrashing out his arms wildly as Birger closed in.

Despite his antimagick inkings, the big man flinched.

That was Marcus' opening.

He sprung forward like a jackrabbit and thrust his fist right into his nose.

It was a good hit.

He felt his nose crunch, and Birger stumbled back, eyes bulging and mouth open wide in a silent scream. Blood gushed out of his nostrils as he tripped over a tent string and landed backwards in a bush.

"Nice," Isla murmured.

"You either have some kind of offer or are ridiculously foolish." The Matriarch's voice cut imperiously through the night, slicing Marcus' moment of jubilation in two.

"Go," Marcus whispered, ignoring the fresh throb in his knuckles.

Note to self: punching people hurts.

He heard Isla's footsteps move away in the night.

Someone must have told her he was coming. She stood beside the campfire, hands folded at her waist.

"Why not both?" Marcus forced a grin. "Both is good."

Song stood beside her, looking as though they were making themself as small as possible.

Marcus' heart felt like it was wringing itself out inside his chest.

Hold on.

Leaning heavily on her staff at the Matriarch's other side was Anabelle, her wrinkled face scrunched in thought as she stared at him.

The Matriarch smirked. "So, tell me...why have you remained here at the promise of death?"

"You tell me. If you wanted me dead so bad, why didn't you already try to make Song kill me before asking me anything?"

Her smirk faltered.

"I think it's because you now know I have something else that's valuable." Marcus folded his arms. "Which is the same reason I didn't leave."

The Matriarch's eyes narrowed. "And what could I possibly—"

"The duck," Marcus said flatly.

The Matriarch raised her chin. "I know you wish to prevent disaster. With the key and power now in place, what remained was the need for a portal. The blood of a three-footed duck may be the means with which to access Theia safely through the veil."

Nope. But good to know you don't know as much as you pretend to.

"So, what you're saying is, I already *had* three parts of the puzzle, and all I *needed* was that fancy knife?"

"Athame," the Matriarch corrected. "Crafted of bone from one of the primordials. Countless souls were lost to obtain it. Having the correct tools is only one part of the puzzle, however."

"Song isn't a tool," Marcus snapped. He cleared his throat. "Song is...my *everything*."

The Matriarch regarded him coolly. "I gather that is often the case with the soul-bonded."

"Then you're crueller than I thought."

She sighed, unfolding her arms. "Cruelty would be failing to act when I am best placed to save this world."

As her sleeves shifted, Marcus saw something at her wrists— slim rings of bone...just like the one around Song's head.

And there we have it.

"Perhaps I was hasty in my previous judgement. It seems you are not a fool. What is it you seek in return for your three-footed duck?" The Matriarch looked down her nose at him.

A thrill ran through Marcus' bones. "I will give you the duck. All you have to do is *not* kill me. Let me stay near Song, and I will help you however you like. I just need to be near them."

The Matriarch scowled thoughtfully.

"If you're scared of me trying to break them out and them dissipating, like you said, I'm not a fool. I'm here because I don't want to lose Song, so there's no way I'm going to do something that scatters them to the furthest reaches of the universe or anything like that. I just want to be with them." Marcus' voice came out harsh. He heard the truth in his words, even if the intent was laced with lies. "Please..."

"I am not one for sentiment," the Matriarch said, "but there may be use in you. Though if you cross me even once, I will not hesitate to—"

"I will be a good boy," Marcus lied again. *That* was always a lie.

The Matriarch eyed him warily before tilting her head to Anabelle.

The elderly woman stared at Marcus so hard he wondered what she could see with those milky eyes. It made him want to cover himself up. •

"I believe he speaks the truth," her reedy voice rang out finally.

Marcus didn't allow himself to smile as another part clicked into place.

The Matriarch's shoulders relaxed. "Very well. Surrender the duck as well as the relics you took from Child Isla, and you may join us."

Marcus let out a breath.

That cunning smile was sneaking back onto the Matriarch's face, the cat that got the cream.

"Sure thing, just uh, give me a sec. Ducky's really...shy?"

The Matriarch rolled her eyes impatiently.

Marcus moved over to the nearby bushes.

Pleaseworkpleaseworkpleasework.

He gave a low whistle. After a moment, there was a pop, and Marcus carefully leaned forward into the bushes to pick up Ducky.

Pleaseworkpleaseworkpleasework.

The Matriarch was tapping her foot impatiently. "The duck didn't seem so shy earlier."

"Sorry, sorry. I just...she's been with me for a while, and she's not great at meeting new people."

"It is a duck." the Matriarch said loftily.

Marcus carried the duck forward, holding its wiggling body in his hands. "She's called Ducky. And I thought you were supposed to be all 'one with nature'. Why are you so weird about an animal?"

"There is nothing natural about *this* duck," the Matriarch sneered.

Marcus shrugged. "Do you want her or not?"

For a moment, the Matriarch stared at the duck disdainfully, then her eyes travelled to Birger. The immense man stepped forward, lips and chin covered in drying blood, ready to take the duck if she commanded. It seemed, though, she decided that power like this was best kept in her own hands. So, she reached out.

Marcus' heart skipped several beats as he handed the duck to her.

She held it out awkwardly at arm's length, and Marcus quickly stepped back.

The Matriarch couldn't hold back the wide smile spreading across her face any longer. "You have made wise choices on this day. Tell me, how exactly does one commune with this creature to have it do your bidding? There is little on how this is achieved in the tomes...more about working with its remnants."

The truth was that Marcus could only commune with Ducky because of the gifts instilled in him through his exchange with Song. Despite that, what he said was, "Hold her up above your head and just imagine where you want to be, then shout 'go!' really loud."

The woman's eyes widened. "Such a simple thing and with unlimited uses. Why did the previous generations slaughter these things so freely when working with them was so simple?"

Marcus shrugged, trying to look nonchalant.

Slowly, the Matriarch raised the duck above her, that beatific smile still on her face. She closed her eyes, took a breath, and then...

"Go!"

That was the signal.

And everything happened at once.

Isla burst forth from the darkness, casting aside the cloak made of skin. She was still in her nightgown, the dark, shrivelled hand-wand clutched in her fist, and her face rapt with concentration.

The shadows flickering around the campfire danced loose.

They formed into the shapes of tentacles, gaping maws, and misshapen men with arms that hung to the ground. The flecks swarmed around the central area, cutting it off from those outside, leaving only Marcus, Anabelle, Isla, Song, and the Matriarch within.

The Matriarch did nothing to stop her, and that was because she was far too busy to notice. The moment she had said '*go,*' the three-footed duck in her hands had not teleported her to some wondrous location. Instead, it bubbled and swelled. The Matriarch gaped as it grew, the transformation happening so fast that before her arms could buckle under the weight, she no longer clutched a duck...but a massive sheepdog. She let out a squawk as she fell back, the massive thing falling on top of her and flattening her to the ground.

Marcus was already moving before she hit the dirt. He rushed toward her and stomped at her wrist. He missed the first time, jamming his foot against her hand and causing her to cry out in pain.

"Shit...I'm not sorry," he shouted and stamped again.

This time, he met his target.

There was a crunching of bone, though not *her* bones. A shard of the bone ring fell from her sleeve, and Marcus moved his attention to her other wrist, hoping to stamp that bracelet as well before she could recover.

"Stop him!" the Matriarch cried.

Marcus froze where he stood, encapsulated in the air like he was suspended in jelly.

His heart sank.

Oh, shit...so that's what this feels like.

"Isla!" he called.

Seeing his plight, the redhead strode forth, brandishing her wand at the Matriarch.

From behind her, Birger strode through the flecks, their dark forms parting around his antimagick flesh like oil on water.

"Isla, look out!" Marcus called, but it was too late.

The massive man's arms closed around her and shook her like a rag doll. She clutched the wand in her hands, but her concentration was broken. The flecks faded, allowing more Filii Terra to flood into the circle. One of them, a white-haired man with cruel eyes, snatched the wand from her hands.

"Get this thing off of me!" the Matriarch crowed.

A second later, Ed was suspended in the air. He deflated down to a furious Chihuahua, baring his teeth at the woman.

"Funny, that," Marcus said as the Matriarch struggled to her elbow on the floor. "All that knowledge and power, and you can't tell a mimick-dog from a three-footed duck. He can turn into pretty much any animal that he's had a lick of."

"Enough!" the Matriarch roared. She tried to stand, but her legs tangled in her flowing robe. "I've had enough of your nonsense! And *you*! You dare betray your own people, Isla?"

"I am *not* betraying my people. I'm doing what you don't have the courage to do, putting trust in someone who knows the way better than we. *I* am trying to have us do the right thing," Isla spat.

The Matriarch tried to rise again but froze.

Marcus saw she was trapped from pressure on her wrist...by a well-worn leather-booted foot. Small, but certain. She turned, staring at the owner of the foot with a stunned expression.

"Anabelle?"

The old woman stared back at her fiercely with her milky eyes. "The girl sees the truth," she said firmly, her old body shivering with effort. Her eyes travelled to Song. "This is not how we should act. You are no fit leader of the Filii Terra."

The Matriarch let out a furious howl. "ETHERNAL, I DEMAND YOU—"

Anabelle pushed her foot down harder, and there was a crunch as the other bone bracelet shattered. Marcus felt the air around him relax, and he moved his arms freely.

Song stood very still.

"DESTROY THIS HAG!" the Matriarch commanded, dragging her wrist from beneath the woman's foot, trying to clutch the shards of bone together.

Song stared at the woman blankly.

"DO YOU HEAR ME, ETHERNAL? KILL HER! AND KILL YOUR SOUL-BONDED! I AM YOUR MASTER!"

Song's golden eyes lit up with rage.

"Oh, there's something else that tells me you're not as smart as you think you are." Marcus' smile was grim as he dusted off his jacket. "You really were so eager to tether an ethernal to this plane, weren't you? Did you ever stop to think how terrible it would be for you if you ever *lost* control of them? If they extended use of their powers to take revenge however they saw fit for your trying to control their timeless being? What it might be like if your fancy little bracelets broke? Nah. Because you're nothing but a basic witch, Linda."

Song's eyes were glowing now, their white teeth bared in a snarl.

The Matriarch let out a cry of fear as Song raised their hands and screamed in pure fury. How a sound like that came from such a tiny form, Marcus did not know. It was the sound of the Earth tearing apart. The fury of a thousand storms and battles won and lost. A bellow of ancient fury.

Marcus put his hands over his ears, but the sound shook through every cell rather than just his ears.

A shockwave spread from Song, a burst of pale golden energy. It spread benignly over him, Anabelle, and the Matriarch too, but it struck the other Filii Terra like a tidal wave, flinging them through the air in a tumble of limbs. Their cries were lost in the torrent of wild magick.

As suddenly as it had begun, it stopped.

Birger still clutched to Isla, and though Song's blast ignored him to avoid harming her too, the redhead twisted in his grip and drove an elbow into his gut. The large man winced, his hands already reaching for her again, but she danced away.

Marcus' entire being was still humming from the unearthly boom when Anabelle's voice rang out once more.

"Birger, stop it now, you foolish boy." She hobbled forward, raising her stick threateningly at the bearded man. He froze, eyes shifting between her, Isla, and the Matriarch, who still lay stunned on the ground. "You listen to me. You no longer follow the commands of *this* woman." She jabbed her stick in the Matriarch's direction to emphasise her words. "You are a Filii Terra. This organisation has long been consumed by her toxic rage. She covered it well. Even I was blind to her poison for a time, but a drop of poison in an ocean is still enough to spoil it. You will stand down."

He regarded the old woman, his lip trembling for a moment, then his massive, tattooed arms relaxed, and he bowed his head.

"Stop this," the Matriarch wailed. "Stop all of this!"

"I think that's about enough from you," Marcus snapped. "You're not my real matriarch, and you never will be."

The woman's mouth flapped furiously, tears welling in her eyes. "I...I just wanted to stop them. I've worked tirelessly for years all over the world. I wanted to protect this world from monsters."

"That's the problem." Marcus sighed. "You can't protect it from them when it's theirs too. We need to work together, not against each other, or whatever we do is doomed to fail. Trust me, I know."

"How can you support this?" she sobbed, jabbing a finger accusingly at Isla. "How can you do this after what happened to your family?"

"We're not the only people to lose someone." Isla looked to Marcus. Her tone was soft, and her voice shook, but her words carried. "But we have to do better. If we act out of hate and vengeance, we're going to hurt more people."

Marcus couldn't help but smile...until his eyes found their way back to Song. They swayed absently on the spot, eyes glassy. He leapt forward, catching them before they could fall, and pulled them into his arms. They felt *different* from before. They were always so small and fragile. Usually, they thrummed with presence and power. Now they felt...weak. A sheen of sweat glistened on their dark skin. He had never seen them sweat.

"What's wrong? Song, please..." He ached for the bond. He ached to share their struggle.

"Please, take this off of them," Marcus begged, looking at Anabelle.

Anabelle's pale eyes fixed on him, full of sadness. "They are tethered to this realm. It must be a jarring experience for one such as them, but..."

The Matriarch began to laugh.

"What?" Marcus' heart hammered in his chest.

"The circlet is fused to their presence," said the Matriarch. "Just like my bracelets were. The only way to remove it is to break it. And doing that would shatter the ethernal, too."

Marcus' heart sank.

If I remove the circlet, it might kill both of us. And if we're gone, who's going to stop this world ending shit storm on the horizon?

But if I leave them tethered, we can't be bonded.

They will have to feel like this, trapped here, all alone and separate.

Bile rose in his throat.

Shivering, Song regained their footing and leaned against him. Marcus raised his hands, his fingers touching the bone circlet at their crown. He had the desperate urge to hook his fingers under its edges and snap it apart. If this was how they had to save the worlds, maybe it was time for it all to be over anyway.

Song's small, dark hands came up to rest on top of his own. Their golden eyes met his, and Marcus stared into them. They were full of pain and fury.

"I'm so sorry," Isla said weakly.

Around them, the Filii Terra were gathering once more. Many held bruised and scuffed limbs or limped with pained expressions on their faces. The cruel-eyed man who'd snatched Isla's bone wand stormed forth, raising it in his hand, pointing it at Marcus.

Song spun out of his grip, and every hair on Marcus' body stood up as they raised their hand. The man froze. His entire body seemed to shimmer. His eyes bulged, and his mouth hung open in a silent scream.

"Song," Marcus murmured.

Tears shone in their eyes, and bond or no, Marcus felt them through their sending. He felt the tempest of fury within them, the will to make this person, any other person, feel their anguish.

"Let him go."

Isla strode up to the man and plucked the blackened claw from his grip.

"Let him go," Marcus repeated gently.

They did, and the man sagged, falling to the ground, face slack with disbelief.

Marcus cleared his throat, looking to the surrounding crowd, his eyes settling on the Matriarch. "We're better than this. Better than *you*. We will do this together, and we'll do it right...no matter what you say. Your time and those like you...it's done."

Marcus reached out, took Song's hand, and pulled them close. Their sorrowful eyes met his once more. He searched them. It was then he knew what he had to do.

He cupped Song's cheeks in his palms, tilting their face up to his own.

Song's lips parted in a smile, their fingers bunching on his shirt as they raised onto their tiptoes.

Marcus leaned down, capturing their lips, feeling the sweetness while their hearts hammered against each other.

He closed his fingers over the circlet.

And he broke it.

24

TRUE POWER

I t was as though the universe was a gong that had just been struck.

Every fibre of Marcus' being screamed with power whilst Song's forced binding on him was torn asunder. But more than that—it screamed as their bond was restored. Song's presence flooded into him like he was a dark room being cast into brilliant light.

Marcus pulled them closer, squeezing them tightly as their fingers bunched his shirt, their lips still locked. The world trembled around them, like reality itself was stretching at its seams, threatening to split apart around them. Then...

He gasped as Song pulled away from their kiss, their golden eyes bright and joyous, sparkling with delight.

"What?" the Matriarch's stunned voice rose.

Marcus grinned, tears streaming down his cheeks. Auras shone around him, rekindled with the restored bond.

Song bounced on their tiptoes happily.

Marcus pulled them back into a tight embrace. "You know, for someone who claims to know a lot about magick, you really don't keep up," he shot at the Matriarch with a chuckle.

Anabelle smiled, clutching her staff to her chest. "Magick is power. Energy captured and unleashed. When conflicting magicks meet, the stronger will prevail. This being was already tethered to this place through a magick more powerful than *yours*, Linda. Your trinkets could not match their love."

"Yeah, *Linda*," Marcus added and stuck out his tongue.

The Matriarch let out a shriek of fury.

"HEAR ME!" Anabelle's thin voice rang out loudly. "As Filii Terra Elder, I declare this Matriarch unfit to serve."

The gathered Filii Terra who'd been cast back by Song's burst of energy now reconvened around the central flame. Dawn crept on the horizon. Song stood closely huddled to Marcus with Ed, still a chihuahua, clutched in their arms.

"You can't do that!" the former Matriarch cried. A few voices in the surrounding crowd echoed her.

"What needs to be done is done," Anabelle snapped, not even dignifying her with a glance. "I knew you were on the wrong path once you started working with that despicable Helios trash. We have a new leader now." Her cloudy eyes moved to Marcus. "One who will lead us to save this world and others. One who will guide us to do what is right and bring us from this tangled path we have become lost upon."

Marcus grinned "That's right. From now on, you will follow *her*." He pointed at the Isla.

Isla's jaw dropped in shock, and even the old woman's wrinkled brow climbed.

"What?" Isla sounded strangled.

"You will lead the Filii Terra," Marcus repeated loudly.

Isla shook her head, eyes dropping in shame. "No. I...I tried to..."

"You did what you thought you had to. But your heart is true, and you are willing to set aside your own feelings for the right things. So, as far as I see it, that makes you a bloody good candidate to lead this bunch of weir—" Marcus cleared his throat. "This delightful sect of Earth-protecting druids."

"I will not—" the former Matriarch began.

"Oh, shut up, Linda!" Anabelle snapped and gave her a clout around the shoulder with her staff for good measure. "We may yet show you the kindness of keeping you here to atone. Keep your mouth shut, and you may do some good. If not, something tells me this ethernal here would see that you spend far longer than you would like suffering before your end."

Song scowled at the woman, raising their hands menacingly. The former Matriarch recoiled in horror, apparently forgetting that free of the relic, Song could no longer cast on this plane.

Isla stalked over to Marcus, her jaw set and face severe. "Are you serious? What do you expect me to do?"

"I...need some time to figure out what's next." Marcus squeezed Song tighter. The Filii Terra that had gathered around them talked amongst themselves. "Will everything be okay here?"

"Everything will be put in order," Anabelle said firmly.

"But...the veil," Isla said, grabbing onto Marcus' jacket sleeve.

"Soon." Marcus released Song, but only for a moment. He looked to where the former Matriarch was still half-sprawled on the ground. "We will open the veil soon, but we need to do it right. And thanks to you, I now have all the tools we need. Well..." He raised a hand and made a snatching motion.

The athame at the former Matriarch's hip pulled toward him, dragging her with it on the ground until the leather cording snapped it free. She tried to lunge for it with a yelp, but it was already sailing through the air into Marcus' hand. "Now I do, anyway."

"If you need us...*when* you need us, the Filii Terra will help," Isla said.

The crowd around them was mumbling, and a few arguments seemed to be breaking out.

"Thank you." Marcus eyed the crowd. "I reckon you have a little work to do here first."

Isla scanned the crowd and seemed to stand a little taller. "I'll do my best."

"You know, you're not so bad for a feisty brat that tried to kill me a few hours ago."

Isla grinned. "And you aren't so bad for a human half-drained by an ethernal with really weird dress sense."

"Don't forget super handsome," Marcus added. He glanced at the deposed Matriarch, who was a shivering, dirtied heap on the floor. "Want me to...erm...put her somewhere weird, like a rain-forest or the arctic or something?"

"No thanks," Isla said. She looked at the woman sternly. "I'll deal with her. Anabelle is right. She may do some good yet."

"I trust your judgement," Marcus said simply.

Isla nodded in return. "Same to you." Her eyes narrowed. "But...don't forget your promise."

"Never." Marcus winked, then pulled Song and Ed tightly against him. He raised his hand and whistled, and there was a pop as Ducky's weight settled onto his arm. He curled the mallard to his chest. "Alright, buddy. Take me to Zara."

TAXONOMY OF MONSTERS: THE ETHERNAL
(SPIRITUS AETERNUS)

Little is recorded of this higher form of transcendent being, and what has been recorded is incredibly difficult to find. A uniquely faceted collective consciousness with incredible power but a limited ability to manifest on the physical plane. Their primary interest with finite beings is to share their experiences due to their inability to experience those things themselves. Transferral of power is liberating and exhilarating for subjects, allowing the exchange of actual or perceived flaws for magickal energies. Ethernal corporealisation is labour intensive but uses free energy and cells to manifest a physical body to partially house the otherwise imperceptible presence of these incredible beings. Aura is unfathomable in colour and shape, but feels like the sun on your skin after you just got out of the sea. Please note: particularly seems to be interested in slippery foods and hot cheese.

— ORIGINAL TAXONOMY ENTRY, MARCUS
WILLIAMS

❧ IV ❧

THE GATHERING STORM

REUNIONS

Broken glass and plasterboard ground beneath Zara's boots as she altered her stance. The flames lapped over Rami's rapidly disappearing corpse. They flickered with the same intense heat as those in Dmitri's eyes, which were casting an eerie glow.

"What...what happened to you?" Zara's voice was brittle.

Not this.

Not after everything.

Don't make me do this too.

Dmitri regarded her darkly, and Zara huffed a tired breath in response.

The flames hungrily crawled up Rami's monstrous chest. The fire had caught one of his arms that rested beside him, consuming both flesh and bone, so a mutated hand lay detached from the rest of him, the flames still eating their way through it.

Zara shook her head sadly, her eyes travelling back to Dmitri's face. She took in his pointed ear and the blistered curl of his other, the white scar across his neck, his burning eyes, and pointed teeth.

He really does look like a monster now.

"Dmitri..."

"He would have killed you," he replied flatly.

"You don't know that." Zara clenched her fists. "You can't just go around murdering people."

Dmitri sneered. It was something she'd never seen him do. Another piece of her heart broke off seeing his previously kind face make such an expression at her. "They were not people anymore. They were demons."

Zara shook her head, heart hammering in her chest. Her nails dug deeper into her palms. "You...you've lost yourself, Dmitri. What they were doing was wrong, but there are better ways to deal with it than killing them."

Dmitri barked a harsh laugh. "There are no better ways. Once a human has fed on Theian flesh, they crave *more*. More strength, more life, more power. It corrupts them. They would have killed their own mothers with a song in their heart if it meant they could keep feeding."

"Still—"

"No. It is not an urge that would pass nor an addiction that can be lived with. It is a sickness that festers within them. What I just did was a kindness."

"A kindness?" Zara bit back. The Ghatotkacha was practically quivering inside her, flooding her veins with fury. "You don't get to decide that. You sound like—"

"Like Lyn?" he replied darkly.

Zara's mouth snapped shut.

Dmitri sighed, his shoulders relaxing slightly. He suddenly looked very sad and tired. "Sometimes cruelty must be done to save people from themselves."

"And you? Who decides when it's kinder to stop *you*? You obviously...you've changed, Dmitri. And it doesn't look like it's for the better."

Dmitri's mouth curved in a mirthless smile that looked strange with those burning eyes. "I followed you here to help. But maybe I was wrong. Maybe you're supposed to be the one to stop me."

Every fibre of Zara's being hummed.

This is it. We're going to fight.

The Ghatotkacha rejoiced within her at the chance of a worthy opponent. A glorious death.

Then, there was a strange popping noise.

"What the fuck? Where in the sweet baby Jesus are we?" a confused voice mumbled.

Marcus?

"Zara! Why are you here? I told Ducky to bring me to you, but it was only after I thought, 'wait, what if she's on the toilet or something', but I didn't expect you to be chilling at some busted fact—WHOA!"

Zara remained frozen on the spot, poised to fight.

To kill.

Marcus—fresh off his babbling arrival—had wandered between the two, still clutching the three-footed duck in his arms.

"Holy shit, Big D. What happened to your face?" Marcus took a step toward him and wrinkled his nose. "Whoa. Kinda smell like you've been travelling for a while."

"Marcus," Zara snapped. "Stay back." She hadn't much detected his scent before, but now that Marcus mentioned it, there was a potent scent of char and musk.

There was a flash of movement, and Song wandered into the fray, bypassing Dmitri and making for the corpse behind him.

"Oh, shit! Is that Rami? What the fuck happened? Why's he all gross?" Marcus' wide eyes shifted between the two of them, both still poised to fight.

"Dmitri killed them," Zara replied hoarsely.

"Them?" Marcus yelled, spinning around, eyes searching for bodies but only finding Beeno's partially bloated remains. He turned to face Dmitri, visibly stunned.

Song crouched beside Rami's corpse...what remained of it, at least. His distal limbs, half a shoulder, and head were all that remained. They stared at the flames eating him away, fascinated.

"Don't touch that," Zara said firmly.

Song turned to Zara, innocently eyeing her whilst still reaching out with one hand.

"I said don't!" Zara shouted.

Song froze, expression unchanging, and slowly drew back their hand.

"Are you evil now, Dmitri?" Marcus asked bluntly.

"Marcus!" Zara hissed.

Dmitri sighed again, his shoulders sagging even more as he dropped his axe to his side. The flames in his eyes dimmed.

Zara allowed herself to relax. Just a little.

"I mean...not judging a book by its cover, but you really do *look* evil. So, I'm just asking if you're evil now and—oh my Gods!" Marcus' expression became worryingly excited. "You two were going to fight to the death right before I got here, weren't you?"

Zara groaned.

"I am not evil," Dmitri grumbled irritably. "I just saved Zara from her cousin, who had been feeding on my kind to gain power."

Marcus whistled through his teeth. "Rami went full dark side, huh? I mean, not totally surprised. I was reading up about that a year or so ago. It sounds like it can get pretty nasty. Are you sure you didn't just kill him out of, you know, that whole 'my lover's ex thing', though?"

The flames flickering in Dmitri's eyes snuffed out, and he hung his head.

A low whining from behind startled Zara, but it only took her a moment to recognise its source. Ed, in the shape of a cocker-poo, tentatively padded up beside her.

"Ed," Dmitri breathed, affection seeping into his voice. His eyes weren't glowing anymore, but they were no longer that shifting grey either. Now, they held a burnt orange with flecks of dark within them, like motes of ash.

Ed let out a low growl, followed by a protective bark, shifting closer to Zara.

Dmitri's face froze, the hopefulness bleeding out of it like the last pumps from a dying heart. His sad, reddening eyes shifted back to Zara.

Her chest ached. The Ghatotkacha roiled inside her, desperate for the fight promised. She pushed it down with great effort, and it grudgingly released its hold on her completely.

YOU OWE ME A BATTLE.

Oh, shut up.

"It's okay, buddy." Zara squatted down, rubbing Ed's head. "It's your master. He's back."

Dmitri opened his mouth as if to say something, but the words died in his throat.

"Something tells me we all need to sit down and have a real good tit-a-tit about all this," Marcus said, thoughtfully rubbing his beard.

Zara shook her head, confused. "Do you mean—"

"I meant what I said." Marcus' grin looked strained, but his eyes were bright with hope.

Zara felt a swell inside her, too.

We're back together again.

The last remnants of her cousin, the man who'd been the boy that tormented her through her childhood—and to a lesser extent, adulthood—disappeared into nothingness as the flames died out on their own. It was yet another person she'd known, if not loved, gone. Zara felt as though another string that attached her to this world singed away. It didn't matter whether that thread had been good or bad, just that it had been part of her.

She took a deep breath. "I agree. Let's talk."

"Perfect." Marcus seemed more relaxed now. Song stepped up beside him and took hold of his hand. "Anyone know where the nearest takeout is? Song's starving. Not literally, of course, because they can't, but they *really* want pizza."

26

THE LONG-SHOT

One hundred and thirty-eight Kinmount street was as eerily beautiful as Zara had ever seen it. Dmitri ensured the contracts were in place to restore it to its pre-Umbran, post-glow-up state before he had disappeared. There *was,* however, two years' worth of dust on every surface. Zara was sure from the scrabbles she kept hearing that more than one family of rats had found themselves a new home. Ed was sure of this, too, and disappeared not long after they arrived in the form of a Jack Russell greedily sniffing after some prey.

Marcus leaned back, his legs spread wide on the couch, with Song beside him. They stretched a piece of hot cheese from a slice of pizza from their teeth and back, eyes wide with fascination. On the floor beside them, Ducky worked on guzzling a two-person serving of shredded duck, making hungry grunting noises that were quite discomfiting.

Zara sat, legs crossed, on the armchair. Her paper bag of prawn toast and curry sauce to dip it in—something Marcus had always called an abomination—sat cooling on the dusty coffee table. Dmitri's arrangements included keeping the electricity running seemingly indefinitely to the house. Though two of the bulbs were dead, the last remaining one gave enough light for their reunion in the living room, the room the Umbran had once torn the window from and almost killed them all.

Dmitri stood watching them quietly from beside the doorway. In the light, he looked even stranger, with his skin appearing paler than it had before, particularly against his black clothes. A pink burn scar crawled up his temple, leaving it hairless. It ran from his curled ear and down his neck on the opposite side of another thick, white scar, which ran to his Adam's apple.

Zara wondered why he couldn't heal those wounds, or if maybe he just chose not to, like Marcus and his scar. He had been an average-sized man when they met him. But ever since shifting in Theia the night Lyn used Oscar to open the world parallax, he'd been larger, and it seemed harder to find clothes that hid his muscles rather than compliment them. His face had been handsome, though more angular and thoughtful. Now, the shadow of those features remained, but the pain, scars, ears, teeth, and peculiar eyes made them difficult to see.

"Marcus…" Zara started flatly.

"Right," Marcus said, giving them a nervous half-smile. "Time for the talking."

"Where do we start?" she asked.

"At the beginning?"

"There are too many beginnings," Dmitri said. "Better to start with an explanation. There are plenty of those too, but at least there can be answers instead of questions."

"Fair point," Marcus conceded.

"Where have you been?" Zara asked Dmitri before Marcus had barely finished speaking.

Dmitri looked at her thoughtfully. "I have been to many places. The darkest reaches of this world and deeper still."

"You said answers!" Marcus pointed at him dramatically.

"That is an answer," Dmitri said. "I can tell you I have been to the Amazon rainforest and the catacombs of Paris. It is not those places that matter, though, but the places beyond them."

Marcus' eyes widened. "You mean like…the in-between?"

"There are more creatures living between the veil than just the Bean-Nighe," Dmitri replied.

Marcus practically bounced in his seat with excitement. "Oh, I know. But what were you doing there?"

"Searching," Dmitri said. "For...chances."

"Chances?" Zara asked.

"We shall get to that." Dmitri shook his head. "Now it is your turn. Marcus, I have heard of your *adventures* from several contacts during my travels. What have you learned?"

"And how did it go getting the, uh...magic pressure release thingy?" Zara added.

Dmitri cocked his head curiously. It was an eerily wolfish gesture she had never seen him do before.

"Oh, you know." Marcus shrugged. "A weird cult queen tried to put a crown of torment on Song. We busted out. And yes, got some magic doohickeys to save the world. Pretty much how you'd expect."

"What?" Zara gasped.

Song looked up from their pizza, tapped their head, and nodded.

"Did you...destroy the witch?" Dmitri asked earnestly.

"Oh, Linda? Nah. She done fucked up, but I figured it was better to cultivate allies rather than corpses..." Marcus trailed off, looking at Dmitri.

An uncomfortable silence settled over them.

"Was there really no other way?" Zara asked, voice tight.

There was another lull of silence, and Zara brought herself to meet those orange eyes.

"Truly," Dmitri said, "if there were, I would have done it. A swift death for him was the most I could do to spare you...and the least I owe you."

Now that Zara gazed into them, she had great difficulty drawing herself away from those eyes. Just like the shifting grey before, those dark motes seemed to dance if you watched carefully enough.

Marcus nodded sagely. "Rami was a douche-supreme and didn't deserve that, at least not before. If he was eating monsters and willing to hurt you to get the Ghato, I'm inclined to agree with Big D."

Zara finally dragged her eyes away. She reached forward and pulled open the paper bag, taking out the pot of curry sauce and popping the lid off. Marcus watched her, evidently ensorcelled by her actions, until she dipped a slice of prawn toast into the sauce and took a bite.

"Why do you want to hurt the world this way?" he whispered.

"Shut it," Zara said through a mouthful.

"So, why are you back?" Marcus chirruped, turning to Dmitri again. "After two years, what made you come back here all scarred and last gunslinger style?"

"And *why* are you scarred?" Zara added. "I thought you could heal from pretty much anything."

"Ever since that night at Stonehenge, my powers have not functioned properly. I suspect it is something to do with this." He unbuttoned his shirt.

"Hey, now," Marcus raised his hands. "I'm not into this..."

Dmitri ignored him, opening his half-unbuttoned shirt.

Zara's jaw dropped.

The burn scar from his head and neck did indeed carry down, its jagged edges crawling over his pectoral and peeking out from under the edge of his open shirt. But more shockingly, right in the centre of his sternum was a pink and puffy scar that looked fresh and on the edge of bleeding.

"What *is* that?" Zara managed.

"Some shard from the bone gate, I think. From the night it collapsed. It's stuck in my chest. I dare not try to remove it. Given the impact it has on my healing, pulling it loose might cause enough trauma to kill me."

"But won't leaving it in kill you?" Marcus asked numbly.

Song took another mouthful of pizza, staring at Dmitri's chest with interest.

"The wound is trapped in an inflammatory state, neither gaining more injury nor healing. Suspended in a perpetual state of trauma," Dmitri replied, staring down at the wound.

"Sounds familiar," Marcus mumbled.

"Have you..." Zara began, mouth still half full.

"Two surgeons of my kind and a shaman," Dmitri replied smoothly. "They all said the same."

Zara pushed her food away, her appetite suddenly gone.

Actually...

She pulled it back and pulled out another slice.

Fuck it, it tastes too good.

Dmitri cast his gaze to the floor as he buttoned his shirt back up.

"So, you came back to say...goodbye?" Marcus asked.

Dmitri shook his head, smiling sadly. "Even when I shift, this barb remains in the same place in my chest. I have shifted three more times since I saw you last, in battles too difficult to prevail without doing so. That is why I am..." He gestured to his face. "Each time I've done it since my brief visit to Theia, I return a little less human. It is better than I thought. Before, I thought I could never change back. Now, I know that may be the truth, but at least not for some time yet."

"What battles?" Zara asked, dipping her toast.

Marcus watched and wrinkled his nose at her.

"Ones I had no right to win, and some that I barely walked away from," Dmitri replied. "I should not be alive by many measures right now. I've battled with primordial beings, those long hidden from this world, who in the past were revered as the first gods."

Marcus' eyes sparkled with excitement. "Why?"

"Information," Dmitri replied simply.

"Is that why you came back?" Marcus asked.

Dmitri shook his head, a small, crooked smile forming on his lips. "No, Marcus. I came back because of you."

Marcus' eyes widened in confusion.

"I came back because what I learned was that my only chance was you."

"What are you talking about?" Zara asked.

"Marcus, you plan to open the veil, to release the pressure building in Theia...to prevent the destruction of these worlds, isn't that so?" Dmitri asked.

Marcus nodded.

"I believe you can do it. And I'm here to help."

Zara chewed, staring at Dmitri.

"You don't want to help me open the veil to save the worlds, do you though, Dmitri?" Marcus asked slowly.

Dmitri's stare intensified upon him as he spoke.

Marcus' eyes shone. "You want to help me open the veil so that you can pass through it."

Dmitri's lips curled in that crooked smile again. "If I am to die, I would take any chance I can, even if it means no return."

"Chance?" Marcus repeated numbly.

Zara's voice practically tore out of her throat. "You want to go through...you want to go through to look for Oscar."

"Why?" Marcus' voice was shaking. "We saw...we saw a sword put through his chest. We saw him torn apart between worlds."

Dmitri's red eyes shone. "Because that's another thing I learned from the primordials. There is something, *someone*, in Theia, holding the destruction at bay."

"What?" Zara breathed.

"It has to be him. I know it," Dmitri said. He was practically shaking with emotion. "It has to be Oscar."

27

AGAINST HOPE

"I want to believe you, I really do, but this sounds like wishful thinking," Marcus said as he stalked back and forth at the edge of the room.

Song had finished their pizza, and it wasn't long before Zara felt a sending of not want—but *need*. She found those golden eyes fixed on her prawn toast and encouraged them to take it. Song greedily began dipping it in the curry sauce, much to Marcus' disdain.

"I thought so too," Dmitri replied gruffly. "But I cannot think of any alternative, so…"

"Once you've eliminated the impossible…I got ya, Sherlock. What I'm saying, though, is you really don't know what's possible in this context. None of us do," Marcus shot back.

"I know. I know that better than anyone, Marcus. I know that after everything, even if it were Oscar, there's no telling if it is *our* Oscar."

"What do you mean?" Zara interjected.

"Being in a place like that, where time moves differently for who knows how long, there's no telling if he would even come back…*right*," Dmitri said.

"What, like he's gonna come and stand on the porch singing

'you were always on my mind' until we bury him under a rose-bush?" Marcus folded his arms.

"What?" Dmitri looked confused.

"My points are, one: you don't know if it's Oscar, or even if it's possible it ever could be. Two: even if it was him, you don't know if it's *really* him. Three: even if you can go through the veil, and who's to say you *can* without me letting all hell break loose, what makes you think you could come back? And finally, uh...six: what if with the shit kicking off over there means you're dead the second you set foot on Theia? Or even that Theia exists in any practical sense of the word anymore as nothing other than an overwhelmed collection of negative energy crushing the bounds of reality?"

Zara frowned. "Marcus, did you give Song your ability to count or something?"

"My point is, well, there's a lot of points. But this shit gets more confusing than a badly written time-travel movie. We're not talking about a multiverse, where effectively any reality is possible based on the right variables. We're talking about a blind unknown with unquantifiable variables, full-stop. It's ludicrous." Marcus rubbed his head.

"But we're going to do it," Dmitri insisted gently.

"Of course we fucking are!" Marcus bounced on the spot.

"Because no matter what..." Zara said softly.

"Even if there's the smallest flicker of a chance," Marcus added.

"I will do anything," Dmitri finished gruffly. At their stare, he corrected himself. "*We* will do anything." He smirked, flashing those pointed teeth.

Zara smiled, too.

"So now we just have to figure out how." Marcus paced again, bristling with manic energy. He patted the blade at his hip. "I have this fancy shmancy bone knife. Apparently, it can part the veil, but the amount of power it needs is enough to burn out my exchange with Song in seconds. I'd never be able to sustain it long enough to do any good. So, if we don't have the power, we need to find the right angle instead. The right pressure points and position to cut with the least resistance."

"I spoke with the Bean-Nighe," Dmitri said. "I thought she may help navigate the in-between."

"She can't." Marcus waved his hand dismissively. "I mean, even if we tried to cut from there, I'd still burn out, but maybe in a minute rather than a second. We need more. Some kind of...link."

Zara's mind raced. She didn't understand half of what was going on, but a fresh hope kindled within her, a hope that she could burn away all the regret that filled her, numbed her, every day.

Dmitri scowled. "The world parallax in the cemetery is no doubt tied to Oscar after the energy it absorbed through him. If the energy were funnelled through some *alternative* link to him, into that very parallax and through that blade..."

Zara narrowed her eyes. *Some alternative link? Did he mean...*

Marcus shook his head. "We don't have the right connectors. That works in theory, but only like your TV and toaster both have power cables. They don't match each other at the right voltage or connector type."

Dmitri shook his head. "We need more time."

"That's the one thing we *don't* have," Marcus replied glumly. "I mean, we have maybe a couple weeks before things are so busted there's no going back."

"We need to think fast," Dmitri agreed.

"You two are hurting my head," Zara said blandly. "I mean, it's great to have the family back together, even if Dmitri is looking a little less Gomez and more Lurch, but isn't there a straightforward way? Like what if I used the power of the Ghatotkacha combined with your energy?"

Marcus shook his head. "We don't know how much power you really hold or what doing that would do to you. We can't do this at the cost of anyone's life, Zara."

Zara thought of the mountaintop gate and the seals it bore.

"We did it at the cost of his," Zara said, her voice brittle.

A stiff silence filled the room.

"This time, we have a choice," Dmitri replied. "We have time to think, even if only a little. We can do this. I...believe in us."

"Me too, big guy. And not just cos I think Oscar, or evil Oscar or whatever, waits on the other side. We can do this because we must. If it's gonna cost our lives to save everyone else, that's what we'll do. But until then, let's keep working on alternatives and see what presents itself."

There was a soft rapping sound from somewhere.

Zara perked up.

That sounded like...

The tapping sounded again.

Zara was on her feet even before Dmitri. She dragged the coffee table out of the way, sneezing when her breath kicked up dust from its surface.

"Oh!" Marcus said loudly as he followed. "I thought it was the bloody Bean-Nighe in the fridge again for a second, but it's the bloody someone else!"

Zara snatched the withered dill from above the mirror and used her sleeve to wipe the thick dust off its surface.

"Paige?" Zara asked, confused.

Paige stared back at her and clearly mouthed a few words starting with 'F'.

Vandle's face appeared beside her, looking tired.

"Vandle, Vandle, Vandle," Zara said quickly.

A moment later, Paige and Vandle spilled out of the mirror, the former staggering and almost falling as her feet hit the ground.

"Fucking hell, I'm really never going to learn to like that. I spent six months on a boat once, and sea-legs are much fucking easier than...mirror legs," Paige grumbled.

"Hi, Paige." Marcus waved cheerfully.

"Alright, Jazz-hands. Zara." Paige smoothed her dress. It was beautiful but spattered with blood. There was a trotting noise as

215

Ed made his way in to check on the commotion. "Dogthing," Paige added before her face twisted. "Uh...and rat?"

Ed threw back his head and gobbled down the second half of a rodent, its pink tail disappearing into his mouth.

Paige cringed. "Bye, rat."

"What are you doing here?" Zara asked, but Paige's eyes fixed on the door behind her where Dmitri had stepped back into the shadows of the hallway.

"Wait. Dogthing looks pretty clean, so why does it smell like hot, wet, dog arse in here?" Paige's eyes wandered to the shadowy doorway, and she gasped. "Is that..."

Dmitri stepped forth into the light, and Paige let out a squeak, putting her hands over her mouth. "Oh, no!"

"He's fine, Paige," Zara began. "He just—"

"Your beautiful face...it's ruined," Paige moaned.

Dmitri looked confused.

"Ugh, it's like someone went into a museum and smashed up a fucking masterpiece. What a crime. Spin around and let me check the arse. At least that—"

"Paige, I think we have more important matters to discuss," Vandle interjected.

Paige sighed dramatically, snatching her purse from under her arm and popping it open. "Fine. I'm going to have a smoke. Later, we're going to talk about how you had me carrying that spicy little bum-bead without knowing how much of a kaboom it made. I could've lost a tit."

The pale woman rolled her eyes.

"That." Marcus pointed at Vandle. "I feel very that."

"Standard," Zara added, forcing a smile at Paige, who was already stalking past her, cigarette between her lips.

Zara waited for the footsteps to fade before she spoke again. "Why is she dressed so fancy?"

"Dinner party," Vandle replied.

"Alright for some." Marcus shrugged.

"The blood?" Zara pressed.

"Not a nice one." Vandle shook her head, her gaze shifting uneasily. "We have been...working with some shady characters in New York. Trading black-market goods for money before stealing them back and replacing them with fakes later."

Zara felt a distant wave of shock bite into her, but the events of the night so far had left her more than a little armoured with numbness.

"I'm...I'm sorry, Zara," Vandle began.

Zara felt a laugh bubble in her chest. "Wait. You're fucking with rich criminals, taking their money and stealing shit back from them later? That's...hilarious."

A pang of concern jabbed into her. She glanced down at Vandle's hands. They, too, were covered in blood.

"Is it...dangerous?"

"Not usually. But tonight, we learned something I suspected was true but had hoped was false. We escaped...but narrowly. You know how dangerous it is for me to enter mirrors when there is a risk of them being broken." Vandle's expression darkened.

Zara nodded, her heart clenching. If the mirror broke when Vandle was too close to the surface, the glass wasn't the only thing that would shatter.

"What did you learn?" Marcus jumped in.

"They were part of an organisation. They have been eating our kind, consuming our flesh in small amounts to augment their states." Vandle shook her head, looking disturbed.

Behind her, Zara heard Dmitri growl.

"I..." Zara trailed off.

Vandle took a step toward her, eyes suddenly full of concern. She stepped forward, touching a hand to Zara's cheek. It felt puffy and raw inside from where one of Rami's punches had mashed it against her teeth. "Zara, you've been hurt."

"I'm fine," Zara said. "I...I'll be fine."

Vandle frowned worriedly.

"Oh! You two are a thing now?" Marcus asked loudly.

Zara did anything but look at him.

"Jeez, Zara, you really got a thing for them monster parts."

"Are you not the one in love with a being that transcends physicality itself?" Vandle turned to him, looking perplexed.

Marcus gave a defeated splutter.

Zara grinned. "Rami and his friends were eating monsters, too. Said they were involved with some group called the Order of Helios. Had a weird tattoo of a sun…"

"A sun?" Paige stalked back into the room, surrounded by the pungent aroma of fresh smoke. "Were you telling them about the culty people at the dinner party?"

Zara's eyes widened. "What?"

"The people we ran from tonight, they had a little symbol with a sun on their ward," Vandle said. "They…they were likely working together, acting in cells around the world somehow."

A stiff tension ran through the air.

Marcus broke it.

"Online," he said flatly. "They probably just have a message board or some shit. Monster-Gobblers dot com."

"I reached out, searching for you as soon as I could. We came straight here. At least this explains where all the missing monsters have gone," Vandle said sadly.

Zara frowned. "Agreed."

"But what are we supposed to do about it?" Marcus moaned. "We have more world-endy problems to deal with right now."

"We focus," Dmitri replied. "We will deal with them if and when it becomes a problem."

Zara remembered his burning axe and the way it consumed Rami. Before they had left the warehouse, he had spoken its name again and set the remains of Rami's friends alight, too. On top of everything else, there were about to be three missing person's cases, two of them active police officers.

This is definitely too much shit to sort out in one night.

"Wait, the world is ending again?" Paige leaned against the wall, deliberately bashing the back of her head against it.

"Of course," Marcus said brightly. "But there *is* some good news!"

"No!" Zara snapped.

Everyone froze.

Zara glowered at Marcus. They couldn't tell Paige. Not when they didn't *know*. They couldn't put Oscar's sister through this if it were all to amount to nothing.

"It's alright, Zara," Dmitri said gently from behind her.

Zara shifted her stare to him.

Dmitri raised his hands peacefully. "She has as much right to know as anyone."

"To know what?" Paige eyed them both. "Wait, is it my fault? Have I ended the world this time? Am I the villain?"

"The pressure cooker of hate is pretty much at an explosion point, and the universe is ripe to go kablooey. But...there is *some* kind of energy in Theia that's holding back the darkness," Marcus said carefully. "Something or some*one* that is holding things at bay."

Paige's eyes widened. "Oscar."

"We don't know that," Zara said quickly.

"Don't we?" Paige spun around on her. "The chosen one? With the touch of Theia and Earth in their veins? The little fucker who was possessed by a weird, slimy hate-monster and sent to another world through a vortex of dead monsters isn't the one fighting off the slimy, hate-monster in the other world?"

Marcus shrugged. "She has a point."

"I believe it's him, too," Dmitri said.

"Fuck that." Paige's grin was wild. "Let's crack this bitch open and get him out."

TAXONOMY OF MONSTERS: THE NUCKELAVEE
(CARNIBUS EQUUS)

A creature strange: horse, man, no skin,
It gallops fast, arms long and thin,
No beating heart nor soul within.
It may not have a head,
But hunts for those that stink of sin,
'Til all of them are dead.

— AMANDA GRACE, DATE UNKNOWN

28

OF SHADOWED HEARTS

The next few days were strange and passed by quickly.

Vandle helped Zara clean the house. Oscar always said Dmitri enjoyed cleaning, but Zara couldn't imagine seeing anything stranger than a red-eyed, pointy-eared Dmitri beating the dust out of the bedsheets. Paige spent most of her time skulking on the porch with a cigarette or bursting into the dining room, shouting non-stop demands. That was the room that held the title of 'the room that had seen far too many end of the world plans' and was currently where Dmitri and Marcus were holed up.

Marcus took to having Ducky just pop Paige right back to the porch. The mallard actually seemed to enjoy the game, seeking to shift her before even a syllable left her lips.

The duck had mastered this the day Zara joined the freshly popped-out Paige on the porch, settling onto the steps beside her and wafting away a plume of frustrated cigarette smoke.

Paige had Vandle pick up her clothes and presently wore a nautically striped summer dress with white socks pulled up to her knees. It had the typical effect of making Zara feel underdressed in her baggy T-shirt and denim shorts. The rest of Paige's clothes were still in several suitcases, now stacked in the hallway.

"Alright?" Paige said sullenly, looking into the sky as though she were speaking to no one in particular.

"Yeah, I'm fine. And you?"

Paige shrugged, looking up at the afternoon sky.

"Paige...I wanted to say to you, but I never really got the chance—"

"You're sorry for impaling my brother on a bloody great sparkle sword?"

Zara cleared her throat. "Uh...yeah."

Paige sighed. "It's alright. It was the right thing to do."

Zara watched Paige take another drag.

How can she say that? How can everyone think that and yet...I'm the only one still not so sure?

"I think...I could have done things differently," Zara said. "I could have tried hitting the gate of bones with the willblade, or—"

"We could all have done things differently." Paige flicked the glowing bud of her cigarette into the gravel.

Zara had the urge to pick it up, but Paige's cool blue eyes turned on her and froze her in place. Before, Zara had never thought she looked like Oscar. But now, she saw him in every angle and shadow of her face...those eyes, a shade or two cooler, but right now full of *uncertainty*.

"I could have not treated him like shit for most of our lives. I could have protected him like our parents weren't there to protect us. I could have stayed. I could have been there when all this shit kicked off. I could have been supportive. I could have..." Paige's voice trailed off in an uncharacteristically emotional choke.

Zara shifted uncomfortably. She had known Paige for many years, and to say they had never been close was a kindness, but this...

Zara reached out and set her hand on Paige's arm. "I think you did alright in the circumstances, Paige. You two got a rough lot, and you did the best you could."

"No, I didn't!" Paige snapped. Tears rolled down her cheeks. "I didn't. At all. I could have supported him. He was a little queer kid who lost his parents and had a bitch of a big sister always treating him like shit. Worst thing is, it was because I fucking saw *myself* in him. Everything I hated about myself; my fear, my weakness, my indecisiveness...I saw all the things I've always been so sure were making me fuck up my own life. And I hated that he was strong enough to wear it all and just carry on. I fought so hard to get away from those things, to be what I thought was *better*. At first, when I was hard on him, I told myself I was doing it because if I could hammer it out of him that he would be better than *me*. Then, I realised I treated him like shit because it felt...*good*. Because making him small made me bigger." She broke off in a sob, rubbing her cheeks furiously with the heels of her hands.

Zara shuffled closer, wrapping an arm around her. Paige's words sent spikes of sorrow into her heart, but they still made her angry. Paige *had* done that. She *had* made Oscar feel like shit.

"I'm not in any position to forgive you on behalf of Oscar or anything. But I think...I think if he were here, he would tell you that what you did is already done. I think he'd say that all he would want moving forward is that you just be a better version of yourself. The version of which thinking about all that makes you want to be."

Paige snorted a snotty, teary laugh. "He would say something like that, wouldn't he? Little bastard."

Zara smiled, rubbing her back.

"Do you..." Paige's voice was suddenly tiny. "Do you think he's there?"

Zara stilled. "I...don't know. I think it's probably unlikely. But I know that if we don't check, we'll always wonder. Even if I don't believe it *is* him, I believe we have to give him every chance possible."

That's the least I owe him.

Paige sniffled.

"Are you going to be okay?"

"I will be if you stop trying to come on to me," Paige said, suddenly smirking through her tears. "Your pasty girlfriend is literally in the house like two feet away, and you're out here trying to cop a feel."

Zara laughed, releasing her and giving her a gentle shove instead. "You're not my type."

"Too human," Paige agreed.

The crunch of gravel announced someone was approaching. Zara stiffened.

"What's wrong with you?" Paige frowned, eyes still bloodshot and skin splotchy.

"Someone's coming," Zara said, leaping to her feet.

She rushed onto the open drive, spinning to face the intruder.

"Who are you?" Zara snapped, not quite adopting a fighting pose but standing ready, joints loosened and Ghatotkacha bubbling within her.

The man was tall, well built, and still far too handsome under the bruises on his light brown face. He stared back at her, shocked. "Uh...sorry, ma'am. I just...I think my, uh, friend is here? Well, more than a friend, I hope." His American accent was slick rolling, but his clothes spoke of money. For some reason, he looked familiar.

On the steps, Paige sprung to her feet and practically shrieked. "Hunter?"

"Paige!" The man's face split in a broad grin, and he half limp-jogged toward her.

Zara let him pass, and in a moment, he had scooped Paige off her feet and into an embrace.

"I take it you know this guy?" Zara asked.

The man set Paige back on her feet. She looked equal parts shocked, happy, and mortified, suddenly trying to straighten her skirt, rub her teary eyes, and fix her hair all at once. She cleared her throat awkwardly. "Yeah, this is—"

"HUNTER OAKLEY?" Marcus crowed from the doorway.

Paige glowed with pride.

Hunter replied with what looked like well-rehearsed faux-modesty, flashing that brilliant smile once more. "Guilty as charged."

Marcus bounced on the spot excitedly.

"How the——" Zara began, confused.

Marcus didn't waste a breath. "This is Hunter Oakley, Zara. THE Hunter Oakley. As in 'Enough is Enough' Hunter Oakley!"

Zara shrugged. "I don't know what those words mean."

Hunter, whose chest had swelled at Marcus' words, somewhat deflated at her reply. "It's nothing. Just a TV show I'm in," he said, rubbing the back of his head.

Marcus snorted. "*Just* a TV show? Man, it's AWESOME!"

Hunter grinned.

"Wait, Paige, is this your..." Zara gasped.

"IS HUNTER OAKLEY YOUR BOYFRIEND?" Marcus shrieked.

Paige's face turned crimson. "Will you two just shut the fuck up, thanks?"

Dmitri appeared in the doorway behind Marcus, his face severe.

The smile that had been tugging on Zara's cheeks froze.

Dmitri looked furious. His axe was hefted over his shoulder, voice molten iron. "Get away from him."

Paige stepped in front of him protectively instead, looking confused. "What?"

"I can smell it on him. He has fed on my kind."

Paige froze.

"I'm sorry," Hunter said. He raised both his hands in the air. "I have, but I...I regret it. I don't want to ever do it again."

"See! He's fine!" Paige said hopefully.

Dmitri growled.

Zara's feet were rooted to the ground. "Dmitri..."

"But...he's really famous," Marcus moaned.

"He is corrupted," Dmitri said.

Marcus scowled, defeated. "Fine. His aura is pretty weird, I guess. Like one big part, then another part, all struggling against themselves."

"I want to help," Hunter shot back. "I will give you as much information as I can on how to find everyone who's done what I've done. I'll help you stop them. And after that's all over, if that isn't enough..." His skin paled. "Then you can kill me."

"Hunter," Paige gasped, spinning around to face him, eyes wide.

"It's what I deserve," Hunter said resolutely. "I always knew what I was doing was wrong. When I met you, I knew you were different. I knew you could help me make it right."

"We're gonna have to put a pin in that," Marcus folded his arms, glancing at Dmitri. "We have bigger problems right now. End of the world style. And we will take all the help that we can get."

"Let me help you with that. Consider it part of my penance," Hunter said.

"I don't think you know what you're getting into," Zara interjected. "Even if we were to trust you, I'm not sure how useful you would be."

"I'm strong. I also have hundreds of connections with powerful people all over the world, from government to security." Hunter puffed up his chest.

"Is that how you found me?" Paige reached out, resting a hand on his thick forearm.

Hunter winked. "The corsage. I had a tracker put on it. I suspected things may go south, and I wanted to be able to find you again after."

"I dunno." Marcus rubbed his chin. "That kind of rich spy shit does sound useful."

"Dmitri?" Zara asked, meeting his burnt orange eyes.

Dmitri stood firm in the doorway, scowling at the new arrival, his axe at the ready. He continued to stare for a long moment before he replied, "I leave it up to you, Zara."

Zara's eyebrows shot up.

"I will trust your judgement as you trusted mine with your cousin. As I ask you to trust mine for what I will do next."

"What will you do next?" Zara asked.

"I am calling for help. Marcus and I agreed we needed more hands, and there is one who is...skilled and knowledgeable in this area," Dmitri said carefully.

Who would...?

Zara's stomach dropped. "Fine," she said, swallowing. "Paige, do you vouch for this guy?"

Paige looked at Hunter for a moment, then back at Zara, nodding decisively.

"Done." Zara fixed Hunter with a hard stare. He shot her that winning pearly grin, and she scowled in return. "But if you set one foot out of line, I'll let Dmitri chop you into fiery little pieces."

❧ 29 ❧

CLEANSING WOUNDS

Z ara didn't go out to greet Lyn when she arrived a couple of days later. Instead, she sat by the front bedroom window and listened. It was the same room she and Marcus had been locked inside back when they found out...*everything*. Now, its walls were a soft grey, and there was a stylish iron-framed daybed with plush cushions freshly beat out of dust.

As she listened to Lyn's voice through the window, she couldn't help but feel a little grateful that Vandle was away. Marcus and Dmitri sent her to Egypt to take pictures of some scrolls they thought may be useful. Not that she *wanted* Lyn or anything, but she didn't want Vandle to see how she dealt with it. She didn't want her calm, red eyes watching her as she put together how to feel.

Zara had no regrets.

Where Lyn was hard and sharp, with keen pressure welcomed at important points, Vandle was calm and deep, thoughtful and intense. Things were *different* with her. Zara felt a future that she hadn't felt with Lyn, and it wasn't like she wanted to rub that in Lyn's face. So instead, Zara listened to her and Dmitri's conversation at the front of the house, only once daring to peek out.

Lyn looks so different.

She'd always been so pristine and crisp, the picture of brisk and efficient beauty. Now, she wore large sunglasses, and her hair was no longer the sleek bob it had been. It was replaced with a loosely knotted plait that ran just below her shoulder blades. Rather than a blazer or blouse, she wore a loose-fitting T-shirt tucked into fitted denim shorts. Zara almost smiled when she saw the cream pumps she wore. The woman *still* couldn't stand to be without a heel.

She thought for a moment that Lyn's gaze flickered to the window. Zara dropped back to the ground, but Lyn's voice continued without a hitch.

She didn't see you.

She didn't see you.

What were they even talking about?

Something about the cemetery?

Zara didn't know why she was so bothered by it all. It wasn't like she wanted to be with Lyn. In fact, her thoughts about the woman had been sporadic for the last few months. They were never right for each other. And Zara had someone else now. Fuck, Lyn probably did too. But that didn't mean they hadn't cared about each other. That they couldn't still care...

"What'chya dooooin?" Marcus' face peered around the door frame, sending a jolt of panic through Zara. She hadn't even heard him coming.

"Shhh!" Zara scowled at him.

The voices outside had stopped. Zara chanced another look.

The drive was empty.

Have they gone somewhere, or are they...inside the house?

"Alright, creeper." Marcus shrugged as he strolled into the room, stuffing his hands in his pockets.

"I'm not creeping," Zara hissed. "I'm just...shut up. They're probably downstairs and can hear you."

"Nope. Big D is downstairs. Your ex is moving at speed away from here. Doubt she can hear much of anything in the house with the wards, anyway. We all need to get some headspace. I'm totally fried. Figured we'd have a little jaunt, in case...you know, this is the end. I just wanted to come and let you know that me and Song are gonna zip over with Ducky to grab some pie in New Zealand. When I say pie, I mean like seven pies, just for Song's delightful little face. We're gonna take Ed and watch him chase some seagulls. Wanna come?"

Zara sighed, shaking her head.

"So, what was it you were doing?"

Zara's scowl deepened. "Creeping."

"Feelin' weird about the old lady of the night being back, back, back again?"

Zara forced a nonchalant shrug. "I...I'm not really sure how to handle it, to be honest. I guess once we have to be in the same room for a few minutes, it will be alright. It's just difficult to imagine that before it happens."

Marcus frowned. "Messy endings. So much worse than happy ones."

"You're one to talk." Zara arched an eyebrow. "If I remember right, you have literally like a hundred exes."

"Flings." Marcus plopped himself onto the edge of the daybed casually. "I mean, I'm sure they're all great. Some of them, at least. But back then, I was just moving through the world, aggravating other people doing the same thing in the same space. I don't think I had a full connection with anyone like that before Song."

Zara nodded thoughtfully.

Marcus grinned. "This room, huh? Kinda different circumstances between us being in here together now. I didn't realise Big D had put in an en-suite. That's handy. No vase for you. Weird thinking back, like almost half a decade how far we've come."

"You mean from being frightened prisoners of a well-meaning monster to the friends of that same monster, only now more sad and pointy but still trying to stop the end of the world?" Zara asked.

Marcus smiled. "We're more than friends. We're family. No

matter how long we've been apart, don't you feel it now that we're back together? Don't you feel—"

"Stronger," Zara finished. Before adding. "Same with Song too, wherever they are."

"They're not spiriting around in the ether or anything," Marcus laughed. "I'm pretty sure they're in the garden looking for beetles to feed Ducky."

"Ah, the sublime power of an ethernal," Zara mused.

"It's the simple things."

They fell into a silence. It would once have been a comfortable silence, but now it felt like a held breath. The wedge between them was unbearable.

"Marcus, I know we have to do this, but...I don't know if I can survive losing anyone else."

Marcus sighed. "This isn't something we're going to solve with the power of friendship, huh? It does feel kinda like the big one."

"It does."

"Is that why you're going with him?"

Zara froze, looking up. "What?"

Marcus smiled sadly. "I said, is that why you're going with him. Are you putting yourself at risk because you'd rather be the one to be lost than survive with other people dead around you?"

Zara stiffened her back. "Marcus, I don't know what you're talking ab—"

"I know you're going through whatever gate we open with Dmitri."

Zara's voice came out a harsh whisper. "How?"

Marcus laughed. "Oh, bitch. Like I haven't met you? Zara, we might have had a rough couple of years, but no matter how separated we were, we've been closer than best friends for years. I probably knew you'd do it before you decided. It's nothing to do with any mind-reading god powers or anything."

"You...told Dmitri?"

"He says it's your decision to make. Right now, it looks like the odds of getting through are slim, which makes the odds of getting back practically nothing. But if he gets in and there is a fight to be had, he could probably do with your help."

"I...think it might be for the best."

"Because if Oscar is in there, you're the one that put him there? Or is it because if you can't absolve your guilt, you don't know if you can carry on? Or, let me guess, you aren't even sure if all these powers—like you and the Ghatotkacha—should even be a part of this world, so what will be will be, and maybe it's just better that way?" Marcus sounded somewhere between resigned and delirious.

Zara sighed, shaking her head. "Yes. No. Maybe. All the above. I don't even know, Marcus. To be honest, I'm tired. There's just so much. And most of the time, I don't know what I'm supposed to be doing. I barely even know who I am half the time. Am I super-nurse-who-wants-to-help-people Zara, or am I fights-monsters-and-saves-the-world Zara? Am I even alive, or am I just a suspended sack of meat being driven around by a ghost?"

"You're a Scientologist now?" Marcus asked slyly.

"I just...when everything's so confusing, and something just feels so right, like a North Star to guide me to what I should do, how can I not do it?"

Marcus nodded. "I get it. Honestly, I do. More than anything since I met Song. Everything we're supposed to be doing, or do next, is like a different TV channel. My whole life, my brain's been overwhelmed by trying to watch and follow all those TV channels at once whilst trying to understand what's going on in them. It's only been since I met Song that I started trying to drown them out and just do what I want. What feels right."

"You're your own North Star, Marcus. You always have been."

Marcus' eyes shone. "I hope so."

"I'm still figuring mine out. I think...I think for the longest time, I thought it was Oscar. Since losing him, I don't know if that was true. I don't know if I just acted like he was *it* because I couldn't be my own."

"You will be," Marcus said with absolute certainty. "And if

doing this feels right, even if it means I lose you...then I support it."

Zara took a deep breath.

I have to do this if things are ever going to be right between us again.

"I needed you." The words came out a whisper.

Marcus didn't reply for a moment, and when he did, his voice was just as strained. "I know."

Silence.

"I'm sorry, Zara. I'm sorry for what happened, and what you had to do. I'm sorry for what we've had to go through, and I'm sorry that I wasn't there for you the way you needed."

Zara finally said it. "Why? Why did you leave?"

"I had to. Honestly, I just couldn't bear being here a second longer. I couldn't stand doing the stuff we used to do with Oscar, but with no Oscar. It...it felt like he was dying every day. Every minute. It was making me sick. So, I ran."

Zara nodded sadly. "I get it. I wish I could have run too. But I don't think there's any running for me."

"You aren't...mad?"

"Oh, I'm pissed at you for a million things. But this? We both needed to process in different ways. It's...I used to think that mental and physical trauma had more in common than most people think, you know? Like, when you break a bone, you need to make sure it heals right. Sometimes that means a cast to hold it in place and let it heal or pins in the bone to hold it together. I thought shit that happened to us was like that, too. And when parts of us get broken, we need our people, our friends or family to hold us together so that we can heal right. Like if we didn't, we might grow back together wrong."

Marcus nodded. "That makes sense. You don't think that anymore?"

"Oh, I do, for sure. Only I think that if you have people in your life that you've loved and who've loved you right back, that they aren't the splint or the brace or the pins in your erm...fractured mind bones. It's the strength you've gained from them and the love they have given you that works toward that. And maybe not for the biggest traumas, not all the time at least. We still sometimes need help, but I know that the strength that Nani gave me is still with me. I know that...Oscar is with me. I know he loves me and forgives me for everything. He would be proud of me and that I have to take care of myself and keep making him and Nani proud."

Zara's voice shook, but it was as though she uncorked something within her. Her words ran on, like everything she had told herself in the lonely dark of night over the last two years was coming out of her at once. "But do *you* blame me, Marcus? Do you think I did the wrong thing?"

Marcus didn't hesitate. "No, I don't. I know you did the right thing. You were the strongest person there that day, and you had the power in you to do what needed to be done. I wish...I wish I could have done it for you, so you didn't have to."

"I'm not as strong as you think I am. I'm not as strong as people need me to be."

"You're wrong," Marcus said flatly. "I...used power from Song to put a charm on my parents because I didn't want them to worry about me if something bad happened. I made it so that they basically constantly feel like they've just seen me. They're always satisfied that they don't need to see what I'm doing or check on me. I don't even know if I can undo it. It seemed so smart and selfless at the time, but now...now I just feel like I dropped a magick bomb on my mom, so I didn't have to deal with another thing or to worry about it. I don't think you'd do that. I think you'd think of something better, even if it was harder. Like what you did with your family and Rami..."

The words hit Zara's chest like a heavy weight. She'd not been able to live with the idea of Rami just disappearing, so she'd told them he was dead...only she told them he'd died like a hero protecting her from a terrible threat. They'd seemed only too grateful to believe the lie, and despite everything he'd done, she couldn't help feeling like it was the best lie she'd ever told. "Marcus..." Her voice barely came out softer than a whisper.

"I know Oscar would think you did the right thing. Dmitri does. I didn't leave because I thought you did the wrong thing, Zara. I left because I *knew* you'd done the right one, but I didn't have the strength to do it myself." His eyes filled with tears.

"Oh, don't!" Zara sobbed. "Don't start crying, or I'll start too!"

"Then cry, bitch!" Marcus laughed, tears spilling onto his cheeks. "Cry, because this is all we have in this world. Because it's hilarious, and awful, and lonely, and probably pointless, but we still have each other. No matter what we do, or where we go, we will always have each other, even if it's just the memories of the times we had together to hold on to."

Zara stumbled up onto the bed, rubbing her eyes, and pulled him into her arms, sobbing and laughing wetly into his neck. "I love you, you weirdo."

"I love you too," Marcus said, squeezing her tight.

PAIGE AND HUNTER were in the living room, surrounded by piles of books that looked even dustier than the house had been. She sat with her legs on his lap. The sight gave Zara...a little hope.

She found Dmitri standing in the kitchen.

He must have heard her enter. In fact, he probably heard her heart beating from the floor above. Even so, he didn't react or turn when she walked in. He stood, leaning against the island, staring at the sink. He wore a thin purple sweatshirt Zara had never seen before. It was certainly unseasonable, but then again, Dmitri didn't have the same issues with temperature as everyone else. According to Oscar, the man's body temperature was always running hot, no matter the season.

"You have made your decision?" Dmitri asked, eyes still fixed on the sink.

Zara grabbed a stool from beside him and dragged it out,

settling on top of it. She propped her chin on her hand, resting her elbow on the countertop. "I don't think there was ever much of a decision to make."

Dmitri grunted.

A few long moments of silence passed.

"Marcus tells me you have...finished studying," Dmitri said awkwardly.

Zara smothered a grin.

Was he trying to make small talk?

"Not much point in worrying about fancy qualifications if the world explodes."

"I suspect that saving the world, as hard as it may seem, will be a far simpler task than returning from whatever remains of Theia."

"We've done difficult," Zara said flippantly. It gave her a thrill. "We might have fucked it up a time or two, but I believe in us. Plus, me and you? I don't see much that's going to stand in our way all teamed up."

Dmitri sighed, grabbing the back of his head. The hair there was shaved as short as his temple's. "The Umbran at close to full power was more than enough for us ten times over. There is no telling how many there are of them in Theia...if anything even remains. Or what state of power or being they are in."

"True," Zara replied. "But there's always hope."

Dmitri remained silent.

"Want to know how I know that?"

"How?" Dmitri asked.

"Because *you're* going."

"How do you know I'm not just going there to die?" Dmitri's voice was barely above a whisper. "All stories have happy endings if you know when to stop telling them. Maybe my story has gone on for far too long."

"You could die anywhere if you tried hard enough. You're going because you believe there's a chance. Marcus believes there's a chance, and so does Paige."

"And you?" Dmitri's eyes shifted away from the sink and to hers. Their burning orange seemed to have sparks of sunburst-yellow today as well as the grey.

"I...don't know."

Dmitri's gaze remained on her.

"I...I believe in him. I believe if anyone could hold shit together that long, it would be Oscar. It's just...I killed him, Dmitri. I felt the sword go through his chest. It's pretty hard to convince yourself things are going to be okay after that."

Dmitri's face was a carefully held mask. "I understand. I have searched many places for texts on the willblade. You know as well as I that if it had been a normal sword, he would not have been able to speak to us in those last few moments. He would have been briefly drowning in his own blood before his brain ceased to function mere seconds later."

Zara stared at him.

That's...true.

She had convinced herself that the blade may have somehow plugged whatever damage it had done long enough to let him have some last words, but the size and position of the blade would have severed part of his heart and certainly his lung.

"You do not believe me?" Dmitri asked.

Zara shook her head. "I guess...I just convinced myself he must have died quickly because I can't stand to think that he suffered. I can't stand to think of him being torn apart in some interdimensional force-field or shredded by hundreds of Umbrans waiting for him on the other side."

"I understand. Sometimes it is far harder to hope than it is to accept loss."

Those words were like a sword in Zara's own heart.

"I...it's not like I knew there was a chance, Dmitri. It's not like I gave up on him."

"No." Dmitri shook his head sadly. "I truly do understand. You could not allow yourself to hope. For me, I could not allow myself to give up. Each of us has our own path, Zara, and we have walked them as we must."

"You sound like the Bean-Nighe," Zara said.

Dmitri smirked, flashing pointed teeth. "I may have gotten a little more wistful in my time away."

"So...what did Lyn say?" Zara asked.

"She is making her way to the cemetery to meet with Gax. I will join her soon. Marcus and I have been discussing that if we open the world parallax in any sense, it will attract attention. Should we even be able to create a one-way flow to release pressure, as Marcus proposes, the breach will surely draw attention from creatures we would rather not encounter on this side."

"Like a mega-monster-magnet?"

Dmitri grimaced. "Exactly."

"So, now we not only have to worry about opening up the breach and getting in and out again but also a whole hoard of monsters coming for whoever is keeping it open on this side's asses?"

Dmitri nodded in affirmation.

Zara sighed. "Fuck me gently with a chainsaw."

"Lyn concurred with our thoughts and proposed making the location more defensible. She also raised concern that someone is monitoring us from outside the house."

Zara cocked her head. "What?"

"There is a van out on the street. It appears we are under surveillance."

"Are you serious?"

"I'm afraid so."

Zara pursed her lips. "Tricky, tricky."

"I was planning on dealing with them on my way to meet Lyn."

Zara smiled. "Nah, you go to the cemetery and let me deal with the van. I need to blow off some steam, and I've got just the secret weapon to take care of whoever it is."

30

NOTHING BREAKS LIKE A HEART

Zara's senses awoke as she dragged on just a shred of the Ghatotkacha's power. She focused on the vehicles neatly lining the street. There were three vans, one of which the hum of various electronic knickknacks and low voices emanated. It looked to be a large landscaping van on the other side of the road. The logo on the side read 'The Tree's Needs', which struck her as such a tenuous pun it actually irritated her.

"I get why *you're* coming out here," Paige grumbled from behind her. "But why in the holy mother of fucks do you need me?"

"Oh, you have such a fantastic way with people. I just thought that no matter who was out here, you'd be able to sweet talk our way through it," Zara said, trying to sound as un-sarcastic as possible.

That stumped Paige, who traipsed silently behind her.

Zara wondered if she was bothered by being taken away from Hunter. The two had been inseparable since he arrived. Paige seemed happy, but Zara still felt...uneasy. Maybe it was the thought of him eating monster flesh rather than the fact Dmitri said he couldn't be trusted.

They arrived at the side of the van, and Zara listened carefully. The hum of electricity continued, but the voices had fallen silent.

"So...what do we do now?" Paige asked, folding her arms.

Decisively, Zara leaned forward and rapped on the sliding door on the van's side.

Silence.

Impatience bubbled within her.

Paige frowned. "Are you going to knock again?"

Zara checked to her left, then right. The coast was clear.

Unless someone is peeping out their window, but fuck it.

She grabbed the handle, allowing a burst of power from the Ghatotkacha to pump into her arm and fill her veins with searing power, then gave an almighty pull. The welding on the door screamed, but only briefly, as it tore free with sheer brute force. Zara twisted her elbow and there was a crunching of buckling metal as she ripped it out of place, and heaved it to one side with the ease of opening a can of tuna.

"Good knock," Paige mused.

The van rocked violently on its suspension, two of the wheels lifting as it almost toppled over before settling back into place.

Inside were two white men.

Or, more accurately, *one* was as white as a lily, and the other was almost as pink as boiled ham.

The pale one looked to be around Zara's own age, and the other seemed to be approaching his middle years. They sat clutched to their chairs with several monitors around them, staring straight back at her with wide eyes and mouths hanging open in shock.

Zara scanned the monitors. They had a camera on the front door of the house, in the trees over the back garden, and at the entrance to the drive and some other places that Zara didn't immediately recognise.

The man on the left, the younger one who had a long face with large, round glasses and slightly wild white-blonde hair, jumped out of his seat, panicking, before banging his head against the ceiling of the van and collapsing back into it. He stared at Zara agog, like she'd been the one to make him do it. The one on the right, square-jawed and face growing more red than pink, eyed her with affront.

"What do you think you're doing? This is government property," he snarled.

"And *that* is private property." Zara waved a hand at the monitors behind them. "So, I might ask you exactly the same thing."

The older man's eyes narrowed. "We'll ask the questions here—"

"Will you?" Paige snapped, marching up and standing beside Zara. "Because it seems that my friend here could pick up your little van and chuck it *and* you in a river...and there's not even a river that close by. So, perhaps you'd better fucking think twice."

Zara smiled.

Glasses suddenly moved again, reaching frantically for the radio sitting in the middle of the two of them, wired to the console. Zara's enhanced senses made the man's move seem even more slow and clumsy. She smoothly leaned forward and plucked it up herself before crushing it into bits with one hand.

Ham-hock snatched at his side, pulling out—what Zara only realised as her fingers closed around that too—a *gun*. The metal of the barrel was cold in her hand and barely offered more resistance than the plastic radio as she closed her fingers. There was a clicking noise, but nothing happened. She released her grip and moved back as Ham-hock stared at the misshapen lump of metal now clutched in his hand.

"Now, now," Zara chided. "We don't use guns. There are far more creative ways we go about solving our problems here. Why don't you tell me who you are, and I won't take you to that river my friend here mentioned."

Glasses looked ready to pass out, his skin suddenly grey and clammy.

Zara heard a sound not too far away and turned to see a

middle-aged woman approaching with a poodle attached to a lead in hand.

Zara froze.

Nobody moved as the woman passed by, as though staying still meant she wouldn't see them. Even the two men in the van stayed stock still, their eyes following her.

The woman stared at them, confused, but did not slow her pace.

Good old London. Could count on people to ignore almost anything here.

Paige winked at her. "Alright, love?"

The woman scuttled away uncomfortably.

When she was several metres past the van and they were alone again, Glasses piped up like somebody had flicked a switch. "My name is Wesley Samuels. I'm an analyst with the Department of Investigation for Cryptids and the Supernatural."

Ham-hock stared at the man like he had sprouted a second head.

"This fellow here is Arnold Dean. He's my partner and a senior agent."

"Jesus fucking Christ, Wesley. Why don't you just give them your birth certificate and bus pass while you're at it?" Arnold spat, with Wesley giving a shrug in response.

"Wait," Paige said flatly. "You're telling me you're...DICS?"

Zara stifled a laugh and ended up snorting instead.

Arnold was practically purple now. "Due to damage of government property and the aiding and abetting of supernatural threats, or...er, being one, you are under arrest under section—"

"Oh, no! You're going to arrest me?" Zara pulled a shocked face. The man's mouth snapped shut. "You and what army?"

"The British Army, if necessary!"

Paige made an amused squeaking sound.

Zara sighed and folded her arms. "Listen, we're trying to sort some shit out, and we really don't need any more hassle. I'm not surprised that the government has an interest in shit like this. In fact, I'm more surprised that we haven't had to deal with you before. But judging by your setup, you're under-funded, and no one really takes you all that seriously."

Wesley's jaw dropped.

"Oh, I'm sure that the threat of Theians is considered legit, but I also have no doubt there are a fair few in your leadership who are pretty invested in keeping the status quo, right?"

"How dare you," Arnold raged. "You have no proof—"

"Oh, I don't need proof. Nor do you. There's no denying this shit's real. And if your higher-ups wanted something done, do you think you'd be sitting out here in a van, just the two of you? Don't you honestly think that if they really wanted to get a handle on all this shit, they'd have a hundred guys with chainsaw-loaded-rocket launchers standing here right now?"

"How do you know that?" Wesley gasped.

Zara shrugged. "It doesn't take much to figure out the government when you've got a handle on apathy. They will put just enough in place to have plausible deniability and scapegoats should shit hit the fan, and they use you guys to monitor everything that's going on and report back. Make you feel like you're doing some kind of high-power job with shit pay when you're just messengers and whipping boys."

"Arnold!" Wesley grabbed the other man's arm. "I told you!"

"Shut up!" Arnold snapped, though the colour was draining from his face.

"I'm guessing you're the smart one, Wesley the analyst?" Zara asked.

Wesley eyed his partner nervously. "PhD in experimental biology and analytical sciences."

"Well, that sounds fucking made up," Paige snarked.

Wesley looked confused. "It isn't."

"So, I'm giving you two options. One, you carry on fucking around and trying to get involved...and things end badly. Or two, you go back to your bosses and tell them the world is just about on its last sigh before it gives out and blows the fuck up. Get them to send us a team to close off the cemetery and evacuate a one-mile radius around it because pretty soon this place is going to look like hell on earth."

"You can't think we can just..." Arnold sputtered.

"I don't care what you think you can do. I'm telling you what *needs* to be done," Zara replied bluntly. "There is about to be a catastrophic event, and I'd wager as shit as you lot are, they'd like to at least try to cover it up, if not help us out."

"Can you tell me more?" Wesley's eyes brightened in a way that wasn't unlike Marcus' when he caught the end of an exciting thread.

It made Zara like him...just a little.

"Not now, but I promise, help us, and I'll tell you as much as you want one day. Just...don't expect to be taking me somewhere to cut me up and experiment on me or anything, alright?"

Wesley looked horrified. "I would never!"

"Good."

"Liz was right," Arnold grumbled. "Maybe she shouldn't have helped this one escape in New York."

There was a pregnant pause before Paige replied, her voice sharp with amusement. "Wait...do you mean Sourpuss? Are you telling me that the reason Sourpuss helped me out is that...she's one of the DICS?"

"Classified," Arnold replied, folding his arms.

"It's looking decidedly less likely you two are going to end up being a meaty paste on the walls of this little fart-cabin on wheels," Paige sneered. "Just don't let us catch you being little shit-weasels again, alright? And you!" She jabbed a threatening finger at Wesley, who let out a squeak. "Sort your hair out!"

Wesley straightened and quickly tried to tame his wild locks.

"We good?" Zara asked menacingly, mainly to Arnold.

The pink-faced man scowled right back, but finally offered a reluctant nod.

∾

"THAT WAS PRETTY FUCKING SMOOTH." Paige grinned as they approached one hundred and thirty-eight Kinmount Street, the gravel crunching under their boots.

"We make a good team." Zara smiled.

Paige gave her a slightly uncomfortable glance.

"What?" Zara asked, pausing just a few steps from the stairs leading up to the front door.

"I just...I never thought we'd end up *friends*." Paige brushed her hair back behind her ear, her eyes shifting away from Zara.

"Me either. I mean...we might have fought in the past, and sometimes I'm pretty sure we can't stand each other, but we're there when it counts. I'm pretty sure that makes us family."

Paige's cheeks coloured, and her eyes shone.

Then, Zara heard something strange.

It was very faint. A dragging thump. A low moan.

She cocked her head, growing still. She pulled on the tempestuous spirit energy within her to sharpen her senses further. With Marcus and Song out with Ed, their new guest, Hunter, was the only person inside the house.

So why are there two *heartbeats?*

"What is it?" Paige hissed.

"Stay behind me," Zara whispered.

Paige's eyes grew large with concern. "Hudson..."

Zara crept up the front steps, allowing more power from the spirit to fill her limbs. Carefully, she reached for the door handle and twisted.

With her enhanced senses, it was practically deafening. To anyone else, it would be inaudible, though the same could be said for the slight creak as she pulled the door open or her footfalls on the hallway floorboards.

Whoever was in there with Hunter was in the living room.

She caught a familiar scent, like cloves and black liquorice.

Vandle.

She was back already?

Zara sighed, shoulders relaxing. She strode to the living room door. "I missed you—"

The coffee table was thrown aside, and the mirror above the faux stove knocked loose. It hung vertically from its remaining nail. Hunter stood over Vandle. The rug was bunched under her body with her limbs twisted oddly. His eyes were wide, and a taser —of all things—was in his hand. The looped wire of the discharged spikes curled from his hand and into Vandle's chest.

"What the fuck?" Zara took a step toward Vandle.

"Stay back!" Hunter snapped, raising his right hand and pointing it at her.

Zara's stomach churned.

A gun.

Another gun. What is with these fuckers and guns today?

"You'd better drop that right about now before I pop your head like a fucking pimple," Zara warned.

"Stop!" Paige cried, bursting into the room. "That's Vandle! That's my friend!"

Realisation dawned on Zara.

Had Hunter and Vandle never actually met?

Hunter must have been sitting here when she sprouted out of the mirror and scared the shit out of him. That rational thought cast some ice in the fire raging in her chest but nowhere near quelled it. Zara fought the urge to pounce forward, to tear the gun out of his hand and break it—then him—to pieces.

"It's okay, Hunter," Paige said as she carefully made her way around the fallen coffee table toward him. "She's one of us. She's just here to help."

Zara tried to focus on Vandle's heartbeat and breathing to make sure she was okay. But as she did, a lead weight dropped in her stomach.

"Paige, stop."

Paige twisted around to look at her, confused. She'd only made it so far as the half-fallen mirror.

Hunter's eyes shifted between them.

246

"This isn't a misunderstanding," Zara said. "His heartbeat. It's...normal."

It was only at *those* words that the man's heartbeat suddenly picked up.

"I said don't fucking move," he spat. To emphasise his point, he pressed down on the taser in his left hand. There was a loud clicking, and Vandle's back arched off the floor. She gasped, eyes rolling back in her head in partially conscious agony.

"Stop!" Zara shrieked.

He did. But then smiled that perfect, handsome smile.

"Hunter..." Paige's voice cracked. "What are you doing? You... you wanted to help. You said you wanted to help us."

"I did." Hunter smirked. "I wanted to help you until I could get hold of *this* one. That's what Valeria sent me for. She knew all along you had someone able to shift in and out of places. How else could you get a hold of all the shit you did? She wasn't sure it was *mirrors,* of course. I've been trying to get that out of you for weeks."

Paige's jaw hung slack. "You...lied to me?"

Hunter's head tilted in mocking sympathy. "I wouldn't say lied, doll. I'm an *actor*. I had my motivation. If I didn't get hold of mirror-bitch here, Valeria would kill me. And you're the one that cast me in that part. Since the first time we met, I saw how your tongue would hang out when you looked at me. We could have been friends, but you just gave me the easiest way in."

A tear rolled down Paige's cheek.

"Aww, don't cry." Hunter stuck out his bottom lip, then grinned. "At least we got to have some fun. Think about it. Both of us got what we want—"

Rage swelled in Zara, and she took a slow step forward.

The clicking noise sounded again, and this time, Vandle screamed, twisting on the floor in agony.

"Now, now," Hunter chided, giving a charming wink. "No doubt normal folk may not catch your movement, but I'm kind of above average, as you know."

"What do you want?" Zara asked through her gritted teeth.

"I told you. I'm going to take this one, and I'll be on my way," Hunter replied. "I'll leave you all to carry on sorting whatever this shit is, which is frankly really boring anyway, and we can all be on our merry way."

"I'm not letting you take her anywhere," Zara snapped.

Hunter narrowed his eyes. "Is that so?"

He raised his gun and pointed it at Zara.

"If you're going to shoot me, you'd better kill me with the first bullet. Because if you don't, you're going to be all over these fucking walls, you smarmy piece of shit." Zara's voice came out as smooth and dangerous as she'd hoped.

She tensed her body, ready to move.

Hunter winked and adjusted his aim, pointing it at Paige instead.

Zara froze.

"From what I gather, killing *you* with one bullet would be pretty difficult. This one on the floor, too. Paige, however, has that pesky bog-standard human mortality. I wouldn't even have to hit her anywhere particularly good, and she'd probably be dead before you could get an ambulance here."

More tears flowed down Paige's cheeks, her mouth twisted in anguish, but her eyes...her eyes were hard with fury.

Zara glanced at Vandle.

The last shock had brought her back to consciousness. She gazed at Zara, crimson eyes bright and calm as though trying to tell her something.

Not for the first time, Zara wished they had the same ability to communicate without words like Marcus and Song.

Vandle's eyes shifted up to the gun in Hunter's hand.

Zara saw she had wrapped her fingers around the taser's wire, ready to pull the barbs when they made their move. Quickly, she brought her eyes back to Hunter. He was watching her cautiously, poised to fire.

"So, what do you say? Let me walk away, and we *all* get to walk away. This monster won't even die. We just want to use her for a bit. Can't be sure the powers would transfer right, so we probably won't even hurt her."

Zara willed calmness into her voice. She took two breaths. "Fine."

"Fine?" Paige roared, stepping forward in outrage. "You can't just let him take—"

There was a deafening crack as Hunter fired.

Paige twisted. Red sprayed the wall behind her. Her eyes bulged, and she staggered on the spot as blood blossomed from the shoulder of her dress and poured down her arm.

At that moment, Zara let the power of the Ghatotkacha fill her.

Everything slowed down.

She dragged a breath into her body and moved.

Paige would live if they got her help fast enough. There was nothing vital where she'd been hit.

She saw Vandle yank the wires out of herself, tossing them away before Hunter had the chance to shock her again. Vandle was already moving when Zara reached Hunter. She had twisted and sprung toward Paige to grab her.

The second shot rang out.

Plaster burst from the blood-spattered wall as the bullet tore into it.

It would have hit Paige square in the face if Vandle hadn't grabbed her around the waist and pulled her aside, dragging her into the mirror beside her, its surface now rippling like a glassy pond with a stone cast in.

Zara's hand closed around Hunter's wrist.

He roared. His body was already changing...just like Rami's.

Her other hand closed around his gun, fingers tightening to crush it. It bucked in her grip, and heat blossomed against her palm as there was another crack.

Something shattered.

Zara heard a blood-curdling scream.

Hunter lashed out at her, his handsome face already monstrous. She danced back before springing at him with a powerful front kick, letting the power of the Ghatotkacha burst from her foot. A large ethereal blast collided with the swollen man. It threw him from his feet and sent him shattering straight through the bay window in a catastrophic shower of glass and flailing, muscular limbs.

Zara took a moment and looked around, searching for Paige and Vandle. Waiting for them to leap out after the man and continue the fight. To end it.

Her eyes found the mirror.

No.

The *parts* of the mirror.

Broken shards hung from the frame, some on the floor, some still half in place. Where cracks remained, traces of dark, red blood leaked out.

At the centre of the wooden backing was a single bullet hole.

TAXONOMY OF MONSTERS: THE TITIVILLUS
(SCRIPTORES PERNICIES)

"Bane of scribes and the origin of niggling errors that plague countless manuscripts all over the world. The tittivilus is a small thing with a nose for trouble and compact wings to facilitate rapid escape, thus avoiding detection. It gains its sustenance not from the frustration of the author's errors it causes, rather the long-term despair and sense of inadequacy that it gradually embeds."

— EXCERPT: THE REVENANT'S ARCANUM

31

MEASURE AND SCALE

"Please, please, please." Zara had already pulled the mirror off the wall. More shards broke loose, tinkling as they fell onto the floorboards. Tears flowed down her cheeks, and she blinked them away desperately. "Not like this, please, not like this."

She set the frame down, frantically seeking the largest fragments and pushing them where they looked like they should fit, moving them around and desperately adding additional pieces.

More blood flowed.

This time her own.

She didn't know when she had cut herself, but her palms stung, and two of her fingers throbbed as they slipped on the surface of the glass, smearing fresh blood to join what leaked from the broken mirror itself.

One of the large fragments cracked in her hands, splitting into three and falling apart. Deep, futile agony bored into Zara's guts.

There was a thump from the hall, and she dully thought that Hunter was back. She didn't care. *Couldn't* care. She needed to fix this.

Vandle told her that if a mirror broke when she was too close to its surface, she would shatter, like the glass itself.

But this *couldn't* have happened.

She has to be okay.

Both her and *Paige.*

They can't be dead...it was too cruel.

"Zara?" Marcus' voice was soft.

She looked up through bleary eyes, blinking.

"I...I thought I sensed Hunter...running like, well, like he'd done this." Marcus stared at the broken, bloody fragments of the mirror.

Zara clutched her shaking hands to her chest, trying to wipe the blood off on her T-shirt. She would heal in a minute from cuts this shallow, and she could keep putting them back together.

"Vandle?" Marcus' voice was distant.

Zara sniffed, wiping her eyes on the inside of her elbow. "And Paige."

Marcus' face dropped. "I'm...I'm so sorry."

"Is there anything you can do?" Zara's voice shook. She didn't know what would happen if he said no. She thought she might shatter into as many pieces as that mirror.

"I...I can try," Marcus said. He looked at Song, who stood in the doorway with Pomeranian Ed in their arms.

Song's large, golden eyes regarded Marcus with a deep sadness. They set Ed down on the floor, who immediately pawed the floorboards and whimpered anxiously as Song stepped beside Marcus.

"What are you—" Zara began.

But Marcus and Song had already embraced, both their eyes closed, and foreheads pressed together.

Zara felt a throb...like something large moved more than she could understand in less than a moment. Marcus' eyes shot open, a rapturous smile on his face.

Did he just exchange something?

No, it does matter.

Nothing else matters right now.

We need to do this.

"Alright, Zara, step back," Marcus said with absolute confidence, raising his hands, eyes closed.

Zara stumbled up to her feet so quickly she almost fell and staggered back, leaning against the wall. "Do it."

Marcus opened his eyes. Pale blue crackling energy shone from within.

It raised the hair on Zara's arms and the back of her neck.

She felt a prickling in her palms and raised them, hissing, as tiny slithers and specks of glass pulled free from her flesh, glittering in the air as they joined others. All of them moved in perfect harmony and unison, none touching the other as they shifted and tuned, sparkling in the air.

Marcus cocked his head, fingers dancing and eyes still shining with that magickal glow. One by one, the pieces found their way into the frame. It was slow at first but unerring. Once each had settled, it didn't move again. As more pieces found their home, the others moved faster until various-sized shards darted and spun into place with incredible pace.

It must have only taken a few breaths before the mirror was complete. Complete, but still broken. Then, everything stopped.

"What now?" Zara breathed.

A look of great concentration came onto Marcus' face, and he placed both his hands out flat in the air. They glowed, too. Static sparks of energy burst forth as he pushed down. The air seemed to compress between his hands and the mirror, shimmering with...*something*. Zara felt a flash of heat against her cheeks when Marcus moved his hands apart as though he were spreading the air itself.

Sure enough, the mirror's cracks faded, and in mere seconds, the surface rippled, then shone smooth.

The bright energy abated, and Zara looked up at Marcus. He stared back at her, a thin stream of blood leaking from his left nostril.

"Did...did you do it?" Zara's voice barely came out as a croak.

"I...I don't know. I wasn't just trying to fix the mirror. I was trying to undo the damage done to a window for magickal energy to travel, so I had to infuse it with a lot of my *and* Song's power. So, I...I hope so?"

"What should we do?"

Song strode forward and got down on their knees beside the mirror, peering in.

"Song," Zara said cautiously.

They tapped on the glass three times, a clean, crisp rap of their dark knuckles. It sounded solid, but after each one, the surface rippled like a pool of reflective mercury.

Song tilted their head, staring into the depths of their own reflection.

After a long moment, they looked up at Zara.

Zara felt their sending.

Sorrow.

Her heart broke.

She felt another part of herself slip away.

Then a hand pushed out of the mirror's surface.

~

Zara watched as she emerged.

It wasn't Vandle.

Nor was it Paige.

The woman that came out was somehow...*both*.

Her hair was patched white and black. One eye was red as blood, the other blue as the winter sky. Across her pale skin were fine, iridescent cracks, which fragmented her flesh—not like a jigsaw, but like the jagged crack on a broken mirror.

Zara's breath caught in her chest. Her heart perched on the precipice of hope and despair.

The woman from the mirror climbed all the way out. Even her clothes were pieced together from what the two had been wearing, patched black denim and blood-stained striped dress. One leg was bare from the knee, whilst the other donned in dark trousers ending in a jagged split like they had been haphazardly sliced with scissors. She stood on shaking legs, staggering to the wall bandy-legged as a newborn foal, steadying herself with one hand.

Zara tried to force her breath, tried to take it in slow and with steady gulps, then deep pulls that made her ribs ache. No matter what she did, it felt like she wasn't getting enough air.

"Uh...hi," Marcus said. "You're..."

"I am....we are." Two voices spoke at once, and the woman from the mirror blinked, raising one silver-crackled, pale hand before her face.

Through her fingertips, her eyes met Zara. From her crimson eye, a single tear formed.

"Vandle...Paige," Zara choked out.

The woman stared at her. Her eyes were full of sorrow. "Yes," her voices said in unison.

"What happened?" Zara dragged her eyes away, her heart slamming against her ribs, and stared at Marcus. "What...did you do something *wrong*? Can you fix it?"

Marcus' mouth hung open, his jaw slack. He turned to Song, blinking as though receiving too much information at once.

"Uhhh, yes...and no," Marcus said slowly, still fixated on Song, who returned his gaze with earnest. "When the mirror broke, it broke *them*. If I had even been a few seconds slower, they might be dead. But because of how things move within the opening point of the space between mirrors, I patched them back together. Only...I did just *that*. Not all of either of them were there anymore. Parts of them had already travelled, shifted away from the surface to different places. My magick put together what was left of them to do all it could to fix them both. They could either have died as two...or live as one."

Vandle...Paige, the combination of the two, watched him from the sofa, their face slack.

"So, can you fix them now?" Zara urged, her voice on the edge of hysteria.

"Yes, but the power it would take me to trace the pieces of them and pull them back together...Zara, I'd have to burn myself out. I'd have to trade everything, or near enough to it. I wouldn't have enough left to open the world parallax and stop the end of everything."

Zara's mouth flapped wordlessly. "Isn't there anything else we could do?"

Marcus' dark eyes met hers sadly.

"I can search," Vandle's voice said from the shattered woman's mouth. It made Zara jump to hear her so clearly when she thought she was gone. "I...*we* could search the fragments, though there is no guarantee we could make ourselves whole again, or how long that would take. The longer we wait, the further those pieces may go. Within mere hours, we could be left searching for eternity."

"Do it," Zara said desperately. "Now."

"Zara, wait." Marcus was staring at the combination of the women. "This...this might be good."

"Good?" Zara screamed, more tears leaking from her eyes. "What are you talking about, Marcus? This...it's Paige and Vandle! Oscar's sister, our friend, and the woman I love!"

Saying those words knocked the breath out of her. She looked at the broken pieces of woman patched together across from her.

I've never...I've never said that before.

"Remember how I said before that we didn't have the right equipment to open a parallax? Like how it's like trying to use the microwave plug to power the TV or whatever? We needed some-thing...*someone* with a link to Oscar, and some way to get closer to the veil, and then *power*." Marcus' eyes were wide with excite-ment. "Vandle, can you hear me? Are you in there?"

"We're both here, jazz hands," the woman snapped in Paige's irritable voice. "It's just...we're both *not*, too. It's confusing, so get to the point."

"Right," Marcus said, frazzled. "Travelling by mirror, Vandle. It's to do with light, right? But more than that, it's involved with the veil?"

The woman was silent for a moment. Finally, she spoke with Vandle's voice, sounding thoughtful. "Light dancing is like skimming a stone on the surface of a pond, except you're the stone and the pond is the veil."

"Right! I think it's kind of like travelling with Ducky. The difference is that with Ducky, I have to be *somewhere*. The second I enter, there's this immense pressure to get out again like the throw's wound up, and I only have moments to direct myself before I'm slung wherever I'm going to go."

"What's your point, Marcus?" Zara said impatiently, rubbing her tears away again.

"When you're able to travel by mirror, like Vandle, you get to aim better. Control the throw as it were, or even stay still. Is that right, Vandle?"

The woman didn't speak, only nodded absently.

"With Vandle's ability and the power I infused them with..."

"You think...you think that she...*they*...can open the world parallax?" Zara said slowly.

"I think they stand a better chance than me," Marcus replied. He sounded breathless now. "It depends on Paige. She has the Tundale blood, but the touch of Theia isn't active in her, so it might not work."

"If we do not search for our pieces now, there is no telling if we can ever separate," Vandle said.

Zara's fists clenched, her nails digging into her palms.

What do we do?

What can we do?

"We need to stay like this," Paige's voice said firmly, hard with determination. "We need to save Oscar."

Zara's head snapped up.

This time, Vandle spoke. "I can't help but think...what if this is what Betty spoke of? Being broken...but carrying the will to save the world. Maybe *this* is why she said those words."

Fresh goosebumps rose on Zara's arm.

Now, both voices came out of her mouth in unison. "We must do what needs to be done to save the world."

"Besides," Paige added. "If we don't, we're all fucking dead, anyway."

❦ 32 ❦

FRACTURED PLANS

Zara didn't know what was worse: sitting beside the new combination of Vandle and Paige or being apart from them.

Zara didn't know how to look at them. She didn't know why it felt so much like both died the moment the mirror smashed. Paige and Vandle died at that moment, and this new thing that came out wasn't both...but *neither*. This person was someone entirely new altogether.

Marcus had been babbling non-stop for an hour about the metaphysics of how they may now be able to open the world parallax. Zara let the words wash over her as she stared at the combined pieces of woman beside her. At her other side, Song—still holding Ed—seemed just as intrigued.

When the front door opened again, Dmitri rushed into the living room, eyes alert, body tense, and ready to fight.

"The window...what happened?" His gaze quickly settled on Vandle and Paige, his eyes widening in surprise before shooting to the repaired mirror now propped against the wall.

"It's uh...compl—" Marcus began.

"The actor was a traitor? He broke the mirror when Paige and Vandle tried to flee? Their relative parts shattered, and the only way to bring them back was by combining what remained of the two with your powers." Dmitri stared at the two women pieced together on the couch.

"Uhhh...yeah, actually." Marcus' eyebrows climbed. "Literally exactly that happened."

Zara opened her mouth to speak, struggling to find the words. "I thought...I thought he might get better. I thought that if he could...maybe Rami—"

"It is not your fault," Dmitri cut her off bluntly, his eyes shifting to meet hers.

Zara's mouth snapped shut.

"After the first day or two, even I thought that the man may have truly meant to make amends. It is...the human in you that sought to allow him to do this. Paige was—*is*—a sharp and discerning person, but her will to see the best in him and his cruel exploitation of that is why this has happened."

Tears prickled the corners of Zara's eyes again, and she looked to the women...*woman* beside her.

"I am sorry that you must endure this. Paige, Vandle...Zara." Dmitri seemed to struggle with those words and could not find any more.

That was when *she* stepped into the doorway behind him.

Lyn's sunglasses were off, hanging from her collar. Her dark eyes took in the room, the people within, and finally came to rest on Zara, impassive and unflinching.

"Hi," Zara said, rubbing at her puffy eyes.

"Hello," Lyn replied in what passed as a gentle tone for her.

"There are military vehicles on the streets outside. They are evacuating the area," Dmitri said flatly, moving to sit on the arm of the closest couch. "I take it what we discussed went well?"

Zara blinked.

That's it?

Paige and Vandle had...this happen, and he's just moving on? Like the two of them aren't gone, perhaps forever? Like my girlfriend and Oscar's sister haven't just shattered apart?

Dmitri's heart really was torn out that day.

She felt cool fingers on her wrist and looked down. Fine veins of reflective cracks lined the pale fingers touching the back of her own golden-brown hand. A chill ran up Zara's spine as she fought the urge to move her hand away. Her eyes met those mismatched ones again, one red, one blue.

"I think there's a good chance this may solve our access problem with the veil." Marcus unhooked the bone dagger at his waist. "Using this, I think that Van...uh...our friend here with the cool hair will be able to step between and cut through. We only get one chance, though, so I guess I'd better head out and call in the cavalry."

Dmitri nodded.

"It's reversible." Zara's voice was ragged. She didn't know why she said it, if it was to tell Dmitri, herself, or...her eyes drifted beside her, then back to Dmitri.

He stared back, looking more tired than troubled.

I guess...does it matter? Fixing Vandle and Paige—if we can even do that—has to wait until we save the world. If we even live.

Zara tried to shake off the feeling of overwhelming despair. She moved her hand away from...*theirs* and set it on her lap.

"If I get the Filii Terra to bring whatever barrier they're using to shield their homestead, it should help protect us when, *if*, we can open the world parallax," Marcus continued.

"We don't even know if it will work yet," Zara said weakly.

"Oh, we don't get a test run." Marcus grinned manically. "Like Big D said, once the veil is open, it'll attract all kinds of fangy no-gooders who want to be involved. Hence the evacuation."

"Things will no doubt unfurl from the earth that may not have surfaced in millennia," Dmitri's voice was grim, and his eyes shone intensely. "The Filii Terra may offer some protection, but whoever remains will need to be ready to fight."

"And they want to go through the gateway? Why don't we just let them?" Zara frowned.

Marcus cringed. "The balance of the world parallax is delicate.

Too many things trying to get in at once, all that chaos, could make it go off like a nuke."

"What?" Zara asked. "That doesn't sound safe."

"Nothing about this is safe," Marcus said proudly. "So, we need to keep the world parallax as stable as possible. If monsters get through in any kind of frenzy and break the parallax...bam. Everyone dies, whether it's with a flash and a bang immediately or with the popping of interdimensional power soon after."

"Your plan has me brimming with optimism," Lyn drawled.

Marcus ignored her. "Once we open it up, the sheer force of what comes out will make it difficult to close, kind of like a pressure-cooker valve being broken off. I have to see what kind of... uh...creepy relics Isla has knocking around. See if we can make it so anything can get *in*, but only things that are from here can get back out. We don't want any surprise beasties coming and making matters worse."

"A barrier would be good," Dmitri agreed.

Marcus nodded. "Yeah, we don't want to have all kinds of eighteen-legged-hell-beasts out the wazoo. Anything could already show up that's living anywhere in travelling distance; gulons, rompos, and finfolk, oh my."

"I think that any of those would be the least of your worries," Dmitri replied darkly. "You could be visited by any number of lesser-known monsters. Yokai, chimera...or things that have barely even been mentioned in centuries, like bloodgannets, soul-winders—"

"Soulwinders aren't real," Marcus chortled. "They're just a bedtime story for naughty magick users."

Dmitri regarded him with uncertainty. "For the most part, the creatures that are drawn forth will be baser in their urges. The Theians, and those of us of Theian descent, will certainly feel the pull but should not be overcome with the urge as the more *wild* of our kind."

"So, the ones that show up will only be the wildest and most bloodthirsty?" Lyn mused. "Sounds like a cinch."

Marcus rubbed the back of his head awkwardly. "It's fine. We have a plan, and Vandle's part can still be done by, uhhh..." He stared at the combination of Paige and Vandle. "What...what shall we call you? Pandle?"

"No, you bloody won't," Paige's voice snapped. The combined woman looked stunned for a moment, as though surprised at how firmly she had pushed to the surface. Her face turned patient, and Vandle's voice came out. "We are still both of us, but I suppose if you want to speak to us both at once, a name does help." She frowned thoughtfully. Next, they spoke together, voices overlapping like two waves merging as one. "You can call us...Paile."

Marcus shrugged. "That works."

Dmitri's eyes lingered on her. "Does it...hurt?"

"Yes," both voices said at once, quickly. Paige's voice alone offered some follow-up. "Worse than trapping your tit in a car door."

"I'm surprised you've ever had that issue," Lyn's cool voice chimed from the doorway.

Paile's head tilted as they regarded her. Zara thought she saw the corner of their mouth lift in a smile.

"I'm sorry—I couldn't resist. I'm sorry that this has happened to you, Paige. And...Vandle, wasn't it? We may have only met briefly, but you have my sincere condolences." Despite Lyn's more relaxed appearance, her tone was as clipped as ever.

"When this is all done..." Dmitri began, but his voice trailed off. "I mean to say..."

Marcus sighed. "Yup. It's gonna get all Blaze of Glory up in here, huh? If we get this done, there's no telling who will even be alive when the dust settles, if any of us."

"If...Paile can open the world parallax, there is no telling how long it will take the pressure to subside," Dmitri said.

"It could take hours, days, *weeks*," Marcus agreed.

"That means a lot more monsters," Zara finished.

"There's no way that the human military can handle any part of this. It would be a massacre," Lyn added. "We will have to convince them to leave if we wish for the streets not to become a river of their blood."

Dmitri smiled wolfishly. "Fortunately, I can be very convincing."

~

WITH DMITRI GONE to deal with the military, and Marcus, Song, Ed, and Ducky back with the Filii Terra, Zara remained in what she realised was a uniquely terrible situation.

She sat beside the broken parts of her girlfriend and the woman whose brother she killed, fused together, with her ex going through the gathered plans in the next room.

Paile's mannerisms already started shifting more fluidly. They spoke more, using Vandle's voice and Paige's, but increasingly both at once. That was when she seemed more *Paile* than Paige or Vandle.

Somehow, that made it so much worse.

"You find it difficult to look at us," Paile said. It wasn't a question.

Zara sighed. "I find all of it difficult. I don't really know what to do, seeing you. I'm just scared you can never come back. I'm scared you're...the other parts of you might disappear forever. Like Paige and Vandle are erased."

Paile nodded slowly. "This is...not a path we would ever have chosen."

"Will you...be okay?"

Paile's back remained straight, their voice firm. "We will do what needs to be done. To save Oscar and protect you. Protect the worlds."

"Not the two of you. Will *you* be okay?" Zara asked sadly.

Paile seemed to struggle to find words for a moment. When they spoke, it was Vandle's voice alone. "I will endure. We will do everything we can to...to be together again."

Zara felt a tear roll down her cheek.

"And you...you plan to go to Theia. We...did not discuss this," Vandle said.

"I have to." Zara had no other words.

Paile nodded, replying again with Vandle's voice. "I understand. Please...come back to me."

Zara met those mismatched eyes and felt the urge to throw herself into the woman's arms, at least, until...

"I expressly don't give permission for any parts of me to be canoodled," Paige's voice rushed out.

Paile looked half shocked they had said that, but their face broke into a crooked smile. "We have been allies, then friends," Vandle's voice replied. Their voices continued together. "We can do this *together*. For Oscar. For you. And us all."

Zara reached out, her heart twisting in her chest. Paile stayed very still, allowing her to take her hand this time. "I...whatever you need. Just let me know if either...both...of you need to talk."

Paile's eyes drifted to the mirror that had been shattered and repaired. "I should begin the task that Marcus set me. He has sent me...many places to travel. I will see you...at the cemetery."

Zara forced a smile. "Be careful."

~

ZARA NEEDED SOME SPACE.

She needed to process what had happened and what it all meant.

Either that or the exact opposite, and to find something sharp enough to distract herself from the horrible fresh and empty ache she felt inside.

She made her way into the kitchen with every intention of sitting with her head cradled in her hands until the first person who turned up dragged her out of it and forced her to get on with preparing for tonight. What she didn't expect was to find Lyn there, sitting on a stool at the breakfast bar, arms folded.

"Hey," Zara croaked as she dragged out a stool beside her.

"Hello, Zara," Lyn said about as softly as her clipped, jagged cadence would allow.

Zara sighed and sat, resting her elbows on the counter and closing her eyes. A few long moments passed in utter silence.

"I'm sorry," Lyn finally said.

Zara didn't open her eyes or reply.

"I need you to know——"

"Don't," Zara cut in, turning to glower at her ex angrily. "Don't try to make me feel better. There's nothing that can do that right now."

Lyn flashed a thin smile. "Zara, you know me well enough that I will not try to mollify you with worthless platitudes. I know what you have been through. I know you will endure, even through bitter misery. What I want to tell you is that you shouldn't give up hope. I must admit, however, it is convenient——"

"Convenient?" Zara snapped, her cheeks burning. "Nothing about this is *convenient*. That's Vandle and Paige, their bodies... their lives. Are you really so cruel you think it's convenient?"

Lyn regarded her coolly. "Cruel? Do you know where I have been these last two years?"

Zara snorted derisively.

"I was in Myanmar for a time. Doing what I could to assist with providing free healthcare. I visited Nanjing after the floods. Auckland after the volcanic eruptions. Most of the wealth I have accrued in my time on this planet, I have now given to relief, development for the underprivileged, and——"

"You think that makes you *better*?" The words spilled out of Zara's mouth before she could stop them. She heard the spite in her own voice and hated it. She hated how vicious it made her sound. More, she hated how it didn't seem to hurt Lyn at all. Most of all, she hated how lashing out didn't even make her feel better, only worse.

"Not at all," Lyn said flatly, looking away. "I hated doing many of those things. I was trying to learn what it meant to use my time, my knowledge, and my resources to do good. I was trying to do what you said. To be...better for myself."

"And did you?" Zara's voice was rough.

Lyn sighed. "I don't know. Maybe? I learned what people *think* it means to be good. But does me doing those deeds to appear better ultimately serve as a selfish act? A desperate bid to throw weight on the other side of the invisible scales of judgement? Who can say if I helped enough people, or if the self-serving nature of my deeds meant that it invalidated the acts themselves."

Zara watched her silently.

"But...I'm glad. I'm glad that I have helped some people, even if I hated every minute. Maybe if I liked it, then I would be good. But I don't think I am ever going to be."

"Maybe you just have to find a better reason," Zara replied.

Lyn met her eyes again. Hers were as dark and unfathomable as always.

Zara swallowed. "Or what if I was wrong about being *good*? I mean, you can do good and evil acts, but do they make you a good or evil person, or is it the *why* rather than the *what* that's important. Maybe nothing is light or dark. Everything is just shifting shades of grey."

Lyn nodded thoughtfully. "What if I'm too late for my *why*, though? What if my purpose was to save Theia, and opening the world parallax that night all those years ago was the right thing to do, just for the wrong reasons? What if leaving it open would have saved...everything?"

"What if I hadn't stabbed Oscar with the willblade? What if the only thing worth saving in this world is love, and I drove a sword through my best friend's heart, destroying the only thing worth saving?"

"Some choices are more...pragmatic than others." Lyn frowned. "Even if what you say is true, think of the countless amount of love you saved for others all over the planet. You did the right thing, Zara."

She groaned. "I just wish things could be simple."

"Is that why you're going to Theia?" Lyn asked bluntly.

Zara stared at her.

"Dmitri told me."

"Maybe." Zara shrugged.

Lyn's gaze hardened. "Do you have *your* why?"

Zara blinked. "To save—"

"To save Oscar...or to save yourself? Because if you don't find him, death will release you from your guilt." Lyn's voice was as hard as her stare.

Zara gazed into those bottomless eyes and wondered if she was right.

33

THE LONG STEP FORWARD

The streets leading to the cemetery were empty. Most of the cars outside the houses were gone, and the dim street lights glowed in the dusk.

But it was not quiet.

Even from streets away, the noise of military personnel and vehicles was audible, becoming ever louder as they grew closer.

Large spotlights were set up around the cemetery's perimeter.

Zara watched as an enormous tank trundled past, taking up both lanes on the street, tailed by several large vehicles full of soldiers in urban fatigues.

As they passed the parallax in the wall, Zara wondered if she still accurately remembered the combination of bricks to push and rub. But that wasn't their way in tonight. Followed closely by Lyn, she made her way further toward the front gate.

More and more vehicles were leaving.

At the entrance, Dmitri was standing beside a dour-looking man with grey hair. Zara recognised the glassy look in his eyes.

"The area will be clear within the hour, sir," the man said.

Dmitri's red eyes glinted in the moonlight. "Make it forty minutes. Help your men if needed."

The grey-haired man looked a little perplexed at the concept of doing the work himself, but saluted and stalked off regardless, already shouting at a group of soldiers trying to take down a tent.

"I'm surprised that it worked," Zara said as she came to Dmitri's side. It was obvious he had used his pheromones to make the commander more suggestible, utilising his status to get the soldiers to vacate the area. It was a kindness. They were not ready for the things that would be drawn here.

"Oh, don't be." Lyn smiled sharply, watching the soldiers work. "These people may seem stern, but they are malleable. They wouldn't have sent anyone who didn't have the desire to follow commands."

Dmitri nodded. "It is not always a matter of will. We were fortunate that their commander was susceptible, or there would have been a lot of dead humans here tonight."

Zara spotted two familiar figures making their way toward them, weaving through the rush of bodies. "Oh shit. Here comes Tweedle-Dum and Tweedle-PhD. Quick, use your stink magic some more."

Dmitri frowned.

"I knew you'd have something to do with this." Arnold's head was just as pink and gammony as usual.

"How did you convince the general to vacate?" Wesley asked excitedly.

"Common sense," Zara said crisply. "Something you two seem not to be familiar with."

Arnold scowled. "The military doesn't have command over—"

"Their DICS?" Zara finished, grinning.

Arnold's face darkened.

"This doesn't really seem so bad," Wesley said, hopefully.

"Oh, that's how it always starts. Then later, there's running and then screaming. Come on, Dmitri. Hit 'em with the funk," Zara said through her teeth.

"The strange one is immune," Dmitri said slowly.

Zara sighed. "I thought you said that was rare?"

"Apparently not as rare as I once thought." Dmitri's tone was irritable.

"If they want to die so much, who are we to stop them?" Lyn interjected nonchalantly.

Arnold's face paled at that. His eyes shifted to Wesley anxiously, as though *he* was the older and more senior agent.

Zara narrowed her eyes. *Like that, was it? Interesting...*

"Dmitri, how about you lower our pink-faced friend's inhibitions and encourage him to say what's really on his mind?"

Dmitri nodded, and the scent of char intensified.

Arnold's eyes grew glassy.

Wesley, however, bounced excitedly on the spot. "Are you saying we can stay?"

"Wesley," Arnold said thickly, swaying slightly on the spot as though drunk. "I...need to tell you something."

Wesley looked at him, confused.

"I...have feelings for you."

The gangly man's jaw dropped. "What?"

"I've...I love you."

Zara thought it would be impossible for the scientist to become any paler, but somehow, he did.

"It seems like you two have a lot to talk about. Why don't you go and hide out in that house you've been monitoring? The wards there should keep you safe, and I promise that after everything's done, if the world is still here, you can come and scrape whatever you want off anything left over."

Wesley's startled eyes shifted between Zara and Arnold, flummoxed. The larger man grabbed his hand and pulled him toward a clumsy retreat, leading him in a half-stunned state away from the cemetery.

Zara smiled and nudged Dmitri with her shoulder. "Stink magick, bringing people together."

∿

WITH THE TWO befuddled agents set ambling toward Kinmount Street, Lyn and Dmitri made for the scar of the world parallax. Zara, however, headed in a different direction after hearing an unmistakable excited voice.

She passed Gax the Bugge, marching behind a man and a woman dressed in hemp robes holding black skulls. He was croaking at them about the history of the cemetery and how they'd better respect it. He barely spared time to nod at Zara before he continued his mobile lecture. Zara suppressed a smile. No doubt the slimy little goblin was having the time of his life bossing people around all whilst pretending to hate them being there.

A little further on, Zara found Marcus talking animatedly with a girl with bright red curly hair between the largest mausoleums. They seemed to be arguing.

"It doesn't matter if the Filii Terra camp is discovered if the bloody world has exploded!" Marcus grumbled.

"And I'm telling *you*, if they're found, you won't have any support left from the lot of them. Half of them already buggered off with Linda when she left the other night!" The red-headed girl folded her arms stubbornly.

"If we don't make it through this, it doesn't matter whose bloody support we have, does it?"

The petite girl simply gave an animalistic snarl in return.

"Everything going well?" Zara raised her eyebrows.

Song, who sat on a nearby broken tombstone watching the two bicker, waved cheerfully at Zara, and Zara waved back.

Marcus jolted as though he had been too wrapped up in the argument to hear her coming. "Jeez, Zara! Don't do that. I've got enough on my plate here with Isla trying to make my head explode without you trying to make my heart stop too!"

Zara shrugged, offering an awkward grin. "Nice to meet you, Isla."

"You too." Isla's eyes grew very large when she looked at Zara, and she rubbed a grubby hand on her hoody before she offered it to her.

She had a firm shake for such pale and dainty fingers.

"I hear you're the leader of the Filii Terra druids?" Zara asked.

The girl blushed. "I...uh...yeah, I suppose." She laughed nervously.

Marcus' face brightened up gleefully.

"Marcus says you're packing some heat. We're going to need you if things go south. How many do you have with you, and what kind of firepower?"

"It's mostly defensive, really," Isla stammered. "With the Elder Sapling here, the barriers should keep out any monsters."

A barb of panic pierced into Zara's chest. She forced it down and plastered a smile on her face as an immense man trundled by. He had a plaited beard, heavily tattooed arms, and two purple-black rings under his eyes that Zara assumed were from a recently broken nose. He carried a huge clod of earth, sprouting from which was the strangest little tree Zara had ever seen. It was white and barely an arm's length high. The twisted little thing had stiff, clawed branches. It looked both newborn and ancient at the same time.

"How does it work?" Zara asked.

Isla sucked her lip for a moment, her eyes shifting like she didn't want to share the secret. "When the first Theian was slain by humans, they buried its body and planted a tree upon it. The tree never grew much...but it never died either. Anabelle says that it may have been the abilities of the creature they killed that infused it, or it was some kind of curse."

Marcus whistled through his teeth. "All these fancy McGuffins are pretty old."

"They're ancient," Isla replied sharply.

Marcus shrugged. "When you date an eternal being, time looks different."

"It looks half-dead." Zara frowned. "Do we have some kind of backup if it doesn't hold up?"

"It should hold," Isla said proudly. "But we have a couple of bone relics if we need to fight." She deflated slightly. "In terms of numbers...the former Matriarch took a good lump, but they weren't particularly anyone you'd want watching your back for something like this. A lot of those left over are too old or weak to fight. My advisor is taking care of things, and them, at the homestead in my absence. I've brought the ones that *can* fight. It's..." She cleared her throat. "Seven of us."

"Hopefully, it doesn't come to that. And if it does, at least that big bloke with the black eyes looks like he will smash a few things up," Zara said.

Marcus and Isla shared an uncomfortable glance.

Zara frowned but decided to ignore it. "Did you sort out the mirrors for Va—Paile?"

Marcus nodded sympathetically. "Scattered them all over the cemetery, and the Filii Terra kindly added some modifications to make them sturdier. They'll be there if we need them, provided everyone does their part."

Zara took a long breath. Her heart was hammering in her chest.

This is really happening.

It's really time.

I'm going to leave Earth and go to...Theia: an overrun world of monsters that has all but melted into a wasteland of creatures bloated with hate.

To try and find Oscar.

That part made it all somehow so much better.

"Good," Zara said, forcing a confidence into her voice that she didn't feel. "Let's get to the world parallax. It's time."

Marcus reached out and took her hand. Song bounced up from the ground, gripping Zara's other hand. Together, they walked toward what might be the end of everything.

~

THE TOMB LYN had thrown Dmitri into almost half a decade ago was still partially caved in. In fact, almost everything looked the same.

Everything, except for the large mirror that stood between the two mausoleums. It took up the space she remembered where the crack between worlds formed, that impossible mouth that spat out shadowy figures that almost killed them all. Lyn stood, arms folded, right in the spot where Zara had shattered the altar that fed upon Oscar's life-force. She had switched from her rather casual attire to a more practical dark grey shirt and wide-legged trousers. She obviously couldn't resist a matte black pump to finish the look. Dmitri wore black too, a thin sweater that looked ready for the buttons to burst apart over his chest, accompanied by dark jeans. Slung over his shoulder was his axe.

Standing by the mirror...was Paile.

Marcus had sent her on mirror hopping errand spree shortly before coming here, and she looked more than a little worn out. She held the bone athame in her hand. The cursed thing was almost as long as her forearm.

"Is everybody ready?" Dmitri asked, bouncing on the balls of his feet.

Zara knew better than to think he was nervous.

He was excited.

He really believes Oscar is in there.

He believes it enough for the both of us.

For all of us.

"Ready as I'll ever be," Zara said, her voice sounding more than a little strangled.

Dmitri nodded.

"There are a few things you should know before we get started," Marcus said, his tone uncharacteristically severe. "The Filii Terra have warded the mirror so that nothing nasty can come out. Only it's impossible to do that. So, what they've done instead, is made it so that anything that *does* come through will get burned to a crisp in searing, magickal energy."

Zara rolled her eyes. "Great."

"Oh, you'll be fine," Marcus said, waving a hand. "You're essentially human after all."

There was a stiff tension in the air, and several sets of eyes shifted to Dmitri, who looked unfazed.

"Big D will be fine, too. I think. I mean...looking at him now, he doesn't look very human, but he's *from* here. The runes should recognise that, provided you are in the right form."

"I must be...like this to return?" Dmitri asked.

"Unless you want to be a lump of charcoal this Christmas." Marcus winced. "Only way we could put the guard up. Sorry, buddy."

"It's fine," Dmitri replied quickly, though his brows drew together thoughtfully. "I will only try to return in this shape."

"Any other deadly catches?" Zara asked.

"This isn't something that has been done before," Vandle's voice said, coming from Paile. She looked troubled. "You will be unmade and remade through the journey. There are potential side effects in any transmutation. We suspect you may need to face your darkest inner conflict. It could create a barrier you must overcome to move forward."

"Or...?" Zara asked.

"I...don't know," Paile said, sounding defeated.

"This is effectively an interdimensional wormhole," Marcus said proudly. "Not just navigating space-time, but dimensions, too. There's also the variable of the mirror being used itself. That's why Paile and I think it might...complicate matters. Hopefully in a less, uh, fiery death way than the other issue."

Zara took a deep breath. "Complicate? I don't know what you mean. We just use Paige's Tundale link Megazorded with Vandle's light travel and Marcus' ethernal powers to open an interdimensional gateway to hell. Then, just defeat some potential dark guardian generated by our id. After that it's just a case of searching for whoever—or whatever—is holding back universe-ending darkness, in hopes that it's our maybe not-so-dead best friend. All that whilst the cult you've gotten to help us uses a weird little tree to hold back legions of monsters that will be drawn here by the pressure levelling between worlds. Then, because taxis are expensive nowadays, we just pop back through the this potentially half-the-party-incinerating mirror. Great. Maybe then we can all go down to the pub or something?"

"I don't know what you're complaining about, it sounds like a lovely night out," Lyn mused archly.

"Remember, time moves slower there," Dmitri added unperturbed. "Hours here could be days there, so we will have more time to search."

"Oh, yeah." Zara huffed. "The time thing too."

There was an uncomfortable silence.

"Well...good luck!" Lyn said with false brightness. "Both of you just...make sure you come back. And if Theia can be saved..."

Zara nodded numbly, several steps beyond overwhelmed.

"Ironic, huh? Being here, all of us, after...everything?" Marcus looked around himself and squeezed Zara's hand.

"What's ironic is that I was unintentionally averting the obliteration of both worlds when last we were all here together. I would have gotten away with it too if it weren't for you darn kids." Lyn smirked.

Marcus' jaw dropped. "Did you just do a pop culture reference? At least I can now die with zero regrets."

Lyn's eyes sparkled with amusement.

Still looking stunned, Marcus made his way over to Paile and put his hand on the surface of the large mirror. He closed his eyes for a moment, and its surface rippled.

"Okay...try now," Marcus said as he took a step back.

Zara's heart pounded harder.

Paile reached up with the athame and pushed it slowly into the mirror's surface.

She dragged it down, then pulled it back out. Nothing changed.

278

"Okay, wait, wait," he mumbled, placing his hand on the mirror again.

"Marcus, are you sure—" Dmitri began.

Marcus raised a finger to silence him, his eyes remaining closed in concentration. "I think...it needs just a little bit more of a magickal jump-start."

Another minute passed, filled with tense silence.

This time, when the mirror rippled, Zara felt like something else shifted, like the whole world rippled, too. The hairs on the back of her neck and arms stood on end.

The Ghatotkacha awoke unbidden in her chest.

It sensed...danger.

"Now," Marcus said firmly as he withdrew his hand.

Paile reached out with the blade again. This time, it touched the surface of the mirror, like it was normal glass...with a resonant *clank*.

Paile froze, but Marcus gave an encouraging double thumbs up. She pushed harder, and the athame slid into the glass.

It didn't crack or break, but light shone from where the blade punctured the mirror's shell. Paile moved her arm, set her hips, and dragged the blade down in one clean line.

A sparkling gash of light trailed the blade like a gouge in the flesh of reality itself.

The strange glowing light spread from the wound, bleeding into the surrounding glass until suddenly, the whole thing face of the mirror lit up like a beacon.

A smell, like thick sulphur and oil, permeated the air. A strange pressure pushed against Zara. It made her feel sick, and weak, and tired, like a sticky balm cloying in her nose and throat.

The light began to break out in splotches, darker than black. Bottomless. The darkness quickly spread, bleeding into each other and filling the frame with a shimmering void, like blotting ink on tissue paper.

All around them, the grass and trees rustled. Branches shifted as birds took to the skies, fleeing the area. Zara caught sight of a family of rats scuttling as fast as they could in the opposite direction.

Good move. Get as far away as you can.

"You did it," Dmitri said, striding toward the gate, his eyes wide. "You really did it."

"It looks...awful." Zara felt her adrenaline surging.

"Having second thoughts?" Lyn asked.

"Maybe Mufasa was right. Where the shadows touch beyond our borders, we must not go there," Zara said.

"Oh, ignore Mufasa, bitch." Marcus grinned, his eyes fixed excitedly on the black mirror. "The stampede that's comin' for us is way worse."

"And we're sure that jumping in and out with time moving differently won't cause...I don't know...some kind of weird timey-wimey stuff to happen?"

Marcus shrugged. "I don't think so. It's a different dimension. I mean...not like a hundred percent chance time won't explode or something, but we don't exactly have other options. Besides, maybe that could be fun?"

Grumbling, Zara moved to stand beside Dmitri, looking up at his face as he stared at the breach. The broken fabric of reality shone in his eyes.

"Lyn," he said firmly, turning his head.

"Yes?"

"I will leave my axe with you. It works best against...I think you will find more use from it than I."

"Thank you," Lyn said, with only the barest edge of sarcasm. "I'll take care of it."

"You know the words?" Dmitri asked as he turned back.

"Oh, we all know the words by now." Marcus grinned.

Dmitri slung the axe. It spun through the air, and Lyn snatched it lazily with one hand.

Nearby, Ed let out a low whine. Dmitri looked at him sadly. The mimick-dog rose, tentatively waddling closer until he was by his master's legs. Dmitri crouched to stroke his face, rubbing his head in a way that made his back legs shiver as he said something low in Romanian that Zara didn't quite catch.

"Zara, be careful." Marcus wrapped his arms around her vigorously. "Don't do anything I would do, and don't get into fights with anything bigger than you. Or, bigger than your spirit-ghost-form-thingy, at least. Only get in fights you can win is what I'm saying."

Zara chuckled, squeezing him. Her heart ached. "What fun would that be?"

Marcus pushed her away playfully, rubbing his eyes.

There was a keening howl in the night. Others joined it, some too close for comfort, followed by a cacophony of rumbling, gurgling growls and screeches.

"They are coming," Lyn said.

"And we should go." Dmitri stood. His red eyes travelled around the group. "All of you...take care. I will do everything I can."

Marcus barrelled into the much larger man. "Be careful, Big D."

Dmitri froze for a moment, then his broad shoulders relaxed. He wrapped his arms around Marcus and returned the hug. Zara thought for a moment that she might have seen him smile just a little.

The howls rose again, and Marcus moved away from Dmitri.

"Zara, I will wait for you on the other side. Be quick," Dmitri said curtly.

Apparently not wanting to waste another moment, he turned his back. A small bag with elasticated straps on his back, containing a few key items, bounced as he ran straight into the mirror. Its blacker than black surface rippled as it swallowed him whole.

Zara took a breath.

"Okay, my turn." She stepped toward it.

Paile stepped forth and wrapped her long arms around her shoulders. "Be careful. Come back."

"I will," Zara said with a certainty she didn't feel. "I'll come back, and we'll...sort this out."

Paile nodded, tears in her mismatched eyes.

"Oh, alright," Paige's voice snarked.

Zara tilted her head in confusion, then Paile's cool lips touched against her own.

It was chaste, tender, and affectionate but not the normal kiss she was accustomed to from Vandle.

Zara broke out in a grin. "Thanks, Paige. I...I love you, Vandle."

A tear shed from Paile's red eye.

"I love you too," Vandle's voice replied before Paile stepped aside.

Zara took another step toward the mirror.

The sense of unease grew stronger with every step, so much it was almost unbearable.

Two more, and she was right by it.

She took a steadying breath and looked back.

"Any last words?" Marcus shouted nervously.

"Like what?" Zara shrugged. "There was room on that door for both Jack and Rose?"

Marcus laughed. "I love you."

"I love you too!" Zara shouted.

She turned back to the mirror and stepped inside.

THE BLACK SURFACE of the mirror pressed into Zara's nose and mouth, cold and unwelcoming. For a moment, it felt like it was pushing inside her, filling her throat and lungs like an icy river welcoming her into its clutches.

She held her breath as it engulfed her body but kept her eyes open as she sunk into its pitch-black depths.

Darkness rushed around her, flecked with bursts of light. Like stars.

Like travelling through a galaxy in seconds.

Then, it stopped.

Zara blinked.

Nothing but blackness surrounded her.

She looked down and found that she was truly there. Her feet stood on darkness no different from everywhere else.

Tentatively, she took a breath.

Why didn't I think to ask if the atmosphere was the same on Theia as it was on Earth? Surely Dmitri wouldn't just let me pop like a blood-filled water balloon. That's if he even knew what to expect.

Dmitri.

Where is Dmitri?

Zara spun around.

She saw something, but it wasn't Dmitri.

Her heart stopped, and she remembered Paile's words.

You may need to face your darkest inner conflict. It could create a barrier you must overcome to move forward.

Zara's heart thumped back to life, but it felt like the blood it pumped was as cold as ice.

Before her stood the bone gate from Stonehenge, red, crackling light erupting sporadically from it. At its centre, amidst the swirling energy, stood a figure.

Oscar.

"Zara?" he moaned, his eyes pleading. "Zara...you came."

She felt something in her hand.

The hilt of the willblade.

No.

She closed her eyes.

I...this isn't real.

"Zara?" Oscar's fragile voice pried into her mind.

Her guts twisted inside her.

"Zara...please."

She opened her eyes and stepped toward him.

"Zara, I did it. I saved myself." Oscar smiled weakly. Tears streamed down his cheeks.

Zara raised the hilt of the willblade. "I'm so sorry, Oscar," she cried. Every part of her shook.

He looked at her pleadingly. "Zara? What...what are you doing?"

Zara let out a sob.

"I...don't want to die, Zara. Please."

The willblade's hilt fell from her fingers. There was no sound as it landed, disappearing into the darkness.

"I'm so sorry, Oscar," Zara cried, reaching toward him.

She could save him right now. She could bring him back.

But she already felt herself being dragged away.

GRASS AND WORN cobblestones rushed to meet Zara's face, and she crashed unceremoniously into the ground with a jarring yelp.

Her head spun as she gasped for breath, rolling over and blinking up at the stars.

"What the fuck happened?!" Marcus' face appeared above her.

Song's face followed, large golden eyes blinking. They waved happily.

Zara groaned, sitting up. "I...I don't know."

"You could not overcome your barrier," Paile spoke with Vandle's voice, coming to her side.

Zara rubbed her face. Her cheeks were still wet with tears.

She took a breath.

It wasn't real.

"I'm going in again. I can do this." Zara struggled to her feet.

"You can't go straight back in. The passage takes its toll," Paile said gently.

"I'll be fine," Zara insisted, but her head spun. "Dmitri is waiting. Remember, time moves differently there, so he might already have been waiting for hours."

"You were literally gone for like a second. It was all dramatic goodbyes, and then that mirror just pooped you right back out."

Marcus frowned. "And I say that because right now, you look like poop."

Lyn stood watching her coolly, tapping the hilt of the axe on her palm.

"I have to go back in. Dmitri needs backup. He...he can't do it alone." Zara tried to steady herself on her feet.

"Here, hold this." Lyn thrust out Dmitri's axe.

Confused, Zara took it, its weight solid and surprisingly well-balanced in her hand.

"Take care of yourself, Zara. Because if you don't, there will be nobody to take care of everybody else," Lyn said, smiling.

Zara cocked her head, then her heart sank. "Lyn, no. You're pure Theian. You won't be able to come back."

But Lyn was already moving, springing through the air, and sinking into the inky blackness of the mirror.

Zara thought that, in that last moment, she might have seen a tear in her eye before the dark mirror swallowed her up.

Lyn...

"Oi!" a rasping voice interrupted.

Zara turned and saw Gax waddling out.

"There's someone in my bleedin' cemetery that int s'posed to be ere...well other'n all you blatherin' idiots anyway," Gax croaked, folding his mossy little arms grumpily.

"Who?" Zara asked.

Was the military back?

"Well...this is already super dramatic, and we've only just started," Marcus said, grinning.

"No...some...well let's just say they *were* 'uman, but it feels like they've been eatin' the wrong sort of dinners. And a lot of it too." Gax shook his head.

"Oh no," Paile said.

"What?" Zara struggled to her feet.

"It's them...the Order of Helios." Vandle's voice dripped with disgust for those last three words.

Paige's voice followed. It seethed with fury. "And...*him*."

TAXONOMY OF MONSTERS: BLOODY MARY

(LUX SALTATOR)

Typically prefers to go by another name at present, however, seems to be linked to dark folklore by some concerning threads. Known to be summoned and granted access by thrice reciting her chosen name. Gifted with enhanced longevity and agility, as well as the power to shift between locations using mirrors and light. Current form and abilities may be related to some lost arts—potentially an opposite to shadowmancy—with full potential yet unrealised. Aura appears to be a pale, silvery grey, and shimmers, but is currently spiked with shards of forest green due to unfortunate events. For someone whose powers revolve around using light to navigate the in-between, likes to dress a bit like a nineties goth.

— ORIGINAL TAXONOMY ENTRY, MARCUS
WILLIAMS

❧ V ❧
INTO THE DARK

34

BACK TO BLACK

The power of Theia drove into Dmitri like an obliterating wave. Towering and crushing, it overwhelmed him. Smothering darkness saturated every fibre of his being. It was all around him, pushing into him, feeding his inner beast with unimaginable energy.

He had felt this once before.

It was the night at the cemetery when he passed through the world parallax. But unlike *that* night, he did not intend to turn back to save Oscar.

Instead, he pushed through.

Parted reality screamed around him in an intangible flux of unmaking, an endless howling void of nothingness, full of...*everything*.

It lasted for an eternity and yet no time at all.

He burst through a bubble of slick, festering darkness.

Dmitri roared—or would have, if he wasn't already drowned by the maelstrom. It battered him with blunt and insurmountable force, tore him asunder, like an overloaded gut filled with oil bursting from within.

The creature ripped out of his flesh. It shredded and twisted and splintered him with agony and ecstasy. Dark fur and scales, gnashing teeth, and a spiked tail lashed in the tempest, wings unable to catch air, and claws unable to find purchase.

As suddenly as reality had been snatched away, it found him again. His ribs rattled and his left flank scraped painfully as he bowled into the cold, hard earth, wings folded defensively.

Stunned, Dmitri—the zburător—lay panting, pink tongue hanging from his jaw, burning eyes staring up at the crimson skies. Though Dmitri's consciousness remained in this form, he was prone to his baser urges. Those urges had embedded themselves more deeply in his human form as he had grown closer to his Theian shape over recent years. Usually, the most powerful was the urge to hunt.

But that did not find him now. Instead, his territorial impulses urged him to retreat. A deep sense of foreboding told him that this place was not for him. It belonged to another.

Gingerly, he found his four-legged footing once more, the small bag still fixed to his back, the elasticated straps tight on his furry shoulders. The stony ground was mottled with red veins. His burning gaze traced the jagged earth to a cliff's edge. A dark panel, the size of the mirror through which he had passed, perched at its edge.

Padding closer and overcoming the urge to leap back through, he saw that beyond the edge was a sheer drop to craggy, emaciated, and scorched land. His eyes dragged back to the portal. A deep forbidding throbbed from beyond.

No. I could not travel back in this form even if I wished to. I must search...but it will take time to control this power and shift back.

He raised his snout, sniffing at the air.

Blood.

Rot.

Death.

Sulphur.

The place stunk of nothing but it. He knew it from before, but now it was enough to nearly make him gag. It was as though poison throbbed in the red veins of the earth beneath him. He could almost taste it.

His fiery eyes cast around for signs of life but found only broken ground and angry red skies. Three great orbs almost identical in size—moons...or suns—illuminated the desolate land.

So, there really is nothing here but death.

Nothing.

How could Oscar survive here for a day, let alone...

Dmitri focused.

The power within him was still overwhelming, and it would not be easy to change back. It took him weeks when he first found himself in this completed form, and over the years since, he reduced that to hours. It might take longer whilst he was here if he could manage it at all.

And if I can't? If there truly is nothing here?

Then what was is point of returning, anyway?

Settling down on his haunches, Dmitri steadied his breath, taking slow drags in through his nostrils and great huffs from his mouth. He felt his heartbeat calm, the urge to fight, hunt, kill—already small—fleeing further still.

Often, this form would resist him, but it seemed even the zburător agreed that this place held nothing but death.

By the time Zara would arrive, which may be an hour or two, Dmitri assumed he'd back in his more human shape...or near enough, at least. He wondered what twisted feature he might be left with this time. Not that it mattered anymore.

His pulse slowed to a deep march, the ever-present sharp pain biting into him. It was a pain he had grown used to, almost welcomed—the pain of his broken heart from that night. From Oscar. The pain of whatever shard remained within him. It had grown safe. Familiar. It was a distraction from the other pain that he felt...the deeper pain. He homed in on it, greeting each stabbing beat as it reminded him of his new fragility.

The scent in the air shifted, and Dmitri felt his hackles rise. He let a low, rumbling growl of warning escape his throat.

More death.

Putrid, rotten, and wrong.

It smells like...

The zburător sprang upright and turned on the approaching threat.

Figures crept from the shadowy crevices, black eyes shining hungrily.

They smell like the Umbran, only...

Countless more glinting eyes and teeth emerged, converging from the darkness.

The first stepped forward.

It was a creature Dmitri only vaguely recognised. It had matted, patchy fur and powerful limbs like a gorilla but large, punching mandibles on its head like a mantis. Its claws dug into the stone. A pair of canid creatures with heads like crocodiles flanked it, jaws hanging open hungrily. More shapes moved from the shadows, all fully formed but also *wrong*. One was pale and vaguely humanoid, limbs far too long, with only one eye on its wretched face and an enormous mouth showing pointed teeth across its gut. Another, a writhing mass of barbed tentacles.

They looked *stained*.

Darkness welled and bled, dripping not only from their eyes but from their mouths and other orifices, too. Their skin was dull and tinged with deep shifting greys, dampening their colours. He thought he could hear the beating of their hearts. The rattling of their breath. They did not seem dead, but—

Beyond them, something loomed...something immense and terrifying. A deep, foreboding power pulsed from within it. It stood on two thick legs, taller than ten feet. The massive shoulders and body bulged with hulking muscles. Vast horns sat upon its head, its eyes full of misery and death.

Panic roared within him like a furnace, burning out everything else.

They are all infested with Umbrans.

The horned one raised its hand and pointed at him.

There are too many of them. I must lead them away, or they will tear Zara apart before she even knows what's happening.

With a roar, Dmitri lurched forward into a pounce. Rather than lunge at the creatures, he instead took flight in the stagnant, windless air above them.

35

TONGUE TWISTED

The Theian creatures followed, far faster than they had any right to with their dead, black eyes.

One hyena-thing snapped at Dmitri's hind legs, and he narrowly avoided its teeth, pounding his wings desperately to carry him out of reach. He banked sharply and opened his mouth to roar, letting a searing flash of fire from his jaws as he did.

The creatures barely flinched, but he let out another. The humanoid with the mouth on its belly seemed to catch fire, even as Dmitri twisted in the air once more and threw himself into the skies.

That should buy some time.

He tried to gauge his speed to ensure they followed him but did not grow too near. He considered checking back because of the lack of whooping and howling when something barrelled into him from above.

The great mandibled ape tore him from the sky.

It must have climbed up one of the nearby crevasses and leapt upon him as he flew. Hard, jagged stone rushed to meet them. Dmitri twisted, expelling another burst of fire before the ground knocked the air out of him.

Powerful fingers closed around his muzzle, forcing it shut. He lashed out with his spiked tail and heard the monster grunt, a splash of hot, stinking blood following suit. The thing's grip loosened only for a second, but it was enough. Dmitri thrashed free and launched himself back into the sky. He had to be quick as the sound of scuttling claws and slithering tendrils grew closer.

He had barely taken a gasp of stale air when something snatched around his hind leg. The mandibled ape twisted its wretchedly powerful grip, and he felt something pop. Dmitri yelped as the creature yanked him back down to the earth with savage force, crashing him against the rocks.

Then it was on him.

Dmitri spun. Strong hands pushed his front paws aside and pinned him to the ground. Then, the beast's massive head appeared before him, its jaw dripping gloopy, viscous fluid.

Hold.

Dmitri contained the panic and fury and stoked an intense burning deep within his chest.

The mandibles moved around his neck. The powerful jaw flexors clicked loudly as hot saliva dripped on the fur of his throat.

Only then did Dmitri release everything he had, a bright geyser of white heat erupting from his jaw. The flames were so intense they nearly burned his own tongue.

The fingers around his chest spasmed. When the flames subsided, the mandibled ape was already dead, its head completely charred to a crisp, pointed maw and all.

Dmitri thrashed, kicking the corpse off him. A panicked glance confirmed his time was up. The tentacled creature from before lolloped down the crevasse beside him, tendrils already extending toward him hungrily. The two canid beasts bounded down beside it, followed by an ominous-looking misty cloud that left the ground steaming in its wake.

Thankfully, the horned thing was nowhere to be seen.

Dmitri tried to push himself into the air, but his left hind leg hung limply and could not yet bear weight. He tried to get air under his wings but only managed an awkward two beats before crashing back to the ground. His left wing had torn during the fight with the ape—that would take time to heal. Desperately, he pushed himself forward, the creatures behind him growing ever closer. His heart hammered, the agonising stab of the shard like a knife plunging at the speed of a hummingbird's wings.

This is how it will end.

It is as good a way as any, but I must get them as far from the door as possible to give Zara a chance.

He felt a stinging touch against his rear and yelped, pushing with his wings to gain a burst of speed once more as one creature narrowly missed its grip on him. Both his hind legs finally found purchase as he bounded awkwardly over another outcropping. His leg was healing faster than his wing, at least.

Dmitri turned sharply, dashing down a narrow inlet between two tall rock formations. He realised too late that it was a dangerous choice. The rock's faces were lousy with burrows and entrances—for who knew what—but the creatures that hunted him still followed too closely behind to change course.

He gained speed and bounded forth, his back leg now almost fully functional, even if it throbbed with pain. If he could get some height, he may be able to glide to gain some distance away and get an opportunity for his wing to heal.

The opening of the gulley grew closer, and hope welled in his chest.

Then, a massive figure landed in that space, with large staring eyes and skin as black as night. A purple tongue hung from its gawping mouth, covered with suckers. It would have looked like a frog if not for the fact that instead of limbs, it had leathery wings even bigger than his own.

That one, Dmitri *did* recognise.

A water leaper.

Llamhigyn Y Dwr.

It was big enough to kill him by swallowing him whole, never mind that its saliva was a powerful toxin.

Dmitri let out a rumbling growl and ran the options through his head.

No matter what he did, death was almost certain. Now, it was more a matter of choosing which way to die.

Forward.

Always forward.

He felt his muzzle split in as much of a jagged grin as this shape could manage and bounded forward to his death.

The water leaper gazed at him curiously, that black stare welcoming him into its depths. Its purple tongue withdrew, and its gullet swelled, preparing to strike.

I'll dodge the first blow and get as close as I can...see how the frog likes flames before it makes me its dinner.

But he never got that close.

The water leaper spat out its tongue like a firing cannon, the air around it displaced in a shockwave from the sheer force of it. The thing fired at Dmitri faster than he could ever have imagined.

The dull realisation that a creature further amplified by the power of an Umbran was beyond anything he expected dawned on him right before the tongue tore through his chest.

For a moment, he felt nothing but searing heat and the air driven from his lungs. Then stone hammered into his face as he tumbled. The pain was fleeting as hot numbness ran over him.

The toxins...

There was a strange crooning noise as something slick wrapped around him, binding his wings to his back. The snarling and scuffling from behind had since stilled, but the ominous crooning continued.

Dmitri realised it came from the winged frog even as its muscular tongue squeezed around him like a boa constrictor and dragged him closer.

It's warning off the others with its song, Dmitri thought numbly as it pulled at him.

He wretched, tasting blood in his mouth, though his head was so fuzzy that the horror of it all seemed distant.

The water leaper stared at him with those huge, black eyes, now mere feet away.

Almost five centuries of life...and I get eaten by a frog.

Dmitri's thoughts were blurry, almost hysterical. His vision darkened, and he was close enough to smell it now. It reeked of stagnant pond water and week-old offal, with that stink of *wrong* that came with everything a corrupted Umbran touched.

Dmitri's breath was weak. His body grew tired, and he let his eyes close as the water leaper unhinged its massive jaw, jerking its head to greedily pull him in.

I'm coming, Oscar.

He closed his eyes.

Its rotten breath stirred his fur as it drew him in.

There was a flash of light, startling even through his eyelids.

He did not have time to open them before the tongue slackened, and he tumbled back against the earth. The released tension from the tongue and thump of the impact made him gasp air back into his burning lungs, or just one by the feel of it. Blood bubbled in his throat as he rolled, the toxins still leaking into his body.

The water leaper flinched back, black ichor spraying from the stump of its tongue, bulging eyes staring as its crooning became a burbled howl.

But between it and Dmitri stood a familiar figure.

Their presence hummed with the touch of two worlds. Long limbs elegantly wielded a staff of straight, white bone, their blue eyes the colour of the ocean on a sunny day. It was a Tundale Dmitri had known and loved, but not the Tundale he had expected to find.

Geraldine Tundale tossed her head, casting the roughly cropped jaw-length grey and blonde hair out of her face. "Hello, Dmitri," she said with the ghost of a smile, as though they had bumped into each other on Oxford Street rather than Hell.

Dmitri wretched again, forcing up blood and bile.

The heaving of his chest forced the water leaper's tongue free from where it impaled him with a wet slap on the stone. Gore gushed from Dmitri's now open wound.

Too much blood.

His vision faded, and all around him he heard the wretched creatures move in for the kill.

36

THE UNDYING

Dmitri heard Oscar's voice.
He heard him speaking.

That's when he knew he must be dead, though he did not know why he deserved to be gifted with such a final destination.

He let himself sink into the deep, chasing it desperately.

He glimpsed Oscar's face—or the echo of it.

He felt so close, but all he could find was hollow pain and fitful flashes of memory and strange awareness. Flashes of pale blue light. Strange and terrible screams, yips, and howls. A dark, oppressive force pressing down upon him.

Fear.

And then...nothing.

Less than darkness.

Absence.

Peace.

For forever and a moment, there was nothing.

Then, he was back. Or *there*, at least, because it was impossible to be back to a place you'd never been before.

Dmitri blinked, turning his head dazedly.

It wasn't quite a room. The stone walls were as stark and

unwelcoming as the earth outside, and the only light source was a round stone set on the ground that gave off a muted glow.

He lay on something spongy which formed around his back.

It was only then that he realised he was in his human form once more...only his head felt too *thick*, his jaw too heavy, mouth too full of teeth.

Tentatively, he reached up with a shaking hand.

His fingers found large, pointed teeth jutting from between his lips, now unable to properly close. Soft fur traced the edges of his jaw—his remaining ear was velvety with it, too. His brow was thicker, heavier.

Dmitri shifted in the dense, leathery fabric that twisted around his body, his flesh slick with sweat beneath it. He forced himself to sit, wincing at the pain in his shoulder as he did. The hair had grown thick as fur on his forearms and in patches on his shoulder. A dark tuft of it sat in the centre of his chest.

A quick glance showed that the tissue where the water leaper's tongue had speared him had healed over, leaving a pink, jagged scar where the skin had knitted back together despite the shard in his heart. It sat on the edge of the dark burn that ran down his temple, neck, and onto his shoulder, given to him by the fire primordial.

He looked at his hands. They were larger, fingers thick and long, nails black and pointed.

Groaning, Dmitri shifted stiffly, glancing around the room. It was empty. But despite that, he felt the heavy sense of being watched, a lingering presence nearby. He searched for its origin, eyes drawing into the shadows in the corner. He swore it came from there...but there was nobody.

Footsteps approached from the mouth of the small cavern.

Dmitri pulled the leathery fabric up, clutching it against his chest.

"Oh, we have become a modest boy," Geraldine mused, smirking as she entered.

"How..." Dmitri's voice was deeper now, ragged. The edge of a growl.

"It's a long story." She sighed, the corners of her eyes crinkled, and she folded her arms. The hooded robe she wore looked to be made from the same leathery fabric Dmitri was covered with.

He moved to stand, holding the fabric to him. His legs shook, and he stumbled back onto the bed behind him.

"Easy," Geraldine admonished. She strode to the corner, waving her hand. Flames leapt from some dry-looking branches beneath a strange pot in the corner.

"Your powers...from Whisper. That's what kept you alive all this time?" Dmitri breathed. His voice was a rumble, and the words were difficult to form in his mouth.

Geraldine had been soul-bonded, like Marcus, though her ethernal was not quite so gentle as his.

Surely that's the only way.

"Alive is such an interesting word. It suggests a life...of sorts. I'm not sure what constitutes 'alive' in this place, but I suppose technically it can be described as that. I continue to exist. For now, at least. What about you? From the looks of you, you were barely alive before you came here."

A cold feeling spread across Dmitri's skin.

The compulsion.

This woman had placed upon him a will-binding that made him need to seek out Oscar when he was in danger. It took any semblance of control or meaning over his own life away and bent it to her will.

And in the process?

Dmitri had found more of a life than he had ever thought possible. He grew closer to humanity, closer to happiness, and was more complete than he had imagined he could be.

Before he had failed...and lost it all.

Despite the joy that he had found, he still felt a spike of revulsion for what she had done to him. She hadn't known he would find that joy, and she used him as a tool. Geraldine Tundale had always been a brilliant woman; intelligent, imaginative, and wise... but 'kind' wasn't particularly near the top of that list. That was where James Tundale had been the balance to her scale.

"Geraldine—" Dmitri began.

"I'm sorry," she cut in crisply. It was a tone considerably unmatched for an apology, yet it was genuine, if not earnest.

Dmitri stared at her blankly.

"I'm sorry for what I have put you through. Truly, you deserved more. But I did what was required of me. So, whilst I can apologise to you for how I treated you, I do not regret what I did."

"You haven't changed at all. Still playing God."

Geraldine's eyes narrowed, and she smirked knowingly.

"James?" Dmitri asked.

The smirk slid from her face, and her blue eyes dulled. "He was not so...fortunate as me. The..." She cleared her throat. "You saw the horned one."

That feeling of heavy dread settled into Dmitri once more. He recalled its eyes and wicked smile.

"That was once a gugalanna."

Dmitri frowned and shook his head. It looked nothing like a gugalanna other than its horns, at least. Gugalannas were more bull-like in form.

"The gugalanna was drawn to Oscar when he was a child. It hungered for him. We knew it was coming, and Whisper warned for a long time about its approach, but we were arrogant." She pursed her lips. "I was arrogant."

"We were ill-prepared for the sheer destructive force of the gugalanna, the frenzy that Oscar's proximity would put upon it. It...it consumed James entirely. I was desperate and didn't have the power to defeat it. So, I fled. I cast a beckoning upon it and travelled to Iceland, where I knew a world parallax lay dormant. I planned to cast it back to Theia. Unfortunately, I was pulled in with it."

"And Whisper?" He remembered Whisper well; tall, lean,

alabaster skin and verdant green eyes, a coif of raven hair, and a penchant for drama.

As with all soul-bonded, the pair had been inseparable.

"It's...complicated." Geraldine frowned. "I assume you came to try and drain the pressure from this world in order to save the other, but unfortunately that will likely be too little too late. Theia is on its final rattling breath. It had already fallen when I arrived. The Umbrans had gorged to such a degree that their power was incalculable. As happens with all beings of power, though, there was dissent. Some wished to destroy Theia—destroy everything—and others still wanted to preserve themselves and continue to feed. The battle was already underway, with Umbrans consuming each other and using powerful Theians as allies by fragmenting themselves and inhabiting their bodies. One such Umbran claimed the gugalanna after we arrived. It twisted its form into its own ideal. It calls itself Belphegor."

An unpleasant sensation ran across Dmitri's skin again.

"Belphegor consumed what remained of the other Umbrans and became ruler of Theia...if one can be the ruler of a wretched wasteland. It spread its influence among the Theians like a parasitic presence. Whatever it touches is tainted by its vileness, forming a hivemind of starving monsters."

"And yet...you live," Dmitri said cautiously, eyeing her.

That knowing smirk returned. "Let's just say Belphegor doesn't like me much. Some part of the damage I left on the gugalanna seems to have left it with a healthy fear of my abilities. And I still have enough power from Whisper to cause it a great deal of pain, if not unmake it."

Dmitri waited for the *but*.

She offered him a resigned smile. "The problem is my power is waning."

"You've been here..." Dmitri frowned, running the numbers in his head.

Geraldine disappeared just over twenty years ago. With the way they thought time moved differently in Theia, that meant...

She smirked. "More."

More than a century?

"As Theia collapsed, pockets of this reality did too. Now, there are places here where time moves a hundred times faster than it did before, and some places where it even crawls backward at a snail's pace. I've been here longer than I can remember, but I'm quite sure it's still less than a thousand years."

"Your mortality..."

She shrugged lightly. "Gone."

"You traded it with Whisper? And how did you retain your sanity?"

"Who says that I did?" She arched an eyebrow.

Dmitri scowled.

"Oh, don't be a spoilsport. By the looks of you, you're not exactly *thriving* either."

Dmitri's stomach sank.

I must tell her.

"You...compelled me to protect Oscar."

Geraldine regarded him gravely.

"And...I...failed." Dmitri's voice shook.

Geraldine blinked.

Dmitri tried to force the words from his mouth, tried to tell Oscar's mother what had happened...to ask the question he already knew the answer to.

Those blue eyes met his patiently.

"Dmitri...I forced something on you and that was the wrong thing to do, but for the right reasons. I know you did your best."

Dmitri shook his head as his vision blurred with tears. "I...I must have been able to do more. There must have been some other way."

"I think you know that is not the truth," she said sadly, eyes sparkling. "I think Oscar knows it too."

Dmitri's breath caught in his chest.

"We always feel like we have more to give for the ones we love, no matter how dry we bleed ourselves."

Dmitri stared, still not daring to breathe.

She stared right back at him.

He wanted to speak, but his mouth wouldn't open, and his voice wouldn't come.

She's talking as though...

"It is him," Geraldine said, though not to Dmitri.

Something shifted in the darkness where Dmitri had looked before yet found nothing.

"I apologise, Dmitri. Many things walk this world that can take the appearance of others. I was quite certain it was you, but I wanted to be sure before..."

"What?" Dmitri choked, staring, eyes wide, at the shadows.

A figure moved from within them, a deep cowl over its head, long-limbed and wary. A scent accompanied them, an impossible scent that did not match their presence at all.

Dmitri shook his head.

It can't be...

Everything inside him stopped.

The figure moved its pale hands up, pulling back their cowl.

His skin was so pale, yet dark circles sat under his eyes like bruises. His messy hair was hacked short and uneven. He had his mother's eyes, down to the now haunted look this place had left them with.

"Oscar?" Dmitri choked.

It...it looked like Oscar. It smelled like Oscar.

But it doesn't feel like Oscar.

There was no deep hum coming from him like it always had.

Hope seared through doubt and confusion.

No. Even if this is a lie, let me have it. Let me die happily in untruth.

Dmitri felt tears spilling. He opened his mouth to speak once more, but only a sob came out.

"Dmitri..." Oscar's voice...*Oscar* said.

Dmitri pushed himself to his feet with no care for his nudity, his head spinning. He took a stumbling step forward. Oscar took a nervous step back to the shadows, eyes wide and blinking.

"It's you," Dmitri sobbed. "I...it's you."

He staggered forth, reaching out with both hands.

Pain lanced the wound in his shoulder, and fresh blood flowed from it. His ears rang and his vision darkened around the edges, but he pushed forward.

Oscar stood frozen in the gloom, mouth half open and eyes brimming with tears.

The ground collided into Dmitri's knees as he fell, head spinning. He crawled on doggedly until his hands found Oscar's feet. His arms wrapped around his legs...his solid, truly *there* legs.

He breathed him in.

Pressed his face against his bare, grubby feet, covered in scars.

Blood.

Sweat.

Death.

Tears.

Dirt and dust

and...

Oscar.

Dmitri's body racked with sobs as he looked up. Oscar reached down, tears in his eyes and lip shaking. One hand reached out, fingers ghosting Dmitri's scarred temple. Dmitri felt himself slipping, vision succumbing to darkness as he fell, head bouncing off the stone.

The last thing he heard was Oscar's voice saying his name, and he had never heard anything so sweet in all his years.

TAXONOMY OF MONSTERS: THE BLEMMYAE
(VEHEMENTI OCULUS)

A man, a man, without a head,
And yet he walks and is not dead.
He sees with eyes upon his chest,
And wields his club to cause unrest.

— NICHOLAS CHLOROS, 1861-1884

37

ALL CHANGE

Dmitri's body was weak when he woke again. The shard in his chest throbbed in time with his slow heartbeat. He stared at the damp stone ceiling for a time, slowly breathing in the stale air around him.

He could still smell him.

It had *been real*.

No matter whether he was dead, and this was the afterlife, he could relish happily in the depths of Hell with a sense of *his* presence so nearby.

He heard movement.

Oscar?

"Now don't you go getting all riled up again," Geraldine mused. "He is...away, for now."

Dmitri let out a breath. Now that he knew she was there, he could sense her...but she had no scent to trace.

No scent?

Just like...

"You're not Geraldine Tundale. You are...Whisper?" Dmitri asked thickly, eyes still fixed on the ceiling.

There was a long pause.

"That is both true and false," she eventually said. "Either way, please say nothing of the sort in front of...him."

Dmitri forced himself up onto his elbows. His muscles screamed, and the wound in his chest ached. "Where is he?"

"He needed some space."

"He...is it...is it really him?" Dmitri tried to contain himself and barely managed it. "He feels...different."

Geraldine simply watched him thoughtfully.

"Geral—"

"Are you Dmitri, son of Catalina Cel Tradat?"

Dmitri shook his head, confused. "I...believe that was my mother's name."

"It was," Geraldine said flatly. "But what I'm asking is, are you him? Are you that person *now?*"

So, it's true. She was my mother.

"No," Dmitri said. "I am...someone else. Something else."

"As is he. As am I. Something I always sought in my prior form was to understand what it was to *give* and not just take to experience humanity. I can't say that I'm all the way there, but I'm closer than I have ever been."

Dmitri growled. "You tricked Oscar into believing—"

"This place has taken its toll on him. I barely think that allowing him to have what he needs to survive and keep his sanity would count as a selfish act."

Dmitri swallowed, unable to hold on to his anger. "But it's... truly him?"

Geraldine nodded.

Relief flooded Dmitri, and he fell back onto the squashy substance behind him. An overwhelming thrill of hope eased into his bones, followed by a sharp edge of...concern.

"Wait. How long? How long has he been here?"

"I will let him tell you of that," Geraldine said patiently. "I will leave it at 'longer than any human soul should be'."

Concern turned to sorrow.

Oscar lived.

He lived.

But he had been trapped here for who knows how long.

Guilt tore into him.

"It is nothing less than a miracle that you are here now. Don't despair that you didn't come faster," Geraldine said, seemingly sensing his conflict.

That made all kinds of sense if she truly was *Whisper.*

Dmitri pushed himself up.

"Go easy," Geraldine warned again.

"You...took care of him?"

"Of course," she chided.

"Even though..."

"Everything that made Geraldine Tundale his mother is within me," she said sharply. "Everything."

"But...how?"

"When the human known as Geraldine Tundale tore open the space between worlds to be rid of the gugalanna, her body was dying. We attempted an exchange, one that would have caused her to lose her humanity and ascend to a greater state of being. However, when we were pulled between worlds, she...perished." Deep sadness hung in her eyes. "I...I took everything that I could from her. Good and bad. She...*what* and *who* she was lives on in me."

That wasn't at all like the normal exchange between ethernals and humans...

"So...she is gone?"

Geraldine nodded sadly. "Everything that made Geraldine is within me. Her being resounds within me like an echo."

Dmitri bowed his head, feeling a pang of old sorrow. He had mourned her death when he heard it—both hers and James'—in his own way, even after what she did.

"I wandered this place, unable to die. I believe I succumbed to madness more than once. The Umbrans, Belphegor...none could end me. Yet a dying star I am, Dmitri. My energy wanes."

There was a shuffling from the doorway to the cave. Dmitri stiffened, eyes seeking Oscar but finding nothing.

But does that mean he isn't here? Or is he somehow hiding like before? How had he done that?

"Oscar, too, has changed. His journey has left more than deep marks upon him," Geraldine said.

Dmitri's eyes still lingered on the entrance. Now, he thought he smelled something...*foul*. "I need to get him away from here. I need to take him home," Dmitri said firmly.

Geraldine's eyes crinkled once more in that smile. "I know."

"Will you help?"

"I would love nothing more."

Dmitri reluctantly allowed his eyes to leave the doorway.

Something else is here.

He stretched his legs tentatively. He felt stronger than before.

"There are...some things you should know," Geraldine continued levelly.

Dmitri tilted his head.

"Oscar...has been..." She seemed to struggle to find the words.

Dmitri listened patiently.

"He has been exceptional," she finished. "I thought he would break a hundred times over under the threats this world put upon him, under the strain of what...what he has become."

Dmitri's back stiffened, his heart lurching in his chest.

"Before he came here, Oscar was infested with an Umbran," Geraldine said gently. "They were parted with a blade powered with pure intention, correct?" She drew an invisible line down the centre of her chest.

Dmitri nodded uneasily. "He...the Umbran is gone, yes?"

Geraldine's lips tightened. "In a way."

An unpleasant chill ran over Dmitri's hot skin. "What do you mean?"

"The willblade is a keen tool, but it was never intended to part human flesh. That is the only reason why Oscar still lives. It was better suited to what it achieved instead. It did a neat job of severing the compulsion I laid on both you to protect him, but the Umbran was more attached than that. I suppose you could liken it to scraping mould from a loaf of bread," she said crisply. "No matter how keen the blade, the unseen roots still reach deep into the loaf."

Dmitri narrowed his eyes.

"Oscar carried the resonant touch of Theia in his cells. Unfulfilled potential. The capacity for change. When he was inhabited by the Umbran, those spaces were filled. Though the thing that possessed his body is no doubt dead, it has left its stain upon him."

Was that why Oscar didn't hum anymore?

"What are you saying?" Dmitri's voice was gruff.

"He hungers," she said sadly. "It...is the only reason he has not perished. He's able to feed upon the same things as them. To use hate. It is the only reason you live and are not controlled by Belphegor's touch. The venom of the water leaper was full of its taint—that is, in part, how this place has been infested. But Oscar leeched it out."

Dmitri's heart felt like it stopped inside of his chest, but the stabbing pain that continued told him that was a lie.

No.

Not Oscar.

Oscar, without an ounce of cruelty in his heart, must endure all that hate.

"I thought that, too, would drive him mad," Geraldine said simply. "But he never gave up, Dmitri. He told me you would come. I did my best to support him, guide him, teach him, protect him. In truth, I'm not so sure he wouldn't have made it without me. He is...he carries a heart the size of a world within him."

Dmitri had tears in his eyes again and couldn't help but smile.

Geraldine, too, dabbed at her eyes. "Of all the things I thought I'd experience from humanity, selfless pride in another is such a joy."

"Will he…be okay?" Dmitri managed.

Geraldine looked thoughtful. "I don't know. Much has changed. He's not exactly human anymore. I think…I think should you both succeed, you will both need time."

Dmitri's heart ached in his chest.

There was shifting near the entrance again, and it seemed to be moving away. But as it did, Dmitri thought he saw a flash of pale green, scaly skin.

"And then, there's you." Geraldine arched her brow.

"Me?" Dmitri frowned.

"You are not the same man I knew, nor the one Oscar knew. At least from what I can tell."

Dmitri's fingers self-consciously drifted to his scarred temple and pointed ear.

"Appearances are one thing. I mean within."

"What are you—"

Geraldine tapped her lips thoughtfully. "I'm sure you've heard the problematic and misappropriated proverb about two wolves fighting within you? Well, let's just say that one of yours is very much not a wolf at all."

"What are you talking about?"

"The wound on your chest. The one that stops you from healing."

Dmitri looked down.

"I used some of my power to close your wounds. I felt it there, what remains. I could have removed it."

"If you remove it, I…I don't think I would survive."

"Oh, I agree! Though no doubt for very different reasons. That broken piece is precisely where it needs to be."

"Why are you being so cryptic? The Geraldine Tundale I knew would have loved telling me exactly why I was wrong, and she was right."

Geraldine chuckled. "I agree. I told you I've changed as well."

Dimitri groaned, annoyed. "We don't have the time. You realise what's happening on Earth, don't you?"

"Of course. Just as you know minutes there are hours here. Just as you know that it's not always important *what* we do *when* we do things, but *how* and *why* we do it." She smiled. "If any one thing is not in perfect alignment, we will fail. Right now, Belphegor will be rallying its creatures and barring the way to the world parallax. Rushing in would as surely spell the end of everything, just as much as ninety-nine of the hundred other options. Trust that when the time comes at which we must move, I will ensure we do. However, some things are better for you to figure out yourself. And to that end, I think you should speak with Oscar."

His heart swelled painfully within his chest, and his pulse quickened. "That much, we can agree on."

❦ 38 ❦

THE SCARS OF TIME

Oscar was gathering food—or at least what Geraldine claimed passed for sustenance here. Though the plant life and water sources had not escaped the Umbran's touch, apparently those were still usable...despite many remaining naturally toxic. The flora did, however, lend itself to a multitude of purposes. Some of the large, squashy fungi had been compressed into the bed he'd lain.

On which Oscar must lay.

Some of the thick leaves could be treated and used as fabric, like the sheets he had been covered in and the robe he now wore. It was coarse, stiff, and leathery, much like Geraldine's.

The same as Oscar wore.

The small bag he had brought through the gateway had been set on the ground in the room where he'd woken. It was stretched and torn at places but still mercifully intact. It currently hung over his shoulder. He longed for the fresh clothes within, but Geraldine told him to wait to don them, though she did let him put on the shoes he'd brought.

She led him out of the cavern and into a network of tunnels. Some were a struggle to navigate in his current state, including a series of steep inclines. Within the tunnels, they'd been able to maintain a small ecosystem of sorts, a place to gather food, water, and plants in relative safety.

At several points, he thought he heard movement from deep within the recesses or saw flashes of spindling legs or slithering shapes fleeing from his sight.

"We have saved a few from Belphegor's influence," Geraldine said, following his gaze as something pale, pink, and frothy with gigantic eyes on stalks retreated around a corner. "It's difficult to provide for them. Some choose to make a life on their own. Oscar has been instrumental in rescuing and protecting those we have been able to liberate from Belphegor's touch. You would be very proud of him."

Dmitri ignored the pain in his body and pushed forward, knowing he would soon be close to Oscar again. Nothing else mattered.

Geraldine paused, gesturing ahead to a crooked little walkway partially blocked with slimy, grey stalagmites. "Down there, second tunnel on the left." She wore that infuriating, knowing smirk once more. "Don't worry. I have warded these tunnels. So long as I live, nothing *too* dangerous should dare enter."

He put his hand on hers as she turned to leave. "Thank you for...for taking care of him."

Her eyebrow arched. "He's my son, Dmitri. Thank *you* for taking care of him. Now, don't you break his heart, or I will use all the energy I have left to pop you like an overripe pimple."

Dmitri followed her directions. The sound of running water grew as he passed through the tunnels and became even louder as it opened into a large cavern.

The red light from the sky punched down through a fissure. Large spikes of dark stone jutted up from the earth like pointed fingers, and a stream of sickly yellow water flowed down one edge of the cave to a pool at its centre. Something scuttled in the darkness, and Dmitri's gaze flashed to track it.

"Oscar?"

The scuttling noise sounded again.

It's far too fast and many-legged to be—

"It's just a headvys," a voice said from right behind Dmitri, jolting him in surprise.

All at once, he sensed him, smelled his scent, and felt his warmth.

"Oscar," Dmitri sighed, not even daring to turn in case it was all a lie.

Oscar stepped beside him, cowl pulled up, head tilted, and blue eyes peering out. "Hi."

Everything inside Dmitri screamed for him to reach and grab him, to take him in his arms and hold him, to tell him that he was here now and would give everything to make him safe.

Oscar seemed to sense this and nervously shuffled back, eyes wide.

The scuttling in the shadows became louder, and Oscar's eyes darted toward it, mouth hardening into a thin line, his gaze focused. It silenced.

There was a shifting movement behind him, and Dmitri spun to face it. Before him stood two very strange beings. One was sugary pink, and its skin looked like melted candle wax. Two small, white eyes were buried in the centre of its round head. The other had a long neck and narrow head with an eelish face. Its body was stretched thin, and covered in skin pale green scales.

"That's Elodie and Garshok," Oscar said matter-of-factly. "They're harmless."

The pink one oozed, staring at him disconcertingly.

Dmitri tried to meet eyes with the eel-faced creature instead, awkwardly raising a hand. "Uh...pleasure to meet you...Gar—"

The creature bore its pointy teeth and hissed.

Oscar made a noise, almost like a chuckle. "That's Elodie, and they don't really speak much."

Dmitri's cheeks heated, and he lowered his hand. "Of course. I'm sorry. Elodie, Garshok." He bowed awkwardly instead.

"You two go down to the burrows. I'll be fine here," Oscar said.

The eel-faced one, Elodie, turned and briskly stalked off. Dmitri recognised the pale green scales on its back.

Had that been the one peering around the door when I was recovering?

Garshok stared on with that strange and penetrating gaze.

"See you later, Garshok!" Oscar repeated, waving at the thing.

It stood and continued staring, pink slime oozing onto the stone below it.

"Oscar, I..."

"Just leave 'em. He'll get bored and follow Elodie soon." Oscar shrugged, turning back to Dmitri. "Have you seen them before?" he blurted. "Anything like Elodie and Garshok, or headvys, I mean?"

Dmitri frowned, looking back to the shadows. "No. And *headvys*...not unless I know them by a different name."

Oscar stepped toward the shadows.

Dmitri's eyes shifted to Oscar's bare feet, wondering how tough his soles must have become to tolerate the sharp and craggy stones. Oscar stood still for a moment. Dmitri saw his posture relax. A moment later, that scuttling noise sounded again.

At first, nothing happened...

Then one long, sharp leg reached out, hard and glossy like an exoskeleton. Another followed. Then another. Its body was unlike any spider Dmitri had ever seen. Not only was the thing the size of a small dog, but its small, black body had two massive fangs on the front that dripped threateningly.

"I have...never seen those before," Dmitri said, his muscles tensing to fight. *Could* he even fight right now?

Oscar's shoulders tensed too, and his focus shifted to the creature. It froze, staring back at him.

"Don't worry about the fangs. They're harmless. Literally just to scare stuff. They feed off fear. Latch themselves with those legs and cling on, scaring you until its appetite is gone, or you stop being scared...or die," Oscar said flatly.

Dmitri eyed the thing's legs. The inner parts looked blade

sharp.

Oscar raised a hand threateningly at the thing, and it flinched before scuttling back into the shadows. He turned to Dmitri, pushing back his hood.

In the light, Dmitri was shaken by how thin he looked. The dark circles under his eyes made it look worse, but his lips were pale and complexion anaemic.

"See," Oscar said, turning his head and lifting a tangle of hair with his left hand. At his temple, Dmitri saw his hair split in three scarred, vertical bands. "Headvys," Oscar added helpfully.

"Oh, Oscar," Dmitri breathed.

"Same on the other side. Three weeks or something, one was on me. No matter what Mum said, I was sure it was going to bite me." His lips twisted in a strange way that wasn't a smile.

"I'm...sorry," Dmitri replied.

Oscar paused, then shrugged, looking a little lost. "I...guess that was a downer. I thought it would be good to tell a cool scar story."

"I hate that you went through that." Dmitri's voice shook. He could weep again just looking at him now, let alone thinking of him suffering alone.

Before Oscar, when was the last time I even shed a tear?

"I...don't know what I should say." Oscar shifted on the spot awkwardly.

"You don't have to say anything."

"I feel weird." Oscar's lips twisted strangely again. "Like...I don't know how long it's been for you, but...I know it's been longer here."

"I..." Dmitri spluttered.

How long?

He suspected he didn't want to know the answer.

Oscar shimmied over and perched on a rocky outcropping with an ease that looked unusual on him. "Are you sure this is a good place to talk? You're injured."

Dmitri realised that the pink slime creature had indeed *slith-*

ered away at some point. A trail of goo absorbing into the stone was all that remained.

Dmitri shifted uneasily. "I'm fine."

"Okay." Oscar took a deep breath. "I've been here, as near as we can tell, for about fifteen years."

Dmitri's breath stopped.

Fifteen years.

"It should have been less, but when I first arrived, I panicked, running away from some weird little spiky things and ended up in a pocket where time moved a little faster. After that, Mum found me, and we've been together ever since."

"It has been...two years," Dmitri said gently.

Oscar's face stiffened for a moment. "Only two?"

Dmitri nodded.

"I..." Oscar looked away with pained eyes. "I'm sorry. I'm so happy to see you. Really, Dmitri. Like, it's everything I dreamed of. Everything I do dream of, every night...for fifteen years."

"Me too. When I can sleep." His hands twitched beside him with the urge to reach out again, but he stayed them.

"I just...it's been so long for me, and...so much has changed."

Dmitri's heart twisted in his chest.

Changed?

"I mean, I'm *different* now." Oscar's blue eyes finally returned to Dmitri.

They looked...*ancient* somehow, in that tired, innocent face. It made the hairs on Dmitri's neck stand up.

"Yes, Ger—your mother told me."

Oscar shifted on his seat awkwardly. "I...I guess I just don't feel very much like *me* anymore."

Dmitri's hand drifted up to his ruined ear. "I know the feeling."

Oscar frowned as if seeing it for the first time.

A long silence hung between them.

"What happened?" Oscar asked finally.

"I fought with an ancient being. But I haven't healed right

since that night at Stonehenge. A piece of shrapnel from the gate is stuck in my chest."

Oscar winced.

"Oscar. I want you to know…I never stopped looking for you."

Oscar grew still and stared right back at him.

"I'm so sorry you had to wait so long. But for all we knew, you were *gone*. That didn't stop me, though. It never even slowed me down. I—"

"I know," Oscar cut in.

Dmitri stilled.

"I knew you wouldn't." Oscar's voice sounded strangely small now. "I knew you would be looking for me. Every time I go to sleep, I imagine you finding me. I imagine you being there. It's… the only way I can sleep sometimes." As he finished, Oscar looked suddenly bashful, as though he had said too much.

Dmitri stared at him, lost for words.

"You want to clean up?" Oscar looked awkwardly toward the waterfall.

Dmitri wrinkled his nose, looking at the cloudy yellow water. "It doesn't smell…*clean*."

Oscar nodded. "It's about as clean as it gets here. Kind of acidic, though. Can't wash too often, or it starts taking your skin off. And it needs special treatment from Mum before it's drinkable."

"Are you sure it's okay?" Dmitri frowned at the cloudy water.

Oscar hopped down. "Come on. Follow me."

THE BACK END of the cave wheeled around into a more closed area, largely obscured by stalagmites. A pool of cloudy water sat at the centre, a smaller fall dribbling into it. As they grew near, it suddenly seemed Oscar realised he'd suggested an activity that included nudity, and his eyes became as skittish as the several headvys scuttling around in the shadows before them.

"Don't worry. I'm not scared of them," Oscar said distractedly. "Well...I guess I *am*. I think they're horrible, but I know I can keep them away, so I don't feel the same fear if that makes sense?"

Dmitri nodded.

Oscar paused, looking around uncomfortably. "So...sometimes I wash up in here. Sometimes I stand under the big waterfall. Depends how I'm feeling." He eyed Dmitri. "Maybe the little pool for you. You look too beat up for the big boy pool."

Despite all the horror, Dmitri felt the corner of his mouth turn up in a smile.

Oscar looked strangely embarrassed at the exchange.

"I'll...stay nearby. Keep the headvys away and look out for anything else."

"Do you...have a weapon or something?" Dmitri asked, eyeing his robe.

Oscar tilted his head. "No. Why?"

"Just...how do you protect yourself here?"

"The Umbran left in me," Oscar said darkly. "Most things don't want to come near me."

Dmitri moved to unknot his robe, and Oscar spun around quickly. He felt a surge of relief at that. There were so many new scars and changes to his body. He didn't know how ready he was to show them all to anyone, let alone Oscar.

"Sorry," Oscar said. "I'm not being weird. I just...I don't know what's normal in this kind of situation."

"Don't worry." Dmitri proceeded to unknot the robe. "I don't think there *is* a normal for a situation like this. We just have to figure it out as we go, and that's fine."

He watched as Oscar shuffled over and settled on the ground.

"Are you...okay, Oscar?" Dmitri shrugged his left shoulder from the robe. The wound was closed again but ached deeply.

"Yeah, I'm used to sitting on the floor," Oscar replied blankly.

"No, I mean...how *are* you? This must all have been...impossibly hard for you." He got his other shoulder free. His natural scent of smoky char and musk was stronger since his changes.

Bicarbonate of soda barely did the job anymore, but he hadn't been so aware of it until his bare flesh was out and he could smell his own dried sweat.

"I'm coping, mostly," Oscar said.

The soft honesty in his voice took Dmitri off guard, and he paused. Carefully, he sat at the pool's edge. "Oscar, turn around, please."

After a moment, Oscar did. His eyes immediately flashed across Dmitri's chest. He had more hair there now, as well as on his unburned shoulder. It was dark and thick but for where the raw, puckered scar sat just off-centre from his pectorals. It had been there for two years, but it looked like a week-old wound struggling to heal.

"That looks painful," Oscar said, eyes fixed on the wound.

"It is...sometimes."

Oscar pulled open the chest of his robe.

Dmitri winced first at the pale skin and tight muscle. It was unlike Oscar's body before. Now, it was hard, thin, and worn from survival.

"See here?" Oscar ran a finger down his sternum. A long, strangely silvery scar the length of his palm sat there.

"That's from...the willblade?" Dmitri asked.

I almost said Zara... I hope she got back quickly.

Oscar nodded. "Mum said the intensity of the reaction with the Umbran is what left this mark. I think you have me beaten for scars, though. Do you think you will heal if we get the fragment out?"

Dmitri struggled not to look away. "Perhaps."

"Oh!" Oscar excitedly popped his shoulders completely free and twisted around. His arms were wiry and toned with sinuous muscle.

Dmitri stayed his face from reacting.

"This here!" Oscar flashed his back. Three white lines ran in a gouge from his left shoulder blade to his right hip. "Weird monkey thing with a pinchy head! Scratched me...a few weeks ago, I think it was?"

Dmitri winced, imagining Oscar bleeding and hurt.

Wait...

"A few weeks ago?"

Oscar nodded earnestly. "I heal fast now, too. Provided I've uh...got some energy on board."

Energy?

Hate.

Dmitri's eyes travelled from the three perfectly healed scars and back to Oscar's arms. More scars stood there. Scratches and splashes of caustic liquids had left their marks on him. All the way around his left arm, just above his elbow, was one thick, jagged band of scar tissue.

Dmitri couldn't imagine what would leave a scar like that. He must have almost lost his arm. His eyes travelled to his lower back and exposed hips, though there were no scars there.

Oscar pulled the robe back up, his face pink.

"Sorry," Dmitri said, feeling his own cheeks colour.

He leaned toward the pool beside him and cupped his hand.

The cloudy water tingled his skin, and he splashed some over his healed shoulder, then more over his chest, and rubbed it in with his palm.

"No, I..." Oscar paused awkwardly. "I just...it's been so long since I've seen anyone but Mum, and I've...I've thought about you so much. I mean, I missed you, but also I'm..."

Dmitri looked back. Oscar was frozen, silenced, like a deer in headlights.

"You do not have to be nervous, Oscar," Dmitri said gently.

"I just...don't want to disappoint you." His voice sounded as small as only Oscar's could.

"You could never disappoint me. Oscar...I feared you were dead. We all did. Finding you...I would gladly stay here with you for eternity if it meant being by your side, even if you didn't want me within ten feet of you."

"What if I've changed too much?"

Dmitri heard more scuttling nearby in the darkness, and Oscar scowled in its general direction. It quickly stilled.

"Oscar...you don't have to be who you were before. I'm just happy to find you however you are. I will help you however I can. But you should know that...I've changed too."

Oscar cocked his head as though confused. "How?"

Dmitri almost laughed in hysteria. "I...I thought you were gone. I...I didn't want to be without you. I did things—terrible things. Whatever I had to do to get more information on how to find you. Whatever amends I made with my search for humanity in the decades gone by, I lost it all again...searching for you. I did anything...I *would* do anything for you. To have you safe. My body..." Dmitri gestured to his pointed, furry ear and his burned neck and shoulder with his clawed hand. "I fear I'm more monster than man now."

Oscar looked confused. "You look just how I remember, though the scars are new."

Now it was Dmitri who stared back in confusion. He looked down at his shifted hands and black, pointed nails.

Swallowing, Dmitri steeled himself before he glanced to his reflection in the pool beside him.

His face was harsher, jaw square and stretched, tufted with fur. His teeth were large and pointed, eyes like burning pools of liquid flame.

I do not even recognise myself. So how...?

"It's been fifteen years, and now you're here. You're everything I've ever wished for. It's like a dream. I feel like now...*I'm* the monster."

"Iubite..."

"I have that thing inside me. It killed people, Dmitri. It's part of me, and it makes me...*hungry*."

"I know."

"Do you think I can ever..." He trailed off.

"Oscar, would you like to come closer to me?" Dmitri asked

gently.

Oscar sat in complete silence for a moment, then nodded.

"Come."

Oscar stared at him blankly for a moment before stepping forward.

Dmitri's heart pounded in his chest, but he remained still.

Slowly, Oscar made his way closer.

The scuttling from the shadows sounded again.

The headvys sensing fear.

"It's okay, Oscar. It's me. I'm here. Take all the time that you need." Dmitri kept his eyes fixed upon him.

Oscar swallowed. The sounds from the shadows quieted as he took another step forward. A little more than a stride away, he stopped and lowered himself to the ground beside Dmitri.

Slowly, Dmitri reached his hand and placed it palm down on the stone between them.

Oscar stared at it for a long time before he did the same.

Dmitri did not move, but his heart continued to race.

To be this close...

To have him within reach was a beautiful torment after everything they had endured, but he kept himself still as the rocks around them.

Oscar's hand edged closer, and Dmitri let out a long breath as their fingertips touched, a shiver running through his body. He clenched his jaw, feeling his eyes well up with tears.

Oscar stared down at their hands but made no move to come closer.

This is what Geraldine meant. It is not just what and when but how and why. Oscar needs to be ready...or as ready as he can be, to go back.

"Everything is going to be alright, Oscar. I'm here now."

He did not know what he expected. For Oscar to break down and cry or draw away? To be overwhelmed with relief? But the one thing he didn't expect was the solemn, doubtful nod that Oscar gave before he looked up into the red skies above.

BE LONGING

Oscar led him to the back of the cavern and left him to wash where it branched off into a more secluded crevice. He had chased away the chittering many-legged things before he did, of course.

Dmitri pulled off the stiff robe and stood beneath the water that flowed from the edge of the cave. It did indeed sting as it touched his skin, and it felt like it was washing away more than the stink of sweat and dried blood. It felt like it was taking away a layer of *him*. A layer he wanted to be rid of.

The scar tissue at his temple and neck heated unpleasantly, like needles pressing into the sensitive flesh. He rubbed the water over his face, palms feeling strange on the fur around his jaw, fingertips catching on his jutting teeth.

There was movement nearby, and he closed his eyes and listened. None of this was what he had expected...but Oscar was close. He could hear him. The beating of his heart, his soft breath, the shift of coarse fabric moving over skin and stone...the change in the sound of the falling water within the main chamber.

Oh.

A different heat spread across his skin.

Oscar is washing, too.

Dmitri tried to push the thought from his head.

I must keep my distance and support, not guide. He has been through so much. All must happen or not happen within his own time.

He turned, letting the stinging water cascade down his back, flowing over the new fur at his shoulders, buttocks, and thighs. He lifted his left arm, gingerly cupping a hand under the water to rub against his armpit. As he twisted to do so, his field of vision picked up Oscar in the main cavern. He stood straight-backed beneath the large waterfall, his pale, lean body barely visible in the cascade.

Just as quick, Dmitri pulled his gaze away, feeling his cheeks heat. That heat spread to his chest and lower still.

He ran his eyes over his own body instead. His muscles were larger, yes. And other things had changed. He was much closer to monster than human now, for sure. He was no match for Oscar, but...he could at least protect him.

Dmitri closed his eyes, turning his back to the main cavern, moving his palms over his chest. He dipped his head under the flow, letting the liquid soak his hair, setting his scalp tingling, and covering his good ear and neck. He rubbed at his face, blinking as he pulled away, shaking his head. His good ear cleared of water, and he realised that the sounds outside had changed.

Oscar had stepped out of the waterfall. He would likely be drying, and then—

Dmitri only caught his scent just as Oscar's fingers gently touched his shoulder, causing him to almost jump out of his skin.

How did he get so close, so fast?

Dmitri twisted, covering himself with his hands in time to see Oscar flinch away at his surprise.

"I'm sorry, I..." Oscar's face reddened.

"No...please. It's fine."

Oscar's eyes travelled down his body to where Dmitri's hands covered himself.

Dmitri felt heat pulse within him. "Is...everything okay?"

"I..." A slight shiver ran over Oscar's body.

"Oscar..." Dmitri's eyes had travelled down too.

Oscar wasn't dressed, but nothing below his ribs was visible. His lower half was fully clothed in...shadows.

Oscar cringed. "I...I'm sorry."

"You have nothing to apologise for. That's...incredible."

Shadowmancy was a high Theian form. For a human to...

No.

Oscar isn't exactly human anymore.

"It's useful." Oscar's cheeks were very pink. "I'm sorry. This was weird. I shouldn't have—"

"Oscar. I have been waiting for you forever. Every second that you have been gone, I have been longing for your return. Come to me whenever and however you please. I am yours."

Oscar's teeth captured his bottom lip, and his gaze hardened. Then, he stepped forward, the shadows slinking away. His face filled Dmitri's vision as he reached up, one hand moving to the back of his head, and pulled him down. The other firm on his chest.

Oscar's smaller body pressed against his, his hardness brushing against the backs of Dmitri's hands where he covered his own.

Dmitri didn't breathe. He let his impossibly tense body be manipulated as easily as possible. Oscar paused before pressing his lips against Dmitri's bottom lip, his large teeth making it difficult to do much more.

A burning heat spread from Dmitri's chest as he felt his hands struggling to contain himself, and Oscar tentatively pushed his tongue into his mouth.

It was a brief kiss.

A taste.

Cautiously, Oscar drew away but didn't step back.

Dmitri felt him twitching against him.

"I...don't know when, *if,* I can ever go back to normal, Dmitri. But...I want you to get to know the new me, too."

Dmitri's breath was hot. It was as if he had a furnace within him.

Oscar's gaze travelled down. "Why are you...covering yourself?"

"Oscar, I...I told you I've changed too. You may not like the ways I have."

Oscar looked at him in confusion. His eyes widened, then a glint appeared within them. "What if I want to get to know the new you, too?"

His hands slid down Dmitri's chest, and Dmitri's breath caught as they continued to his own, gently pushing them aside and releasing him.

"Oh!" Oscar stared down.

Dmitri closed his eyes, not wanting to see Oscar's facial expression shift.

Instead, he heard his voice. "Wow."

Dmitri stayed very still.

"Well...that's going to be interesting."

Dmitri gasped as both Oscar's hands closed around him at once. He opened his eyes, groaning as Oscar leaned forward, offering Dmitri his lips while his hands continued to move. His own skirted Oscar's shoulders and arms, fingertips barely glancing his skin.

"I...it has been a long time since..." Dmitri growled.

Oscar pulled away, his nose crinkling. "Dmitri...I've been living in a cave with my Mum."

"Point taken."

Oscar bit his lip in that irresistible way, looking down at his hands as they worked.

"Oscar...may I...touch you?" Dmitri tensed as pleasure welled in him.

Oscar paused, eyes drifting up to meet his. "Please."

Dmitri leaned forward, pressing their bodies together, trapping Oscar's hands between them, and placed his arms around him. His left shoulder keened, but he forced the pain away. Nothing would stop him from doing this.

This close, he could feel Oscar's ragged breath, his lightly shivering body and racing pulse. Dmitri realised that he himself was shaking just as much from the barest of contact.

Oscar tilted his head to meet his kiss, his already small body seeming to shrink into his touch. Dmitri pulled him closer, as firmly as he dared without breaking Oscar's body. Oscar wriggled his hands from between them; one grabbed onto Dmitri's arm, and the other moved up to his face.

Dmitri flinched as it connected with the burned tissue of his neck and ear.

Oscar pulled away. "I'm sorry. Did I hurt you?"

"No," Dmitri replied, his voice trembling. "Just...I know how I look."

"You're perfect. You're the most perfect thing I've ever known."

Dmitri silenced any words that might follow with a kiss. His hands moved lower, gripping Oscar's buttocks, taking care that his claws did not bite into his pale flesh. Oscar whimpered, put his arms around his neck and pulled himself up, wrapping his legs around Dmitri's waist.

He's so light...

Or have I just gotten stronger?

He pushed his tongue into Oscar's mouth as he wriggled against him. Dmitri shifted his arms, moving to adjust Oscar and gain an advantageous angle, but pain lanced his shoulder, and he cried out instead.

Oscar slipped from his grip as Dmitri's left arm gave out, landing adroitly back on his feet.

"I'm sorry. I..."

"I guess we're a little out of practice," Dmitri said weakly. His voice shook, and his body hummed with need and anxiety. He had never dreamed he could have this again, and now that he did...he could barely contain himself.

Oscar bared his teeth in that strange way again.

Dmitri paused.

Is he...trying to smile?

Dmitri's heart broke in his chest all over again, and he gently cupped Oscar's cheek and brought their lips together.

Oscar's hands roamed his body as Dmitri pressed his tongue into Oscar's mouth once more. Oscar gently squeezed at Dmitri's uninjured bicep, raked his fingernails down his chest, and reached between his thighs, pressing just so.

They slid to the uncomfortable rocky floor, Dmitri sitting back against the wall, lost in a haze of pleasure. His head spun as Oscar moved down, setting to work hungrily with his mouth, bringing him close, then closer still. He seemed to sense the heat flushing across his skin and the electric jolts of pleasure that Oscar's touch sent through his body, knowing just when to stop and when to move.

Dmitri's hands set about doing the same to his returned lover. Kneading, gripping, pulling, pushing, relishing in the squirms and moans he elicited. He barely had time to register the absence of Oscar's mouth below before lips were on his own once more. Oscar moved to sit on his lap, grinding against him maddeningly, blue eyes alight with passion, working patiently until he could have him. Until they could be one.

Moments or hours could have passed in their joining.

Moans of pleasure and whispers of lust echoed, words of promises fulfilled and yet to come.

At least for now, time went away, and Dmitri forgot they were in a very special place in hell. Instead, he had everything he had ever wanted.

THE RED SKY hung ominously above, like a blood-soaked blanket.

Dmitri didn't dare close his eyes for long. Not here and now. But he wished for nothing more than to fall into a deep sleep, holding Oscar close to him until he awoke restored and hungry to have him again. For all he knew, they could both do that now, be without nourishment or water for weeks, until they would need anything but each other.

Oscar's head rested heavily on his chest, but his body seemed tense, paused on the brink of rapid movement—like a spring ready to uncoil into violent motion at any moment.

They had discussed as much as Dmitri could manage in the time they had. He had feared overwhelming him, but Oscar already knew about the world ending pressure, and Geraldine's belief that it was already too late. In fact, Dmitri got the distinct feeling that Oscar may know more than he did himself. So, instead, Dmitri told him about Zara and how he had led the creatures away from the gateway to buy her time to escape. About Paile, and that somehow, they would return Oscar's sister and Vandle to their rightful selves.

He tried to lay out the pattern of Oscar's life where he had fitted before, to show him what he had to go back to. What more they all had to lose if they weren't ready when the time was right —which was *everything*.

Oscar had taken it all stoically, each thing another straw on his back. He quietly processed the horrors until they had fallen into a long and easy silence.

"Does what count for a sun ever set here?" Dmitri murmured.

Oscar sighed tiredly. "I don't think you'd want it to. Things are horrible enough in the day. I can't imagine what might happen in the night."

Dmitri pondered that in silence for a while, pulling the smaller man closer.

"Did you...really never stop looking for me?" Oscar asked finally, his voice very soft.

"I couldn't."

"Couldn't?"

"Not even had I tried for years. There is a word in Romanian. It cannot be translated into any other language. *Dor*. I knew it, of course, but never truly understood what it meant until I was absent of you."

"What does it mean?" Oscar asked.

Dmitri sighed.

How can this feel so different?

How could he feel like there was hope again so quickly after sinking so low? And yet, how could his grip on that hope feel so weak, like its threads were thin and slippery, escaping his grasp even now?

The way he answered or wanted to answer Oscar truthfully, easily...felt *alien*. It was like he couldn't fathom not speaking like this again after what they had been through. But it wasn't so long ago this *had* been his life. And it had been longer yet for Oscar.

"Some would say it means longing or the profound absence of someone important. Now, I understand it as the utter compulsion to seek out what I am missing. To bask in its glow. *Your* glow."

Oscar was quiet for a moment before he replied, "I'm not so much the fountain of light these days, Dmitri."

"Is the light of the moon so different from that of the sun?" Dmitri ran his fingertips gently down Oscar's spine.

Oscar flinched at his touch, and Dmitri froze for a moment.

Then, Oscar nuzzled closer to him. They lay for a time, breathing and existing together, until Dmitri spoke again.

"Soon, I will take you home. And things will be—"

Oscar stiffened, squirming away from him.

Dmitri frowned, letting him move. "What's wrong?"

Oscar pushed himself up on one arm, looking away.

"Oscar..."

"You say it like I can just go back. Like everything will go back to normal."

Dmitri sat up, placing his clawed hand on Oscar's back. "I am sorry. I know it will not be that easy."

Oscar shook his head fiercely. "I don't know if I *can* go back, Dmitri."

"Is this...because you have changed? I told you, the runes that the Filii Terra placed on the mirror should not affect you. You were born on Earth and will be returning. You should be just as safe as me if I am not in my other form."

"I don't mean that." Oscar sighed, and his shoulders slumped. "Dmitri, I dreamed of being back. Being with you. With all of you. I dreamed it so much and for so long. Now, I'm not even sure what's really happened and what's dreams. When I dream it, I'm never...*me*? I'm still who I was. When I imagine really going back, I worry I won't know how to be that person anymore. I just feel like everyone will stare at me, wondering who I am. Maybe I really *did* die that night. I feel like that was a different life for a different person, and now...this is where I belong."

Dmitri opened his mouth, stunned. "Oscar...I don't understand. Are you saying you want to stay?"

"I can't stay. I know I can't," Oscar said miserably. "We have to go back. Mum and I have talked about it for ages. Going back is the only way to save everything from Belphegor and the pressure on the veil. It's just...I don't know where I *belong* anymore."

Dmitri nodded slowly, carefully unpicking Oscar's words. He let a silence settle before he spoke again.

"I will not say you belong with me, Oscar. I feel that in my heart, but I also know that you are more than that. You belong with yourself. That you share yourself with me has been the greatest thing in my life. You helped me realise that being a monster made me no less of a man. But when I lost you...I was reminded that being less of a man made me more of a monster.

"I have seen and done many things over the years. I cannot imagine the marks left upon you from all that has happened or how difficult they will be to manage. Going back after all this...it's never easy, even if it is possible. Still, I think it is better to move forward."

"But how can I do that? Everything will be different. I'm different." Oscar's voice was tight and shaking.

"I know. But you will have time to figure that out once you get out of here."

"*We* will have time," Oscar corrected.

"We," Dmitri agreed.

Oscar leaned against him. He smelled...different. It wasn't just the absence of humming in his presence or the deep scent of this place and its horrors in his skin. It was him.

Dmitri was accustomed to the scent of fear from humans; he had caused it himself enough. He also knew blood and sadness just as well. Oscar smelled of all of those. But also, Dmitri thought, of darkness itself.

"I can't do it without you," he said. "Until I saw you...I didn't know how far away I felt from who I'd been. But with you here, even though there is horror all around us, I feel safe. I feel like together we can do anything."

Dmitri felt his lips pull up in a smile, his teeth stretching against them oddly. "You sound like Frida Kahlo."

Oscar cocked his head. "Is she an ex?"

Dmitri chuckled, tracing his lip on Oscar's shoulder blade and earning a shiver. "No, iubite. But she wrote a beautiful poem about the lover you deserve. Everything I wish to be to you, forever. I will fly with you and never be afraid to fall."

Oscar rested against him again, his fingers trailing gently through the fur in the centre of his chest, eyes looking far away. "What about Zara and Marcus?"

"They will be happy to have you back, no matter what you have been through. I think they, too, know dor now, though I have not told them of this word. Even if you are not the same person, that doesn't mean you aren't *you*. Those who love you will always have a space for you to return to. They will still love you, Oscar. You just have to let them."

"I don't know if I can..." Oscar whispered. "These last few years, I've thought of nothing else but going home. But now, I don't know if there's a place for me anymore."

"There is," Dmitri replied firmly. "There always is."

"But I..."

Dmitri reached down, brushing his fingertips over Oscar's cheek, feeling the wetness of tears. "Oscar...I will not tell you that you are a better, stronger version of yourself. I cannot. You are no stronger than you have ever been. These terrible things that you have had to face...they have only stripped away layers that did not make your truth more obvious for you to see. No part of you is broken, Oscar. And when you leave, you will leave no part of yourself here."

"Everything that's happened...it's been because of the thing that I thought made me special." Oscar sniffled.

"But the strongest part of you—the part that truly makes you special—is the part of you that was always the most human. The parts that make you persevere."

"Sometimes...I wonder what's more powerful," Oscar said, his voice shaking. "Being the chosen one, or just being able to choose."

"It's okay," Dmitri said so softly he thought Oscar might not even hear, as though he might have been saying it to himself. "No matter what you choose, I will always be with you."

And then, Oscar wept.

TAXONOMY OF MONSTERS: THE SOULWINDER
(ANIMA VISCUM)

"Vile remnants of dead magick shaped by residual malice, the
soulwinder is oft dismissed as a cautionary tale for budding spell-
weavers. Able to nullify castings, it is fuelled by a powerful disdain
for magick users, and seeks kill them with prejudice. It is said that
the last soulwinder seen was in 1431 when it brought the famed
Maid of Orelean's her untimely death."

— EXCERPT: THE REVENANT'S ARCANUM

A TANGLED WEB

After as long as they dared to wait, Dmitri and Oscar put on the clothes he had packed in the bag he'd brought through the portal. Oscar put on a thin sweater. One of his favourites. The navy cotton swallowed up his slim body, and he had to take the tie from his robe to weave through the loops of his jeans to make them tight enough as to not fall. His feet remained bare. Dmitri cursed himself for not having thought to bring him shoes, but little practicalities escaped thought when planning to rescue your loved one from a dark dimension. For himself, Dmitri had jeans and a simple black shirt that had gotten caught on his teeth and felt stretched and close to tearing at his shoulders.

"So, are you ready?" Oscar asked, looking at his clothes as though they, rather than the leafy robe, were the abnormal attire.

"Yes. Let's return to your mother. She will travel with us back to the gateway. Let's go home."

Oscar kicked a stone, staring into the darkness where it saw off a few more lingering headvys in a chittering scurry. Then they made their way back through the jagged corridors, hand in hand.

Oscar moved slowly, despite this being his home. It was as though he did not quite know the way or want to take it.

Movement in the burrows was livelier now. Two strange, pale

insectoid beings with four arms and chitinous, pale bodies followed them for a while. Dmitri eyed them anxiously, but when the pink blob creature and eel-thing found them again, the insects dropped away.

"What's happening?" Dmitri whispered.

"They like me, but they don't much like each other." Oscar shrugged. "Elodie and Garshok keep the others in line—" He stiffened, then released Dmitri's hand and darted ahead.

"What?" Dmitri asked, trying to follow as quickly as he could.

Oscar bounded through the darkness smoothly. Dmitri cursed as he clumsily scraped his shoulder, unused to his new size.

Dmitri heard the voices before he smelled her. He launched himself faster down the tunnels, arriving only a moment later than Oscar, albeit panting.

Geraldine Tundale sat on the edge of the fungi bed, arms folded and tapping her foot.

Before her, dried blood streaking one side of her pale, angular face was...

"Lyn?" Dmitri panted. "What happened? Is Zara..."

"Zara is fine," Lyn snapped dourly. "It seems she could not overcome her barrier to make it through the gateway."

Dmitri grimaced.

"What do you mean she couldn't overcome her barrier?" Oscar shook his head, confused.

"Apparently, there was some kind of metaphysical challenge to gain passage. She is still very much human, it seems, no matter how powerful she has become."

Dmitri did not miss the hint of pride in her voice.

Geraldine cleared her throat, her eyes fixed on Oscar significantly.

Oscar nodded. "It's really her..."

"Of course it is," Lyn snapped. "I got through relatively easily. Nothing can quite prepare you for seeing the shredded faces of former victims of your spite, but knowing they weren't exactly *real* helped me handle it."

"What did *you* face?" Oscar tilted his head at Dmitri.

Dmitri frowned. "Nothing."

Lyn's eyes widened, and she folded her arms. "I had to go through that, and you got the fast-pass?"

Oscar reached out and took his hand, a look of understanding in his eyes.

"Maybe it's because I'd already had the worst thing I could imagine happen," Dmitri replied.

Lyn rolled her eyes. "Spare me. Anyway, *that* wasn't the worst of it. The mirror challenge I was ready for. What I wasn't ready for was a wretchedly powerful thing bleeding darkness with giant horns."

"She met Belphegor," Geraldine clarified with a knowing smirk.

Oscar made a noise that sounded almost like a hiss.

Lyn's scrutinised him, and she smiled. "Oscar. It's...surprisingly good to see you."

Oscar tried another smile. He almost did it this time. "You too, Lyn."

"No hugging, though, if you'd be so kind. I'm not sure what stinks more, this place, you, or the dog."

There was movement behind them as the pink blob and the eel-faced Theians arrived.

"Oh, Zara, Marcus, so glad you could make it," Lyn continued drolly.

"Lyn," Dmitri warned.

"Oh, please let me spend some venom. I just got chased by an Umbran-fuelled gugalanna."

"Thank you for coming," Oscar replied instead.

Lyn's dark eyes twinkled. "I'd be lying if I was to say I came for you. I have unfinished business with this place."

Dull realisation settled on Dmitri.

"Lyn. Now you're here, you cannot—"

"Don't start." Her eyes flashed at him in warning. "We don't have time for happy reunions, bickering, or lamenting. Whatever you two were fiddling about at, I've been here long enough for our kind host to introduce herself *and* catch me up on what's been going on. That horned thing...it's close, and it looks like it's bringing an army."

"Yes." Geraldine arched an eyebrow, smirking. "You have been gone some time. What kept you?"

Dmitri glanced at Oscar, who looked right back before his cheeks coloured, and he quickly averted his gaze.

"Uh...nothing. Just...there was a situation. I handled it," Oscar said ungracefully.

Lyn sighed. "I bet you did."

Oscar choked in response.

"How did you get away from Belphegor?" Dmitri asked.

"You forget yourself, puppy. I am stronger than you. Seconds in this world restored me to a strength I have not had since, well, a very long time." Lyn's eyes flashed yellow. "I can even hold the form of my choosing. Imagine that!"

Dmitri narrowed his eyes, rubbing the fur on his jaw.

"Good," Geraldine said curtly. "You will need every bit of that strength and more. And don't tease him. He's still figuring himself out."

Lyn pursed her lips. "He'd better figure fast."

"It seems we are presented with more of an ultimatum than an opportunity, but with Belphegor coming to us, the parallax should be relatively unguarded." Geraldine smiled sadly, her eyes drifting to Oscar. "We're going to have to move faster than we ever thought, love."

"Really?" Oscar breathed.

Geraldine cocked her head toward Lyn. "If the world parallax truly is draining the excess hate from this place, Belphegor will be desperate. Since it cannot pass through the gateway, it will do everything possible to stop *us* from doing so out of spite."

Cold panic spread across Dmitri's skin. "So, its forming an army? For us?"

Geraldine nodded.

"What do we do?" Dmitri's voice was barely a rasp.

Oscar moved beside him, fists clenched and knuckles white.

The shadows seemed to throb around him.

"We fight."

~

LYN'S FACE had been difficult to read when she was properly introduced to the un-cursed Theian remnants living in the warrens. Dmitri was introduced at the same time, but with Lyn being a pure Theian of high standing, all their attention was on her. Elodie and Garshok were but one thing to handle. She had visibly flinched when the snivelling, tentacle-faced Rayth reached out with one gooey hand, only to bump up against the bloated, translucent body of Guber. It was at this point that Dmitri realised Oscar had named these creatures. Oscar continued the attempt of pleasant introductions as the Theians filed past the entrance of the room. Some snapped, pinched, and bit impatiently at each other whilst waiting for their turn.

Of course, this was Lyn Ocampo. So, when things looked to not be under her control—which took only about a minute—she snarled to the creatures using a harsh tone that Dmitri knew in his bones was spoken in Old Theian. He could feel what she was saying himself, though he didn't understand the words: *I'm here now, listen to me, and you just might live.*

"How many are there?" Dmitri asked as a tall thing with several eyes on stalks and four crabbish claws clicked excitedly at Lyn before she waved it away.

"In total, a little under two hundred at present, though the venemwhirlers are currently hatching," Geraldine replied. "All of the high Theians perished early on in the Umbran's war from what I understand, so having one such as Lyn here is quite the novelty."

"I SAID DON'T TOUCH ME!" Lyn barked at Garshok, who was tentatively reaching to prod her with one gooey, pink finger.

346

"Weird that there're more high Theians on Earth now than here, right?" Oscar said thoughtfully as he turned to Dmitri. "I mean, even though you're not high Theian, the fact that you can shift and use a form of glamour means that you're like...second generation or something?"

Dmitri's eyes shifted to Geraldine, and she smiled knowingly.

"My mother. She was a high Theian. Catalina Cel Tradat," Dmitri said carefully.

"Your mother was Catalina?" Lyn's head snapped around, black eyes brimming with curiosity.

Dmitri cleared his throat. "Apparently, yes."

Lyn sniffed. "She was one of the oldest of your kind. The most powerful. She lived for longer than anyone even knows before she disappeared. Strange to think that *you* are the progeny of one such as her. I mean, you didn't even have wings when we first met."

"He's got them now," Oscar said defensively. "He just needed a Theian protein shake, is all."

Lyn shrugged, turning her attention back to a short, stony thing that looked suspiciously like a gaeant. "I suppose it depends on the quality of the father. Perhaps she chose a runt of another litter to breed with."

Dmitri frowned.

My father.

He had few memories of his childhood, other than starving in solitude and dripping blood in the worn backstreets of Romania.

As far as he knew, he'd never *had* a mother. That was, until he had been taken in by a woman named Natalia who'd claimed to be his aunt, who had taught him to fight, hide, and hunt. She had been the one to tell him who his mother was, that she had fled with him from the Russian Empire but been forced to leave him on the streets.

She was the one who had originally held the axe, Nenorocitul Dracului. But they had never spoken of his father.

Beside them, the stream of Theian creatures was at its end, and Lyn shooed Elodie and Garshok out of the entrance.

Lyn turned to the group, one of her thin eyebrows quirking irritably. "So, we're facing overwhelming odds, power, and numbers. What we have leftover of my kind are effectively the dregs. I mean...I've worked with worse ragtag groups of misfits, as you know, but what's the good news?"

Geraldine met Oscar's eyes for a moment. "That when Oscar goes through the gateway, the remaining parts of the Umbrans here should all substantially weaken, then die."

"What?" Lyn cocked her head.

"Oscar has been imbued with abilities similar to an Umbran. A fragment of one's essence fused into his cells. He can absorb hate as they do and release it, either as benign energy or through the manipulation of shadows."

"The runt can do shadowmancy now?" Lyn flashed a glance at Oscar and smirked, impressed.

"What does that have to do with Belphegor?" Dmitri asked anxiously.

Geraldine's expression hardened. "I have placed a casting upon Oscar—"

"What..." The hair on what passed for Dmitri's hackles felt as though it wanted to rise.

"I understand your apprehension, but again, this is quite necessary," Geraldine replied primly.

"When will you stop playing at being a god?" Dmitri spat, missing the irony in his own words until they left his mouth.

"The partition in the veil that your friends have created is not enough. It is not sustainable, even assuming they can survive long enough to hold it open and weaken Belphegor's hold on this pace. But without a patch to the broken ecosystem, Theia will continue to shrivel and die. And thus, Earth."

"Oscar..." Dmitri looked at him.

Oscar would not meet his eyes.

"The casting that I have placed upon Oscar will bond him with the gateway, merging their energies to allow filtration even after it is closed."

"That sounds…impossible," Lyn said crisply.

"Thank you." Geraldine took the compliment smoothly. "I used a substantial portion of my power to do it."

"What will it do to him?" Dmitri felt like his chest had been hollowed out. Oscar still would not look at him.

You were keeping this from me, iubite?

"It will give him an incredible supply of power, albeit to a rather explosive degree in the first few moments when it really kicks in."

"You're describing bonding interdimensional energy with a human—well, *mostly* human body. I highly doubt the most significant concern is 'it makes him strong'." Lyn's tone was cool, and her eyes were fixed on Geraldine with distrust.

Dmitri felt a rush of gratitude. Geraldine once again looked to Oscar, and it was he who replied.

"I…won't be able to be far from the world parallax. I will need to be close for the energy to channel through properly."

"You will be…stuck in the cemetery? Forever?" Dmitri's voice sounded strangled even to himself.

Oscar shook his head. "If it works, and I, uh…don't get overwhelmed by the energy."

Lyn huffed. "That's an interesting way of saying 'explode in a shower of entrails'."

"I won't be stuck exactly. And not *there* precisely."

"He should be able to travel a mile or two from the location itself, but the bond will be permanent," Geraldine said.

The heat that lived inside Dmitri went ice cold.

If we were to go back and not do this, everything would end anyway. If we do this and then go back, Oscar will never live a normal life again. But…would he ever have?

"It may not be a permanent solution because we don't know how long Oscar will live. It may be fifty years or fifty thousand." Geraldine's tone was matter-of-fact, as though she weren't discussing the potential eternity of a utilitarian function for her child.

349

"It's okay, Dmitri," Oscar said resolutely. "I want to do this. I need to do this. We can be together, forever, if I live that long."

The chill in Dmitri was passing, but he was still as stone.

Would death be kinder?

Not if it was the death of everyone and everything.

Swallowing, he looked down at Oscar, his voice gruff. "Forever still would not be long enough."

This time, when Oscar's lips upturned, the corners of his eyes crinkled too, and a smile found its way back onto his face as though it had never forgotten where it belonged.

Lyn rolled her eyes. "Oh, do stop it. It's as nauseating as it is tedious."

Oscar ignored her. He shuffled awkwardly on his feet, pulling at the loose fabric of his jumper. "I'm going to go to the top of the caves to see if I can tell how long until they arrive."

"I will come with you," Dmitri said smoothly. Oscar shook his head in response, and Dmitri frowned.

"Mum will need to tell you the whole plan. We don't have enough time to, uh...get caught up again."

Lyn scoffed a laugh, and Dmitri felt his cheeks heat.

"Will you be okay?" Dmitri asked worriedly as Oscar stepped not toward the doorway but the shadows in the corner of the room.

Oscar nodded, looking a little confused. "Of course, I'll be fine."

Then, the darkness consumed him, and he was gone.

Dmitri stared into the space where he had been, longing to rush into it so perhaps he could follow.

Geraldine smirked. "Oh, don't start with the puppy-dog eyes. He'll be back."

"It's safe?"

"Oh, Dmitri. You don't think we spent the last decade cross-stitching quaint cushion covers out of plant fibres, do you?" Geraldine spared him a glance, those blue eyes sparkling enigmatically.

Dmitri grimaced. He did not like the idea of Oscar having to fight alone. Tentatively, he rolled his shoulder.

The pain is almost gone now.

"So, you have some kind of battle plan?" he asked.

Geraldine smiled. "Something like that, yes."

"No," Dmitri said, for what felt like the hundredth time.

Lyn had grown silent and was sitting at the edge of the mushroom bed.

Geraldine's eyes just regarded him with cool amusement. "You think I am asking for permission? Or even an opinion from you?"

"You can't do that to Oscar." Rage wound around his every syllable. And for the first time, he was grateful for his new rumbling tone.

"You seem to forget the most important thing," Geraldine said, folding her arms primly. "Without worlds, there is no Oscar."

"You said yourself that you could hold Belphegor at bay—"

"With my power as it is now, yes, for a while. But not indefinitely. I fear that waiting would likely lose any advantage we might have and reduce any chance of escape. I can think of far better ways to spend the power which remains to me." Geraldine turned and fussed over a concoction that involved some bloated-looking, blood-red berries. They popped as she mashed them with a rudimentary stone mortar and pestle.

"It is too dangerous. You cannot expect for Oscar to—"

"To say you love him, you have an alarming lack of faith," Geraldine cut him off sharply.

Dmitri seethed. But it was true.

When Oscar stood in the shadows with that dark energy throbbing strangely around him, he seemed so certain that he could fight whatever came.

But could he really?

Could that gentle soul really stand against...

Geraldine set down the pestle and moved to the hollow in the wall where various dried leaves hung. "I told you the plan, Dmitri, only because we can't risk you ruining it. You only really need to know one part. It's the most important part, and it's the only thing I want you to think about."

"Get Oscar out," Dmitri replied, even as the words left her mouth.

Content, Geraldine plucked a long, shrivelled leaf from one of the branches.

"Can you at least heal me? Can you take this thing out of my chest so that I can be at my full strength? Surely that is...something your powers could do?"

"Absolutely," Geraldine said curtly. "But I think that's something that is best to stay where it is for now."

"Geraldine..."

"Trust me, Dmitri." She winked, adding the dried leaf into the mix, followed by a pinch of crystalline powder she scraped from a rock with her thumb.

"How is it you have even more secrets than before?" Dmitri grumbled.

"Countless years to accrue them."

"And what do you think of this, Lyn?"

Lyn rubbed her chin thoughtfully, tapping one heel on the stone below. "Of course, I don't like it. I know when to run and when to fight. And usually, I prefer the latter. It seems like we're putting all our eggs into one...very fragile, pale, and thin little basket. In terms of the Theians, the slimy one will be relatively useful, and the one with a head like an egg has a knack for illusion that will be of use for hiding them from some of the lesser beings. Other than that, the rest of them are relatively useless. A bunch of party tricks so far as fighting is concerned. Couldn't you have rescued some more useful Theians?"

"As I said, most of the stronger ones died early on," Geraldine answered sadly. "Due to damage to the ecosystem, there hasn't been time for higher Theians to develop in some time. All the most powerful beings remaining carry the Umbran's touch and are not easily overcome."

"I am...not sure if this will succeed," Lyn said doubtfully.

Geraldine sighed. "If all goes to plan, this will keep all of us alive and two of you through the portal. It is Oscar that takes the greatest risk, not you. I wish you would both just trust me as he does."

"Would he say the same if he knew what you really were?"

"Don't." Geraldine raised a pointed finger to him, her blue eyes suddenly burning with a flash of power. Her voice was harsh. "Don't you say a word to him. You could ruin everything, and it changes nothing. Do you understand?"

"Fine," Dmitri snapped, staring at her a moment longer before he spun and headed toward the tunnels.

THE PAST, PRESENT, AND FUTURE

The warrens were difficult to navigate, but now that he was stronger, at least, it did not take long to find a hole that went almost vertically up to the top. That was where Oscar said he was going.

With his returning strength and agility, Dmitri quickly scaled the complex, though sweat and grime made short work of his clean clothes. As he neared the top, his sense of Oscar grew stronger. It was that familiar energy clouded with foreboding darkness. Soon, the red sky bloomed as he left the darkness of the caverns, entering a rocky outcrop at its peak. There, Oscar perched with unusual balance on a pointed ledge, hunkered down in a squat, staring into the distance. Dmitri wanted nothing more than to cry out in alarm and tell him to come back and be careful, but he stayed his tongue. Instead, he watched, breath half-held, until Oscar spoke without looking at him.

"There's a lot of them. Probably all that can still live under his influence."

"Your...mother. She has told me the *plan*." Dmitri tried not to sound sullen.

Oscar remained silent. He stood and walked back on the stone spike like a tightrope artist.

Dmitri's heart stopped in his chest, but Oscar never mislaid a foot. Dmitri stared at him, bile burning like fire in the back of his throat.

"I guess Lyn will be in charge of protecting the surviving Theians now, though I wish she hadn't nicknamed them 'The Dregs'. She will take them deeper in the caverns to give them the best chance possible whilst we make Belphegor's forces chase us..."

"That's not the part I have the problem with," Dmitri said weakly.

"Mum says that the pressure being released by the doorway is draining the ambient hate. Even I can feel the air is less thick with it. The hate that built up, the pressure, is easing. I get why Belphegor is coming. It's now or never."

Dmitri stared in the direction Oscar had been looking. He could see them. A dark mass of shapes on the near horizon.

"Oscar, I can fight," Dmitri said. "I'm almost healed. I will be able to—"

"No," Oscar said flatly. "You'll die."

"I would gladly—"

"No." Oscar's eyes widened, and he grabbed onto Dmitri's arms, squeezing tight. "You can't die. I...I need you."

"And I need you, iubite," Dmitri said softly, still staring at the approaching death. "As do your friends. I will die with a smile on my face and a song in my heart if it means you can live."

"You don't need to!" Oscar cried. "I...can't go back without you. I'd rather stay here with you and die together if it comes to that."

Dmitri clenched his jaw.

If it comes to that, I will not give you the choice. After the things I've done...

"Don't look like that. Don't look like you're going to throw yourself in front of them for me," Oscar snapped.

Dmitri gave a start.

"We need to do this *together*. Live or die, we do it together, okay?" Oscar put out his hand. "Promise?"

Dmitri stared at it. "Oscar...I..." He looked down.

Oscar's mouth was set in a straight line, his eyes burning with intensity.

"I cannot let you do this."

"I don't think it's your choice," Oscar said bluntly. He raised his hand.

Slowly, jaw clenched, Dmitri reached out, took it, and gently pulled Oscar into his arms.

This can not be the last time for this.

It cannot.

It was as they stood on the ledge that Dmitri first heard the wretched shrieks and howls approaching from the horizon.

DMITRI MADE his way back down into the caverns.

Going down was worse than going up, and he obtained a few more scratches and a split in his shirt over his shoulders at the back before he found the bottom once more.

Lyn had been waiting, leaning against the craggy wall, arms folded and face severe.

"Do you trust her?" she asked bluntly.

Dmitri rubbed at his sore palms and rolled his shoulders. "I do not trust anyone except Oscar."

A smile quirked Lyn's lip. "And yet it seems he kept this from you."

Dmitri scowled. "You are not exactly the person I would seek relationship advice from."

Lyn raised an eyebrow. "Wise."

There was a moment of tension.

Dmitri tried to relax and took a deep breath. "I... Thank you for coming. I know it means nothing—"

"It means something, dog." Lyn's tone was almost *affectionate*.

"Odds are, we're all going to die. I just chose which side to die on."

Dmitri grunted. "In any case, I am grateful for your help."

Lyn sniffed. "Not much use since I'll be running away with The Dregs. We shall see about that when the time comes."

"I think it may be best to follow her plan."

"The ethernal's?"

"That is not what she is anymore. I think that the human in her has *grounded* Whisper. He was cool and...difficult. Geraldine was not so different, barring her temper. But together, what they have become seems...*better*."

Lyn nodded thoughtfully. "Funny, the impact that humans can have on us."

Dmitri smiled. "You still love her, don't you?"

Lyn's eyes fled from his, scouring the tunnels as though Zara might pop out at an inopportune moment and hear the admission. "Do you know why I like these shoes?" She tilted her impractical heel. Though grubby now, it still looked...*expensive*.

"It will do as another weapon in a pinch?" Dmitri guessed.

Lyn smirked. "They're fragile. Temporary and beautiful, but strangely...powerful."

"Are you comparing humans to shoes?" Dmitri raised one thick brow. Not as easy as it used to be with his now altered face.

Lyn sighed tiredly. "No. I mean, maybe a little. But sometimes what you want isn't practical or right, but it makes you feel...*good*. Safe, strong, or better than you were before. Shoes like this were my first experience of that. I suppose the relationships I made with humans were a kind of...natural evolution from there. Would you like to know the *worst* thing I've learned from them?"

"Is it something terrible?"

"For certain kinds of love, there is no past, present, or future tense. Only...*love*." Her mouth twisted in distaste for her own words.

Dmitri chuckled. "I understand that."

"Do you think this is going to work?" Lyn asked.

Dmitri cocked his head.

"I mean...going up against what is effectively a primal being formed of millennia of condensed festering hate and—against all odds—fleeing miles across a treacherous terrain to leap through a doorway between worlds and suck the poison from Theia like drawing venom from an already rotting corpse?"

Dmitri shook his head. "I...don't see that we have any other choice."

"Oh, don't get me wrong, I'm not saying that I don't want to. Honestly, at this point, we're all probably going to die anyway, so we may as well make it fun..."

"You're really something."

Lyn tapped her lip with one nail. "I was also wondering...do you think that you might have more in common with them than you think?"

Dmitri tilted his head. "With humans?"

Lyn nodded. "A child of Tradat would be a savage foe. Given the stories..."

"I had my times," Dmitri said softly, feeling a stab of shame. "I have my stories."

"I just wonder whether your father was..."

Dmitri looked at her sharply, frowning. "I mean...I suppose he could be? I've never much thought on it."

"Hmmm."

"What?"

"I just wonder if that's what *this* is about." She gestured languidly at his altered form.

Dmitri frowned deeper as he remembered Geraldine's words about something inside him not being a wolf at all.

There was a deafening crash from above.

THE TURNED TABLES

Geraldine rushed down the burrows, her eyes wide, bone staff clutched in her grip. A moment later, Oscar emerged from the shadows beside her. He looked even paler than before.

"They're here," was all he said.

"Are you sure you do not want me to fight?" Lyn's tone was sharp, as though she already knew Geraldine was making some incorrect decision.

"When the tainted break the defences, you will be all that stands between them and the ones we have been able to save. Escape is the absolute priority, followed by survival, with battle as the last resort. But should battle be required, they would not stand a chance without you," Geraldine said firmly.

A Theian with a face full of tentacles ambled behind her and made a strange barking noise of discord. A hiss from Lyn set it to silence before she sniffed irritably and kept her peace.

"I would feel greater at ease if you were using the weapons afforded to you," Dmitri said.

"I am well aware of the weapons available," Geraldine replied tartly, that eyebrow arched once more. "I have survived here for longer than you can imagine, so I suggest that you have faith in my capabilities."

Dmitri growled in unsatisfied concession.

"When they arrive, the Theians and Lyn will head deep into the burrows. We will draw them off and lead them on a chase to the gateway."

"Lyn," Oscar said. "Please be careful. I want to tell Zara that you are safe."

Lyn looked uncomfortable. "Oscar...we have not been together for some time."

"I know you're important to her. Important to me. To all of us," Oscar replied.

A slow smile spread across Lyn's face. "You are a good...mostly human, Oscar Tundale. I am sorry for trying to use up your life force to part the veil between worlds."

Oscar stared at her for a moment and let out an awkward chuckle. "I forgave you for that ages ago."

"I am sorry nonetheless," Lyn repeated.

"Good." Geraldine's eyes twinkled. "My son may have forgiven you, but I may have had a few choice words before we parted ways if not for that apology."

"Good luck," Lyn said firmly. "If you succeed, Theia will need one to lead the way to recovery. To protect it and..." Her lips twisted with distaste. "*Nurture*."

Dmitri shot her a grim smile. "A queen, you mean. To *rule*."

Lyn grinned, her eyes gleaming yellow. She did not reply but instead looked to Oscar. "I left quite abruptly, so I would like you to do me one last favour, though I doubt I deserve it. If you return—*when*...tell Zara that I found my *why*."

Another thunderous crash sounded from above. Dust and rock showered all around them, followed by a howling roar.

"Oscar. Just as we discussed, you know what to do," Geraldine said firmly, bracing herself against the wall with one hand.

Oscar spoke quickly. "They're attacking from above, trying to drive us out by threatening to bury us in the mountain. No need to break the wards that way. It's one of the big ones...the fliers. There's a few of them, um..."

Geraldine waited patiently, even as another crash sounded from above and more debris showered.

"A snallygaster?" Oscar finished.

"Yes," Geraldine agreed.

Snallygaster? Dmitri had merely only heard of those before.

"If they're attacking from above, we head out from the side and draw them away," Geraldine continued.

Another crash.

Oscar's words came out in a rush. "When you leave the tunnels, however, the wards will weaken enough to break, given enough distance and pressure upon them. So, the forces will likely divide in two; one to give chase to you, and the other to enter the caves."

"So..." Geraldine prompted.

"So, for you to head out from the side, I need to aggravate them. Draw them into a frenzy and encourage more of them to pay attention to me."

Geraldine nodded. "Good."

"And then..." He trailed off, his eyes shifting between Dmitri and his mother.

"You run," Dmitri finished.

Oscar's eyes met his anxiously.

Something gnawed inside Dmitri's chest.

"You are ready for this, Oscar. You have prepared," Geraldine said.

Oscar flexed his arm, frowning while rubbing at the place where Dmitri knew the thick, white scar separated below his elbow and forearm.

"Oscar," Dmitri urged. "Are you sure you can do this?"

"It's okay, Dmitri." Oscar shifted nervously on his feet. "I can use the shadows. If I draw enough energy, I can shape them into the scariest things I can imagine."

"You don't have to do this alone." Dmitri reached out and took him in his arms.

"He must," Geraldine said firmly. "You need to *let* him, or you will not survive to take care of him afterwards."

Dmitri hissed through his teeth, torn between his need to protect Oscar and his desire to believe in him.

Another crash sounded. This time it reverberated so loudly, several clumps of stone fell loose. Dmitri thought they had delayed too long and that they would all soon be entombed.

But the caverns held, and the dust settled among the sound of panicked breathing. There was a keening wail, and the pink, gooping creature, Garshok, emerged from one of the tunnels.

"I will take them," Lyn said imperiously. She looked slightly grey and suddenly not so keen to fight anymore. "All of you...die well, and preferably on some other day." With that, she moved to Garshok, snapping at him in Theian before they disappeared into the tunnels.

"Oscar..." Dmitri started.

Oscar wriggled out of his arms, his small hands taking hold of two of Dmitri's large, clawed fingers. He squeezed once and let go. "It's okay, Dmitri. You protected me more times than I can count or even know about. Now it's my turn to protect you."

And with that, he disappeared into the shadows.

GERALDINE LED the way down a narrow passage Dmitri had not seen before. Red light broke into the tunnel as they reached the outside. A huge millipede-type creature on hovering wings loomed. It waited with several other dark insectoids, all somewhere between oversized crabs and ticks scuttling around, discoloured and dripping with the wretched darkness of the Umbran's taint. Geraldine held out her staff and, in a flash of blue light, burst apart the earth amidst them, sending them scuttling away, screeching and buzzing.

"Oscar," Dmitri moaned.

"Oh really, Dmitri? You've been around centuries, and your

vocabulary is so limited to be my son's name and a handful of miserable complaints?" She cast another blue bolt at the millipede, scorching away one of its wings. It fell to the ground, thrashing, its long stinger dripping viscous poison as she sent it away with concussive force.

"Will he be okay?"

"I really think that question can be extended to us all right now." She scowled. "He is ready for this, has been ready for this, for some time now. That is the best that any of us could ask."

Dmitri nodded and tried to swallow down some of his fear.

"Now move, or they'll all be on us before anything comes to fruition." Geraldine cast a shimmering wall of pale blue light, using it to push away the advancing shadows.

A surprisingly low number of them followed as Dmitri and Geraldine fled. So few that Geraldine stood atop a low outcropping, goading them with blasts that parted their numbers. They still lingered at the caverns, jaws snapping and pressing against the wards.

"It's worse than I expected," Geraldine grumbled, grinding the base of her staff into the stone beneath her. "Belphegor must have told them not to let up on the warrens, even with us and Oscar as bait."

Dmitri glanced among the bizarre and twisted shapes crowded around the mountainside. He did not have to look long to find Belphegor.

The enormous creature's body appeared amidst them. Its vast horns pointed at the sky, ichor dripping from its every orifice, crusting its eyes and nostrils as it stared up...up toward the mountain peak.

Dmitri followed its gaze.

Up above...the snallygaster? No, two of them. Three.

Massive wings hammered by the peak, their giant serpentine bodies arcing through the sky as they attacked the mountaintop again and again.

The mountaintop? Or Oscar, who is already up there?

A chill passed over Dmitri's skin as he imagined Oscar trying to fend off the things, huddled behind a rock and shaking. His eyes were drawn back to Belphegor.

The cursed bull stared straight back at him, rolling its impossibly muscular shoulders. Its eyes were like holes that had been punched into reality itself, a draining vacuum of nothingness.

For a moment, he thought he saw it smile.

It opened its mouth, black ooze dripping from its crusted lips, and let out a single bellow, still staring in their direction.

Above, one of the snallygasters broke off from the others, its serpentine body sailing through the air. Dmitri saw its face was long, jaw almost like an alligator's, though the whole thing was roughly the size of two articulated lorries strung together.

"Move," Geraldine snapped, placing an arm before him.

A bitter sense of dread set into Dmitri as the snallygaster let out a screeching roar and twisted its body in their direction.

Belphegor has sent it after us.

Dmitri's muscles tensed, ready to fight or flee as molten power pumped from his chest into his limbs.

But the snallygaster paused halfway, not attacking, simply barring their path.

A sick feeling settled in Dmitri's stomach. Belphegor hadn't sent the snallygaster to attack.

It...wants us to watch.

Then, something else moved from the mountaintop. The fire pumping through Dmitri's veins snuffed out and became ice in an instant.

No.

Not something.

Someone.

Oscar's small, thin body tumbled through the red sky, arms and legs splayed.

Dmitri let out a small moan, stepping forward, but Geraldine's arm pushed hard against his chest.

"Wait," she said simply.

Dmitri's heart froze, eyes uncaring for the advancing snally-gaster focused only upon Oscar, though the two *were* growing rapidly closer to each other.

Oscar...had not been knocked from the top of the mountain. He had leapt.

With unerring accuracy, Oscar collided with the snallygaster.

The dark, slithering, winged shape curled in the sky, body spasming and twisting as though in pain, trying to buck him loose. Dmitri lost him for a moment in the chaos, but then something incredible happened.

The snallygaster's black wings lightened. Like oil being drained, the dark feathers became paler. Flecks of lurid blue and gold became visible in its plumes. Its body, too, altered, with dark scales fading to a polished green.

For a moment, it stilled, falling like a stone in the sky.

Dmitri would have spoken, but his breath was trapped in his chest.

Then, those brilliant wings opened, and it spun in the sky. It let out a howling roar of victory.

No. Of freedom.

The snallygaster swooped down low, buffeting the snarling and growling creatures on the ground with a blast of its wings.

Atop it, Oscar clung tight, teeth bared, eyes wide and filled as black as the deepest night.

Oscar and the snallygaster soared through the air before advancing back and charging the hoard of monsters, aiming directly at Belphegor.

"He has cleansed it of Belphegor's touch," Geraldine explained. "I imagine it has quite the bloodlust for its tormenter right now."

Indeed, the thing wasted no time lashing out with its dripping fangs and barbed tail. Several beasts got knocked aside, but Belphegor stood firm, massive hands rising to take on its challenger.

Its huge, knotted fingers clutched at its jaws, forcing them shut. Dmitri saw dark spreading up its maw, taking over its eyes once more. But Oscar reared up behind its neck, and the darkness faded faster than it appeared.

The monstrous bull roared and twisted viciously.

Dmitri heard the popping of vertebrae from where he stood.

The snallygaster's body twitched and grew limp.

"The beast grows desperate," Geraldine murmured.

"Oscar..." Dmitri hissed.

Belphegor released the snallygaster's head, letting its body drop to the earth.

Dmitri saw Oscar roll out from beneath one of its beautiful wings.

Belphegor raised one massive hand and barked gutturally. The creatures that had been tentatively approaching Oscar edged back.

The massive, cursed bull strode forward, fingers gripping the air as though they were already crushing Oscar's bones to dust, a look of ruthless hunger in its eyes.

He looks so small and fragile.

"Trust him," Geraldine said, though her voice was very stiff. "He can do this."

Dmitri watched as Oscar turned...and ran. He ran faster than Dmitri had ever seen him run before, faster than he had ever seen any human run. It took him a moment to realise it wasn't just Oscar running.

The shadows at his feet, the shadows from him, weren't resting as normal shadows would. They were rising to meet his pounding soles and pushing him away, propelling him at break-neck speed from the Theians that chased him.

Only, that still wasn't fast enough.

Belphegor roared and its creatures gave chase.

The snallygaster barring their path banked in the air, joined its fellow, and circled overhead, ready to swoop. Several of the tainted Theians moved with incredible speed. Forms with loping grace and bodies like panthers with massive snapping jaws gained on him rapidly.

Oscar ran as fast as he could, but he was still too far. They were almost upon him.

Dmitri stepped forward, opening himself to the well of energy roiling within his chest.

"No," Geraldine said flatly, raising a hand to stop him. "Let him be."

"He's not going to make it," Dmitri moaned desperately.

"He's not. But you must have faith in him."

The first of the monsters reached Oscar, its jaw latching onto his calf, and he cried out, tumbling.

Dmitri roared, lurching forward, but Geraldine's hand pushed him back with more strength than she had any right to.

The pack of Theians huddled around Oscar's fallen form, twisting and writhing. Fighting over their meal, or...

Dmitri noticed that one of them had changed. It was no longer dark and oily but a pale grey with darker spots. It lumbered back from the frenzy, looking confused, then dashed away. Others were changing too, almost as quickly, breaking away from the pack and following the first to do so.

"It's better he starts with the smaller ones. Running is a good way to separate their ranks. The energy he takes from them will help him deal with the others, though no doubt cleansing a snallygaster has fuelled his power significantly already," Geraldine mused.

Dmitri stared at her, aghast. "What is he doing?"

"Oh, Dmitri." She smiled coyly. "As I said, we haven't been out here playing eye-spy. Oscar has been training. He's going to *fight*."

TAXONOMY OF MONSTERS: THE ZBURĂTOR

(ALES LUPUS)

Legend of the zburător includes the pterolycus, kludde, Managarmr, and Fenrir. Wings may be absent in modern descendants, but can be restored through the veil. Aura like midnight streaked with patches of moonlight. Territorial, fierce, proud, and prone to bouts of lonely brooding, it seems that the zburător can adopt a pack, and mate, to enrich its existence. Crossbreeding capacity remains unknown but hopeful in humans of all biological structures.

— ORIGINAL TAXONOMY ENTRY, MARCUS
WILLIAMS

VI

THE MONSTER MASH

THE UNINVITED

"Marcus! The barrier," Isla shouted. "It won't keep them out. The tattoo they all have...they're like Birger's. Magick won't work on them. They paid Linda for that and a bunch of other things."

She and a couple of the Filii Terra huddled not far away, stationed by the strange little Elder Sapling. They earthed the infant tree amidst a circle of tombstones. The mass of muscles, beard, and anti-magick tattoos shifted in anticipation beside Isla. Marcus was glad that Birger was on his side this time. The rest of their sparse number were stationed around the larger tombs nearby. All held weaker relics than Isla, but they could act as watchful eyes, at least.

"Paile, go!" Zara said. "If you don't, there might not be time."

Paile grunted, her eyes narrowing at the approaching figures. She spoke with Vandle's voice first. "These *people*. They are trouble. They are no longer human." Paige's voice followed. "And they're right fucking wankers, too."

Zara hefted Dmitri's axe over her shoulder. Marcus followed her line of sight and saw that she had spotted a familiar figure amongst those approaching.

Hunter.

Paile muttered curses in two voices.

"We'll handle it," Zara said firmly.

Marcus saw her knuckles whiten around the haft of the axe.

"Marcus..." Isla repeated.

"Let them come," Marcus said, his breath tight in his chest. *This is not what we need right now.*

Marcus watched the approaching figures as their auras swirled violently. Unlike most, their auras weren't clean with shifting shades. There was a raging torrent of conflicting forces, angry reds and violets crashing into yellows and greens as though they were at war. They were so intermingled they seemed to fight themselves into a constant, muddy flux. The woman walking at the front had an ocean of energies warring within her that made Hunter's aura look like a sad puddle.

The night sky rippled as the first of them stepped through the barrier.

Marcus guessed by the cut of her pristine, white pantsuit and the lustrous fur shawl over her shoulders that this was a woman accustomed to nothing but all the most beautiful things. She even posed like she was the most sublime figure there. Her pink flesh was puckered and raw, with not a single hair on her head. Behind her followed two dozen others, most of them suited in snappy matching outfits, though a few wore more fashionable garb.

Hunter lingered near the rear beside a small white woman with a white and purple punk haircut.

"Valeria Sands," Paige's voice dripped venom. It was followed by Vandle's. "She must be the head of the Order of Helios."

"Good evening," Valeria said smoothly. "Which one of you should I be speaking with about obtaining the mirror leaper?"

"Sorry, no swapsies," Marcus replied quickly.

Valeria frowned, a difficult expression with her burned off, snakeish lips.

"I bet the DICS wish they were here now," Zara said, barely in a whisper.

Apparently, Valeria had excellent hearing because she cackled in reply. "Oh, please. You think they have any power to stop us? We only let one of them infiltrate us long enough to keep track of what information you were being fed."

"Sourpuss?" Paige gasped.

"Don't worry. She died fast. Barely even had time to scream." Valeria bowed her head, smiling beneficently.

"You'll pay for that," one of Paile's voices hissed.

Marcus *thought* it sounded like Paige, but it had such a keen edge that maybe only Vandle could inject that much promise of death into the words.

"Paile, you need to go," Zara urged.

Grudgingly, Paile shifted away, only releasing her gaze from Valeria at the last minute before she sprung into a separate tall, gilded-edged mirror propped up nearby. It rippled as she disappeared to fulfil her tasks.

Marcus sighed.

So it begins.

That wasn't exactly true. This had all begun before tonight… before the girl shaped monster had turned up at the hospital years ago even. Marcus knew the worlds had been ending since the decision was made by the Filii Terra to barricade the veil. *This* wasn't the beginning at all.

This was the end.

"You should summon the mirror leaper back right this minute." Valeria's voice was imperious as she sashayed between the tombstones. Marcus saw now that her skin was not just burned, raw, and blistered, but rather raised, healing flesh.

Marcus forced a grin. "We're not really in the habit of doing what we're told, especially by rich white women wandering around where they've got no business."

"'specially ones that weren't invited and aren't welcome," Gax added.

Her gaze shifted to him, and the Bugge shivered.

"I wouldn' bother tryin' to eat me. I'll give you a right sore belly, you 'orrid cow," he mumbled, shuffling awkwardly under her scrutiny.

Valeria smiled, then cast an interested glance over at Isla and the others who watched her warily, then back to Marcus with one eyebrow raised. "Filii Terra? I'm surprised you can afford their rates."

Marcus shrugged. "Special discount when you're fighting the good fight."

"That's not how the *true* Matriarch tells it." Valeria smirked. "From what I hear, you're nothing but a usurper and some troublesome children playing at stopping the end of the world, and—"

"You need to leave." Zara's voice was burning with rage. Her eyes were fixed on Hunter, who was scowling and looking amongst the gathered faces.

He's looking for Paige, Marcus realised. *He really doesn't know what he's done.*

"Is...she—" Hunter began.

"None of your fucking business, dickface," Zara snapped.

Hunter's eyes hardened.

"This doesn't have to get nasty," Valeria said. "I have little to no interest in any of you. We are here looking for the one who can move between mirrors. I'm sure you can imagine her talents are worth a million times their weight in gold. Literally. We'll be taking her and the relics these rebels have stolen from the Filii Terra and returning them to where they belong. I'm assured we will then have unrivalled services for eternity."

"You'd better check yourself before I wreck yourself, Val. That's not gonna happen," Marcus growled.

Valeria's smile was slow and wide. "I won't lie. I was quite hoping you'd say that."

"You don't know what you're getting into, do you, you deep-fried bitch?" Zara asked flatly. She pulsed with spiritual energy, though just for a moment.

Valeria regarded her warily and took a few steps back toward her entourage. "I will say it once more: give us the mirror leaper and the relics you stole, and we will leave you be. I'll even let Paige live if she's still around, despite..." She gestured a hand to her blistered face. "*This*."

There was a moment of heavy silence, and then Zara let out a harsh bark of laughter. "Paige was the one that burned you? Good for her. Shame she didn't get any flames on pretty boy over there, too."

"We're not fucking around," Hunter snapped, stepping forward. "I didn't want to hurt her, but you don't know who you're messing with. The Order is *everywhere*, involved in all the most important power systems in the world. You don't stand a chance."

Marcus and Zara shot each other a look, and both grinned.

"What are you idiots smiling at?" Valeria snapped.

Marcus smiled in her direction. "Those are our favourite odds."

"Yup," Zara agreed.

Marcus felt Song step closer to his side, their fingers linking with his.

Valeria sighed, folding her arms. "Fine. I suppose we start pulling off limbs until you give up and make her come back then. I would suggest you don't take too long. You don't really have that many limbs between you."

Zara throbbed ghostly light like a warning beacon once more. "You might be surprised at that, too."

Nearby, Ed let out a rumbling growl, swelling to three times his previous size.

Valeria's eyes narrowed. "Maybe we'll start with the dog."

"Don't you dare touch my son." Marcus hardened his gaze. "If you do, I'll—" His skin prickled, and a cool sensation spread through his bones.

Then, there was a wretched, bellowing howl in the night, followed by an echo of snarling cries.

Valeria stiffened, looking around, her eyes wide. Her lackeys moved uneasily, scanning the surrounding night. "What the fuck was that?"

The horrible howl came again.

Marcus shot her a grim smile. "Those, my good woman, were the *real* monsters. They're almost here, and they won't be going anywhere soon. So, you really have two choices; settle in here with us and be good little monster-eaters or fuck around and end up out there and become a horrible paste on the cobblestones."

❦ 44 ❦

THE ENEMY OF MY ENEMY

The first monsters to arrive were a pack of scuttling things that looked almost like crabs but with birdish beaks and spiny shells. They bucked and scratched against the invisible barrier, letting out shrill, keening whines.

It wasn't long before more arrived.

Next were figures shaped almost like men, but with their limbs and bodies stretched, almost alien. Dangling fingers ended like talons, and their heads bore no faces at all, just flesh the same pallid grey as the rest of their bare bodies. They swayed and lurched, their talons scraping against the air where the Elder Sapling kept them at bay.

"What are you doing? Stop this right now," Valeria barked. She was eyeing the monsters with disdain, her burned fists clenched at her sides.

"You're attracting them here. Why?" Hunter sounded more afraid, at least.

The earth rumbled.

"That's the problem when you blow your cover before you find out all the details of the plan, Hunter Oakley of 'Enough is Enough'. Fuck, saying that is so cool. We're trying to save the worlds." Marcus' eyes travelled around more newly arriving creatures outside of the barrier. He saw some familiar shapes. He ached to sit and add the ones he didn't have to his taxonomy.

Large flapping monsters with heads similar to pincered insects circled above. Something else was humming in the night, too small to see.

Some kind of cool monster-bugs?

Many of their auras were beautiful. They weren't quite as bright and glittering as say Lyn's, but they shimmered wonderfully in vibrant hues. Each thrummed its brilliant colours with primal purpose and drive.

Drive to reach the gateway.

"What the fuck are you talking about?" Valeria snapped.

Zara sighed. "How much do you know? It's a long story."

"They know plenty," Isla said sharply. "The Order of Helios has access to information almost as detailed as the Filii Terra, not to mention a history of...working closely together."

"Fine. The short version then." Zara raised a hand, signalling Marcus to cover it.

"Barrier on the veil stoppering inter-dimensional energy leading to pressure-fuelled, world-ending clusterfuck. Releasing pressure with magick mirror until things are okay. But monsters like the energy, so keeping them out with little magick tree thing." Marcus grinned at Valeria as she shook her head, spluttering.

Outside the barrier, a huge moth-winged entity with a body that looked far more humanoid—though strangely translucent—was hovering nearby.

"Oh, shit! That's a mothman! It's so pretty! I thought they'd be creepy as hell!" Marcus cawed.

"Are you insane?" Valeria spat.

Zara shrugged. "Jury's out."

The ground shook again.

What was that?

"You can't just summon a hoard of monsters to a place like this! People will—"

"Got that covered, too. We're a government-approved rogue bunch of weirdos now. You probably noticed the evacuated streets and abandoned military set-up outside," Marcus supplied.

"It's the mirror," Hunter barked, pointing at the black, shimmering mirror beside Zara. "That's the thing that's attracting them all here."

Valeria's eyes were more than a little wild. "So, we get the mirror leaper, smash that thing, and get the fuck out of here."

"Oh, no single part of that sounds like a good plan for anyone involved," Zara said crisply. "Least of all, *you*. Let's make it easy for you. Burnt bitch hit mirror. Mirror go boom. Burnt bitch dead."

"Nice," Marcus added.

Valeria barked a harsh laugh. "We see things very differently. You think you've trapped us in here with monsters outside. I say you've trapped yourself in here with us. And we're far worse than whatever is out there."

"I think you need your eyes tested, then," Marcus mumbled.

"I count only a dozen of you and three times that of our number. Tell me, what's to stop us from just taking what we want?" Valeria's voice was growing more and more excited as she convinced herself of her certain victory.

"Just about everything?" Zara's voice was iron.

Valeria sneered. "You? With the spirit thing inside? Like I don't have ten men stronger? The one with the magick fingers and the scraps of the Filii Terra? Like we don't have repulsion runes on us? Or don't tell me, it's the ugly puppy that can get bigger, or turn into a poodle if it wants. And is that...a duck?"

Ducky gave a nonchalant quack.

"Ducky says she doesn't give a three-footed-fuck what you think," Marcus translated.

"You're pathetic," Valeria scoffed.

The earth rumbled again. Something tickled in Marcus' mind.

It was something that *definitely* was in his taxonomy.

It can't be. The barrier would work underground, too? Right?

"Take the woman first." Valeria raised a hand. Several of the burly men behind her broke off, walking toward Zara.

"Trust me, you *really* don't want to do this," she replied with a growl.

"Oh, I do." Valeria shrugged, and her fur stole slipped from one singed shoulder. "Don't worry, I'll try to leave you alive. I still need motivation for the mirror-witch to leave with us."

"Marcus," Zara said firmly. "Protect the mirror."

Something big shifted outside of the barrier.

Several of the smaller monsters let out cries, making space and moving away.

Marcus narrowed his eyes, staring at the space where whatever was frightening them *should* have been, *must* have been. But there was nothing there. No aura. A complete absence of—

The other auras faded in his vision. For a moment, the world looked entirely...*normal.* And then everything returned. He shivered.

No. It can't...

A deep sense of dread blossomed in Marcus' chest. He swallowed. "Zara, I uh...think there might be a soulwinder here."

"Marcus, do you hear me? Protect the mirror!" Zara bellowed. A bright glow erupted from her skin, and her ghostly armour projected from her being, encasing her within it.

Copy that. We need to keep the world parallax open, or this is all for nothing...

Marcus swallowed, and Song's fingers squeezed his in response. He looked to his side and met their eyes.

Fear.

He didn't need a sending to confirm.

Soulwinders weren't supposed to be real. They were bereft of...*anything.*

They could become invisible with a turn to the side and were untouchable by magick. But what was worse, they were also drawn to it with a bloodthirsty vengeance. They were a living nightmare.

"MARCUS!" Zara bellowed again, launching herself forward.

"Gotchya," Marcus yelled back, releasing Song's hand and striding to stand before the mirror. He rolled his neck. "None of these jumped-up monster gobblers will get by me."

Zara collided with the men with a thud of ethereal energy on flesh. Half of them bore the brunt of the collision, their bodies expanding with muscle and meat, skin stretching and tearing as the night filled with their roars.

One of the Order, a pale fellow with enormous arms and squashed features, was catapulted by the blow, and his swollen body sailed through the air, rolling even further when he landed. He was quick to recover, though. His snarling, veiny face looked furious, right until the moment he realised he had been flung outside of the barrier. Then dull shock echoed on his features before a set of massive jaws took off his head.

There was a harsh jet of blood from the stump of his neck from his over-inflated body before countless other monsters fell upon him, biting, scratching, clawing, and *feeding*. It was a ravenous frenzy of gore. The millipede creature that had taken off his head swallowed. It was the size of a giraffe. It had little interest in the man's remains, however, and instead began bashing its yellow segmented body against the barrier.

Marcus shook his head. "Oh. That was really gross."

Zara flung another one of the men. His body was torn, and bleeding muscles peeked through his flesh. He was thrown so hard that his body broke through several gravestones and tumbled limply beside Valeria. She pushed it away with one black boot and a look of disgust.

Two of the men clambered on the back of Zara's spiritual armour, and two others grabbed one of each of her massive, ghostly arms as she wrestled with them.

Marcus raised his hands, drawing on his power, feeling the spark of life bursting through his body like a boosted circuit. He focused his energy on Zara's attackers and tried to pull them away —like pulling ticks from a dog—but they were far too *slippery*.

The runes. Isla said they had anti-magick tattoos like Birger's.

"Take the boy. Do not fear the ethernal. They have no power here." Valeria smirked at the remaining figures around her, gesturing at Marcus.

Three of the Order of Helios made toward Marcus, though Hunter hung back with Valeria. The frontmost was the woman with the shock of white punk haircut streaked with purple.

"You don't want to fight us, magick-boy. Valeria only needs one of you alive," she sneered.

Marcus scowled, then snatched out a hand and lashed out with energy, flinging a clump of a broken tombstone with as much force as he could manage.

The punk woman yelped as it clipped her shoulder. It connected fully, however, with the gaunt man behind her, barrelling into his chest and carrying him through the air and beyond the barrier. A moment later, there were screams and snarls accompanied by the tearing of flesh and crunching of bones.

Marcus smiled darkly. "Funny thing about runes, Punk. Good for keeping off direct magick but not so good if I just chuck a fucking rock at you."

The woman snarled with a ferocity that belied her size and rolled her shoulder. It popped back into place with an audible clunk while veins bulged in her neck and face.

Marcus grabbed out with both hands, pulling at more of the stone Zara had broken loose with the second man's body, and hurled them forth.

Punk twisted with horrifying grace, slipping through the air between them. Most of her compatriots followed suit, dodging and rolling as the stone soared through where they previously stood, crashing into the night. They moved alarmingly fast, closing in on Marcus with a pincer movement with Punk in front.

"Ed!" Marcus snapped.

Ed barked in response, leaping to the left even as his body grew, swelling beyond the size of any natural Rottweiler. In an all too familiar way, Ed dragged one invader to the ground by his trousers as the man desperately batted him away.

Marcus let out a whistle, and the goon to the left disappeared with a pop.

Punk pulled up short, blinking at the space they'd been a moment ago.

"What did you—"

There was another pop from some distance away and a howling scream as the man was dropped from the sky into the waiting clutches of the monsters outside of the barrier.

There was one last pop beside him as Ducky returned and let out a disgruntled quack.

"Good work, buddy. Now...help Ed out?"

Ducky let out another quack and waddled over to Ed and the struggling man.

Punk sneered and lunged at Marcus with savage grace. He twisted his body, dodging her lunging blow, then raised his hand, catching her fist from her second strike.

Her eyes widened.

"What, you think I'd have the ability to trade flaws and not trade anything for being able to fight real good? Bitch, please." He waggled his eyebrows and then gave her a solid kick to the abdomen that sent her staggering back. "I told you. No one is getting by me."

The man struggling on the floor let out a gurgling cry, and Marcus saw that Ducky's pointy-toothed beak had found his throat, and blood was flowing freely as his struggle weakened.

Marcus turned his eyes back to Punk. "You're lucky you're fighting me, and not Ed and Ducky. They're way worse."

There was a pulse of light behind him. Marcus heard the cries before he saw the four men who'd been on Zara tossed loose. One landed outside the barrier and was made short work of by the crab-things pincers and beaks, but the other three survived the blast.

Zara flexed six massive arms of light and power.

"Holy shit, Zara. That's just about the coolest thing I've ever fucking seen."

385

Zara's smile was dangerous. "Toss me the axe."

Marcus flicked his wrist, and Dmitri's axe tore from the earth and spun through the air. Zara snatched its haft in one massive, glowing hand.

"What was that you were saying about not being a match?" she shot at Valeria.

Valeria hissed in response. She still had a few men and women whose bodies had shifted and swollen. Some barely resembled humans any longer and were closer to giant, fleshless apes.

"Enough of this," she commanded. "Kill them all. We will make the mirror leaper join us by other means. GO!"

The goons around her surged forth at her command.

Marcus heard Zara cry the activating words for Dmitri's axe. Enchanted flames lit the night as she carved through two of their number in a single blow, their burning remnants falling to the ground. More of them were on her, though, stronger than before.

Hunter rushed forward from Valeria's side, and his hands closed around the axe in Zara's fist, trying to pull it away.

Marcus sent a blast of earth, but it only aggravated him. He quickly turned his attention to the assailants making their way toward *him* now.

Punk had changed even more, her face scaled and eyes yellow. There was really nothing so different that would set her apart from some of the monsters he had seen. Well, nothing but the fact she'd eaten them to become that way.

Marcus dodged to the left, evading her fingers, which had now morphed to claws, as a bulky man with a shaved head lumbered closer, pulling out a gun.

Marcus whipped out with a hand, flicking the weapon from his grip. They hadn't been clever enough to put a rune on *that*, but the distraction meant that Punk's claws found a soft spot in his defence, and pain blossomed as they raked deep into his flank.

He stamped a foot, sending a shockwave of magick into the air. It pushed her away in a cloud of dust, but that meant the large man was closer now, and he snatched out with meaty fingers.

Marcus danced back, let out a low whistle, and raised his hand. A rush of feathers and webbed feet landed in his palm before he disappeared with a pop.

Marcus reappeared behind the large man in a flurry of space and colours, reaching out with one hand and pulling in a hefty slab of stone. He flagged it through the air into his back with a sickening thud as the man's immense body was thrown forward. He collided with Punk, sending them both into a sprawling pile of struggling limbs.

There was a wet *pop*, and the man started screaming. He writhed on the floor, rolling onto his hands and knees, retching.

Gax scuttled away as Punk lashed out at him.

"Bleedin' 'ell!" Gax squawked. "I don't think they're immune to me poison, but they might be resistant."

The large man vomited, his body shaking.

Marcus wrinkled his nose. "You stay out of the way, Gax. Keep an eye on the Filii Terra on the outskirts of the barrier for me?"

Gax nodded his mossy little head, black eyes flashing. Punk lunged at him, her claws lashing out, but he had already slipped between the cobblestones with the slimy smacking of loose flesh.

Marcus rewarded her effort with a blast of energy into the earth, which sent a shower of dirt and stone into her face, leaving her rolling back, howling.

Then sharp teeth bit into his ankle, and he let out a yelp.

Ducky let out a disgruntled quack, staring up at him angrily.

"Sorry, buddy. I know you don't enjoy fighting. Why don't you...stick with Ed? Keep each other safe?"

Ducky quacked again and waddled off.

A pink, bloated body flew within inches of Marcus' head, and he ducked belatedly as it continued through the barrier and into the waiting mouths in the night.

"Careful, Zara! Don't just yeet people fucking all over the joint. You nearly took my head off!" Marcus spun just in time to see her mash a man into a pulp with two of her ghostly fists.

"STOP!" Valeria shrieked piercingly. She had moved since he last saw her to...

Oh no. She hasn't.

Sure enough, she had taken the opportunity of their distraction and stood with Hunter amidst the small group of Filii Terra. His bulked-up body had withered somewhat—his suit hanging loose and torn—but somehow he'd gotten a hold of Dmitri's now flameless axe. The last few of the Order of Helios bore firearms. The Filii Terra, including Birger, were on their knees, with the weapons pointed at them. Valeria herself gripped Isla by her wavy hair, pulled back her head, and held a gun to her pale jaw.

"That's just about e-fucking-nough of that!" Valeria shouted. "Do you have any idea who these people you're mashing up and feeding to monsters *are*?! How dare you!"

"You started it," Zara snapped back sullenly, her ghostly-shaped hands wiping gore off one another.

Marcus felt a flash of petty pride.

"And I'll finish it," Valeria snapped.

Marcus tentatively reached out, lifted his fingers, and gently tried to grip the weapon. His magick slid off like water from Ducky's creepy little back.

This bitch was smart...

"Now, I assume you don't want this girl's brains all over the place, whereas I have no particular fucking commitment as to where they end up. So, I suggest you give us what we want, and we'll all be on our fucking way." Valeria's hands were shaking, eyes wild, her finger twitching on the trigger.

Marcus met Isla's eyes, and she looked down. He followed the glance to her hand, hovering by the wand at her hip. His head shake of warning earned a scowl in return, but he was certain her shadows would just slide over these people like oil on water.

"Fine," Zara growled. "Marcus?"

It hadn't been long enough.

Vandle...Paile could travel between mirrors in seconds, but she'd had plenty of stops to make tonight.

"Copy that," Marcus said. "We'll give you what you want, alright."

"Oh, don't act ominous." Valeria pushed the barrel of her gun harder into Isla's jaw. "I hold all the power here."

Marcus smiled grimly. "You know what? A tiny part of me might even wish that was true."

"Paile, Paile, Paile," Zara said flatly.

Marcus saw the way she winced as she did. That wasn't the name she was used to saying three times, and using it admitted that still fresh loss.

The mirror shimmered, and Paile stepped out.

Marcus held his breath until his eyes met with hers—one red and one blue—and she gave him the barest of nods, face stoic.

Marcus smiled.

At least there's some backup...

"That's not her," Hunter shouted, pointing. "That's not fucking her!"

"What is this?" Valeria snapped, her eyes flashing angrily. "Some kind of trick?"

"That looks like..." Hunter's eyes were wide.

Paige's voice replied. "Yeah, it's me, dick-face. And you'd better not get too close to me, or I'm liable to attach your actual dick to your actual face."

"You did this, back at the house," Zara said angrily. "You did this to them."

"You think we're here to fuck around?" Valeria's voice was low and dangerous. "If you have two mirror leapers, I want them both. I've *had it* with you kids."

Marcus saw that final decision snap into place in Valeria's cold eyes. It was the flat line of her mouth and thrill in her voice, that spike of violence in her swirling, muddy aura.

When her arm moved, and the tendon in the back of her hand flexed, he raised his hands. As she pulled the trigger, he pushed with all his finesse and will to form a paper-thin barrier, harder than steel, between the barrel of the gun and Isla's skin.

He knew from Song that time was not a linear path. Time was more like lots of things happening at the same time, but at slightly different rates. He hadn't, perhaps ever, been quite so aware of it as he was in that moment right then.

Time stopped but also hastened. Zara's cry of warning was a moment slower than the crack of the gun, but that was a sudden and short thing...unlike Isla's scream, the scream of horror and pain as the barrier cut through her skin. Then, there was the sound of the gun. That was a wretched thing. It gave its own scream as the powder and gases and fire burned it from within. He'd never really known what it meant for a gun to backfire, but this must have been it, as that was literally what it did. The explosive scream of metal on metal, and then...the expulsion of that violent pressure tearing back through Valeria's hand, mincing flesh and bone. *Her* scream was not instant or even fast in the scheme of things.

Isla fell away from her in a cry of shocked pain, clutching her head, where blood poured freely. Her severed ear fell away as she did.

Valeria's howl of hysterical agony came next, a garbled, horrible wail as she staggered back.

Marcus was too shocked to try and grasp out at her. His own passage of time was somewhere between that and Hunter hefting the axe, looking horrified. Even if he had tried to grab her, his magick would have slid off, and he didn't have the speed or focus to place another barrier. Instead, Valeria Sands fell back, directly onto the twisted, little Elder Sapling with a horrifying and final crackling crunch.

Isla stared in horror, her eyes flashing straight back to Marcus with realisation.

"Oh." Marcus swallowed. "Now you've *really* gone and fucked it."

Around them was a flicker of dying energy...and the excited, ravenous cries of monsters as the barrier dropped.

FULL HOUSE

"Oh fuck, oh fuck, oh fuck..." Zara moved back, raising her fists as the snarling cries of the monsters closed in. "What do we do?"

Valeria was still shrieking on the ground, expensive clothes caught on the splintered branches of the Elder Sapling. Her henchman turned their attention from the Filii Terra to the beasts now closing in.

Isla staggered forward, pale and shivering. Her eyes were glassy and wide, and one hand clutched the side of her head where blood still gushed. Marcus rushed to her, catching her in his arms. He raised a hand, sensing the damage he'd done, felt the broken vessels, the damaged cells. Her ear was completely gone. His barrier had cut into nothing else important, at least. He focused his energy, closing the vessels and stabilising the damage. Given time and power, he may have been able to rebuild the ear, if not restore the hearing. But with things as they were right now...

"Thank you," Isla said numbly from within Marcus' arms, looking up at him.

"I chopped off your ear," he said apologetically.

"Better than getting shot in the head," she replied, blinking.

Around them, a few of the Order of Helios fought the monsters with varying success.

Two of the bloated, muscular men were stamping on the crab things. At least until one of them was half-gobbled in one bite by the giant millipede, and the other made a break for it only to end up falling into three of the long, thin, faceless men who then hacked at him with their claws. The woman with the punk haircut leapt into the air, clawing at the mothman and tearing into one of its wings. It fluttered back, letting out a keening wail. Its translucent face looked pained before it promptly vomited a yellow substance onto her arm, which hissed and seared through to her bone in seconds. He lost sight of her a moment later but didn't expect she would live much longer.

"Pretty great time to call in reinforcements, I'd say," Marcus shouted, glancing at Paile.

She nodded, stepping toward the tall, gilded mirror.

"Get me out of here!" Hunter shouted, panicking as he rushed to cut off her path. "You, whichever...whoever you are. You can use the mirrors. Just get us out of here. I'm sorry for what I did!" His eyes bulged, skin shining with sweat.

Paile regarded him with a disdain that was all Paige, but it was Vandle's voice that spoke. "You would be the last person I would choose to save."

"I don't know how long we can hold these things off," Zara warned loudly. She was turning around, trying to decide where to fight first.

The ominous rumbling of the earth sounded again.

So much closer now.

"Let me by, or we're all dead," Paile said firmly to Hunter.

He raised Dmitri's axe as she raised the bone athame ready to fight. They were both stayed, however, by that rumbling in the ground again.

It was like an earthquake building, but Marcus knew exactly what it was. "Everyone...get back."

Even the monsters that closed in around them were cowed, retreating with higher yips, snarls, and caws.

Marcus focused on the ground. If he concentrated really hard, he could just about see its shimmering aura.

"YOU FOOLS!" Valeria wailed. She staggered into their midst, pristine white suit splattered with blood as she waved her ruined hand before her, now little more than pulped meat and splintered bone. "YOU ABSOLUTE IDIOTS. YOU HAVE KILLED US ALL!"

"Last I checked, you were the one that fell on the magick tree," Marcus grumbled.

The swirling tumult of power within her swelled. The auras of her own and the monsters she had consumed grew.

The aura *below* grew closer, too, seemingly fixated on her changing...drawn to her power.

"Everyone. Get back," Marcus repeated.

Valeria bucked and twisted, her body growing and limbs swelling with unnatural muscle as she released the energy within. "I WILL DESTROY YOU ALL! I AM THE MOST POWERFUL OF THE ORDER OF HELIOS, THE GRAND HIGH MASTER OF THE COUNCIL, AND I WILL—"

The earth groaned. Stone and soil shook and split as the shimmering energy below burst upward. There was a shower of dirt and debris as the ground tore open beneath her.

The force of it put Marcus to his knees, but he saw others fall completely as the earth caved in and opened.

Valeria let out a cry of surprise as she tumbled into the massive jaws below, jaws large enough to swallow a car whole, with a mouth and gullet lined with rows upon rows of razor-sharp teeth.

"Earth-wyrm!" Marcus shouted.

Paile quickly moved away from Hunter, who had fallen from the quake, and stepped to the edge of the opening. Her hand darted into her patchwork leather and striped jacket, pulling out a bunch of what looked like glass marbles.

Marcus saw the magick energy compressed within them. Violent and beautiful.

Valeria was still screaming from inside the earth-wyrm's maw. Its barbed throat shredded her mutating flesh as it sunk back into the ground to enjoy its meal.

Paile cast the handful of marbles into its open throat. Her silver-cracked face wore a grisly smile. Marcus didn't know which one of them it belonged to.

"Get back!" Marcus cried right before there was a thrumming burst of energy.

The condensed power within the glass ruptured. Fire and lighting tore up from the earth in a violent explosion, followed by wet hunks of meat and a shower of blood that he managed to keep mostly away from himself and Isla with a quickly conjured shield of air. His ears were still ringing as he blinked around the aftermath.

Zara remained by the black mirror, still clad in her spiritual armour, six arms ready to fight, and gore dripping from the light around her. Paile was beside the hole in the earth. The edges had collapsed, filling it partially in. She was covered in slime and blood and still smiling. She popped a hand in her pocket again, and in a moment, had a cigarette in her lips, sparking it up.

"I'm not sure now's the time for that," Marcus said.

She took a deep drag. "Let people enjoy things." Paige's voice left Paile's mouth with a plume of smoke. "That was for Sourpuss."

Around them, Marcus saw the shimmering auras of the monsters closing in once more, no longer afraid now that the earth-wyrm was dead. He couldn't see the auras of any of the Order now, other than what felt like Hunter, who was snivelling in the debris.

"Isla, you and your people stay close together. Protect each other."

Isla nodded, brandishing her bone wand. Her skin was tinged grey, but her eyes were full of determination.

"How about that backup?" Zara shouted, batting one of the winged monsters out of the air as it swooped down upon her.

"Fine." Paile took another puff, waving a dismissive hand and striding to the mirror.

She was almost there when there was a burst of movement.

Hunter flashed through the dark, tears streaking his dark cheeks. He was swinging Dmitri's axe.

Paile saw him, but a moment too late. She twisted to the side, the blade of it missing her entirely, but Hunter had already let it go. He collided with her bodily, his growing form bowling her over and gripping her in his powerful fists.

Marcus moved to help, but something shimmered in his near vision. His world dulled, and their auras disappeared. That sickly shivery feeling washed over him again as every drop of magick within him was silenced.

The soulwinder. It's close.

Something large and shrieking rushed toward him from the darkness. He raised his hands but couldn't channel any power at all.

No.

No, no, no.

Pain lanced into Marcus' shoulders as the talons took purchase, and his feet left the ground. He screamed in pain and terror as he was lifted into the sky. Darkness rushed around him, panic welling in his chest. The talons bit deeper, and Marcus felt hot blood flow from where they punctured his shoulders. His voice was lost in the rushing night.

I'm going to die.

...I'm going to die.

Fear consumed him. He desperately lashed out with his fists, finding scales and feathers. Marcus thrashed and batted at them desperately. His fingers found something warm and slick, firm.

An eye?

He jabbed his finger into it. Whatever held him let out a rattling squawk of pain. The talons released him.

And he fell.

He pushed out with his power.

Nothing.

Still falling.

The wind whistled in his ears.

From this high, the impact will kill me.

Panic.

He tried a desperate drag on magick again, aiming down.

A bare echo of power blasted out like a dying cry. Marcus felt it push him back up—slow him—just enough. His fall ended as his chest collided with hard earth and grass, knocking the wind out of him.

Marcus lay for a moment, trying to find his breath.

That...that was almost it.

Marcus blinked, swallowing. He tasted blood in his mouth, and his shoulders throbbed with deep pain from whatever had grabbed him. Before he even tried to stand, he reached for his power and found...nothing.

Song.

He forced himself to his feet. His left ankle hurt, and he could barely carry his weight on it.

I need to find Song.

He had to trade something, something to deal with the soul-winder, if that's what it really was. There was nothing they couldn't deal with together.

"Song?" he croaked.

Something growled nearby in the darkness. He heard a blast up ahead and somebody screaming. Marcus blinked in the darkness, desperately trying to get his bearings.

A corpse lay on the ground nearby—a woman, her throat torn out, blood spattered on her robes. One of the Filii Terra. Beyond one of the gravestones nearby, he thought he saw the remnants of another.

Marcus limped past her, realising the thing dropped him beyond the outer crypts where they had been stationed.

There was another blast from the direction of the world parallax.

Marcus raised his hand hopefully and whistled, reaching out for his magickal link with Ducky.

Nothing happened.

That cold, sick feeling grew stronger.

"SONG!" Marcus sobbed.

He staggered forward, cutting between mausoleums, and took a moment, resting a hand on the wall, breathing raggedly.

Nearby he could hear...

A deep, rattling breath.

Marcus looked up in alarm.

There was someone there.

Someone in the darkness.

Separated from his powers and from Song, he couldn't make out their aura, and it was too dark to see properly.

The figure turned around, and Marcus' heart froze.

The soulwinder was almost the shape of a man but impossible to mistake for one. Its face was a skull. No mask or missing flesh, but pristine, sculpted bone with two ram-like horns atop it. Marcus had seen pictures, heard whispers, but nothing could prepare him for the dread it engulfed him with. Unlike its skulled head, its body was naked, with ancient-looking mottled flesh, sagging and torn, and at parts, hanging in tatters.

Tears fell from Marcus' eyes, and he was unable to blink, unable to even swallow as he stared at the thing.

"Marcus?"

Isla?

The soulwinder took a step toward him.

Marcus tried to move. He tried to scream. His muscles spasmed as he attempted to do anything at all. Its fetid breath was on his face.

"Marcus! I have Song with me, I...I don't think they can feel you anymore. Please, where are you?" Isla cried.

Marcus forced a wailing gasp out of his throat and twisted his head.

He forced every bit of energy he had into one word. "HELP!"

He felt a blow punch into his chest. The air was knocked out of him, and he heard something crunch. He fell back, his head bouncing off the ground, ears ringing.

"MARCUS!" Isla cried.

There was a flash of movement as the surrounding shadows rushed forth.

He heard the soulwinder let out a rasping hiss.

Song's face appeared, their golden eyes full of tears. They blinked, and those tears fell onto Marcus' face.

They feel so warm.

I feel so warm.

His chest burned.

Isla appeared above him. Her eyes were wide with shock and horror.

He tried to open his mouth to tell her she was supposed to be with the others. Instead, blood bubbled at the back of his throat, and he was forced to either swallow it or choke.

Dazed, Marcus tilted his head to look at the soulwinder. Isla's attack had disconcerted it and pushed it back a bit, but now it was regarding her with interest.

"Marcus...what is that thing?" Isla's voice shook.

Marcus blinked, staring at the soulwinder. For some reason, his vision was blurry.

One of its pointed arms was coated in dripping, red blood.

Marcus looked down at his chest.

Oh.

His shirt was soaked with crimson. He felt it now, still pouring out of him. So much blood. *Too* much blood. His body was so numb with the shock of the injury that the pain itself was only a distant echo, but his arms and legs felt so *heavy* already.

"GET AWAY!" Isla sobbed. She was crying as she lashed out at the soulwinder again with her black bone wand.

Dark shadows reached out, gripping onto the monster, but it tore them off easily and took another step forward.

"You can't die," Isla wept. "We have a deal! You haven't helped me find a family yet."

Marcus felt blood bubble in the back of his throat as he replied. It was getting hard to breathe. "I think...we've...got that...covered."

Isla wailed and lashed out with her wand, again to no effect.

Marcus focused on Song's eyes. With the soulwinder near, they couldn't send or even feel each other.

Please. I don't want to die.

I don't want to leave you.

I don't want to ever leave you.

"I can't stop it!" Isla wailed as the monster stepped closer. "I... what do I do?"

Marcus blinked, his vision fading.

He wasn't warm anymore.

He was getting cold.

The soulwinder stiffened suddenly, arching its back, its mouth opening wide.

Then, a long, sharp bone pushed through its sternum.

Its strange body spasmed, and as it died, Marcus felt the distant thrum of magick returning to him. He felt Song's presence welcoming him back. Isla was shouting something, but it sounded faint and tinny in his ears.

The bone blade pulled back, and the soulwinder fell to the ground.

From behind it stepped a figure wielding a great, thin blade of bone almost as tall as she was herself. Her dress foamed around her unnaturally like frothing cream, her long hair the colour of mouldy oranges. She came close and leaned down to him, staring with those large, round eyes, lidless and lashless, and gave him a sad smile.

"Hello, little one," the Bean-Nighe said softly. "Now, aren't you glad I didn't tell you this was how it ended?"

TAXONOMY OF MONSTERS:
THE NIX
(DRACO FLUMINIS)

Eyes that burn like cold blue flame,
Scales rock hard and cool as rain.
They lurk close by the riverside,
Take many forms, and like to hide.
So, take care, sweet, unwary swimmer,
Or else you'll be the Nix's dinner.

— DEBORAH LOVE, 1905-1942

46

WHAT I AM

The last of the four-legged beasts fled away from Oscar, who stood all in one piece, facing the oncoming wall of snapping jaws and death.

Belphegor loomed in their midst, its massive horns dripping with darkness. It raised one muscular arm.

A loping army of Theians surged forth, larger than the first in both size and number. Several ogre creatures that must have been twice as tall as Oscar, and several faceless, humanoid shapes with too-long limbs, galloped grotesquely on all fours, leading the way.

Dmitri watched, expecting Oscar to turn and run once more, but he simply watched until around half the distance between them was closed, then burst into motion. Except this time, he was running *at* them. Dmitri's jaw hung open as Oscar darted toward the oncoming Theians, and the gap closed in seconds.

One of the massive ogres lunged out, but the shadows at Oscar's feet pushed up, sending him into the air. He spun, reaching out a hand, and a tendril of shadow shot up from the ground and into his palm, pulling him down at a new angle and onto the thing's shoulder.

He placed both his hands over its head, and it convulsed, its dark, oily skin and hair becoming a rich purple instead. As the ogre returned to itself, one of its compatriots connected with its jaw, knocking it down.

Dmitri lost sight of Oscar in the fray. He soon realised, however, that Oscar leapt from the victim to the attacker and now had his hands closed over its head, too.

"He...how?" Dmitri breathed as the darkness sapped from the second.

"Amazing what you can achieve with time and power," Geraldine said smugly. "I thought he told you he could fight them?"

"I..."

"Didn't believe him?" Geraldine quirked an eyebrow. "I understand it's hard to let someone you love put themselves in harm's way, but from what I understand, this must be very much what it was like for Oscar to watch *you* protect *him*."

Dmitri turned his eyes back to Oscar and the Theians. More of them had altered in colour. Two of the large ones were wrestling on the ground, apparently confused, while others were fleeing. Oscar danced between the faceless beings as they snatched out at him with their too-long fingers and arms. Everywhere he touched, the darkness sapped from their skin, faster and faster as he moved, his speed increasing to a frantic ballet.

"He is taking on the energy stored within them. Not only does it cleanse them, but it also feeds his power. If you simply fled to the parallax, in the time that passed between your passage and the release of pressures here, Belphegor would likely destroy all life that remains here. Hopefully, by subduing it first, we will be able to—" Geraldine's voice cut off.

Dmitri saw it too.

The army of Theians had parted. Belphegor's massive form strode forward, its void-like eyes fixed on Oscar.

"I had hoped that Belphegor's arrogance might mean it would take a little longer for it to realise. That Oscar could take on more of their energies before they battled." *Now* she sounded concerned.

If Oscar had the same anxiety, he didn't show it. Small and

thin as he was, his back was straight and proud as the giant bull-monster approached.

Dmitri looked back to Geraldine. She watched cautiously.

"Should we...help him?" Dmitri asked. He had never felt so weak.

"Not yet," Geraldine replied crisply. "Let's just see..."

Belphegor smiled a grin that dripped with ichor and death. It was three times taller than Oscar, but Oscar still faced it unflinchingly.

Iubite...you have become...so brave.

No, you were always this brave. Now, you just know it.

Belphegor stamped one cloven hoof. When the monster spoke, it carried like a rasping hiss of snakes slithering through dead grass. It was not loud but audible through the sheer power of its presence. "Finally, it is time for this to end...*human*."

"Finally," Oscar agreed. His voice did not shake.

Belphegor's black eyes travelled over Oscar to Dmitri and Geraldine. Its gaze sent a shiver through Dmitri's bones.

"You seek to protect them?" Belphegor asked.

"I seek to protect everything," Oscar replied.

After a moment of silence, Belphegor laughed softly. "It has always been this way." Its voice dripped with as much disdain as its mouth and eyes dripped darkness. "Humans...reaching too far."

Oscar stared back. "Wanting to exist isn't too much to ask."

The massive monster looked pained. "Isn't it? When there is...such agony. Such violent hate. Would it not be better to rest?"

"I will help you rest," Oscar said so gently that Dmitri barely heard it.

And then, he attacked.

~

THE SHADOWS PUSHED Oscar into the air, but with a gesture from Belphegor, those same shadows reached up and snatched him by the ankles, dragging him back down to the cracked, stony earth.

Dmitri saw the struggle it took from Oscar to unravel them before they drove him down with bone-crushing force. He barely disentangled himself and rolled aside before the shadows around him opened, like mouths themselves, full dark, pointed teeth bursting up like bear traps trying to hungrily gobble him up. Belphegor tore forth with powerful speed and a cascade of stomping hooves.

Oscar fled. He leapt straight into one of the opening mouths of darkness, hands grasping, and with a look of great concentration upon his face he disappeared into the dark.

"Oscar," Dmitri moaned. He cast a desperate look at Geraldine.

"He is travelling," she said, though her eyebrow twitched with anxiety as she scanned the shadows. "He will not be gone long. Only so long as he can hold his breath."

Dmitri swallowed. "Belphegor is too strong."

"The beast has more power," Geraldine agreed. "And *far* more skill with shadowmancy."

"Then...why is *this* the plan?" Dmitri still looked for Oscar, who had not yet resurfaced.

"Oscar may not be able to defeat Belphegor...but he'll make the wretched thing burn through a lot of power, so then I can finish the job." Geraldine smiled knowingly. "And power and skill are not everything. You've spent this long around humans. You know how effective pure stubbornness can be."

Amidst the ranks of tainted Theians, a commotion began. There were roars and howls of panic and fear and a spreading amount of movement within their number. At a bellowed cry from Belphegor, they parted, and Dmitri saw Oscar.

He rode the shadows themselves, like a swelling wave among them. Wherever he touched, their darkness was absorbed.

The cleansed and panicked Theians either fled or attacked

their surrounding former compatriots, some simply becoming reinfected by Belphegor's taint.

The air around Oscar flickered with power and darkness.

"Face me, human!" Belphegor hissed, raising a hand. Tendrils of darkness rocketed from the surrounding. shadows, seeking out Oscar unerringly, spearing through cleansed and tainted Theians alike if they got in the way.

Oscar dodged and wove around them as they sought to capture or kill him. When it appeared he could no longer outrun them, the darkness below gave a massive thrum and launched him high into the air.

Oscar rocketed into the sky, arms open. The snallygaster above had no time to move as he connected, sapping the darkness from it almost at once and clambering onto its back.

"FACE ME, HUMAN!" Belphegor bellowed.

Oscar stood soaring a hundred feet in the burning skies on the snallygaster's back, then leapt.

Dmitri's heart stopped beating as Oscar—sweet, kind Oscar Tundale—careened through the air. Darkness flickered around him like a cape. He thrummed with power.

Belphegor roared, and any tainted Theians with the ability to fly launched themselves from the ground to meet Oscar.

Oscar twisted and wove as he rocketed toward Belphegor, dodging them all, raising a hand. Darkness swelled around his fist like a glove of night.

He's going to do it...he's really going to...

Belphegor raised a fist, gloom swarming around it, and met Oscar's blow with its own.

A reverberating pulse blasted forth with a deafening crack, sending Dmitri and Geraldine staggering back.

Dmitri shielded his eyes from the resulting dust and debris. Gasping, he focused through the haze, not even daring to breathe.

The tainted Theians had been blown back, too, leaving a clearing where Belphegor now stood.

Dmitri's heart turned to ice.

In one of Belphegor's massive hands...was Oscar. His body was limp, his eyes closed.

"Do you see?" Belphegor hissed. "This is the way things always needed to be." It shook its fist, and Oscar's limbs swayed weakly. "Nothing so pathetic as a human could ever hope to stand against me. This...is..." The monster reached up and, with a massive finger and thumb, gripped Oscar's arm by the wrist.

"Geraldine," Dmitri whispered, stepping forward.

She didn't stop him this time.

Belphegor laughed, wrenching Oscar's arm in its grip.

Dmitri cried out as flesh broke and joints gave way. Blood sprayed as Oscar's arm tore off. He awoke for a moment to let out a horrible, guttural cry of pain and then fell into unconsciousness...or shock.

"You thought this was your saviour?" Belphegor cackled, black ichor running down its chin. It flung Oscar's arm disdainfully to the red, cracked earth, then took one of Oscar's legs in its grip instead.

Dmitri wailed in anguish as the monster pulled again, leaving ragged flesh hanging from Oscar's ruined hip as blood surged out.

"This is what humans do to insects, is it not?" Belphegor smiled. "I...see the appeal."

The blood pumping from Oscar's torn hip was weakening. Dmitri let the fire inside him loose. It spread into his veins, and he felt his body begin to change.

"Dmitri!" Geraldine barked.

"Pathetic," Belphegor sneered and tossed Oscar's ruined body into the rising mass of monsters that fell upon it with glee. "You thought you had a chance? Have you no idea what you are?"

"Do *not!*" Geraldine snapped, coming up to Dmitri's side and grabbing him by the arm. "If you change, you cannot return, correct?"

"You did this," Dmitri spat, tears streaking his cheeks. "You tried to make him into your soldier. I will not return without him." His voice almost failed him. He turned, snatching her shoulders in his claws.

She stared past him, her eyes widening. She was...smiling.

Dmitri released her and turned as the monsters that fell upon Oscar's body yowled and yipped in fear, trying to get away.

They were...cleansed.

Dmitri focused on that space as more of them moved away, willing it to be true.

Belphegor let out a furious growl.

Please...

Please...

Oscar's thin body pushed up, held in place by the shadows, soaked in blood and pale as death, his eyes still closed.

"Impossible..." Belphegor hissed.

Oscar raised his remaining hand. Threads of shadow danced around him, rushing out with perfect accuracy. They were dragging something...two things.

Oscar's limbs were pulled back onto his body by the darkness. Dmitri thought he saw tiny threads of black stitching him together even as blood flowed from the healing wounds.

"Oscar," Dmitri said, staring in awe.

Geraldine smiled. "Darling."

Oscar raised both his hands and dragged on the shadows, pulling them close to his body, condensing them around him. Shaping them into...something.

Something...*terrible*.

What was it he had said at the cave?

'I can make the darkness into the scariest thing I can imagine.'

Long claws stretched from his fingertips. Above his head were two long, pointed horns bleeding with shadows.

Dmitri could feel and smell what it was that Oscar had pushed into this shape. It might have been built from the power of hate, but it dripped with...fear, anxiety, loneliness...

Oscar opened his eyes. They burned blacker than infinity. "I know exactly what I am, Belphegor. Do you?"

47

FROM THE START

Belphegor let out an infuriated roar and raised its fist, shrouded in pulsing darkness once more.

This time, Oscar did not meet it.

Instead, bolted through the air, a barely visible black flash. He leapt up at the last moment, raising his dark, clawed hands as he did, pulling the darkness from the ground up with him. The shadows beneath Belphegor clutched and clawed at its legs, and it stomped them away angrily, tearing them like dark fabric.

"You are too weak!" Belphegor snarled, bringing down a fist as Oscar landed beside him.

Oscar rolled, but the shadows burst forth in a tidal wave. He bounded over them with absurd agility. The shadows beneath Oscar propelled him, even while Belphegor's wave of darkness cast its ranks aside and hurled him into the sky.

But Oscar did not fall.

From his back burst two wings of jagged, burning darkness, holding him, framed by the largest of the three red suns.

Irate, Belphegor turned its dark gaze upon Dmitri and Geraldine. It smiled, and a large contingent of the tainted Theians broke away in their direction.

"Its trying to distract him." Geraldine couldn't keep the smile from her face. "Draw his attention into two places at once."

"Because...its scared," Dmitri added.

Geraldine laughed, raising her staff, ready to fight. "Don't worry. Shouldn't be anything I can't handle. Although..."

The tainted Theians approached rapidly. Several strange lizard-type beings at the front of the ranks were making the fastest progress.

"Dmitri...why don't you try your pheromones?"

"What?" Dmitri said numbly. He watched as Belphegor hurled lances of shadow from the earth into the air while Oscar twisted and banked, avoiding them smoothly.

Geraldine's eyes shone with excitement. "Let's see if its strength is faltering."

Dmitri swallowed, stepping forward. He focused on the Theians, on the snapping jaws and slathering mouths, and the dark claws tearing into the ground as they grew ever nearer. He formed his intentions.

Stop.

Calm.

And he pushed.

Using his ability wasn't so different from pushing a thought, though that thought was pushed from his whole body. Over years of use, it had become second nature, but now...it felt different. Easier. Smoother.

But the advancing ranks did not falter.

"Never mind. Let me—" Geraldine began.

Dmitri pushed harder.

STOP.

One of the scuttling lizards came to a halt far too quickly for its own good, tumbling over its own legs and sending the things that followed it into a flurry of confusion.

STOP.

Heat pulsed from Dmitri's body.

It hit them like a wall, and the approaching creatures froze mid-motion or fell into a confused writhing mass of flailing claws and gnashing teeth.

Dmitri gasped, holding the heat firm, pushing his will.

"Very good," Geraldine mused beside him. "Perhaps there is hope for you yet."

Dmitri shifted his gaze away from the creatures to where Belphegor's hooves stomped deep cracks into the ground. Darkness burst from them like erupting lava but missed Oscar time and time again.

Belphegor huffed and lunged again, missing Oscar by inches as he swept by, his new, dark claws rending a gouge in the monster's back that oozed inky gore.

"Dmitri, I told you before that there are two things fighting within you," Geraldine said softly.

Dmitri nodded, staring ahead as Belphegor lunged out again, desperately trying to pull on the shadows that Oscar formed around himself. But he'd made them too solid, claimed them as his own. So instead, the monster drew on its *own* power, forming a massive blade of darkness that it wielded in both hands.

"You would do well to accept that perhaps you are not just one of these things. That perhaps neither should win. Rather, both should prevail together. Ask yourself, why is it that Oscar can accept all of you...and yet you cannot? That is the only way to hone your *will*. When all parts of you hold the same intent, that is the only way to separate yourself from your past and become who it is that you are destined to be."

Dmitri shook his head distractedly, his eyes unable to leave Oscar as he fought on. Oscar needed to gain more distance as the beast lashed out with the extended range of its shadow-formed blade. Oscar beat his jagged, black wings, pounding his way into the red skies.

"He's not strong enough to finish it," Geraldine grumbled beside Dmitri. "He just needs..."

Belphegor staggered, and Dmitri's eyes searched for the trap in the shadows that Oscar must have planted but came up with nothing of the sort.

Belphegor tried to pull up a hoof, but thick, pink mucusy sludge pulled it back to the ground.

"What?" he bellowed.

Dmitri heard a familiar voice.

"More!"

Over by the rocky outcropping were Lyn and her Dregs, who had hidden in the burrows.

The dripping sludge monster, Garshok, had its hands buried into the ground, and sure enough, more thick goo oozed around Belphegor's hooves. The massive beast let out a cry, trying to pull itself free.

"Now!" Lyn cried.

The sad-looking eel-faced creature stepped forth, aiming its slithery fingers toward the goop. The sludge creature stepped back.

"Spending too much time around humans has rubbed off on her," Geraldine mused, smiling. "She couldn't resist stepping into a practically un-winnable fight to save the day."

The one Oscar called Elodie let loose a torrent of crackling electricity that surged through the liquid sludge on the ground and sparked around Belphegor. The monster roared in agonised fury.

Lyn burst from the outcropping with a brief click-clack of heels before they were pushed from her feet, her body shifting, reverting to its true form. It was a form that their previous encounters had only hinted at, a form Dmitri had never seen when she was full of her natural power in Theia.

The mottled, grey flesh he had seen before was barely a dull echo of her real skin, a silvery grey and almost scaled like armour. She opened her arms, and leathery wings burst out of her back as her body swelled and grew. Her eyes shone yellow and a long, black tongue hung from her mouth.

She beat her way into the sky beside Oscar.

"You fight well." Lyn shot a large, pointed smile at Oscar. "Care to help me save this world, then go and save your own?"

"Deal." Oscar grinned, his black eyes leaking shadows down his cheeks.

Lyn nodded. "Then let's go!"

She swooped down, twisting and twirling around the recovering Belphegor's sloppy strikes.

Oscar used her distraction and surged through the air, pulling on the shadows to sink Belphegor up to its knees in the ground, before landing on its shoulders and taking the bull by the horns.

Then Oscar pulled.

Belphegor snarled, and Dmitri saw its dark energy fading, being pulled away. The bull monster thrashed out with its blade, and Oscar was forced to disengage.

"ENOUGH," Belphegor bellowed.

Dmitri watched as the darkness sapped from the creatures under Belphegor's hold and the others whose bodies lay limp on the field of battle. That darkness pulsed through the shadows, away from hundreds of the creatures at once, like dark blood returning to a festering heart through swollen veins, returning to its origin.

Belphegor released its hold on the now cleansed Theians, most of them fleeing immediately. Some few remained, lethargic and confused, while others stayed unmoving. At the same time, Belphegor *grew*. Its body swelled with dark energy.

"This is it," Geraldine said, stepping forward. "Belphegor has drawn in all the free energy that Oscar does not hold. Be ready. We must soon part ways."

The black blade flashed through the air with alarming speed, separating Lyn at the waist.

She twisted and hissed, her intestines hanging loosely. Rather than retreat, she darted in, her intestines wrapping around Belphegor's face, smothering it like a bundle of slithering serpents.

Dmitri swallowed. "What are you talking about?"

"Oscar will try to weaken Belphegor as much as possible, and then I should be able to hold it. You must go back to the gateway immediately. As Oscar draws the power from this place from the other side, it will leech the power from Belphegor and end it."

"And you?" Dmitri asked, though he knew the answer.

Geraldine smiled darkly. "Don't go getting sentimental on me now. I told you I was dying. Can you think of a better way to use the last of my power?"

Dmitri blinked and shook his head numbly.

"OSCAR!" Geraldine shouted. "NOW!"

Oscar nodded, taking higher into the sky and opening his arms.

The darkness around Oscar hummed, and he drew the shadows that clothed him into his palms. First, the armour at his arms and legs, then chest, and the horns on his head. By the time the wings he'd worn were sucked in, a pulsing maelstrom of power seared in each of his hands, the sheer energy alone seemingly keeping him aloft. When he brought his hands together, the two balls of power greedily combined, consuming each other and becoming one spiky, crackling ball of black energy sculpted from chaos and hate.

Lyn sensed this, banking hard to move and carrying herself as far as she could with a few powerful beats of her wings.

Belphegor roared.

And Oscar released.

To Dmitri's eyes, it was a streaking bolt, though the afterburn it left looked more like a beam.

The roar of power it sent out followed less than a second later and after the blast had already hit. Another wave of earth and debris was sent out, swallowing Belphegor in a cloud that pushed out like a blanket of destruction.

And then Oscar fell, his body limp and spent.

"Catch him!" Geraldine barked at Dmitri, slapping his shoulder.

Dmitri bolted forward, but he never had a chance.

Lyn moved too quickly. She grasped his body gently in her arms and brought him down to the torn earth.

Dmitri waited, panting and desperate to feel Oscar's weight in his arms for seemingly an eternity, though it must only have been seconds.

"He lives," Lyn said, smiling.

Dmitri reached out, and she handed Oscar to him with great care.

He is so light.

"Thank you," Dmitri said.

Lyn gave a slight harrumph. "I am only doing what is best for Theia," she replied. Then she looked at Oscar's unconscious form, and her eyes twinkled. "Though I will say, he really should have been one of us."

Dmitri smiled, but it faltered a moment later.

There was a deafening roar from the debris.

Through the clearing dust, Belphegor strode out. The monstrous bull had shrunken somewhat. It was soaked in blood, dark and thick as oil, covering half of its muscular torso. Its shoulder was split in two, and one arm ended in a charred nub just below the elbow.

"Allow me," Lyn growled, not waiting for a reply before she lunged forth, colliding with Belphegor in howling fury.

"Oscar...can you hear me? We need to go," Dmitri said softly as Geraldine reached his side.

"Be quick. He has used too much power." Her eyes moved over Oscar with concern. "I do not think he has the strength to regather it and heal here. If you do not get him through the gateway, he will die."

"Mum?" Oscar croaked weakly, shifting in Dmitri's arms.

"Oscar, I...I..." Geraldine blinked, her eyes shining with tears.

"You can't come." Oscar opened his eyes. They were his ocean blue once more.

Dmitri held him closer. "Iubite."

"You can't come because...you're not Geraldine Tundale. At least...not who she was before."

"Oscar," Geraldine gasped, her eyes wide.

"You're not...are you?" Oscar asked.

Nearby, Lyn howled in fury.

Geraldine blinked.

"You're...her ethernal."

She bit her lip in a painfully familiar way. "How...how long have you known?"

Oscar smiled. His eyes shone with tears as well. "Since the start. I...it got easier to pretend. It helped me...but I think it helped you, too."

Tears flowed freely down the ethernal's cheeks. "Your mother...she is a part of me. I wasn't pretending."

Oscar sniffled and smiled. "Even if she wasn't...you were a wonderful mother."

"Is anyone going to help me?!" Lyn cried as she sunk her claws into Belphegor's shoulder and was battered away once more.

Geraldine sniffled and smiled, raising her staff. "Of course," she replied, turning to the fight.

She looked back over her shoulder to Oscar and nodded. "I am very proud of you, Oscar. You *and* your sister. Always have been."

Oscar rubbed his eyes. "I love you," he said weakly.

Geraldine turned. Dmitri knew it was because she didn't want Oscar to see the look on her face.

"I love you too," she said. "Now go. Go and save everything."

❦ 48 ❧
AT ALL COSTS

Dmitri ran as the bright glow of Geraldine's magickal energy illuminated the red sky behind him. The sheer power of its release vibrated his bones and made the hairs on his neck and arms stand on end. All he could hear was the sound of his boots hammering the dry earth, his racing heart, panting breath...and Oscar.

Oscar's heartbeat was growing weaker and weaker. He was white as a sheet, his breaths rasping and ragged, and his blood-shot eyes were barely able to open.

I will save you, Oscar.

You are going home.

Dmitri clutched Oscar's body to his chest as if he could will his own heat, his own life, into him as he ran. He raced through the deep gulley and beyond the jagged crevices. His mind must have played some trick on him when he fled the tainted Theians because he seemed to reach the cliff's sheer drop, where the gateway had been, far too quickly. He returned to the jagged outcroppings, feeling confused and lost. Panic welled in his chest.

Oscar's breathing was becoming very quiet now.

He doesn't have long.

Dmitri closed his eyes and breathed. He tried to extend his

senses beyond the putrid stench of hate and rot of this place and search for the strange, magickal presence of the world parallax. He *could* sense it. It didn't seem to be anywhere different, only *further* somehow.

The earth groaned. Nearby, a large portion of the outcropping of the edge fell away.

This place is falling apart...

Dmitri blinked.

No.

He narrowed his eyes, peering into the red skies. It was there. The parallax was suspended in the air, about a mile above them.

A dull weight dropped in Dmitri's chest.

"Dmitri?" Oscar said weakly in his arms.

Dmitri tried to steady his breath. "Yes?"

"Did I do it?"

Dmitri fell to his knees, cradling him closer.

"Did I?"

"You were incredible, iubite. I...I've never seen anybody do anything so brave." Dmitri's shortness of breath had nothing to do with running.

Oscar smiled. His eyes searched hazily for Dmitri, though his face was only inches away. "I've seen you do braver things..."

Dmitri chuckled, feeling the tears begin. "Anything that I have ever done that was even a fraction as brave as that, I have only done for you. Because you made me better."

Oscar smiled and closed his eyes. "Is the gateway gone?"

Dmitri looked up into the sky.

Oscar sighed at his silence. "At least we're together."

His heart fluttered. Dmitri swallowed and forced the words out of his mouth, though they burned more than fire. "Oscar... listen to me. I need you to hold on to me. I am going to take you home."

Oscar's eyes opened. "What?"

"I'm going to change, iubite. I'm going to carry you through the world parallax."

"No!" Oscar's eyes widened, suddenly more alert.

"I must. If I don't...then everything will end. I understand what you must do. I know that you have to go back and drain this place of the hate that has infested it."

"But...you said...you said you wouldn't survive."

Dmitri smiled sadly. "My body will not...but I will always be with you, Oscar. I will always be watching over you."

Oscar sobbed, shaking his head. "I...I can't...go back without you."

"You can." Dmitri smiled, his tears falling onto Oscar's cheeks and mixing with his. "You can because it's the right thing to do, and I need you to do it. Not just for everyone but for me. For *us*."

Oscar forced a great shuddering breath into his body, his hands reaching up to touch Dmitri's face weakly, tears still flowing. "You did it. Just like you promised. You found me, no matter what. You..."

"Before you, Oscar, I did not have a reason to live. You have given me better. You have given me something to die for. If I can, I will always find you." Dmitri's voice cracked. "When your time comes, I will find you again. I will pull the moon from the sky and tear the earth in two. *Again*." Dmitri eased himself down to his knees, setting Oscar on the ground.

"Please...I love you." Oscar sniffled. "I only just got you back."

"And I love *you*, Oscar. Now please...*please*...carry our love on for us? Let me fly with you and not be afraid to fall."

Oscar sagged in silent defeat, blinking away stunned tears.

Dmitri leaned down and gave him one last kiss. A gentle kiss, like a glimpse of a shooting star, a fleeting promise of all the possibilities that could have been and all the places they could have seen together. He allowed himself only a moment, for even if he waited an age, the kiss still would not have been long enough.

Then he pulled away, his eyes fixed on Oscar, wanting to savour every moment. He stepped back and let the power tear free from his core. Dmitri embraced his other form, welcoming it with joy, not disgust, for the first time. He pulled the zburător free rather than unleashing it.

His flesh split, revealing dark fur and scales. His bones twisted and reformed in brief, excruciating ecstasy as the beast emerged. In moments, he was looking down at Oscar once more. He looked even tinier now, precious and powerful and perfect.

Dmitri lowered himself carefully on his front paws, bowing his head, and relished Oscar's touch as his fingers knotted in the fur at his neck.

It took three tries and a little nudging from Dmitri's snout before Oscar managed to get onto his back. His weak heartbeat and ragged breath were so close...but not for long.

Dmitri closed his eyes, giving Oscar a moment to right himself and hold as tightly as he could. He felt Oscar's hands pull his fur, burying his tear-streaked face into the back of his neck.

"Dmitri...please," he whimpered.

Dmitri looked up at the world parallax, taking a few tentative steps back to allow a smooth take-off.

Oscar pulled himself closer as Dmitri loped forward, leaping from the edge and into the nothing, opening his wings smoothly and keeping himself as level and steady as he could so as not to lose his precious cargo.

He soared through the sky, the parallax growing ever closer... his *end* growing ever closer.

"Please," Oscar whispered. "Find a way back to me."

Dmitri closed his eyes, tucking his wings tightly into his body, and rocketed into the gateway.

His heart overflowed with enough joy to numb the agony as his fur and scales were seared away with magick and his muscles charred. Even the pounding within his chest was absent of its usual stabbing pain from the shard. Instead, it felt bright and buzzing with glorious power. He held one thought close until the end.

I saved him.

TAXONOMY OF MONSTERS: THE UMBRAN
(UMBRA LAUTUS)

"A helpful thing of mindless function that helps cleanse energies passing betwixt the veil, most commonly the energy of hate. Once consumed, the energy is redistributed to service more useful functions. The umbran is harmless, a massless entity with no means of attack or defence, though it has been remarked that some seem to become quite sullen when overtaxed."

— EXCERPT: THE REVENANT'S ARCANUM

❦ 49 ❦

WILL THERE BE PARTY BAGS?

Zara cringed as a huge furry ball that was almost all glowing teeth threw itself against the shell she'd formed from the Ghatotkacha's energy. Countless other entities swarmed around her, keening and wailing frantically, leaving smears of blood and slobber dripping down the translucent, glowing shield she'd thrown out.

Zara's body shook, and sweat poured down her skin.

I killed people.

Horrible, twisted people, but I still have their blood on me.

But what else could I do...

She didn't know how long she could hold whatever barrier she'd created. She'd never put the energy into this shape before. When the monsters swarmed, she got as close to the black mirror as possible. On instinct, she let the Ghatotkacha fill her until she thought she was going to explode with power. As the countless eyes, teeth, and claws grew closer, though, she knew no matter how many arms she had, she wouldn't be able to protect the mirror. Instead, she had thrown up a cocoon of spiritual energy to encapsulate both her and the mirror.

When she tried to think about *how* she had done it, her focus would drop, and the cocoon would flicker or crack. What she *did* know was that it was draining her energy fast.

WHAT ARE YOU GOING TO DO NOW, LITTLE GIRL? the Ghatotkacha rumbled from within her.

Why did it have to feel so smug?

"Shut up," Zara spat. Her eyes darted around the gaps between where the monsters swarmed. Not for the first time, she tried to expand the shell.

Creatures whooped and shrieked as she pushed them away. "MARCUS? PAILE?" she shouted hoarsely, but her voice was lost amidst the din.

YOU KNOW WHAT IT IS THAT IS REQUIRED.

"I said shut up!" Zara snapped, glimpsing something shimmering in the moonlight on the ground.

A weapon?

An axe.

Dmitri's axe.

She took a careful step forward, and the cocoon flickered, almost collapsing under the weight of the monsters outside. Desperately, she clung to her power, solidifying it in time before it dropped. Zara wiped sweat from her eyes, and through the movement outside, saw something else.

Hunter.

He was only a few feet away. The monsters had little interest in him when they were this close to the parallax. Either that or the feeble, shattered remnants of the Elder Sapling beside him was deterring unwanted attention. He was struggling with something, though...*someone.*

Paile.

She thrashed on the floor, her pale, silver-cracked hands grasping at his thick arms. He was using his superior mass and strength to overpower her. His hands were around her neck, and blood leaked from her nose and temple. He was shouting something at her.

"PAILE!" Zara cried as the swarm of monsters shifted, and she lost sight of them again.

He's going to kill her.

I need to get out of here, but how can I...

CLOSE YOUR EYES, LITTLE GIRL. GIVE ME CONTROL. I WILL HOLD THE LINE.

What?

YOU KNOW WHAT YOU MUST DO. IF YOU DO NOT, THIS FIGHT IS LOST.

Zara realised immediately what it spoke of. She could practically see the vast red and gold gate covered with seals already.

You don't know that...

I HAVE WON AND LOST MORE BATTLES THAN YOU HAVE TAKEN BREATHS. RELEASE THEM AND FACE THE CONSEQUENCES, OR YOU AND YOUR FRIENDS ALL DIE HERE.

Release them?

So, the seals truly do contain something powerful behind the gate.

She didn't know what was behind that gate, what she might let loose. Nani's voice echoed in her mind, '*You don't know what it is you bear.*'

What good is bearing it if it means we all die here tonight?

"Fine," Zara hissed out loud. "But if you're tricking me..."

The Ghatotkacha chuckled loudly, and Zara scowled in reply, closing her eyes. Giving up power over herself wasn't easy, not whilst holding onto the cocoon around her. The searing energy of the spirit surrounded her, holding onto her. She took a deep breath, trying to ignore the screaming, snapping, and snarling around her.

She felt herself on the surface of the Ghatotkacha's power, like floating on her back atop a dark ocean of immeasurable age and strength. She let out a long breath.

Here we go.

Zara let herself sink as the Ghatotkacha took over.

THE LIGHT of the sky on the mountaintop should have been blinding after the darkness of the cemetery. But somehow, her eyes were completely adjusted. The vast, red doors stood were arm's reach before her, pulsing with ominous power. It was so close it was smothering. Zara raised her hand and rested it against the red wood. She felt the immeasurable pressure beyond.

"So, you want out?" she asked softly.

Silence. She took a deep breath of anticipation, waiting expectantly.

"Fine." Zara reached for the handle and twisted it. "Get your asses out here and help."

She pushed and was blown apart in an explosion of multi-coloured light.

CAN I GET A REWIND?

Zara's eyes opened wide, and she gasped, immediately regaining full control of her body, even as her senses reeled.

The barrier of energy she was holding in place faltered and fell. The monsters moved in on her like a hungry swarm with shining eyes and dripping jaws.

She raised her hands, and a blast of pale violet energy forced her to her knees. The blast also forced back the swarm...but it wasn't only a blast. The violet power solidified into a solid spiritual form, standing ten feet tall and...

She is beautiful.

It took the shimmering shape of a woman with long hair plaited over one shoulder, chin proud, and eyes fierce. She bore a long halberd tipped with a great curved blade.

As Zara watched in awe, her body convulsed again, this time with a blast of aqua.

A short, fat spirit bearing a mace, with not a hair on his head, sprung forth, eyes full of malice and glee.

Zara gasped as the force of the eruption pushed her onto her backside.

There was another pulse from within her, and her back arched. A deep red light erupted from her mouth as she let out a cry. A man just as big as the first spirit, with a large beakish nose and a disdainful stare emerged. He wore a long cloak and bore two long, curved blades in his hands.

The next blasts, yellow and green, came in rapid succession. These two looked to be androgynous twins, handsome and beautiful at once, eyes wild with mischief. One carried a bow, the other a short, narrow blade.

Then something shook deep within her, and Zara felt herself being separated from within.

She screamed.

From her mouth and eyes, a beacon of pure light shone, and she felt *him* burst out of her. The sheer force of it threw her back into the ground and left her blinking tears from her eyes. Gasping and ears ringing, Zara looked up...at the Ghatotkacha.

He was pale as the moonlight, the largest of all of them, and thick with bulk and muscle. He smiled at her, folding his arms.

Zara twitched weakly on the ground.

I...released him.

Released them all...

"We should leave," the red spirit rasped, lashing out and felling three monsters with one of its blades.

"No," the tall, violet woman said imperiously. "The human released us to win this battle. Let us honour that before we find our joys."

"KILL?" the squat, teal man squealed excitedly.

"Kill!" the twins agreed in unison.

And then the spirits went to war, their luminous bodies fanning out into the masses of shrieking monsters.

Zara struggled weakly to her feet in their wake. Her body screamed with exhaustion and useless mortality. She ducked behind the crimson spirit as it drove both its blades into the big, toothy furball but was promptly knocked down by a long, faceless creature being blasted through the air. Her body crashed agonisingly on the stone.

The screech of battle and stench of blood, bile, and excrement filled her senses. Zara's ankle gave out under her as she stumbled painfully to her knees. There was a strange hissing from above, and Zara looked up.

The translucent, glowing body of the mothman regarded her with interest, its large grey wings fluttering against the moon.

Zara tried to crawl away. She'd seen what that thing could do. Sure enough, it spewed out its acid. She screamed, raising her hands and closing her eyes.

There was a squelch and a high-pitched shriek.

Zara opened her eyes, peering between her fingers. The tall, violet spirit of a woman stood before her, one large hand dripping with the thing's acidic bile, the other holding her halberd, poised gracefully as it speared the mothman through its face. The mothman's body twitched, its wings fluttering feebly.

"Thank you—" Zara began.

"Move!" the spirit snapped, pulling her halberd free.

The mothman fell to the ground, its translucent body bulging and bubbling.

Zara had barely hobbled up when the thing's middle split like a seam. Wriggling larvae poured from its gaping abdominal cavity. She watched as they immediately turned to feed on the dead mothman. One of them turned its attention to Zara. Its small, milky eyes shone in the moonlight. It opened a tiny mouth full of sharp teeth and let out a shriek like a whistling kettle.

She limped back, horrified, as the violet spirit danced to her next battle.

Zara's good foot bashed against something on the ground, and she fell, her head bouncing off the stone cobbles with jarring force. For a moment, she blinked dazedly up at the moon, hearing the snarling cries of monsters fighting and dying around her. She tilted her head to the side and found a familiar face.

Half of one, at least.

The large, tattooed man who had been with Isla lay there, his remaining eye staring sightlessly.

Zara retched and rolled the other way, finding what she had tripped over.

Dmitri's axe.

She grabbed it, pulling it up with both hands. It felt far heavier than she remembered, and her joints screamed in protest as she rose.

It's not heavier. I'm just weak again now.

Zara heard another shrill cry and glanced to see several of the larvae now wriggling her way. She pulled the axe close to her chest and turned in the direction she thought she'd seen Paile struggling with Hunter and ran as fast as her now mortal body could carry her.

THERE WERE STILL SO many monsters, and more appeared still from the surrounding darkness, arriving from more distant locations, drawn to the power of the world parallax.

Zara ran past a huge, bloated-looking frog lying on its back. It was full of bright yellow arrows, with the green twin sitting atop it, ramming their blade in and out of its throat with a merry look on their face. The one with the bow was standing behind them, sending streaks of glowing light from their bow, felling flapping creatures in the night sky one after another.

There was a snarl, and Zara turned to find something like a large, black wolf—but bigger—with red, glowing eyes stalking her between fallen bodies. She ran faster, hoping to lose it amidst the battle.

"I'm sorry. I'm so sorry," she heard a voice moan.

His voice.

Zara ducked beneath the clumsy swing of an enormous creature that looked to be made of mud and grass. She twisted in the direction she had heard him. Something caught the back of her trouser leg, and she fell, dropping the axe with a clatter, palms and elbows scraping sharply on the ground. She didn't have time to wonder what it was before she felt teeth close around her calf, her flesh being punctured in multiple places. She screamed as searing pain shot through her leg and hot blood flowed down her ankle. Twisting desperately, Zara kicked out with her free leg, but the black wolf attached to her was unfazed, her boot glancing off its face ineffectually. It tugged at her fiercely, jaws tearing into flesh and muscle. Letting out a sob of agony, Zara twisted again, trying to reach the axe.

"Zara!" Paile's strangled voice called.

Lying on the ground along with her, Zara could see Paile still struggling with the man who had done this to her, the man Paige thought had loved her. His handsome face was stretched and contorted as much as the bulging muscles that had torn through his shirt were.

"It doesn't have to be like this!" he moaned, eyes wide, even as he tried to wrestle his hands free of hers and get them around her neck. "If you'd just do what you were supposed to!"

The wolf yanked hungrily at Zara's leg. Her head swam with pain, her vision darkening around the edges. Then there was a yelp, and the pressure around her leg eased and released.

Zara looked back.

The pale, glowing form of the Ghatotkacha stood proudly, the black wolf clutched in one of its massive hands.

Zara swallowed, and the spirit regarded her flatly, then squeezed the wolf to a bloody pulp.

"GO," he boomed.

Zara rolled back, panting, fingers closing around the haft of the axe.

"Paile!" she cried.

One red eye and one blue met hers at once, and Zara pushed herself forth, leaping as close as her wounded leg would allow. She flung the axe.

Hunter slapped out a hand, knocking it away with ease, before attempting to wrap his hands around Paile's neck again.

Zara stumbled and fell once more, tears of frustration stinging her eyes. She scanned for where the axe had landed and found it by the broken remnants of the Elder Sapling.

So close, but so far. At this rate...

A strange, familiar humming joined the surrounding din, followed by shrieking, gurgling cries. Between the shifting bodies, a shape emerged, dress billowing like frothing cream as she danced gracefully between foes, a long bone blade, almost as tall as she, striking out with perfect aim.

The Bean-Nighe felled one creature after another, and Zara watched, hypnotised by her movements, as one pale bare foot slid beneath the axe's haft and launched it smoothly into the air.

Zara's heart and breath failed her for a moment as the axe travelled the space between them. The Bean-Nighe looked her way, and Zara thought that if she had eyelids, she might have winked before she disappeared back into the fray.

Paile released her hold on Hunter's hands, allowing his thick fingers to close around her throat as her long fingers reached out and closed around the haft.

Zara took a gasping breath, and the world moved again.

Paile whipped the side of the axe with blunt force into left of Hunter's head. He gave a strange barking yelp of surprise, and his hands came loose from her throat, his eyes bulging as he tumbled off her. Paile rolled, gasping for breath and spun to stand protectively before Zara, axe clutched in both hands.

"Are you okay?" Vandle's voice asked.

Zara coughed, pushing herself up. She tasted blood. "Oh, I'm just fucking dandy. Here at the end of the world in the middle of a war with monsters..."

A waddling monstrosity with three yellow eyes on stalks approached them. Paile leaned toward it and bared her teeth, hissing. Its three eyes widened with panic, and it waddled rapidly away.

"Okay, but why was that weirdly hot?" Zara managed a smile.

"Alright, pervert, we'll have less of that," Paige snapped. But Paile was smiling.

"About that backup," Zara said.

"On it," Paile replied, using both her voices. Then, only Paige's. "A little unfinished business on the way, though. What were them magic words again? Necrotic scrotal Dracula?" Her mismatched eyes were fixed on Hunter, who was staggering to his feet, looking somewhat deflated. "I know them," Vandle's voice replied before Zara had a chance. "Oh goody," Paige said.

"Paige...*Paile*...you can't undo this," Zara said.

"I know," Paige's voice snapped. "I won't want to undo it." She strode forward.

"Wait," Hunter said thickly, raising his hand.

Dmitri's axe spun in Paile's fingers, whistling in the night. And just like that, Hunter's hand was gone.

His eyes bulged, and he opened his mouth, a horrific scream escaping as blood squirted from the severed arteries in his wrist.

Paile changed the direction of the axe, swinging it around and up from below.

Zara closed her eyes as the blade struck home between his thighs, burying itself the full depth of the blade and instantly being lost in a torrent of rushing gore.

Hunter's scream became a strangled squeak.

"Nenorocitul Dracului," Vandle snarled. Hunter's crotch and abdomen erupted in searing flames. Paile popped a hand inside her jacket and pulled out one of the glass beads. "Last one. Lucky you," Paige's voice said sharply as she popped it into his mouth, then slammed his jaw shut with the heel of one palm.

Zara heard a crunch.

Paile was already walking toward a nearby mirror when his head erupted in a geyser of fire.

The mirror had tumbled but not broken, thanks to the strengthening glyph from the Filii Terra. Hopefully, the other mirrors scattered around the graveyard remained just as intact.

Hunter's burning corpse struck the ground.

"Are you...going to be alright?" Zara asked.

Paile turned and shot her a feral grin. Zara couldn't place which of them it belonged to. Maybe both? Maybe neither.

"We will be." Her eyes travelled over Zara's shoulder, and Zara followed them, finding a new wave of monsters bounding, slithering, and scuttling into the cemetery. "I'd worry more about yourself. Don't be a hero."

"I think those days are over." Zara forced a smile and limped over to Hunter's remains. She lifted Dmitri's axe from where it had fallen. Its handle was wet and slippery with blood.

"Good luck, Zara. Be safe," Vandle said. She winked with her blue eye, and Paige added, "I'll be right back."

And then, she disappeared into the mirror.

❦ 51 ❦

ALL IN

The axe felt almost impossibly heavy now in Zara's grip. She leaned against the mausoleum wall. In the distance, she could hear the smashing of glass and crunch of metal and could only imagine that the surrounding houses and cars were being trashed and destroyed as the larger, slower, and more distant monsters were drawn to the parallax. These sounded bigger.

In the cemetery, the first wave of monsters that arrived was growing thin in number. The yellow and green twins had seemingly grown bored with the fight and had bounded off somewhere in the night. Zara couldn't stand to think about that right now. Shortly after, the crimson and teal spirits disappeared, too.

The Ghatotkacha was visibly frustrated with this, destroying his foes with increasing vigour. The violet spirit worked in unison with him, covering his inelegance and lumbering strength with the precise power and swift accuracy of her halberd. Beside them, the black mirror remained untouched under their protection, and a swathe of monstrous bodies was piling up. The spirits had been seemingly using the hole that Valeria and the earth-wyrm collapsed into as a landfill for monster corpses, and even *that* was overflowing.

Zara's breath rattled in her chest, with either cemetery dust or blood from injuries, she didn't know. Either way, it wasn't worth thinking about too much. From the sounds of the approaching monsters, they wouldn't survive another wave.

The spirits didn't seem to have much interest in protecting them and had only wanted to fight until they'd had their fill.

Who knows what mischief they've gone to find now?

She wondered how long they had been locked away and what for.

Had it been Nani that did it or someone before?

What will happen now that I've unleashed them?

I suppose that's not much of my concern anymore.

"Quite a night, huh?" a voice said beside her.

Zara jolted, turning and smiling in surprise. "Marcus!"

Marcus nodded, leaning against the mausoleum wall like he had been there all along. His shirt was stained dark with a huge amount of blood, but it couldn't have been his, as miraculously, he seemed completely uninjured. He was practically glowing.

"I thought you might be dead," Zara admitted.

Marcus cocked his head, umber eyes twinkling in the moonlight and winking. "Never gonna happen. Hey, speaking of dead, I saw...a bit of Hunter on my way here. Shame he had to split."

Zara smiled, shaking her head.

Marcus looked aghast. "Oh no. Did somebody already do the pun?"

"Nah, you're fine. I don't know for how much longer, though. This next lot sound nasty."

"No doubt, no doubt," Marcus agreed. "But you sent Paile to do the thing?" His voice carried a predictable amount of excitement.

"I did."

"Even if shit goes sideways, at least we'll go out with a bang."

"Is there any other way?" Isla said sharply. She strode forward, looking more than a little ragged. Her neck and collar were dark with blood, hair matted on one side, and eyes wild. Song walked

434

beside her, their large, golden eyes fixed on Marcus balefully for some reason.

"Have you seen Ed?" Zara asked.

"Ducky and Ed are together. Last I saw, they were eating some big, fuzzy monkey crocodile thing. Fucking cute little weirdos."

Zara laughed.

There was a deafening roar from far too close.

Zara swallowed, pushing herself upright. She could barely move now, and her joints all screamed with stiff agony.

"Marcus—" she began.

"No more powers," Marcus cut in. "I know. I feel it."

She took a deep breath...at least, as deep as she could right now.

"Don't worry, sis. I got ya. How are you holding up, otherwise?"

Zara forced a smile. She tasted blood when she swallowed. "I'm still here. Almost got taken out by that mothman, though."

Marcus shook his head. "Stupid, sexy mothman."

There was another roar.

Zara glanced at the spirits by the black mirror. All the monsters around them were dead, and they seemed to be...arguing about something?

"They're close," Marcus warned, staring into the darkness. "Watch the skies. The ones with the long necks...they have poison breath. Three hearts in their chest, so aim for the head if you can. Stay away from the big snakes. Their eyes don't turn you to stone, but their skin will rot you through in seconds. Everyone got their packed lunch and ready to play?"

Zara barked a bitter, painful laugh and watched as the violet spirit sprung away into the night. The Ghatotkacha watched her go, then turned and regarded Zara with glowing eyes.

Don't you leave me now...

The earth rumbled beneath them.

"Oh, and there's like five more of those earth-wyrms," Marcus added brightly.

Zara sighed. "We're fucked."

"Let's get to the mirror with that big ghost thing and buy as much time as we can. May as well make it worth it at least," Isla said resolutely.

"Welcome to the team," Zara said tiredly. "Looks like you're part of the family now."

Isla shot her a grin and blushed.

Zara smiled in return. "I'm not too hopeful we're gonna last much longer than a full five seconds, though."

Something lit up the night beside her with bright, blue crackling energy.

Zara turned toward it. Marcus floated in the air, eyes bright with sparkling magick, fingers already working excitedly.

"I reckon I can do better than that," he said. "Shit's about to get real. Somebody bust out the Bon Jovi."

ISLA AND SONG helped Zara down the hill toward the mirror whilst Marcus flitted through the air, harrying the approaching creatures with bolts of blue energy that struck like lightning, leaving shrieking fire and ruin in their wake. When they arrived, the Ghatotkacha watched carefully as Zara leaned on the wall beside the mirror.

"What? Aren't you going to leave like the rest of them?" Zara grumbled. She coughed and spat. It looked like mostly blood.

"ARE YOU DYING?" the Ghatotkacha boomed.

Zara rubbed her mouth with the back of her hand. "Maybe? We've all got to die sometime. I was on borrowed time with you, anyway. I guess that time's up."

The spirit regarded her with interest.

"You told me you'd help us win this fight, then all your little ghost mates fucked off," Zara said bitterly.

The Ghatotkacha gave a remorseful growl. "THEY ARE

BEINGS AS OLD AS I, BUT FEW KEEP PROMISES AS I DO. AND NONE RELISH WAR SO MUCH."

"So, they helped until they got bored and decided to cause different trouble?"

"YES," the Ghatotkacha said bluntly.

Zara rolled her eyes.

That sounded familiar.

There was a flash of light nearby as Marcus spun through the air, catching himself before he collided with the earth. Zara heard him cackling as he took flight once more, aiming straight back at the hoard.

"YOUR FRIEND FIGHTS WELL," the Ghatotkacha said, watching him.

"Yeah."

"*YOU* FIGHT WELL."

Zara chuckled weakly. "Not so much. I think most of it was you. I just let you out as much as I needed to help get done what needed to be done."

The Ghatotkacha stared at her, then boomed, "YOU HAVE A WARRIOR'S HEART, AND YOU ARE...HUMBLE."

Zara frowned. "Listen, ghost-boy, I don't know if you're trying to get in my pants, but—"

"NOT ALL FIGHTS ARE FOUGHT WITH FISTS, LITTLE...CHATTERJEE." The massive spirit placed one hand on its barrel chest. "YOU FIGHT FROM THE HEART."

Zara smiled. "Only way worth fighting."

A long cry grew closer as Marcus was once more catapulted through the air. This time, he collided with the ground with brutal force, rolling in a tumble of long limbs, coming to a stop before them.

"Marcus!" Zara cried, certain he was dead.

Marcus twisted then sprung upright light a jack-in-the-box. "I'm okay!"

Zara stared at him blankly and then turned her gaze to Song.

Those large, golden eyes looked back at her sadly.

"YOU ARE...IMMORTAL," the Ghatotkacha said.

"No shit," Zara scowled.

"I can explain!" Marcus began.

"He was dying!" Isla added defensively.

Marcus shrugged. "Ran into a soulwinder...and the Bean-Nighe. She didn't do a very good job of saving me. Three out of ten would not be saved again. Then she did a bit of stabbing and said she had business to attend to and buggered off. Main point being, we better hope there are no more soulwinders around, or we're in the shit. I had to give up a lot just to stick around."

Zara sighed. "If there was ever a time to trade the big chips, I guess it's now. I saw the Bean-Nighe too. She saved Paile and was definitely...*busy.*"

The first of the creatures erupted from the night, a row of furry monsters with multiple legs and snapping jaws. Among them were two, no three, lumbering creatures that looked almost like large trees but with wicked faces carved upon their trunks with cruel, flashing eyes.

"Well...here we go." Zara hefted Dmitri's axe weakly.

There was a flash to her left. At first, Zara thought Marcus must have used magick, but then she saw it was one of the mirrors, the one propped high on top of one of the tombs. A few huddled shadows were moving atop it.

There was another flash from the right, where she knew another mirror was propped between the trees.

A wild smile crept onto Marcus' face. "At first light...on the fifth day...look to the east, motherfuckers."

The Ghatotkacha turned to Zara. "BOND WITH ME AGAIN."

Zara blinked. "What?"

"BOND WI—"

"I heard you. But...why?"

"I SEEK TO FIGHT WITH THE BEST." The Ghatotkacha's reply was short, simple, and full of truth.

Zara shook her head. "I'm not the best."

The Ghatotkacha's large face split with a broad smile. "YOU WILL BE."

More things were yipping and howling as they approached in the night. One of the massive serpents Marcus had mentioned slithered toward them.

"Fine," Zara agreed, smiling grimly.

There was another flash from the left, then another. Then one from the right and one from behind. A suited figure leaped down with feline grace, landing on all fours. He cocked his head at them, offering a handsome smile.

"Mr Sato!" Marcus whooped.

"I heard there was a party. I hope you don't mind that I brought a few friends?" The man offered a sly grin.

Zara looked again and saw that the shapes scuttling atop the tomb were a group of hideous little goblins with long noses and even longer claws. From the trees to the right, a beautiful East Asian woman emerged, propelled entirely by her thick, dark, lustrous black hair. From the left, another woman emerged, just as striking. She was completely nude, though her body was not the same colour as her peachy face but a chitinous black. She stretched her arms, including the six spindling limbs that protruded from her back, as several dog-sized spiders scuttled around her.

Marcus smirked. "A party? I forgot to bring my poppers."

"I don't think he means that kind of party." Zara sighed, unable to stop herself from grinning.

There was a loud crash as one of the mausoleum's doors smashed open. An enormous beast tore out, standing eight feet tall with stubby horns atop his head. His eyes glowed red, and he roared, showing a large mouth filled with sharp teeth. It was strangely intimidating, despite the bright yellow trousers he wore. Zara spotted a human with glasses nervously peering from the tomb behind him.

There was movement beside her, and Zara turned to find Paile, looking worn and tired but smiling excitedly. She held the bone dagger in one hand, ready to fight.

"Well, now that everybody's here," Marcus said brightly as the horrible little goblins leapt from above the tomb and swarmed, tearing chunks from one of the tree monsters that had just arrived with the latest swarm.

The black mirror pulsed beside them.

Zara stared at it.

What?

No...

Marcus let out a raucous laugh. "YOU'VE GOT TO BE SHITTING ME!"

Zara gasped. "Marcus..."

"Here he comes to save the dayyyyy!" Marcus sang, doing a dance that was entirely inappropriate given the war looming before them.

The spider woman leapt forward and decimated one of the tree creatures with her powerful legs. Her scuttling children swarmed over several of the hairy, many-legged things. The woman with the long hair was...*eating* one of them with what looked like...the back of her head?

"We will hold them off," the catlike Mr Sato said merrily before them, flexing fingers that shifted to paws with long claws like daggers. "Hopefully, that's a good sign, and the world isn't ending. Some of us like it just fine here, thank you very much!" He pounced into the fray, landing atop a tall lizard creature, claws gouging into its face.

The massive, hairy thing ploughed through one of the tree monsters, shattering it to twigs and smithereens, then was set upon by the other. One of the snakes lunged at him, but he shifted aside, snatched it by the tail, and set about beating the tree monster with it.

Zara's eyes shifted back to the black mirror.

It bulged...like something was struggling to come through.

Only a few things had passed through the mirror from Theia —or at least *tried*. All that was left of them was hunks of steaming meat and bone. But whatever *this* was seemed to be bigger...and alive.

Zara's heart stopped in her chest. She stepped back, mouth open, staring as the mirror's dark face stretched, the blackness expanding until...

A heaving mass exploded from the mirror's face, tumbling in a smouldering heap of ruined tissue and smoking wings. Zara stared at it in shock.

What was that?

She swallowed.

It can't be...

He wouldn't.

A pale, slim figure rose from behind the dead thing, visibly disoriented.

Zara froze.

His hair was longer.

He looked so thin.

But he was...

Alive.

He was alive.

He's alive.

"I'm going to say it!" Marcus squeaked excitedly.

"Oscar..." Zara started.

His eyes were wide, his body shaking, and his face streaked with tears.

"I'm going to fucking say it..." Marcus clearly couldn't contain himself.

Oscar was stared at him, blinking and confused.

Zara shook her head.

Marcus let it rip.

"GAYVENGERS, ASSEMMMBLEEEEEE!"

TAXONOMY OF MONSTERS: OSCAR TUNDALE

(STELLAM MATUTINAM)

Descendant of the Irish Knight Tnugdalus, the only known human to travel to and from Theia in history, whose accounts were recorded in Visio Tnugdali. The impression left upon Tnugdalus' cellular structure translated into a genetic mutation that took multiple generations to manifest, resulting in a human with perfectly attuned Theian cells within their body. Fusion with a rogue Umbran, followed by acute magickal separation, seems to have resulted in a permanent presence of Umbran characteristics. Host's own peaches and cream aura is intermingled with dark threatening clouds. Longevity and power of Umbran origin have combined with the resilience of human nature, allowing consumption and redistribution of negative energies, shadowmancy, and enhanced durability. Prefers only to be addressed as 'Oscar' rather than something cooler.

— ORIGINAL TAXONOMY ENTRY, MARCUS
WILLIAMS

VII

VITA POST MORTEM

MORNINGSTAR

O scar felt it.

His ears still rang from the rush of the world parallax, the flashing bright rush of infinity. The smell of charred fur and flesh filled his nostrils. The power of darkness from Theia pressed against him tentatively like thin threads of energy, latching onto him and pulling at him as though he was a patch being sewn into a tapestry. He staggered forward, blinking.

They were there.

"Zara...Marcus." He took a heaving breath, his eyes falling to Dmitri's ruined body beside him.

"OSCAR!" Zara cried.

He turned his head dazedly—too slow.

Something like a massive wasp, but the size of a man, buzzed through the air directly at him. Its long, barbed stinger dripped threateningly. He raised a hand weakly, but nothing happened. He didn't have any power...the connection had not taken root properly yet.

Zara rushed forward, leaping into the air. At the same time, the large, bulky figure glowing with intense energy standing beside her did the same. In the air, they became one.

Oscar watched in awe as she reached out with a massive,

glowing hand—extended from her own—and snatched the monster, crushing it into a green, oozing pulp before she even landed back in front of him.

"Zara," Oscar said feebly. He couldn't get out another word before her arms were around him, pulling him to her desperately.

"I'm so sorry. I'm so sorry, Booboo. I'm so sorry," she sobbed.

Oscar squeezed her back, feeling beyond tears, but they flowed anyway. "It's okay...it's okay. You did the right thing."

How many times have I dreamed this moment? And yet...it happens like this.

"I DON'T KNOW ABOUT YOU TWO, BUT I'M FIGHTING A WAR RIGHT NOW!" Marcus yelled. He was...*floating?* He threw a handful of searing magick at a gigantic snake that had been about to sink its fangs into a big, hairy creature. "I COULD HAVE SWORN I SAID ASSEMBLE, NOT HAVE A FUCKING CUDDLE."

"Sorry," Oscar said before adding an awkward wave.

Marcus grinned and waved back, then rocketed forth, both his fists glowing with bright magick.

"That's new," Oscar said, watching his friend fly into the fray.

"Wait...isn't Dmitri coming?" Zara asked.

Oscar swallowed. "Where is the world parallax?"

"Oscar..."

"Where is it? We can't wait any longer."

Zara looked at him with concern but pointed to the mirror that stood several feet away. Its face was darker than night.

Now, Oscar could see it. It was as though the threads that had been searching for him took root in his bones and pulled him toward it. He wasn't sure how he hadn't found it before.

"Oscar, aren't you going to wait for Dmitri?" Zara asked, her voice high with panic.

Something that looked like a relative of a water-leaper approached, just as big but with no wings. It spat out a massive tongue, and Zara snatched it out of the air with a ghostly hand before it struck Oscar. He blinked, walking closer to the mirror as

Zara reeled it in and clobbered it with a ghostly punch. The dark surface of the mirror shone before him. Behind him, though, Oscar heard the chaos of battle.

"Oscar, what are you doing?" Zara cried.

Oscar turned his head in time to see Zara tear the frog-monster's head from its body. "Whatever happens next, Zara...you have to trust me."

"What are you talking about, Booboo?"

"Just *trust me*, okay?"

Zara nodded, and Oscar touched his fingers to the black glass...and became one with the space between worlds.

OSCAR HAD DRAWN in hate and darkness countless times since he had bonded with the power of the Umbran. He had pulled it in like draining a glass through a straw and spat it out immediately or consumed it when it suited his needs.

This was nothing like that at all.

This was like having the contents of all the world's oceans forced through that straw and into his mouth until the fluids burst from his stomach, filling the space around his organs and bloating him like a balloon. Thankfully, because of the mark the Umbran had left within him, Oscar had quite a big appetite for what flowed forth.

He was submerged by the putrid darkness. It was like a bottomless oil slick, and it filled him with life. He felt the wounds he sustained in the battle with Belphegor heal within an instant. He pulled and pulled until he felt ready to explode with it, and then he pulled some more. And yet, he could feel that beyond the veil, there was an eternity left.

"Oscar?" Zara's voice called to him from somewhere far away.

Oscar paused.

"Oscar, what are you doing?" She sounded closer now.

He felt something pulling him.

Pulling him back.

Pulling him out.

Oscar blinked, and the night sky was around him again. He stared at the black surface of the mirror, of the world parallax. He felt Theia beyond.

"What did you do?" Zara breathed.

Oscar wriggled out of her grasp. He could feel it now. The threads that sank into his skeleton before were like dark, invisible veins now connecting him to Theia. Not through the dead mirror...but through this place.

"Oscar...your eyes. They're black like...the Umbran's."

He tried to force a reassuring smile but wasn't sure how good a job he did based on the look of horror on her face.

"It's okay, Zara." He felt so strong now. Full. Yet more energy pulsed into him through those dark veins, force-feeding him with all the pressure built up in Theia. He needed to release it, *fast,* before he was overwhelmed.

"Zara. I need to use power. Who do I fight?"

"What?" Zara asked, looking shaken.

"I need to use the power poisoning Theia," Oscar repeated, turning and scanning the night.

"Oscar...what's happened to you?" Zara asked, voice full of worry.

A stab of fear drove into Oscar's heart.

What if I can't go back?

He heard Dmitri's voice as if in reply: *'Then you go forward'.*

Oscar raised his hands and pulled on the darkness. A group of lizard creatures that were nipping at a woman propelling herself away using her dark hair were captured by their scaly feet. He dragged them toward himself as they whined and bit at their own legs, trying to release themselves in confusion.

"Look out," Oscar warned, stepping to the side.

Zara stared wide-eyed with shock. He was forced to drag the shadows at her feet to move her out of the way as he bundled the lizards into a writhing ball of shadow and forced them through the world parallax.

Black power sparked from its surface as it swallowed them. He felt them moving *between*. He pushed, holding his grip on them. Though his awareness faded the further through they got, he *thought* he pushed them far enough to not drop them into the space below.

Zara stared at him. "Oscar, what the fuck?"

A world of power battered Oscar through the threads between worlds.

"I need to use more," he said flatly. "It looks like some monsters are helping us. Find me more of the bad ones that you want me to put through. Tell Marcus, too. Get anyone on our side out of the way and try to funnel everything to me."

"The world parallax," Zara said, staring at its surface. It sparked with angry power. "Marcus said if it becomes unstable, it'll blow up like a nuclear bomb."

Oscar nodded. "I'll hold it. Now, bring me more monsters."

OSCAR WATCHED as Zara darted into the night, energy pulsing at her feet to enhance her speed. From behind him, the dark power that drowned Theia continued to push into him. Sweat poured from his brow and ran down his back. Ahead, he saw Marcus—standing on the ground now—with Song beside him as he cast out a bolt of power. He heard Zara shout something at him but couldn't make out the words exactly. Marcus, however, took to the air once more with a whoop and flew up into the night sky.

Oscar heard a voice call from his left. "Please...be careful, Knud!" He looked over and saw a spectacled man peering out of one of the tombs, though *he* was definitely very much alive.

The large, hairy monster with horns—or Knud, as the man had called him—growled and started stomping one of his massive feet on one of the termite creatures with big snappy jaws. Oscar had seen nothing like *that* in Theia.

"Daniel, stay back," Knud rumbled as he retreated from more of the creatures.

There were so many of them, each the size of a small dog, their heads unnaturally large. They moved too quickly for his powerful but clumsy stamps, and as they reached him, their powerful jaws began biting into the monster's hairy flesh. He roared as blood flowed from him.

Oscar felt a stab of empathy and let the shadows at his feet lift him, carrying him like a wave, propelling him toward the poor thing. "Stay still!"

To the monster's credit, he did his best, staying as still as he could even as the little things continued to bite, staining his bright yellow trousers with crimson blood.

Oscar stretched out his hands, concentrating on forming fine fingers of shadow that reached out from the darkness like tentacles. Forming so many at once wasn't easy. Worse still was the delicate touch, as not to harm the big monster with this much power in him begging to rush forth. As he worked, several of the termites scuttled toward the human, hungrily snapping their jaws.

Oscar panicked. He didn't have focus over this much power to save them both, but he wasn't forced to choose. Just as they neared the man, a figure appeared out of nothingness, gobbling one up with a chomp. It vanished, then reappeared with a pop, and wolfed down another, this time accompanied by a victorious *quack* before it disappeared.

Was that Ed? With some kind of bird on his back?

Before he knew it, Oscar had plucked all the small creatures off the thing called Knud and bundled them with those on the ground into another bundle of shadow and cast them behind him and into the mirror.

"Th...thank you," the man with glasses said, rushing out of the tomb to his...*Knud*.

Knud reached out with one massive hand and pulled the

human toward him, embracing him protectively. "Daniel, stay safe," he admonished softly.

Oscar's heart wrenched.

The human, Daniel, struggled from Knud's loving grip, looking at Oscar fearfully. "Thank you...for helping him. Whoever you are."

Oscar forced a smile, but the man only blinked, looking even more nervous.

Oh.

My eyes...

"Knud came to help, and I didn't want him to be alone. Sato said that this might be...the end. Is it really going to be? Are we... all going to die?" Daniel asked, swallowing anxiously.

Oscar stared at him for a moment, then shook his head. "No. No one else is going to die tonight."

A nervous smile lit up Daniel's face.

"You two...take shelter in that tomb. Take care of each other, and...be safe. Just...hold on."

You won't lose each other.

Not like I lost Dmitri.

Not if I can help it.

"Thank you," Daniel said again, reaching out and taking the monster's large hand, pulling him toward the tomb.

Knud eyed Oscar curiously but allowed himself to be dragged away. There was certainly no way the human could have moved him if not.

Oscar heard a crash from the side and a rumbling in the earth.

A gigantic cloud of dust was forming. From it, cloaked in the glowing armour of the Ghatotkacha, ran Zara. "OSCAR, I HOPE YOU'RE SURE ABOUT THIS! MARCUS HAS DEFINITELY MADE THEM MAD, AND THERE'S A LOT OF THEM COMING!"

Oscar nodded, letting the wave of shadow carry him back to stand before the world parallax. The thick veins between worlds grew, beating and pushing more and more power into him. He hoped it was enough.

"I'm ready," he said.

Ready to end this.

For Mum and Dad.

For Dmitri.

Oscar raised his hands as Zara pulled to a stop beside him.

"No. Stay back. I...don't know how well I'm going to be able to control this."

Zara shifted away, but he could see her lingering at the edge of his vision, close to the tomb where Knud and his human were hidden. Ahead of him, a dark shadow of roars and snarls advanced.

Oscar swallowed, preparing to release himself. There was a bright flash of light, and Marcus burst out of the din, eyes wide but mouth in a fierce grin as he rocketed by, followed by...

Everyone's worst nightmares.

Eyeballs with wings.

Spiders the size of caravans.

Flapping, biting, slithering, crawling monstrosities of all kinds. The earth groaned with something big below, and the sky darkened with winged shapes of different sizes.

Oscar licked his lips and allowed the power to consume him. He pulled on the night itself. The sky bled with darkness, and the shadows on the ground stretched up. Oscar screamed as the sheer force of the pressure threatened to tear him apart. He stitched the darkness together, enclosing all the hideous advancing monstrosities like a giant blanket, and wrapped them within it. He pulled more and more greedily on the power pouring into him as fast as he spent it.

He squeezed, feeling them, hearing them roar and snarl and cry as their bodies pressed together in the darkness. A few escaped his grasp, but Marcus whizzed around, snatching them up and tossing them into Oscar's growing maelstrom of shadows.

Oscar pulled. More power filled him.

The crushing ocean of putrid hate pressed into him, still seemingly endless.

Oscar shifted his stance, turning to push them into the mirror, warping the darkness like a huge, black funnel full of horrors. It would all have worked wonderfully if he was perhaps more adept, or the mirror was bigger and monsters smaller.

As it was, he felt countless lives snuffed out as he forced the thrashing column into the world parallax. Severed limbs, tentacles, heads, and gore of all varieties fountained from the dark as though he'd put half of them into a blender and forced them through together. He had no idea how many would survive or what state they would be in when they arrived, but he couldn't think of any better way to handle it. He pushed them as far as he could, hoping to save them from immediate death upon their arrival. At least this way, some of them could live. And hopefully, Theia was in a fit state to take them.

The mirror screamed under the pressure, threatening to blast apart a thousand times over, to flatten London and beyond. But he held that, too, winding vessels of shadow up and around the frame like delicate vines full of nothing but power.

Oscar's body screamed. He felt blood and darkness leaking from his eyes, nostrils, and ears as he forced the last of them through and released.

With the cacophony of roars and screams silenced, the night was eerily quiet, so the thud of his kneecaps hitting the ground as he fell made him cringe even before the sharp pain jolted through him.

His body was weak, and yet more power pressed into him.

There is still so much.

What can I do?

Oscar felt himself being washed away by the unending torrent of darkness.

Surely I have done enough. Surely whatever has been released through the parallax already could ensure the survival of Earth for centuries to come.

Now...I can rest.

Now I can be with...him.

Oscar surrendered himself. He started to let the darkness overpower him and burn through him like a blown bulb. He felt his body shaking, his heart fluttering...

Then, he felt something else.

A small, warm hand linking fingers with his own.

Oscar turned his eyes.

Song was on their knees beside him, their large golden eyes fixed on his with a deep sense of knowing.

And they sent to him.

Oscar felt their understanding of the love they had seen for him.

Felt for him.

Oscar was buffeted by the adoration and grief that Song had witnessed since they had been there. He felt it all...each person's powerful and distinct love. Marcus' burning fiercely, Zara's endless and warm, Paige's sharp and firm...and Dmitri's: an undying tide of bottomless hope. He felt them wrap around him, hold on to him.

And he held onto himself.

Song smiled.

"Oscar?" Zara asked gently, approaching with caution. She, too, came to her knees, reaching out and taking his other hand. "What's happening?"

Oscar moaned. "There's...too much."

"Use it!" Marcus hollered, settling beside Song. "You're the valve, Oscar! Stop trying to control it all and just let it rip! We're here with you. You can do this!"

"The valve?" Zara repeated loudly, then gasped in realisation.

Oscar looked up at the night sky and tried to relax his body.

Let it out?

Stop trying to control it?

That's everything the opposite of what Mum taught me...

Oscar felt a different weight settle on his shoulders. Not the crushing weight of hate and death, but a solid, certain presence full of promises.

"You can do it, iubite. You can do anything."

The thought came to him in Dmitri's voice so vividly that for a moment, he almost turned to look for him.

No.

He was gone.

But...I'm not. Everyone else isn't.

Oscar took in a deep breath and closed his eyes and...

Released it all.

The power flowed through him, arching his back and making his arms and legs spasm as it tore up through his chest and out of his mouth in a great geyser of darkness. Oscar screamed, and more flowed through him. He bled shadows and misery and all the hate that had built up over centuries, releasing every moment. He felt like he couldn't bear it any longer but knew that he must. He counted in seconds, promising his body that he would give up after just one more but forcing it on and on, until he felt like he had lived and died in a thousand moments of pure, beautiful, exhilarated agony.

And then...it was over.

He gasped, swaying wearily, his face turned up to the moon where the darkness he'd released continued to dissipate like parting clouds fading into the world, returning as energy in the cycle.

Oscar pulled his hands free and fell forward, heaving. There was nothing left in him to come up, only an inky splotch of blackness that slid out of his mouth and seeped into the earth below. He rolled onto his back, relishing the cool feel of the ground through his ruined clothes. The blood that had stiffened the fabric on his torso and waist had been soaked through once more with a fresh spattering of gore.

He could feel the power from Theia still, like a gentle tide lapping at him.

There was a cracking sound.

Oscar tilted his head and saw a large splinter of light had spread across the dark mirror's face. It was followed by another larger one, accompanied by its own cracking sound.

It's over.

The tendrils of shadow holding the frame together weakened, fading as his power ebbed. But the mirror didn't throb with energy anymore. It was dying.

More cracks appeared, and the darkness faded further. When its face shattered apart and the pieces of frame fell loose, they were just glass and wood.

Oscar swallowed and dropped his head back, panting and staring up at the moon.

It's over...and Dmitri isn't here.

Oscar's heart ached.

Something furry appeared before his eyes, and a big, wet, pink tongue licked up the centre of his face.

"Hi, Ed. It's good to see you too." Oscar gently pushed him away. His breath smelled of death.

Another face appeared above, round and smiling, eyes the colour of freshly fallen autumn leaves and full of tears. "You did it, Booboo."

Another followed, russet eyes sparkling with mischief, glowing umber skin, a long nose, and a massive smile. "Bitch, this cinnamon roll got SPICY! You're literally like a fucking God. What is your cool monster name going to be? Shadowprince? Morningstar? Oooh, what about Shadowspinner?"

Oscar blinked the tears out of his eyes.

"I think I'll just stick with Oscar."

❦ 53 ❦

FATES END

Fortunately, the link with Theia's flowing energy meant Oscar recovered quickly. The threads were back, steadily feeding him with power. Soon, he was strong enough to be on his feet again and was greeted by a strangely familiar figure.

"Oscar," Paige's voice said.

Oscar blinked.

But it wasn't Paige at all.

It's just like Dmitri said.

He stared at the tufts of white and dark hair and the silvery cracks in her pale skin.

"Oh, Paige," he moaned, lurching forward.

She moved just as fast, grabbing him and pulling him fiercely against her.

"I'm sorry about what happened to you two," he said into her shoulder. She smelled like cigarettes and death.

"It was a bad break-up," she said flatly.

He pulled away and looked her in her eyes. One was as red as blood, and the other her shining, cool blue. "You..." He shook his head, confused.

"We are okay," Vandle's voice softly replied. "I will take care of her."

Oscar smiled gratefully and hugged Paile again.

"This is lovely, Oscar, but I'm not a fan of your redecorating," Paige said snarkily from their embrace, booting aside what looked like a lion's head with large horns on it.

"Sorry," Oscar said.

Paile shrugged. "I've seen worse," she said, this time with Vandle's voice.

"You two did great," Marcus intervened as she released Oscar. "I saw you jumping between mirrors, stabbing things up something rotten!"

"I mean, I expect it from Vandle, but...Paige Tundale, hero extraordinaire," Zara said musingly.

"Marcus, can't you..." Oscar waved his hands at Paile. "You seem kind of all-powerful now."

"Nah." Marcus shrugged. "Not enough time."

Zara's head snapped around. "What? What do you mean? Oh, is this another one of your jokes? Do you have a table reservation in Sicily or someth—"

"Is this him?" a sharp voice snapped.

Oscar turned to see a very petite and pale girl approaching, hair red and frizzy, her throat and collar caked with dried blood. She clutched what looked like a shrivelled claw on a long, blackened forearm. Ed moved toward her, panting merrily in the shape of a chocolate Labrador. He head-butted her legs affectionately, almost knocking her over.

"Ah, perfect. Oscar, this is Isla. Isla, Oscar." Marcus grinned.

The girl, eyed him fiercely. "You don't look like much. But that was a lot of power."

Oscar rubbed his head. "I...don't think I'll be able to do anything like that again any time soon. Probably never. The pressure in Theia shouldn't ever get that high again. Not with me here."

Isla shrugged. "Still pretty cool."

Oscar narrowed his eyes. There was something...*familiar* about the girl. "Have we met before?"

The girl eyed him thoughtfully with her sapphire eyes and then shrugged. "I don't think so. I'd never heard of an Oscar Tundale before."

"Nor I an Isla…"

"Barlow," Isla said.

Oscar froze. His mind flickered back to Harry Barlow.

When they had shared minds in the clutches of the Umbran, he had seen him fighting with a woman. *Laney, was it?* And the little girl, sitting on the stairs with tired eyes like she saw the same fight every day.

Those eyes that were in front of him right now.

He stared blankly at Isla and forced a smile onto his face. "Isla Barlow. Thank you…for helping stop the end of the world."

Her pale cheeks flushed. A ruckus kicked up nearby with some of the strange little goblins as they fought over some bloody remains. Isla was forced to rush away and mediate, followed by a yapping mimick-dog for assistance.

A wet pop announced the arrival of a more familiar presence.

"Gax!" Oscar spun around and found the Bugge looking even more sombre than usual.

He shifted on his mottled green feet and gave Oscar what looked strangely like a bow. "'Orrite, urrr…Morningstar." Oscar flashed a look over at Marcus, who winked and gave him an excited thumbs up.

He shook his head. "Oscar is fine."

Gax continued to wring his little hands. "You 'ave to come with me. Quick."

Oscar frowned. "What's wrong?"

Gax was already waddling away toward the copse of crooked trees, half of them torn down and leaning askew.

Oscar followed.

"Oscar?" Zara shouted, rushing to join him. "What's wrong?"

"No idea," Oscar replied. "But I doubt it's anything good."

THEY RUSHED through the dark trees and past the remains of several monster corpses severed into bits by some sort of blade. They weren't like any monster or Theian that Oscar had seen before, with large, skeletal heads, ram-like horns, and bodies tattered with loose flesh. Even in death, they exuded a deep sense of dreadful foreboding.

Above, the branches reached up to the sky like thin, jagged fingers trying to clutch at the moon. At the centre of a small clearing was where they found her.

The Bean-Nighe's dress was covered in blood. She lay amidst its voluminous fabrics, fanned around her as though she were a blood-stained cloud.

Zara gasped, but Oscar rushed forth.

"Here he comes, here he comes, all is saved, for here he comes," the Bean-Nighe cooed softly.

Oscar fell to his knees beside her, where a long sword whittled from bone was driven into the ground. He looked desperately into those large, orb-like eyes. They seemed fainter than usual, dull almost. Her long, pale fingers reached out and touched his face.

So cold.

The Bean-Nighe smiled. "Hello, Cricket."

Oscar tried to smile back but found he couldn't.

"I'm so very glad you chose this path," she crooned softly. "Even if I got lost on the way, it was the best route to take. I got all the ones who'd make it fail, but the cost is the cost, so now I must sail."

'All the ones who'd make it fail.'

Was it her that had killed those strange monsters with the skulls all alone?

Zara slumped to the ground beside him, her fingers gathering the Bean-Nighe's dress and pressing it against the deep gash at her waist.

The Bean-Nighe crinkled her delicate nose and tssk'd, her fingers moving from Oscar's face to rest on Zara's hand.

For just a moment, those big, lidless eyes shone. And then she laughed. It took a few moments for her to stop. And then she smiled at Zara.

"Definitely not the damsel in distress. Just remember to have fun."

"What?" Zara frowned, pulling her hand away.

The Bean-Nighe sighed. "It's getting late. My work here is done, but I have so many places yet to be...sons of skies and princes of sea...hearts to find and hearts to free."

"Bean-Nighe, is there...anything we can do?" Oscar asked.

She smiled, gesturing with bloody fingers for him to come close. For a moment, he heard only her weak, ragged breath, then...

"*Live*," she whispered.

Oscar moved away and stared at her.

Her face was fading. She shimmered like a mirage.

"Please...don't go," Oscar said. He didn't have any tears left, but his chest ached numbly.

The Bean-Nighe smiled. "Goodbye, Cricket."

Her empty, bloodied dress collapsed onto the ground, and Gax let out a gruff, wailing cry.

As Oscar made his way back in silence, Zara's fingers linked within his. They didn't speak. Despite their time apart, right now, it felt like there was nothing to say.

The deep ache in Oscar's chest only got worse when they arrived back.

Marcus was squatting on the ground beside the ruined corpse of the zburător...of Dmitri. He was speaking to a man Oscar heard him call Sato, who was holding a duck...with three feet.

Wait...

Zara's fingers squeezed his. "I'm sorry about Dmitri."

Oscar swallowed. He couldn't bring himself to meet her eyes.

"Nani said to me, before the end, that nothing is as dangerous as a broken heart. I don't think she was wrong, but there's more to it than that," Zara said. "Having a broken heart is dark and lonely, and sometimes there isn't a way back, but sometimes it forces you to find parts of yourself you wouldn't know were there otherwise. Wisdom, resilience, strength, or courage. Horrible things happening to us won't ever make us *better*, but they might bring us closer together or make us stronger. I just want you to know that you don't have to do this alone, Oscar. I'm here. All of us are, no matter what happens. No matter how far you feel you've fallen or how far apart we have to go, we will always be together. Whatever you have to carry; power, responsibility...grief. We will help you carry it so that we can move forward together."

Oscar swallowed and squeezed Zara's hand tighter but could not find the words to respond.

~

PAILE WAS STANDING in the middle of the ruined cemetery, speaking to the woman with the long black hair and the nervous man and his big hairy lover. Oscar edged toward her rather than face Marcus and...*that* right now.

"I need to take them back," Vandle's voice said as they neared.

The long-haired woman folded her arms irritably.

"This one's got a right mouth on her...two, actually," Paige added.

Oscar forced a smile.

"And then?" Zara asked. "Are you going to...search for your missing parts?"

Paile nodded smoothly. "There is no telling where they will be. I have some other tasks to fulfil first, though. I plan to finish the Order of Helios. We cut the head off the snake tonight, but the hand that fed it remains. After that...Isla says that the Filii Terra may have some relics that might assist me in locating my parts and has asked me to help track down their former Matriarch in return. It sounds as though she has a score to settle."

464

"Can I join you?" Zara asked.

The fractured combination of his sister and Betty Blumpkin's former bodyguard stiffened, cocking her head. "I told you, no funny stuff," Paige said.

"The spirits that were locked away...uh, *inside* me?" Zara said carefully. "I have to track them down. It's not just that I have a bad feeling...I literally feel like I'm being pulled in several different directions inside my chest. I'm not sure I could stay even if I tried."

Paile's face twisted in a half-smile. Oscar wasn't sure which half.

Zara's eyes flashed back to Oscar. "I mean...Oscar will probably come, too. Right, Booboo? Use your new found shadow-magick to save the day?"

Oscar shook his head. "I uh...can't go too far from here. I'm kind of...tied down. I'll probably stay at the house."

Zara's face stiffened, and she let a long breath out. "I guess that makes sense, given what you did. I...don't want to leave you, Booboo. Not with..." Her eyes travelled over to where Marcus still sat with the zburător.

"I'm fine," Oscar replied hoarsely, then cleared his throat. "I mean...you have to do what you have to do. If you have to go, I'll manage. I can wait. I've waited longer."

Zara's eyes shone sadly. "How long was it for you there?"

Oscar opened his mouth. He almost told the truth and broke her heart. He almost lied and twisted his own. He took a breath instead and then spoke. "Let's talk about it later. I have so much to tell you. But I will tell you everything. I promise."

"Distance shouldn't be an issue," Vandle's voice said gently. "You will be fucking fed up with us in a week," Paige added in a similar but mocking tone.

The nervous man with glasses, Daniel, tugged gently on Paile's jacket sleeve. "Erm...excuse me. Can you take us home, please? That woman with the long hair keeps smiling at me with the back of her head, and I don't like it."

Paile sighed tiredly and nodded. She cast a look at Oscar and smiled.

Oscar smiled back.

She turned and led the way to a mirror propped against the mausoleum.

"Nice to see you DICS alive. Make sure you stay out of trouble!" Zara shouted to two unfamiliar faces wandering into the devastation around them.

A thin man with white hair waved excitedly back at Zara, and his companion, looking very grumpy, put a protective arm around him in a way that made Oscar's heart swell.

As the two of them moved away, one scraping samples from the fallen monsters, Oscar spotted Song, standing close to where the world parallax had fallen apart. They looked small and anxious, their golden eyes shining in the moonlight.

"Hi, Song." Oscar waved.

They shifted on their feet awkwardly.

Oscar frowned.

Then he felt a gentle sending.

Guilt, sorrow...an edge of regret.

What?

There was a low whistle, and Oscar saw Marcus waving them over. That hollow space in his chest grew larger until he thought it would swallow him and turn him inside out.

Zara squeezed his fingers again. "Come on, Booboo. Let's go together."

❧ 54 ❧

BEYOND

Marcus stood beside Dmitri's body, though it barely resembled him anymore. One of his formerly proud, leathery wings was a charred nub on the blackened shell of his corpse, the other a crumpled ruin. His fur was scorched off, scales split and burnt.

A wretched sorrow filled the void in Oscar's chest.

Misery.

Loss.

Helplessness.

He pushed it down...for now, at least. He had time to feel this, would feel this forever. But for now...

"So, Sato is going to take care of Ducky. Apparently, he knows some great places she can indulge her...*appetites* without attracting too much attention from people that want to turn her into a fast-track pass to trouble. I trust him to take care of her, and she was totally sick of me for getting her involved in all of this."

Oscar frowned. "Who's Ducky?"

Zara turned her head and raised an eyebrow. "The duck."

"Anyway, I'm sorry I can't help Paige and Vandle. I really am," Marcus said, his eyes shining.

"You said before...that there wasn't time?" Zara replied warily.

Marcus nodded.

Song edged closer to him, their hands tucked at their waist.

"What did you mean?" Zara said bluntly.

Marcus sighed and looked up at the moon.

"You...gave up too much, didn't you?" Oscar asked softly.

Marcus didn't look at them. He didn't say anything, but Oscar knew it was true. Somehow, he could feel it.

"Marcus, no..." Zara's voice shook.

Marcus tutted. "Bitch, half an hour ago, you were all like, 'here we are at the end of the world together' and ready for me to die. Flash forward to Oscar cramming a bunch of monsters into a mirror, like a finished fucking gruesome Jumanji game, and suddenly, you don't even want me to become a higher being."

"Marcus!"

"It's fine! We knew the deal! It's not like I'm DYING! I'm literally *undying*."

There was a cautious nudge from Song.

"*Fine*. I probably technically already died, but not really... because I'm still here. Like a tune that you can't get out of your head."

"Marcus...I just got back," Oscar breathed. "I...I need you."

Marcus smiled and strode forward, grabbing Oscar in one arm and Zara in the other. They fell together in a clumsy hug, sharing each other's breath and warmth, if only for a few moments longer.

Zara started to cry, and Oscar cried too, though he held back his tears as much as he could. He didn't want to lose these last few moments to weeping.

There was a small nudge as Song burrowed their way into their huddle, standing at their centre and blinking up with those golden eyes contently.

"Anyway," Marcus said, "I can learn how to reform and come back to see y'all. Like Song, but without their, erm...life-sucky powers?"

There was a cautious prod of doubt from Song.

"What now?" Zara asked, rubbing her eyes.

"Nothing, nothing," Marcus said, stepping out of their arms. "You both know I love you, right? Like...I would make babies into hamburgers for you if you wanted."

"I don't want that," Oscar said flatly, sniffling.

Zara laughed, but it broke into a sob.

"Good, because I don't want to do it. I just would, ya know?" Marcus rubbed his head. "Just promise me you'll take care of yourselves. And I, uhhh..." He reached down and rubbed Oscar's belly. "Make good choices, okay?"

Oscar frowned, putting his hand to where Marcus had touched a moment ago.

What?

Marcus stepped back. He was shimmering now, like the moon was showing thousands of tiny diamonds hidden in his umber skin.

"I always knew you were too good for this world, Marcus," Zara said through her tears.

Marcus grinned. "Me too. But I'll be back—promise! Terminator-style."

There was that worried sending once more, and Song glared at Marcus.

"For Christ's sake, what are they saying, Marcus?" Zara asked loudly.

Marcus grinned nervously. "Uhhh...they're just reminding me it usually takes people a few thousand years before they can recorporealise after ascending."

Zara groaned loudly.

"What? It'll be fine! One thing I've learned is that when conflicting magicks meet, the stronger will prevail. I'm kind of an expert in finding myself, and you two aren't exactly human anymore. It's not like we know how long you're even going to live. You might still be spring chickens in a thousand years!"

The twinkling light shone through him now, and he looked up at the moon, smiling.

"Besides, you're forgetting one really important thing," he added with a wink. "I'm a *really* fast learner."

And then, he was gone.

~

SONG ONLY STAYED a few moments longer, filling Oscar and Zara with a sending full of hope and love that cushioned their sobs before they, too, disappeared. They spread into motes of light and dissipated, following Marcus to wherever he had gone.

Everywhere, Oscar supposed.

Ed had found his way back to them. He huddled beside the scorched body of his master in the shape of a golden retriever. When Oscar sat down, the mimick-dog let out a low whine and came to rest his head on his lap, the fur around his dark eyes damp with tears. Oscar stroked his silky ears, and he nuzzled in closer.

Zara joined him, and for a time, they let the tears take them. He let Zara hold him, and he held her like they were the last and only thing each other had right now. And in some ways, he knew that was true.

Finally, eyes puffy and face covered in tears and snot, Zara spoke. "You'd...you'd..." she huffed through tiring sobs.

"What?" Oscar asked weakly.

"You'd better hope..." She started to laugh, tears still streaming from her eyes. "You'd better hope Marcus didn't put a zburător baby in your belly with magick before he popped off," she wheezed.

Oscar felt a moment of panic, then a delirious laugh bubbled from the void in his chest and broke through his tears. And they laughed and cried until his eyes were sore and his chest hurt from it.

"So...should we...bury him at the house?" Zara asked finally, looking beside them at Dmitri's charred remains.

Oscar sniffled, nodding. "I think...he would like that. I should be able to get far enough from here to live there, so that way...he will always be near." He felt tears flow again, even though he thought he was all cried out.

"What was Marcus even doing over here, anyway?" Zara wiped her nose on the back of her hand. She leaned forward, her attention fixed on something in the zburător's corpse.

Oscar saw it too.

Something *shiny* was lodged in its sternum.

"What is that?" Zara frowned, reaching forward to touch it, then pulled her hand away and looked at Oscar.

Oscar roused Ed from his lap and climbed to his knees. Very slowly, with one hand, he reached out, pressing his fingers through the brittle, charred flesh of the zburător.

The thing was lodged firmly, but he pulled, and the burned tissue gave way, though it slipped from his fingers as he did. It had barely clattered in the cobblestones when it disappeared into Ed's mouth.

"Oi! Ed, stop! What is that?" Zara grabbed his head firmly and wrestled it from his jaws. Ed didn't put up much of a fight, surrendering his prize and watching Zara turn the spittle-coated thing over in her hands.

It was a shard of golden, brilliant metal, barely the size of her thumb.

Zara frowned. "Dmitri said he had something stuck in his chest that stopped him from healing. He thought it was from the gate of bones when it exploded, but that's..."

Oscar's breath caught in his chest. He stared at the metal shard.

A piece of the hilt.

From the willblade.

Oscar swallowed.

There was no way.

But hadn't the hilt shattered that night in Stonehenge? Part of it must have been what was lodged in Dmitri's chest all this time.

He crawled on his knees, the words of Betty Blumpkin ringing in his memory: *'If your will is strong, it will part night and day...or any number of things, really.'*

He lurched forward, throwing himself against the zburător's remains. Ruined scales, fur, and flesh crumbled under his touch, and the stink of burned flesh and sulphur filled his nose.

It was...still warm.

"Oscar? What are you doing?"

Oscar closed his eyes, resting the side of his head against its chest, and concentrated.

Then...

something inside...

moved.

THE END

LIFE AFTER DEATH

Though friends and loved ones may part through time, distance, and death, the way they shape one another will always persevere. A body's return to the earth can nourish new life, just as the memories they made with others can shape endless futures. Every action brings potential, and the impact of a single soul can cast ripples across the surface of the pond of reality, even within a cascade of others.

Stories can be the same way, too. Memory's mark, and the infinite possibilities of what might happen next, will always be there. Some stories are told far and wide, others known only to a select few, but all carry an endless potential for secrets and change.

Like the story of the girl who fought through hate and turmoil to become a better person than she should have been. Her bold heart still has far to travel, and there are challenges ahead, including protecting her people from the harm of the one that came before her, to ensure that those who follow can live the lives that they deserve.

Or the monster, survivor, and woman who was willing to trade everything to save her world. The story of how she became a battle-scarred queen of harsh lands full of challenges yet to come. Old wounds may heal poorly, but scarred tissues can be thicker and stronger than they were before, and few are as suitable for the task as she.

And the two broken women, clinging their pieces together to survive as one. Who knows if they will ever find their pieces or what lies in wait when they do? This is a story that a powerful businesswoman called Margaret Dettweiler does *not* know. She will wish she did when a package arrives at her home; she opens it up to a simple dictaphone that causes a puzzled look to cross her face before she clicks play. The message is brief. One word, three times out loud. Or was it a name? She catches movement in a mirror to her left. Hers is a story that has little left to tell.

A story that can barely be imagined is that of the man who found himself, fought to *be* himself, and then expanded that self beyond the constraints of knowledge and power. He knows life. He will explore and become one with infinite possibility. Where that will lead, and what semblance of his former self remains, is yet to be seen and may forever remain unknown.

And then there's a woman; proud, brave, and strong, leading with her heart and fighting fears that are not hers to face. Will the fuel of her determination be enough to see her through? Will her bold spirit persevere as she seeks to recapture ancient powers of chaos and catastrophe that should have remained forever contained?

There is also the lesser-known story of the man who learned that being a monster was not his darkest part and that being human not his best. Only then could he hope to mend the tear in his heart and consider how he might live as who he was always meant to be. But what *will* would it require to conquer death? Enough to tear the earth in two...or maybe bring it back together?

Finally, there's the tale of one frightened, feeble, and fragile; a boy who became more than a man through the strength in his heart and the many scars he learned to bear. Some will speak of him for many years to come, though they may not know that they do. Legend will tell of a pale youth with messy hair and eyes blacker than night who appears in the cemetery in Highgate. He is often seen with a dog, though accounts vary of what kind.

Some claim that he is a sign of death or of the end of the world, but some very few know the truth is quite the opposite. They will know that not all heroes start off that way and that courage comes in many shapes. They will know not all happy endings are the same and that darkness and light live within us all. But what *really* counts is what we do and who we love, and how we are loved in turn.

One thing that they will all agree on is that he is *never* alone. Other shapes accompany him, those that some have astutely related to these prior stories told. Some even say he is seen with one man whose eyes burn like cinders and whose love knows no bounds.

Only a select few know what really happened—and now that includes *you*. So, carry this story, and remember:

This was the story of when the world was ending...and how Oscar and his friends *didn't* let it happen.

ACKNOWLEDGMENTS

Before I say anything else, I need to thank Oscar.

He was created to be cowardly, clumsy, and average in many ways (...and less than average in more). Instead, he became a character that no matter what I threw at him, and how bad things got, would always do his best to make it through. That is his true power. Oscar overcame the worst things that could happen to him with nothing other than perseverance and the bonds he cherished with those he loves. Oscar overcame me, as the author, no matter what I tried to do to stop him. I will miss writing him, and his beautiful heart, but I will always remember the lessons he has taught me. Oscar Tundale—it turns out he was always my hero, and I hope now he's yours too. I hope we can see in him how we can all be the heroes of our own stories, even if we often don't feel strong or brave.

Jayme Bean has been an utter champion of the series. Founder of the tiny but powerful 'Lesser Known Monsters fan club', cheerleader, coach, marketing manager, safety net, and inspiration. I can do nothing to repay the impact of what you have done for me whilst writing these books, but I hope knowing how grateful I am for your friendship and kindness helps. Shimaira's energy and passion for the series (and help, along with Jayme and William in going through every word to look for last-minute errors) is another incredible act that I can never repay. Publishing books can be exhausting, and I don't know if I could have managed without all of your support. Ash, who encouraged me to even consider publishing, your tireless enthusiasm and sparkling joy for everything is something I wouldn't have started this journey without—let alone ended it.

I absolutely could not have done this without my editor Charlie, who excels at providing honest, direct, constructive and supportive feedback. Their hands have touched the bare bones of all my character nuances, plot twists, and revelations, and helped shape these stories into what they became. Dean Cole is skilled, talented, and tolerant of my constant requests for development of the covers. I can't imagine having anyone else do what we have done with this series. Axel Toth (UrbanKnight Art) has been an absolute blessing, with the incredible knack for seeing and creating what I imagine, and bringing it to life. I can't wait to work together on more projects in the future.

The huge padded cushion of kindness, support provided by the writing community has been such an incredibly safe and encouraging space for me. Thank you to the amazing Halo Scot, Sarah Bell, Gideon E. Wood, Katherine Shaw, Mario Dell'Olio, M.E. Aster, Gabriel Hargrave, Brittany Weisrock, Chris Durston, and AC Merkel. Queer Lit book store in Manchester has also been a fantastic friend to the series, and I am grateful to you and the great work you do for me, and the rest of the queer community.

Thank you to my one. We take pride in being complete versions of ourselves—but as complete as I am, you add more to my fullness. You brighten my stars and make everything better and more. You are never surprised when I achieve something great, because you believe in me more than I do myself. May our adventures never end.

I'm going to do something really fucking weird now. I'm going to thank myself. Thank you, Rory-who-is-reading-this, for somehow finding energy and headspace to let these books out of you in a difficult time. Having the courage to share these stories is not something that came naturally, but I am glad that you found it.

Maybe I should thank myself more often...

This counts for you too, reader of these words. Thank yourself. For every moment that you can share your heart with others, and the beauty and power that comes with it. Thank yourself for being someone that those you love can depend on and making their best even better. I hope that the memories of these stories stay with you, and you recall the characters like old friends. I hope I made you smile, or your heart skip a beat. Thank yourself, because I thank you too, for joining Oscar and his friends on their adventure, and joining me on mine...now, go have yours.

ABOUT THE AUTHOR

Rory Michaelson is always doing too many things, and rarely the ones that they ought to be. The Lesser Known Monsters series includes Rory's debut novel and short story collection. They were born and raised in the UK, love stories in all forms, and are easily bribed with cookies.

You can follow Rory on Twitter (and other social media platforms) for shenanigans @RoryMichaelson, or subscribe to their newsletter at RoryMichaelson.com.

ALSO BY RORY MICHAELSON

The Lesser Known Monsters Series

Lesser Known Monsters

The Bone Gate

The Torn Earth

The Little Book of Lesser Known Monsters

Made in the USA
Las Vegas, NV
12 May 2022